MICHELE
PAIGE
HOLMES

Copyright © 2025 Michele Paige Holmes
Paperback edition
All rights reserved

No part of this book may be reproduced in any form whatsoever without prior written permission of the publisher, except in the case of brief passages embodied in critical reviews and articles. This novel is a work of fiction. The characters, names, incidents, places, and dialog are products of the author's imagination and are not to be construed as real.

Interior Design by Cora Johnson
Edited by Cassidy Wadsworth and Lorie Humpherys
Cover design by Rachael Anderson
Cover Image Credit: Photography by Alyssa Howard. Cover model: Hannah Fackrell

Published by Mirror Press, LLC
ISBN: 978-1-952611-47-6

HEARTHFIRE ROMANCE SERIES

Saving Grace
Loving Helen
Marrying Christopher
Twelve Days in December
Love Unbound
Love Undying

HOLIDAY HARBOR SERIES

A Holiday Affair
Home Sweet Holiday
The Heart of Holiday

To Mom, for all she has sacrificed for me throughout her life, and the many things she has done for my benefit—including the writing of a letter in 1987 (to the man I would one day marry) that changed the course of history and led to my own happily ever after.

Prologue

Saint Kitts, Caribbean, 1829

THE HOUSE, LIKE THE REST of the island, could have been beautiful. It should have been with its elegant, white columns stretching to the roof of the second story and the wide veranda that encircled the entire building on both floors. Palm trees flanked the large, square plantation house, their brown trunks and green leaves a stunning contrast to its yellow paint and the brilliant blue sky beyond.

So different from the smoke of London. Little wonder Katherine had stayed, had loved it here. He had loved it, too, on his last visit, over two years ago. *Why didn't I return sooner?* A lump lodged itself in Graham Murray's throat as he thought of his sister in this place, imagined her smiling and happy, waving to him from the balcony as she'd welcomed him at long last—after years of begging him to visit.

Various flowering plants—none of which he was familiar with—boasting red, orange, and yellow blossoms, lined the long drive. Yellow had been Katherine's favorite color. The pit in Graham's stomach told him he'd probably detest it for the rest of his life now. Just as he'd be loath to remember these moments, and this house—where she had died—forever.

The ancient, withered handler pulled the phaeton to a halt at the top of the drive. Graham hadn't expected him to actually get them here and would not have been surprised had the old man keeled over en route. Fortunately he hadn't, so Graham paid him twice the quoted fare, thanked him, and asked him to wait. Then, with heavy heart and steps, he made his way up a half dozen stairs to the double front doors and knocked.

"Mas'r not home," a Negro woman informed him before the door was even halfway open. A bright red wrap encircled her head, and her apron sported several green stains, as if she'd been shelling peas or snapping beans over it. She kept one hand on the door, as if prepared to slam it in his face.

"I'm not here to see the master," Graham said, his teeth grating at the term. So much the better if he didn't have to see the man who'd wrongfully taken over Katherine's plantation, claiming it as his own. There was much to be settled in court later, but all of that could wait. "I am looking for two children. A girl, Ayla, and a—"

"Mas'r not home," the woman repeated, her eyes darting to the left as she spoke this time.

He's right here. Graham's jaw clenched, refusing to utter such a declaration. No man should be another's master, and he'd no intention of taking on that role, no matter what his supposed rights were. "I don't care where he is," Graham said, impatient with the woman and her still-shifting eyes. "I am here for—"

The sharp crack of a whip, followed by a scream, cut off his response.

The Negress's hand clenched in her apron, and tears flooded her eyes as they sought his imploringly. A second crack sounded, the scream that followed piercing his heart. Graham pivoted and ran the length of the veranda.

He rounded a corner and vaulted down a set of wide steps to a side yard where a tall post had been erected. *A recent addition. Not Katherine's doing.* A child hung by bound wrists, her back exposed by the vicious lashes that had torn her dress.

"Stop!" Graham shouted as he ran, then immediately regretted it. Years of experience with his father had taught him the futility and foolishness of asking a bully to desist. He'd only given his adversary warning of his presence.

The man spared Graham half a glance over his shoulder before the whip cracked a third time, sending its victim into a jerking spasm of pain.

Graham reached the man wielding it, grabbed the hand holding the whip, and twisted it behind the man's back, jerking the arm upward until he heard a satisfying snap.

The man writhed and cursed, bucking against Graham. "I'll have your head for this. Just like I had your sister."

Higgins. With a powerful surge of anger and hatred, Graham shoved the previous foreman away a split second before his head could slam backward into Graham's jaw. Higgins stumbled forward, his arm hanging. The hateful man deserved far more than a broken arm, and Graham dearly wanted to pummel Higgins's face until it was unrecognizable. *To shatter every single rib. To—*

A pitiful cry from the girl still hanging at the post silenced Graham's violent thoughts. He drew his gun and started toward her as Higgins caught himself and whirled around, a pistol in his good hand.

A shot echoed through the yard, ricocheting off the surrounding buildings. Bright red blood seeped through Higgins's linen shirt, over his heart, as he crumpled.

Finally gone for good. Katherine had dismissed him immediately upon her husband's death, ending the reign of terror he'd inflicted upon all who lived and worked here.

Or so she had believed. *What part did Higgins play in her death?*

Graham strode forward, bent, and swiped the gun from the dead man's hand. Keeping it drawn, his eyes darting in every direction, he tucked his own weapon into his belt as he ran to the child.

He pulled a knife from his boot then tucked Higgins's pistol beside his own. He cut the girl free, catching her as she fell. She cried out again as his arms connected with her torn flesh. Graham crouched, lowering her gently to the ground. "Can you stand?"

She nodded and lifted her face to his. Two light blue eyes peered up at him. Graham startled. *Ayla?* It had to be. He took in her features—hair long and sleek, pulled into a tight plait that wound around her head, and her skin a beautiful mix of color. Not nearly as dark as the driver's or the woman's at the door, but also not as fair as his. Perhaps the most beautiful child he had ever seen—exactly as his sister had described in her many letters. And exactly what he had thought of Ayla when they had met two Christmases ago.

Her beauty was still evident, though there was a hardness to her that had not been present before. Her childlike features were still there, but the innocence was gone. She looked far older than her years—weary, worn, and wise now to the cruelties of the world. Or at least of the island. There would likely be more cruelties in life ahead of her. He hoped they would be significantly less than those she'd endured already.

"Where is your brother?" Graham asked.

Ayla's lips pressed together and her small chin lifted defiantly as she took a step back from him and nearly fell.

Graham reached for her, holding her arm briefly until she'd regained her balance.

"I've no wish to harm either of you," Graham said. "I've come to take you both far away from here. My sister wished that. She asked it of me. I have her last letter." As he reached toward his pocket, Ayla's eyes widened and flashed upward.

Graham whirled around, and a shovel connected with his

cheekbone, slicing his skin and shooting pain up the side of his face. "Run!" he shouted to Ayla, blood trickling down his cheek as he faced this new assailant.

A tall, burly man held up the shovel and circled him. "You'll pay for this." As he inclined his head toward Higgins's body, Graham reached for the gun at his waist, the one that hadn't been fired yet, but it wasn't there.

A screeching noise and laughter sounded to his right. A boy, only slightly taller than Ayla, pranced around, both weapons in his hands.

How— It didn't matter. Graham was facing a giant, weaponless. *I'm not dying here.* Even more important, he wasn't leaving his niece and nephew here to suffer. He'd let Katherine down in many ways, but not in this.

The shovel swung toward him again, and Graham jumped back, barely avoiding a strike to his head. He ran to the side and ducked, avoiding a second swipe. How long before his attacker gave up and made use of the more efficient weapon the boy held? Or maybe the boy himself would shoot.

"I'm here to help you," Graham called as he ran past the child and the other boys clustered around him. "I want to free you as my sister did."

The laughter ceased. The man holding the shovel barked a command, and the boys scattered.

Sweat beaded on Graham's brow as he studied his attacker, noting the similarities to Higgins. *His son? A younger brother?*

The blood trickling down the side of Graham's face made it into his mouth. No time to spit. He tried not to swallow. He backed up again as the man wielding the shovel stepped closer.

He intends to pin me against the house. Graham glanced quickly in either direction. A wood pile. A chopping block. A calculated calm descended, and he staggered back, feigning confusion and fear as he took one more look, moving his head back and forth as if panicked and desperate.

An evil glint shone in the madman's eyes as he moved closer. Almost within striking distance. "I can't wait to dig your innards out and feed 'em to the dogs."

Three steps. Reach. Throw. "I didn't come here for trouble," Graham said, hands out in front of him as he moved back, his body angled so the axe remained unseen. *Just a little closer.* "I came to collect my niece and nephew—there." He nodded to a spot behind his attacker, where Ayla had stood. It was vacant now.

The man didn't quite turn, but in the half-second he hesitated Graham snatched the axe and threw it. It flew one turn, end over end, just missing the shovel and striking its target in the center of his forehead. A howl rent the air. The shovel clattered to the ground, the man crumpled, and Graham ran. Behind him a shot rang out. He whirled around and caught sight of the boy with his gun, standing on the balcony above, the smoking weapon aimed at the unmoving body of the man with the axe in his head.

The boy raised his hands high. "Make free!"

One

London, England, 1831

MISS SOPHIA CLAYBOURNE WAS A practiced flirt—a disappointing observation that Graham ascertained in the first five minutes he followed her every polished move around the overcrowded drawing room of her father's London townhouse. She never conversed with any one man too long before becoming caught up in conversing with another, only to leave that gentleman in favor of another's company, and yet another's after that. *An age-old ploy to encourage jealousy.*

Graham had seen it previously, and he'd seen enough tonight to know that he disliked what he saw. His position behind three potted palms—trees Lord Claybourne had imported from Saint Kitts, no doubt—afforded him an excellent viewpoint while keeping him out of sight. Lord Claybourne had invited more guests to this little soirée than his townhome could comfortably accommodate, and thus far that had worked in Graham's favor, both in his ability to enter on the coattails of his friend, Lord William Fitzgerald, and to remain unseen. Dinner would likely prove more challenging, but Lady Claybourne had arranged for him to be seated at the far end of the long table, among the lowest of the fifty or so guests and hopefully out of sight of her husband, who would no doubt be preoccupied impressing those guests of greater importance seated near him.

But remaining anonymous until later was at present the least of Graham's concerns. What to do about Miss Claybourne was the far more pressing matter. He'd been led to believe, by one of her previous suitors, that she was a bookish woman. Graham saw no signs of that now but instead saw only the insipid demeanor so prevalent in females of the ton, whose only thoughts most often involved which titled and wealthy men they might ensnare to elevate their own statuses and fulfill their every desire for jewels and gowns and the like. If that was the case with Miss Claybourne . . . *Newsome can have her.* They deserved each other.

But the men and women of Saint Kitts who would suffer because of such a union did not deserve that. Graham's jaw clenched. No matter what he saw in Miss Claybourne, he had to steady the course. In addition to fulfilling his own purposes, he'd given his word to her mother as well.

Her mother . . . Graham's eyes strayed from Miss Claybourne to Lady Claybourne, busy in her own gossip circles. She appeared about as intelligent as her daughter, yet the letter she'd written to him had definitely sounded otherwise. Could it have been a ploy? Was a viscount perhaps not good enough for her daughter, and Lady Claybourne had hatched a plot to snare a duke instead—even one with as dark a reputation as his?

Graham mulled this over as he searched the room for Miss Claybourne once more and could not find her.

"Ill-mannered, loathsome toad," a female voice muttered behind him.

"Beg pardon," Graham said gruffly as he turned and discovered the object of his thoughts standing with her back to him, speaking under her breath all manner of egregious insults as she rubbed her hands up and down her arms, as if to rid them of something unpleasant. He was used to being called names—several of them—but not usually so early in the evening and not before he had made someone's acquaintance. It seemed his reputation preceded him more and more.

Had the chit's mother alerted her to their plans? He reached a hand between the palms and snagged two flutes of champagne from the tray of a passing footman. It would not do to start out poorly with Miss Claybourne, no matter how much he already disliked her. Guessing that she had not heard him before, he cleared his throat.

"I understand congratulations are in order, Miss Claybourne." He held one of the glasses out to her as she turned to face him.

Suspicion flashed in her eyes, and she frowned, making no move to accept his offering. "I do not believe we have met." She tilted her head slightly, looking up at him, and he noted the magnificent blue of her eyes and the hint of intelligence behind them.

"We haven't."

The bell announcing dinner rang, signaling that he had but a minute to complete his business and discover whether or not she was already betrothed. Formalities would have to wait. "I hear congratulations are in order," he repeated.

Her brow furrowed and her frown deepened. "I am not certain for what, unless you wish to congratulate me on keeping my temper thus far this evening. I am rather proud of myself for not smashing a glass over any of these fops' heads." She snatched the glass from his still outstretched hand and raised it to her lips but did not drink. "Oh, dear." She sighed heavily. "I did not mean to imply that you were one of them." Her gaze drifted over him, as if fully seeing him for the first time, and she took a step backward, as if preparing to run.

"No offense taken," Graham said, offering her a lazy smile. "I am not one—not a gentleman at all, or so many say."

"What a relief." She sipped her drink. "Then my father would not approve of my marrying you, and I have no need to fear that our conversing will lead to your interest and another unwanted proposal." Miss Claybourne returned his smile, and he felt sudden pity for all those fops. He realized that she had not been flirting but attempting to avoid encouraging anyone's affections and to shake the pack of pups that had been following her about. And still were, he noticed as he glanced through the space between the palms at a room of searching gentlemen.

He could hardly blame the men for wanting to be in her company. If women of the ton were guilty of chasing men with money, the men were equally so, and Lord Claybourne had provided ample incentive. But men also chased beautiful women, and Miss Claybourne was not lacking in beauty either. Rich, honey-colored hair was swept back on either side by a set of jeweled combs, before being caught up in a mass of curls that revealed a slender, elegant neck and bare shoulders. Those glorious eyes were topped by long lashes and defined brows. Her skin looked not porcelain white, as so many of the women's of the ton did, but had a healthy glow, as if she walked outside frequently and often forgot her bonnet.

But he sensed that her beauty was perhaps more burden than blessing. Certainly her unusual dowry was.

"We should probably go in," she said, looking past him to the doors that had opened to a large dining room.

Graham gave a little bow and stepped aside so that she might pass. "My many congratulations on your *betrothal*, Miss Claybourne." He said her name again, so there could be no doubt that he was talking to her, *about* her.

Her gaze snapped back to his. "I am not betrothed."

The intensity of his relief took him by surprise. He feigned confusion and then regret. "My apologies. I had heard that Lord Newsome—"

"Lord Nuisance and I?" She shook her head, and her nose crinkled as if she'd encountered a foul odor. "He is annoying, to be sure—mostly to our beleaguered staff—but he is merely my father's business partner. Nothing more. We have spoken less than a dozen words to each other over the past weeks since their arrival from Saint Kitts." She shook her head again. "He is *not* interested in me."

Graham lowered his voice and spoke with urgency as she moved past him. "He is more than interested. Lord Newsome visited with your father last week and offered for you. Announcing your engagement is the reason for this gathering."

Miss Claybourne's gasp of revulsion and utter expression of horror told Graham all he needed to know. She had not been aware of her father's plans. She did not wish to marry Newsome.

Miss Claybourne turned back to him, arms wrapped around herself protectively even as she shook her head in denial. "No. No, he wouldn't."

"I am afraid that he already has," Graham said somberly, imagining how it must feel to be a female, whose fate depended upon the whim of her idiot father. His sister had suffered similarly.

"You're wrong," Miss Claybourne insisted and stepped out from the shelter of the palms. Her chin lifted as her eyes landed on Lord Newsome—a slight, slimy worm of a man, in Graham's opinion.

Newsome caught sight of her as well and started toward her, a smug grin plastered across his ugly face. Miss Claybourne swallowed, then closed her eyes briefly and brought a delicate hand to her throat.

Graham imagined she felt as though a noose rested there.

He took a step closer, and his fingers brushed her elbow briefly before they parted. "Don't lose hope."

He wasn't certain she'd heard him until she glanced his way once more, her magnificent blue eyes glittering, not with tears, but with determination.

Oddly enough, he was the one who left their brief encounter more hopeful than he had been in some time.

Two

"OF COURSE, REMOVING ELEPHANT TUSKS is no *small* matter." Lord Harrelson guffawed loudly, apparently under the impression that he had made some sort of joke, though most of the others seated near him at the long table merely looked annoyed.

Sophie forced a smile and even one, small, rather false-sounding giggle as she feigned amusement and continued the charade she had engaged in since the start of dinner. She leaned closer to the older baron, pretending keen interest in the nabob's story, when really she wished she could use his ivory-ring-laden hand to cuff his own cheek. *The old fool.* If she ever had the good fortune to see one of those magnificent creatures, she wouldn't be so stupid as to kill it.

"Hunting interests you, does it?" The voice to her left—far too close to her person—turned Sophie's smile into a frown. Even her irritation faded in the face of this imminent threat. Viscount Newsome had spoken in private with her father last week. This was not an unusual occurrence, given that they did business together, but the stranger's warning just before dinner suggested that this interview had been about something different, something *personal.* That might not have signified, but the seating arrangement at dinner, that her parents were hosting such an elaborate and carefully orchestrated party, the viscount's excessive attentiveness to her all evening, and her father's unusually good spirits all did. She was in danger of a betrothal—this one planned so she dared not refuse.

"Hunting does not interest me in the least." Sophie kept her gaze straight ahead, staring at the candelabras and the flowers lining the center of the table. She took a deep breath, inhaling the slight scent of roses, and closed her eyes briefly, wishing she were at their family's country estate or the park—anywhere besides London, this townhouse, and seated beside the viscount. "It is the prospect of travel to exotic locations that appeals. I find Lord Harrelson's tales of India intriguing."

Lord Newsome leaned closer yet, forcing Sophie to lean away, though she turned slightly in his direction, hoping that her look of disdain would discourage his attentions.

"Why should anyone wish to venture to such a wilderness, when London offers the *best* that is to be had?" His eyes raked over her from her head down to the bodice of her gown.

"Crowded streets, smoke-filled skies, excessive poverty. Why, indeed?" Sophie faced the center of the table again and resisted the urge to cross her arms protectively in front of her. She edged farther to the right—the farthest she could without falling off her chair. She returned her attention to the baron and found two others observing her. Lady Harrelson's eyes were narrowed, her piercing gaze warning Sophie away from her husband.

Sophie smiled in return and wished she might verbally assure the woman that she had no need to fear. It was only Lord Harrelson's proximity and his penchant for boisterous, entertaining tales that Sophie currently sought refuge in. Were a pig seated next to her, she would find its company more tenable than that of the man on her other side.

The second set of eyes upon her were those of the stranger who had apprised her of Lord Newsome's meeting with her father, and of his intentions. She was not certain who the man was—unusual, though their dinner guests numbered fifty this evening. Whatever his name, he was, as he had proclaimed, no gentleman, as he was seated toward the end of the table, on the opposite side. He had probably only been invited because of some association concerning her father's plantation on Saint Kitts.

A pity. She imagined she might have enjoyed conversing with him. And doing so would have held no risk, as her parents would never approve of such a match. She wanted to ask the man how he'd known to warn her of Lord Newsome's intentions. Possibly she would have asked him how he came by the scar above his cheekbone, the one that marred an otherwise handsome face.

But an interesting dinner conversation was not to be. Sophie sighed inwardly. Instead, she must encourage boorish Lord Harrelson to regale her with his tales.

Her mysterious benefactor gave her a knowing look, as if he understood what she was doing—or trying to do, anyway—in avoiding the viscount's attentions. Sophie gave a slight nod of acknowledgment while wishing she'd had more than a moment to speak with the stranger. His warning had been helpful, and she wished she knew who he was. His gaze held intelligence, and—something else. Something intriguing.

Lord Newsome placed his hand on her knee, and she jerked away from his touch, nearly falling off her chair in the process.

He met her accusing stare with an unnerving, proprietary gaze, as if he already felt that he owned her. Perhaps he did, if papers had been signed. Six months ago she had promised her father that she would agree to marry the next man who asked—it was either give her word or be disowned; cast out and penniless. She'd no doubt her father had meant every word of his threat, given what had happened to her older sister two years before.

Faced with the choice between having a roof over her head in the middle of winter or becoming a street urchin, Sophie had found the promise to accept her next offer a necessary one. If only to buy herself some time.

Because she had agreed only to *accept* her next proposal of marriage, not to actually marry the man who gave it. Since then she had been doing her best to avoid proposals altogether—and had managed to dissuade three potential suitors. Her tactics had worked—until now. She barely knew Lord Newsome. Recently he had begun frequenting their home as one of her father's business partners. He was her elder by at least twenty years and, by all counts she could tell, stuffy, rigid in his thinking, boring.

Lecherous.

Dangerous. From the top of his oily, slicked-back hair to the tips of his polished shoes, everything about him bespoke of a predator. On more than one occasion before tonight she had noticed his beady eyes following her, looking at her in a way that made her most uncomfortable. Her maid had complained to her of the same, and the staff had taken to calling him Lord Nuisance. Footmen were often sent to do the work of a maid when Lord Nuisance was in the house, so the women could avoid him.

Whenever Sophie had had the misfortune to be in the same room as him, he had made it a habit for his hand to brush against her elbow or her back. He lingered excessively long over her gloved hand when greeting her. *A snake with legs* was how she had come to regard him. And now, tonight, it appeared the snake was about to strike.

Even if he hadn't repulsed her—and he very much did—she could not imagine a life with him. He knew nothing of her personality or intellect, but she knew enough of his to recognize that they would most certainly *not* suit. Which left her to reason that his pursuit was based on something else, perhaps a favor to her father. She did not think he was after her sizable dowry—as she'd suspected many of her past suitors were. The viscount had wealth of his own, and she doubted hers would signify. But perhaps her father had made an arrangement with him, as Father seemed eager to marry her off, especially now that her younger sister Olivia was out as well. Most of the ton based marriages off similarly shallow standards of financial gain or social climbing. But it was not what Sophie wanted from her marriage—if she must marry at all.

"If it is travel you are keen for, perhaps you would be interested in hearing of my visits to the West Indies," Lord Newsome suggested, his hands back upon his silverware where they belonged. A good thing, else she would have been tempted to use her own utensils to fend him off.

Had it been anyone else offering to tell her of a far-off place, she would have been most attentive, but to show the slightest interest in anything he said would only encourage his suit.

"Will you be returning there again soon?" One could only hope business might call him away. Tomorrow.

"It is possible, and possible I might be persuaded to bring a companion." Lord Newsome cast a glance toward her father, as if speculating whether or not he would be amenable to having his daughter so far removed once she was wed.

Sophie could have answered that question easily enough. Neither of her parents would give a fig for her whereabouts once she had made a good match—her duty to the family name. *By marrying a viscount, no less.* It was a step up that no doubt had her mother swelling with pride already. The imaginary noose tightening about Sophie's neck felt even more snug. Getting out of this one was going to be difficult.

She would have to do her very best the entire night to avoid Lord Newsome's company—a difficult task, given that her parents would be doing all they could to encourage the two of them to be together. If she did manage to avoid him tonight, he would likely call on her tomorrow, and she would have to be unavailable then as well. And the next day and the next. She felt a true headache coming on.

She looked away, catching the eye of the man at the far end of the table again as he watched her, his brow furrowed, as if concerned.

"I have the finest plantation house on Saint Kitts. It is quite grand, with a bevy of servants, luxurious furnishings, and as excellent a cook as can be found in those parts." Lord Newsome's head raised proudly as his statement earned a few admiring murmurs from Lady Fredericks and her daughter and others seated nearby.

His apparent self-confidence and belief that he was impressing Sophie only confirmed her dislike of him. What did she need with a fine house and servants and an extravagant cook? He knew nothing about her. *Nothing at all.* She did not wish to marry him, nor even contemplate it. She must prove this to him, and quickly. "Does your plantation have an extensive library? Have you discovered a great deal of new wildlife there—both on the island and in the sea surrounding it? Is the water as exquisite a blue as they say it is?" She lowered her voice to a whisper and dared to lean slightly closer. "Does the sand feel glorious beneath your bare feet?"

Lord Newsome drew back at her last, most inappropriate question, his mouth twisting as if he were put off, though his eyes shone with renewed interest, as if imagining her bare feet and ankles.

Sophie's stomach heaved as she realized her error.

"I would not know about the sand, having never removed my shoes outside of my bedroom. I will say it's the devil of an annoyance though—gets everywhere, in everything, and is quite impossible to remove."

"How—unfortunate." She was referring, of course, to his never having walked barefoot on the beach. *What a pity. What a waste.* That such a gift of nature should be squandered on one so unappreciative.

Lord Newsome's brow furrowed. "I have not bothered with a library at my house in Saint Kitts. Most of the population is illiterate, so I would have to bring books over with me. I am never there more than a few months at a time, not long enough to require any. As to your question about the water—it is blue, as all water is. The climate is hot, and the air is sticky. Truth be told, I find the island altogether unpleasant."

"Then why did you wish to tell me of it?" Sophie frowned her displeasure of his report.

"Because it is not without its merits altogether." A sly smile curved Lord Newsome's lips. His voice lowered. "The island would be a very good place for a couple to be *alone*, with ample time to get to know one another—in detail."

"I don't believe I should *ever* like to visit Saint Kitts." Sophie looked away from him, ignoring his low chuckle, and forced herself to remain in her seat, when more than anything she wished to bolt, to run from this room and this house and most especially from the man beside her. She returned her attention to her plate, though whatever appetite she might have had was gone.

She would sooner die than marry Viscount Newsome. He might have an elevated title, but it was apparent he'd no brain to match it. To go months without reading? To have lived near the ocean and a beach and not once walked barefoot on the sand? What was wrong with these men that they would butcher magnificent animals and take beautiful, turquoise water and the exotic creatures who lived in it for granted? She could not understand them, nor this wretched Society that she was expected to be a part of for the remainder of her life. If forced to live in such a stale environment, her life might be short indeed. She would die of boredom and frustration. Her spirit would die, suppressed under the demands of a man she could barely stand to look at, let alone imagine giving herself to.

I could die in childbirth. The chilling thought swept through her, further dimming the light and hope she almost always maintained, despite the limited opportunities life afforded her as a female. If she married Lord Newsome, a year from now she might bear his child—and die from it. Before she ever had a chance to really live at all.

At least Victoria had known a short life of freedom and love before her death.

If I am forced to wed Lord Newsome, I'll not have even that.

The conversation around the table faded to a hum and buzz, as if swarms of insects encircled her head. Indeed, those might have been better—certainly more harmless—than Viscount Newsome and his intentions. Half-heartedly, she turned toward the baron again, though she guessed that no amount of ignoring the viscount or pointing out their differences would dissuade him. The look in his eyes, his suggestive words, the way his hand had wandered to her knee, all implied that he already owned her. Or believed he did.

Attempting to pick up on the conversation going on to her right, Sophie shifted her gaze to Lord Harrelson, only to intercept the stranger's at the end of the table once more.

He held his glass aloft, swishing the wine aimlessly. He

seemed to be considering something, and then—when their eyes met once more—it was suddenly decided.

He set his glass down rather forcefully and rose from the table, a tall, striking figure that commanded attention. Conversation ceased almost immediately as all heads turned toward him.

From the other end of the table, her mother spoke, sounding both alarmed and apologetic. "Your Grace, is something amiss?"

A duke? Why was he seated so far down the table? Sophie felt shame staining her cheeks, though it was her parents' blunder, not hers. Except that it could not be a blunder, but a bold, intentional slight. *Why?*

"Several things are amiss, but I shall put the most important item right presently." The duke stared down the length of the table at her father.

Sophie's gaze shifted momentarily to her father, as well, and noted that he did not appear the least apologetic but wore his mask of forced calm. She knew what anger simmered behind that face and prayed it would not be unleashed here, in front of so many witnesses. There would be talk of this tomorrow, regardless. And Father no doubt would wish to minimize the damage. It had not been so very long since her family recovered from the scandal of her sister's marriage.

Sophie's gaze swung back to the mysterious duke.

"Earlier this week I spoke with our gracious host, Lord Claybourne, and this evening I was fortunate enough to speak with his daughter, Miss Sophia Claybourne." The stranger turned to look at Sophie, his expression softer, yet determined, and . . . something else she couldn't quite decipher.

He pinned her with that gaze, so she couldn't have looked away if she'd wanted to. To her surprise, she found she did *not* want to, but wanted to know everything about the man behind it. As she had been during their brief conversation before dinner, she felt strangely drawn to him. Curious. *That is all.* He was a riddle she must solve, even more so now that she realized he was a duke. He did not act like one, did not seem wont to lord his position over those beneath him—as every person seated at this table was. And he certainly did not bother with convention or fear gossip, with his current, bold actions.

He is fearless. Regardless of his high rank, to be so outspoken right in the middle of dinner . . . Would he have done so had others of his social standing also been in attendance?

The Duke and Duchess of Devonshire had been invited tonight but, much to her parents' disappointment, had declined, as they were traveling. Which left her duke—this duke; he was not *hers*—the most prestigious man in the room. Yet he had not been treated as such. *Why?* Had there been some scandal? He certainly looked the part, with his suit cut from the finest cloth, his dark hair styled precisely, his angled cheeks smoothly shaven, and that mysterious scar . . .

A corner of his mouth lifted. Sophie felt her face warm again, afraid he'd caught her admiring him. His gray eyes changed, darkened, and she desperately wished to know what he was thinking.

"I am most pleased to announce that Miss Claybourne is to be my wife."

Sophie bit back a gasp, held in by years of strict social training and the way his eyes practically pled for her to go along with whatever scheme this was. The rest of the room did not school their reactions quite so effectively, and whispered gossip flew up and down both sides of the table, as all eyes were upon her.

"Preposterous." The table vibrated as Lord Newsome's fist met the wood. "I spoke with her father as well."

"But you failed to consult the lady." The duke's tone dared him—or anyone else—to question his announcement. None did. "And Miss Claybourne was under *strict* instructions from her father to agree to marry the next man who asked for her hand."

Sophie sucked in a breath. How had he known that?

The mysterious duke sent her an almost apologetic look before inclining his head toward Lord Newsome, spitting and sputtering at her side. Sophie's lips curved in an unbidden smile, and she suddenly felt like laughing. Her eyes met the duke's once more, and she sent him a silent thank you. He had just saved her from Lord Newsome.

And she wasn't truly betrothed at all. Because her mysterious savior hadn't actually asked her to marry him.

Three

"THERE IS TO BE A wedding! How delightful," Olivia squealed before Sophie had even taken her seat in the withdrawing room. Her younger sister's enthusiasm was met by near silence or tight-lipped smiles from the other ladies settling at the table, as well as those scattered throughout the room. Almost immediately after her sudden and unexpected betrothal, her father had excused the ladies to take their leave.

Head still spinning, Sophie sank into her chair. Her friends studied her, their expressions grave and concerned. The questions would come any minute, and she was at a loss as to how to answer them.

"A *duke*," Olivia gushed. "However did you manage? I saw you speaking to him before dinner, but I did not know what it signified."

Nor did I.

"He *is* magnificent," Miss Violet Beaumont offered, her smile encouraging as she grasped Sophie's hand. "Easily the most dashing man here. Wherever did you find him?"

"He found me. Truthfully, we are not well acquainted yet." From the corner of her eye, Sophie watched her mother, surrounded by her own friends and deep in conversation. Their frequent, furtive glances in Sophie's direction gave little doubt that she was the subject.

"Tell us *everything*," Olivia drawled. "Has he kissed you yet? What was it like?"

"Livie," Sophie warned, even as her friends leaned in close, eager anticipation on their faces.

"Do tell us," Miss Anne Simms implored. "Some of us may never be kissed, let alone by a dark and dashing duke."

We have not kissed. We are not betrothed. Sophie could speak neither of those truths, and the realization that though she had avoided one messy situation this evening, she had landed herself in another, potentially worse one settled over her. *Mother will move heaven and earth to see me married to a duke.* The intense conversation coming from the matrons on the other side of the room practically guaranteed that.

A cloak of foreboding settled over Sophie, driving away the relief she'd felt earlier at having thwarted Lord Newsome.

"If you had a black gown on right now, you'd look like you were in mourning," Anne observed as she shuffled the cards for their usual game of whist.

"Of course she's in mourning. She's finally caught. Everyone knows Sophie never intended to marry," Olivia declared with a toss of her chestnut curls. "She'd rather go to university than to the altar."

Sophie glared at her sister across the table. Their parents would be the ones mourning soon—the untimely demise of their youngest daughter if Livie did not choose her words more carefully. She was fresh out of the nursery, and now Sophie wished her back there. She excused her sister's outspokenness—this time.

"Did you expect his announcement tonight?" Violet picked up her cards and began studying them.

"No," Sophie replied honestly. "Not yet," she amended. There was no point in starting the gossip already. "We had spoken of marriage . . ." Her marriage to another. The feeling of melancholy passed quickly, replaced by a much stronger anger and the realization that she'd been duped—they all had.

Likely His Grace had only spoken to her before dinner to ascertain whether or not she was engaged yet. When he'd discovered she was not, that had cleared the path for him to make such a bold announcement. And what was she to have done but go along with the charade when there were fifty of Society's elite in attendance to witness it? At least Viscount Newsome, unpleasant as he was, had not forced her hand in front of an audience.

And as to the fact that she had never actually agreed to marry this mysterious duke—*I do not even know his name.* None of that mattered now. The other guests knew him. Her parents did. The papers would, and by tomorrow news of their betrothal would be all over the city. She would be stuck. "How *could* he?" she said, unsure whether she felt angrier with her father or with the unnamed duke. Her hands fisted in her lap, and she felt the need to strike something.

"How could he *not*?" Violet asked. "You have turned down *four* offers of marriage in the past year and a half. No doubt you would have turned down this one as well—unless the situation forbade it. What parent could pass up a duke? I think it likely they seated him far from you so you would not suspect."

"It was rather brilliant of Mother," Olivia said. "She promised me she would do whatever necessary to see you wed soon, so she would not have two daughters competing for the same suitors."

"It would not have been a competition," Sophie said, further stung by her sister's words and her mother's scheming. "I would have gladly given them all to you."

"Including the Duke of Warwick?" Anne asked.

For the third time that evening Sophie struggled to hide her shock. The *Duke of Warwick* was her betrothed? Her savior? *Impossible.* The man was a blackguard and given wide berth by most of the ton for good reason. Among other things, it was well known that he had killed two Englishmen on Saint Kitts last year. There had not been evidence enough to prosecute him here, but by the numerous accounts she had heard, it had to be true.

No wonder her parents had seated him so far from her. They couldn't have known of his plans. Had he even been invited? Perhaps when a murderer showed up to dinner, one made room for him at the table, regardless.

"Though you seemed startled at first, you also seemed happy," Anne continued. "And the way you two were looking at each other at dinner . . ."

"We were?" Sophie didn't even bother attempting to explain that away. She had been curious about him, and then she had been so relieved to be free of Lord Newsome that she hadn't considered how her reaction might look to others. It was better that everyone believed her pleased with the duke's announcement anyway. No one would suspect that she would do anything rash. Or perhaps they thought her rash or desperate already, for accepting his offer.

But she hadn't really, and she didn't have to marry him or the viscount or any man. It was time to put her long-laid plans into effect. She'd been preparing for the unfortunate eventuality of an unwanted betrothal for months, saving all of her pin money, researching different cities and neighborhoods—and the best avenues for getting to them—procuring letters of recommendation from various teachers she'd had over the years. Running away to be a governess wasn't her first choice, but it had just become the only one.

If she could not tolerate marriage to a man like Newsome, she could certainly not be married to the Duke of Warwick, whose dark reputation was known throughout all of London.

Four

"It appears your bride-to-be has fled already." Lord Newsome *tsk*ed unsympathetically. "At least you don't have to worry about her jilting you at the altar."

"Actually it is *your* company she was hoping to avoid by retiring early." Graham clenched one hand into a fist and tucked it inside the other at his waist. He leaned closer, speaking slowly and clearly. "A good thing too, because if I ever see you treating her as you did tonight, your family will be naming a new viscount. You are never to touch Miss Claybourne, look at her, speak with her, or even think of her again." He straightened, a false smile in place. "Unless you would like to meet at dawn, of course."

Newsome's face was mottled and his mouth twisted, making his tiny eyes even beadier than usual.

Graham arched a brow. "Are we clear on those terms?"

"Very," Newsome spat out, then turned on his heel and stalked away.

"Pity, that," Graham murmured to his friend, Lord William Fitzgerald. "It would have been rather satisfying to shoot him."

"You have bigger problems." William inclined his head toward the doors leading into the drawing room, where their host glowered at them. "It looks like Lord Claybourne wishes to shoot *you*."

Graham waved the comment away. "He has felt that way for some time. I've only given him another reason now." Graham grimaced, bracing himself for a conversation with one of the most despicable men in London.

The pudgy curmudgeon marched directly up to him. "Where is my daughter?"

"I assume she is upstairs in her bedchamber, resting," Graham said calmly. "That is what your charming wife told me minutes ago when we joined the ladies." He had taken this as good news. He was relying heavily upon gossip from the servants—Miss Claybourne's maid, Mrs. Shelby, to her husband, the groundskeeper, and the groundskeeper to his new assistant, who was actually one of Graham's men. When servants held no respect for their employer, there was no loyalty, and thus it had been almost too easy to learn what he needed and even to arrange a private interview with both Mrs. Shelby and her husband.

It was from them Graham had learned of Lord Claybourne's edict to his middle daughter, information Graham had used to his advantage tonight. From Lord Claybourne's own wife he had learned of Newsome's frequent visits and that there was more to the arrangement in Saint Kitts than he had first imagined. Rescuing Miss Claybourne from an unwanted marriage would be mutually beneficial—keeping her from Newsome's clutches and also preventing the merger of the two largest plantations on the island and the imbalance of power that would have ensued. That it came at the price of a marriage neither Graham nor Miss Claybourne had planned on nor wanted did not particularly bother him. She would likely be amenable to his suggestion that they live separate lives, married in name only as it mutually benefited them.

He had been told that she did not wish to marry at all but had been begging her father for years to allow her to further

her education. She valued her independence and was not close with her family—little wonder, with the way they had disowned her elder sister for marrying below her station and the manner in which her father had attempted to use Sophia as a bargaining chip with Newsome.

Graham would have to be careful that she did not feel forced into a marriage with him. He would have to help her see that marrying him would protect her from men like Newsome, and her father would lose much of his leverage with her. With any luck, the two estates—her father's and Newsome's—on Saint Kitts would never be joined, and conditions on the island would continue to slowly improve.

Depending upon Miss Claybourne's feelings and/or prejudices, he might also gain somewhat of a mother for his sister's children. If she was kind and caring, they could live with her, and Miss Claybourne would still have plenty of free time to pursue her own interests. It was a perfect plan.

If she truly was upstairs, preparing to make her escape tonight.

He very much hoped that was the case, as he was not overly fond of kidnapping. He'd done it before as a necessary means to an end, and he would do it again if left no other choice. But somehow, he didn't think that would be the best way to start out with Miss Claybourne. Ayla had not been particularly cooperative when he had rescued her and her brother. He still bore the scar of a bite mark on his arm as a reminder and did not wish for another to match.

"Raymond, my study. Now," Lord Claybourne hissed.

Graham held in a grimace at the use of his father's surname, and instead flashed a sardonic grin at William. "Care to join us?"

"Wouldn't miss this for the world." He stepped in line with Graham, following Lord Claybourne from the room.

Their host led them down a short hall, the butler trailing behind.

The butler stepped forward when they entered the study. "May I offer you some refreshments?"

"No. They don't need drinks. It is bad enough I was forced to feed them tonight." Lord Claybourne dismissed his servant with a glacial expression.

"I do believe I was on the original guest list," William said. "And as Lord Arnold was unable to join us this evening, I had hoped you would have no objections to my bringing another old friend, one of higher social standing to elevate your event, as it were."

"You should choose better friends," Lord Claybourne snapped. He strode around to the other side of a garish, gold-leafed desk and sat. He waved his hands at the chairs beside Graham and William. "Sit."

"I prefer to stand," Graham said, not intending to be here long and pleased to be looking down on the man. "What did you wish to discuss? Since it appears my welcome is worn out at this party, I would prefer to be on my way."

"What you did in there tonight—" Lord Claybourne shook an angry finger at him. "Lies. All of it. You did not speak to me about marrying my daughter."

"You are wrong," Graham said. "I told you to call off the plantation merger or there would be consequences. If you did not believe me, that is your fault."

"I—you—" Claybourne jumped up, slapping his hands upon the desk. He leaned forward, the bright hue of anger blazing across his face. "How was I to know you meant Sophia?"

Graham shrugged. "You ought to have. You're the one who made her part of the collateral. I have simply removed your ability to use her."

"You've done nothing of the sort," Claybourne shouted. "So long as she is under my roof, she is mine to do with as I see fit. And I don't see fit to have her marry *you*."

"That is unfortunate, as the papers will be reporting just that in a matter of hours." Graham stifled a yawn, bored of the conversation already. "Your guests will bear witness as well. It will be more than gossip by noon tomorrow. It will be fact, relayed repeatedly all over London."

"You will have difficulty refuting it, when everyone here saw Miss Claybourne's reaction," William added.

Graham gave a nod of thanks for William's support. "If she was not in agreement, surely she would have shown it." It was what he had feared, what had made him wait so long into the meal before acting. Had she rejected him outright, he would not have cared—for himself, at least. But he had feared hurting her, humiliating her, and causing her further duress than she was already under, seated next to Newsome with his lustful touches and looks. Who knew what the man had said to her that had her looking so abjectly miserable and leaning away, practically into Baron Harrelson's lap.

It was at that moment Graham had decided to act. How could he not—at least try to give her hope of rescue? He had stood, and her gaze had followed him, as it had much of the evening, since their encounter before dinner. He had announced their engagement, and then . . .

She had smiled. At him, for him. He'd wanted to help her before—because it also suited his cause—but in that moment his motives changed, shifted with the sweetness and innocence of her smile. A surge of protectiveness, much like he'd felt for his sister, took hold inside of him. He had let Katherine down, but he would not make that mistake again. He would see that Miss Sophia Claybourne was safe from Viscount Newsome, and so help anyone who got in his way.

"She was merely putting on a brave face. Sophia has never wanted to marry—*anyone*. Least of all a scoundrel like you." Claybourne's eyes burned with fury.

"Yet you intended to force her to wed Newsome," Graham said. "And you sat back and allowed him to treat her little better than a common whore during dinner."

Lord Claybourne sneered. "As if you'd treat her any better. Everyone knows your reputation as a despoiler of women."

Claybourne's insult bounced off Graham harmlessly. He knew what his reputation was, and he couldn't have cared less. He followed his own moral code, the one a loving mother had instilled in him during his youth. He had only to answer to his own conscience, and to no one else, least of all the ton with its backbiting and double standards. And Lord Claybourne had it entirely wrong. *If his daughter and I were to marry . . .* It would not be a traditional marriage. They would live far apart, where he could be certain never to do her harm in any way. "Do not pretend to be the doting father now. You've already thrown away one daughter, so it was rightly assumed you cared little more for the next."

"What? I have not—Victoria chose to marry a commoner, a *merchant*. That was not my doing."

"Was it not you who cut her off from her family and fortune completely? And who brought ruin to her husband's previously successful business? And you who sent her husband away, when he came to your house, pleading with you to send a doctor to help her through childbirth? Because of you, Victoria and her child died. If that is not throwing away a daughter, I don't know what is."

"Allowing her to marry a murderer," Claybourne retorted. "Which I will *not* do!"

Graham noted that the older man hadn't missed a beat, hadn't flinched or shown the least amount of remorse regarding the death of his eldest daughter and his grandchild. It was telling and troublesome and made Graham want to march up the stairs this instant to remove Miss Claybourne and whisk her to safety.

Claybourne's eyes had taken on a reddish hue and bugged out, looking as if they might dislodge themselves from his face altogether.

"If murderers are out, that takes Newsome off the table too," William muttered under his breath.

But Claybourne heard it. "Unlike your *friend*, Newsome has not killed anyone."

"Hasn't he?" Graham met Claybourne's eyes, his own seething with hatred and the strong desire for revenge that had been building inside of him the past two years, since he had learned of his sister's death—her murder. Some days he thought he would explode with it. "You had both better pray that I never find out otherwise."

He turned to leave before he did something that would get him arrested and disturb his carefully laid plans. "I will return tomorrow afternoon to take Miss Claybourne for a drive. Banns will be posted this week. We will marry next month. If you do not wish to be ruined completely, you will not interfere."

Five

GRAHAM BADE WILLIAM GOODNIGHT IN the privacy of the earl's carriage, with a promise that he would see William and his wife at Caerlanwood, his secluded estate in Scotland, eight days hence. "Don't delay," Graham warned in low tones. "If her father finds us, I'll need a second when I face him at dawn."

"You won't have to wait until dawn," William said. "You can shoot at each other as soon as he arrives. No one for miles around on that wild land of yours to hear or care."

"True enough," Graham agreed with soberness. "I hope to avoid it, all the same—if only for Miss Claybourne's sake. If I am fortunate, it will take Lord Claybourne some time to locate her. But if he does, it's bound to be a messy business. I'd like you there to witness that Claybourne came after me, and not the other way around."

"And to attend your wedding," William's wife, Elizabeth, reminded him.

"Aye." Graham felt suddenly weary. He had not set out on this journey intending this course of action but could see no other way to keep Miss Claybourne from Newsome's clutches and to avoid the merger her father had arranged. Beyond his musings during dinner, Graham had not had time to think on the reality of marrying Miss Claybourne. He only knew it must be done and he should make it as painless as possible for her. "She shall have a proper ceremony in a chapel—even if it is the small one at Caerlanwood. There will be none of this marrying in the blacksmith shop at Gretna Green. I want her to be able to hold her head up in Society in the future."

"Which is why you announced your betrothal this evening. So it will not seem as if she eloped but that it was planned all along," Elizabeth said.

"One can only hope." Graham frowned, thinking of all the scandal Miss Claybourne's family had already endured. "It was either speak up or clobber Newsome with the roasted pig from the table. Did you see his odious behavior tonight? No lady should be treated that way."

"I was not near enough to hear their conversation," William said quietly. "But I caught the way he was looking at her—it was hard for anyone to mistake."

"And her father *encouraged* it." Graham's anger spiked again as he rapped on the door for the footman. He had been too young to do much about his father's mistreatment of his mother and sister, but now he could right the injustices he saw, particularly when an innocent woman was involved.

The door swung outward, and Graham stood and ducked beneath the opening. "Goodnight," he bade his longtime friends. "Safe travels to you." He stood on the sidewalk and watched as William's carriage drove away. Then, after making certain no one else was about, he walked two houses down to where a pair of his own vehicles were parked. Last week he'd had them stripped of their crests and painted a solid black to match the public hackneys found around London.

He peeked into the farthest one and saw Mr. Shelby and his toddler son, along with an array of hatboxes, carpet bags, and a trunk piled on the opposite seat. Graham was impressed that Mrs. Shelby had been able to pack Miss Claybourne's belongings so quickly and without being noticed. He'd already decided to increase the Shelbys' wages when they came to work for him, and now he wondered if perhaps they ought to receive an even larger raise. For as much as the servants here were not loyal to Lord and Lady Claybourne, it seemed that a few of them, at least, cared greatly and would do anything for their middle daughter.

The second carriage, and one closer to the Claybourne residence, stood empty, save for the woman seated inside. Graham peered through the window and noted her clasping and unclasping her hands repeatedly. What he had asked of Lucy and Adam Shelby was no small thing, and he appreciated the immense risk they were taking, as well as the great trust they had placed in him. He supposed he had his own, extremely loyal servants to thank for that trust and for speaking well of him to the Shelbys.

Graham stepped back from the carriages and into the shadows between the houses. He pulled out his pocket watch to check the time and found it nearly too dark to read. According to her mother, Miss Claybourne had gone upstairs forty minutes ago. When delayed by her father, Graham had feared he might miss her, but neither his drivers nor the footmen had seen her emerge from either entrance to the townhouse yet. *Any minute now.*

He clenched and unclenched his fists, much like Mrs. Shelby was wringing her hands, as he wrestled with both an overwhelming desire to throttle Newsome and a fervent hope that the remainder of this night would go as planned. He needed Miss Claybourne to come and, in addition, found he wanted her company as well. Some part of his mind rang out a vague warning at that. There was not room in his life for wanting of any sort, particularly when it came to a woman. He told himself it was just that so much hinged on her leaving with him tonight, free from her father and Newsome's clutches. And effectively ceasing the merger of the Saint Kitts plantations.

If she ever came.

Six

Sophie brushed dust from the front of her gown, then picked up the heavy carpet bag from her bed. Minutes earlier she had hauled it from beneath her wardrobe, where it had been mostly packed and ready to go at a moment's notice for nearly three months.

If only Mother hadn't come up to check on her, she would have been gone already. As it was, she'd barely managed to hide her bag when Mother knocked on her door. And then it had been such an odd conversation.

"You're all grown up and to be married to a duke." Mother's eyes had glistened as she spoke. No doubt she was overcome at what to her must seem a brilliant match, never mind that the man Sophie was to marry was probably a murderer. A duke was a duke regardless, as far as her mother was concerned.

Sophie longed to tell her that she would be doing no such thing and marrying no one, but she could not alert her mother to her plans. "I'm glad you are pleased," Sophie said, sitting at her dressing table and reaching for a hair pin, as if she were preparing for bed.

"I am—hopeful," Mother said, coming to stand behind Sophie. "Hopeful that you will be happy."

Surprised, Sophie looked up and met her mother's expression in the mirror. Her happiness had never concerned Mother before—had it?

"I know I should have done more to help Victoria," Mother said quietly.

"*More?*" Sophie turned in her seat to face her. "You should have done *something*—anything. Instead you stood by and let Father ruin—"

"You are right." Mother glanced toward the door and sounds in the hall. "I should go back to our guests."

Sophie stood and walked toward her bed and the bag she'd hastily stowed beneath it a few minutes earlier. "I will not be back down tonight. My head aches."

"I'll tell everyone you are resting," Mother said, following her, then placing a hand on her arm. "I do love you, Sophia. I loved Victoria too, and I failed her. I pray I have not failed you as well."

With that her mother had left the room, leaving Sophie confused and experiencing a compassion for her mother that she did not usually feel.

She'd waited a few minutes until her mother's footsteps had receded. Now Sophie clutched her bag in her hands and crossed the room and opened the door slowly, peeking out into the hallway. *Deserted.* The maids, including her own lady's maid and her mother's, should all be below stairs for another hour at least, and she would be well on her way by then. She stepped into the hall, closing the door softly behind her, then hurried toward the back stairway at the far end. Thinking of the servants who regularly used it, she suffered a pang of regret at leaving some of them, particularly Mrs. Shelby—Lucy—who was only a few years older than she and had been a loyal servant to Sophie since her twelfth birthday. Many times Sophie had debated confiding her plan to her maid but knew it would go better for Lucy if she could truly say she'd no idea of Sophie's whereabouts.

Pausing before the door to the stairwell, Sophie shifted

the heavy bag temporarily to one arm. She turned the knob and stepped through the doorway, then shut it tightly behind her. Step one accomplished. Next came traversing the wood stairs without sounding like one of Lord Harrelson's elephants. Keeping her bag in one hand, she used her other to grasp the railing. Then she tiptoed down the steps to the ground floor. Pressing her back along the wall, into the shadows, she made her way toward the service entrance.

Voices carried from the kitchen, and she heard snatches of her name, along with the Duke of Warwick's.

"Her mother was in on it, I tell you," Cook said. "She knowed he was coming—told me first thing this morning to plan for an extra guest."

Livie was right. Tears stung Sophie's eyes at this confirmation. Had Mother invited him here? Told the duke of the promise Sophie had been forced to give her father? Her mother had always seemed the more reasonable of her two parents, and though they had not been particularly close, Sophie had never felt so betrayed as she did at this moment.

"Poor dear. 'Tis like throwing her to a lion, all for the sake of a title." Fanny, one of the upstairs maids, sounded on the verge of tears.

"That's the way of it for their lot. We spend our whole lives laboring in this hot kitchen, and they have to marry who they're told." Cook's matter-of-fact tone brooked no sympathy.

"Better she marry the duke than that despicable Newsome," one of the other maids said.

Better I marry no one.

"The Duke of Warwick is more than despicable. He's a murderer."

On that pleasant thought, Sophie reached the door and opened it slowly, letting in a blast of cool air. The wind had picked up, and though it was well into May, she felt a chill pass through her. She shivered at once in the ridiculous evening gown not meant to be worn outside and wished she'd thought to bring a shawl. Changing into something more practical had been impossible without Lucy to assist.

Sophie clutched the bag tighter. All the books crammed inside wouldn't do much to protect her from inclement weather. *No matter.* The inside of a coach would be warmer, and summer was practically here. By the time autumn came and the weather turned cool again, she would have been working as a governess for some time and have the funds to purchase a proper cloak.

Sophie kept to the shadows along the side of the house—easy enough, as the street lamp did not reach that far. With less than an hour until the house party ended, she expected carriages to begin arriving soon, including at least a few cabs for conveying guests who had not brought their own vehicles.

A careful, guarded glance at the street proved her theory correct, and Sophie let out a breath of relief at the sight of the two plain carriages parked a short distance away. With hurried steps she approached the nearest.

A footman jumped down and opened the door.

"Twenty-one Palace Gate, Kensington." Sophie rattled off the address of the London Governess agency. The office would be closed at this time of night, but she would either find somewhere nearby to stay or wait on the doorstep until morning, if necessary.

She accepted the footman's outstretched hand, climbed into the carriage, and settled on the seat—directly across from her maid.

"Shelby?" Sophie squinted across the dark space, certain her eyes must be playing tricks on her.

"I wouldn't have done it, but for your own good, Miss. Please hear him out."

Him? "Hear who—"

A tall, masculine frame filled the doorway, blocking out what little light from the street had made its way inside the carriage.

The man, head lowered as he ducked to enter, hesitated, then chose the seat beside Mrs. Shelby. The footman passed a lantern inside and closed the door, but Sophie was already moving, out of her seat and reaching for the handle. A large hand clamped over hers. "Please do as your maid has requested and allow me to explain myself and why you are here."

That voice. The warm timbre of it washed over her again. But instead of bringing to mind a pot of rich, delicious chocolate, as it had the first time she'd heard it, the deep tones sent a shiver of fear along Sophie's spine.

"You!" She turned on the Duke of Warwick as she wrenched her hand free. He tapped on the ceiling, and the carriage gave a lurch, sending her sprawling backward into her seat.

"That was an ungentlemanly thing to do," she snapped, barely managing to hold onto her heavy bag.

"I warned you earlier that I am no gentleman." He attached the lantern to a hook in the middle of the roof, and a soft, yellow glow lit the small space, making it almost cozy.

Too cozy, too close, too confined. Panic rose in Sophie's throat, but she lifted her chin and faced him head on, unwilling to show her fear. "Every bit the knave you are reputed to be." She'd been duped again. She scowled, furious with herself as much as with the man across from her. She was not usually so foolish. This was no public coach but a luxurious private coach with wide, plush seats, and the finest glass windows. Had she but taken a second before entering—She looked toward the door longingly as they picked up speed.

"Don't even think about it. You'd break your pretty little neck, and then my reputation would be beyond repair."

Her eyes narrowed, though she doubted he could tell in the shadowed space. "Then stop this vehicle at once and allow me—and my misguided maid—" she spared a glance in Shelby's direction— "to remove ourselves."

He shook his head. "Allow me to explain myself, and then if you still wish to leave, I shall deposit you anywhere you would like to go."

"Why should I trust you?"

"Because in this instance you have no choice. I apologize for that. I wish there had been another way."

"Another way to force me into marriage? Aside from tricking me and announcing our betrothal to a roomful of people before abducting me?" She couldn't be certain, but she thought she saw his mouth twitch.

"Yes, other than all that. It was rather bad form. Had the circumstances not been so dire, I would not have acted thus."

She huffed and scooted to the far side of the carriage, as far from him as possible. Directly across from her, Shelby was wringing her hands and looking generally miserable.

"I have—arranged—your company here tonight so you might avoid marrying Lord Newsome."

"How gallant," Sophie muttered. "I was trying to escape *you*!"

"Also understandable," he acknowledged, surprising her. "You do not have to marry me. I was not in the market for a wife and only recommended marriage for your protection."

She harrumphed again. "From whom? Surely not yourself."

"From Viscount Newsome, specifically, and from your father and any other way he might see fit to use you as a means to an end."

"Explain." Sophie set the carpet bag aside with a thud that earned raised brows from the duke.

"Your gowns appear to be rather weighty."

"Books," she clarified. "I am going to be a governess. One does not need fancy clothes for such a position."

"Ah." He nodded. "Well, that is good news, as I am currently in need of a governess. Perhaps you would be amenable to that position instead of marriage? I am a guardian to my sister's children," he added, answering the question that had come unbidden to her mind.

Not his, then. Obviously, he was unattached, since he had pretended they were to marry. She didn't care whose children they were. She wouldn't be teaching them anything if they were within one hundred miles of him.

He leaned forward, elbows braced upon his knees. "I believe we can be of mutual benefit to one another, Miss Claybourne. Your father and Lord Newsome were planning to merge their plantations on Saint Kitts. As your father's plantation is considerably smaller than Newsome's, you were part of that agreement. In exchange for an equal partnership, Newsome was to have you as his wife."

Shelby gave a grunt of displeasure as Sophie suppressed a shudder of revulsion. She crossed her arms in front of her, warding off both the chill of the carriage and the cold fear that crept over her at how near she'd come to being trapped in a situation she might not have escaped. Not that she wasn't trapped now. But the duke, for all his ill reputation, seemed somehow less abhorrent and threatening than Newsome. He'd not once eyed her as if she were a meal for him to devour.

"How do you know all of this about my father?"

"I have interests on Saint Kitts as well. I make it my business to know everything that goes on there."

"I assume you are against this merger."

He nodded. "Your father and Lord Newsome keep slaves—and they don't keep them well. Not that there is such a

thing, but some owners are worse than others." His jaw clenched, and he brought a fist to his mouth, as if holding in anger.

Sophie swallowed uncomfortably, but she met his eyes, which glittered with a rage that frightened her.

She'd known about her father's plantation and the slaves he kept—on some level—from snatches of conversation she'd heard here and there. But saying it out loud, thinking of what it meant, made her ill. The food she ate, the gowns she wore, her pin money, the books in her bag, had all been gained by the forced labor of others—backbreaking, torturous labor, from what she understood.

"The slave trade ceased in 1807," she said, more to herself than the duke. "But the islands still practice slavery. They're just not to import more, is that it?"

"Oh, they still import them," he said. "Just not as many, and not legally. And you are correct, not much has changed on Saint Kitts or the other British colonies so far as slavery is concerned."

"My father said that to give it up would be to give up what we have here. Our lifestyle." He'd said a great many other things too—none of which she particularly believed—about the slaves being incapable of learning to read or write or to provide a living for themselves. Such judgments sounded all too similar to those passed upon women in England. They were untrue for her, so it seemed likely they were untrue about the African slaves as well.

The duke's jawline sharpened as he frowned at her. "It is a lifestyle that comes at the price of human life. On the islands business and humanity intersect at a most horrendous junction. It is collision and calamity, foul and depraved."

His passionate words reverberated through the small carriage and pierced her heart. She had known this was happening, had heard her father speak of the unspeakable from his visits to Saint Kitts, and she had ignored the prick of conscience that always followed and kept her thoughts to herself until they faded and were forgotten. *That was wrong.* She ought to have been speaking out for others, doing all she could to promote their welfare, instead of always being so concerned with her own.

"In your father and Lord Newsome's case, they stand to lose much. A considerable portion of their livelihoods are derived from their plantations. Like many, they have made a fortune there and wish to continue."

"Are you the same?" she prodded, unable to believe such after his ardent speech. "What is your specific interest in Saint Kitts? Why do you wish to prevent this merger?"

"Because I am slowly and systematically buying up plantations and freeing the slaves there. My sister owned a plantation on Saint Kitts."

"Your sister," Sophie exclaimed. "*Owned?* A woman—"

"She became the owner when her husband died. Unlike estates in England, it did not come with an entail. So yes, she owned it. For a very brief period—while she was still alive." The duke's face clouded. He broke their gaze to stare down at his hands a moment.

"I am sorry for your loss," Sophie said quietly. His pain was recognizable, a reflection of her own for the sister she had lost.

She looked away, affording him a moment of privacy, or as much as might be had in the confines of the carriage.

Across from her, Shelby had quit wringing her hands and leaned her head against the side of the carriage, her eyes half closed.

"As wretchedly as her husband treated her," the duke continued, "his abuse of the slaves was even worse. Katherine could not stand it and secretly did all she could to aid them. After her husband died, she freed every last one. Those who stayed on were paid a fair wage and became her loyal friends. She had a dream that all on the island might be freed. I have tried to continue her work."

Sophie studied him closely, doing her best to determine if he spoke the truth. At the moment he did not look like a murderer or speak like the blackguard he was purported to be. Yet he had fooled her twice already. "And this merger will somehow interfere?"

"You're very astute for—" He broke off and had the decency to look chagrined.

Sophie sighed with exasperation. "Go ahead and say it."

"For a young lady of only twenty."

"So you would expect an older woman to have more intelligence?" She wasn't going to let him off so easily.

He shook his head. "No, unfortunately. I would not."

"But you should," she challenged.

To her surprise, he agreed with her again. "When in the company of females like my sister and yourself, I feel you are correct."

"Continue your explanation," Sophie urged, granting him temporary forgiveness for his insult. She glanced out the window, aware that the neighborhood outside was unfamiliar and he was taking her far from home. She ought to tell him to turn around, but their conversation was intriguing. He was discussing things with her as if she were a man, treating her as an equal—or more so than most other men whose company she had been in. Her instinct was to believe all he had told her so far. His ready admission of his faults might also be a ploy to gain her trust, though, so she remained skeptical. But with every word, she felt more and more that he was being truthful with her.

"The merger will give your father and Newsome more influence, more governing power on the island. It is possible that they could actually prevent slaves on other plantations from being freed."

"Then I am doubly grateful not to be a part of it." Her mind spun, thinking of the ramifications, and wondering that the supposedly wicked Duke of Warwick took such interest in the affairs of enslaved people thousands of miles away. He piqued her curiosity, that was certain, but "curiosity killed the cat," or so she had heard Cook say on numerous occasions, to servants asking too many questions or wanting to know about things that had little to do with their stations. The duke had nothing to do with her station, particularly now that she was going to be a governess. The sooner they parted ways, the better.

"I gave your driver an address, and I would like to be taken there posthaste. I intend to seek employment as a governess, preferably as far away from London as possible. My father shall neither know my whereabouts nor even what has become of me. I appreciate your assistance in conveying me the first leg of my journey. Once I have departed, I respectfully request that you return my maid to her place of employment."

"You don't look much like a governess in that gown," the duke observed, with the same lazy smile he'd bestowed upon her earlier in the evening.

"I intend to change before interviewing." Though she wasn't exactly certain where, now. But the two dresses in her bag were more than suitable for a governess.

"Were you planning on giving your new employers a false name? If your dress and jewels don't give you away, your name will, and your father will be there to collect you in a matter of days, if not hours."

Sophie bit her lip, displeased with this flaw in what she

had considered carefully laid plans. Her name was on her certificate of schooling and her letters of recommendation, and without those, without proof that she was worthy of hire . . ." You are right," she admitted reluctantly. "I had assumed Father would simply let me go, that he would be happy to be rid of me." She smiled ruefully. "Some months ago he threatened to throw me out on the street if I did not agree to accept the next offer of marriage. But if what you say is true—"

"It is."

"Then he won't wish to forfeit his plans."

"Which is why you are here in this carriage. I can take you somewhere he is not likely to find you for some time. And if he does, I will offer you my protection."

"By marriage." She looked down her nose at him. "You must think me a complete imbecile if you expect me to wed a stranger—one reputed to be even worse than the man my father chose for me."

The duke leaned forward again, and when he spoke his words were soft, almost soothing, meant to console while imparting a harsh truth at the same time. "Your father did not choose a husband *for* you. You were not any part of his selfish machinations, but a means to an end for what he wanted. Choose for yourself now. Judge for yourself. I have not accosted you, though I've had ample opportunity. I arranged for your maid to be here to see to your comforts—" he glanced sideways at Shelby, snoring softly, her head lolling against the side of the carriage— "and as a sort of *chaperone*, though her usefulness there leaves much to be desired."

Sophie laughed. "It's not her fault she fell asleep. She is with child again and often exhausted." Little wonder, with all of her duties and a two-year-old to care for between. *Oh no!* Sophie turned back to the duke. "What do you mean you arranged for her to come? *Mrs.* Shelby has a husband and a child. You must return her at once!"

"Her husband and son are in the carriage ahead of us," the duke said, a hint of reproach in his voice, as if he were offended that Sophie had thought him careless. "I would not steal a mother from her child or a wife from her husband. I am trying to end slavery, not contribute to it."

"Oh." Sophie leaned her head back against the seat in momentary relief, then immediately recalled his previous deceptions. "Stop the carriage," she commanded, reaching up to pound on the roof. "I wish to see Shelby's family for myself."

"Very well." The duke rapped on the roof and shouted to the driver. The carriage rolled to a stop, and a minute later a footman appeared and opened the door.

"What is wrong? Are we there already?" her sleepy maid asked from her corner of the coach.

"Nothing is wrong—aside from the fact that we have been abducted by the Duke of Warwick."

"You climbed into my carriage of your own accord," he reminded her.

Ignoring him, Sophie focused her attention on Shelby. "I intend to see for myself that he has kept his word and that your husband and son are indeed making this journey with us."

"Thank you, Miss," Shelby said, casting a wary glance at the duke.

Sophie stood and moved toward the door, then accepted the footman's hand as she stepped down.

"It's pitch black out there. Take this to assist you as you walk." The duke handed her the lantern from inside the carriage. "I don't desire to have a wife *or* a governess with a broken leg." Once he had handed the lantern off to her, he leaned back in his seat, apparently unconcerned.

The chill spring breeze made the gooseflesh on Sophie's arms rise again, and something sharp attempted to poke through the thin sole of her slipper, a reminder that she was attired very poorly for any type of journey and especially not for midnight explorations outside. Nevertheless, she held the light aloft, faced the front of the carriage, and walked several steps. They were still in the city—somewhere—as houses lined either side of the dark, quiet street. The neighborhood was not nearly as fancy as her own and had no streetlights at all. She walked another dozen steps, past the carriage with its lanterns and the horses breathing heavily, then peered down the street in front of her as far as she could.

It was silent and empty, with no other carriage in sight.

Seven

LADY CLAYBOURNE SETTLED ON THE edge of her middle daughter's bed and absently stroked the lump beneath the covers that she knew very well was not her daughter.

Like Victoria before her, Sophia was gone. But not gone for good. Not forever, Lady Claybourne reminded herself while simultaneously praying she had done the right thing.

"I owe you so many apologies," she said to the unmoving lump of pillows under the quilt. "I should never have let Victoria be cut off. Or if your father insisted, I should have defied him and visited her and helped her myself. I will never forgive my part in her death." Lady Claybourne drew in a shuddering breath as her hands clenched—one in the folds of her gown, the other in the blankets. The pain of losing her eldest daughter—sweet Torie, as her sisters had called her—was never far from the surface, a constant throbbing of loss and sorrow. All of which Lady Claybourne felt she deserved. What kind of mother was she, to have disowned her daughter simply because she had married below her station? Far below her station, into abject poverty thanks to the way her father had set out to ruin her merchant husband. But Torie hadn't cared because she'd loved Jonathan so very much.

Lady Claybourne had never known such love. Her marriage, like so many of the ton, had been arranged. It was simply the way things were done.

And it was wrong.

"Yet have I not done the same to you now, dear Sophie?" She sighed, her anguish and regret weighing heavily tonight, along with worry that she had done wrong by her middle daughter as well.

But no. It was right. Or it would be—eventually. Lady Claybourne straightened her shoulders and sat up taller. She had been thorough and careful. She had studied all the solutions and come up with the best. Her research and logic had all been very Sophie-like. She could only hope that someday Sophie would see it that way.

"I wrote a letter to the Duke of Warwick," Lady Claybourne began her explanation again. "Your father had mentioned him so many times—in anger, of course. It seemed that, right and left, the duke was thwarting your father's efforts on the island. I took it upon myself to learn everything I could about the Black Duke, as he has come to be called here. And everything I learned led me to believe his name was earned from his work as a champion of slaves' rights more than for any deeds he had done."

He *had* killed at least one man on Saint Kitts, and possibly two. But the circumstances surrounding those deaths were murky, at best. Everything Lady Claybourne had learned—and a lady of her position seeking to gossip or hear such could learn a great deal—led her to believe his actions had likely been self-defense.

"I knew the duke was the only one who could possibly stop your father from completing his plans and marrying you off to that wretched viscount."

Lord Newsome's presence in their lives had come at a steep price, as far as she was concerned. His influence upon her husband was more than evident in Lord Claybourne's increased temper and sour disposition. It was shortly after his return from Saint Kitts a few years earlier that he had so cruelly disowned Victoria. And now he wished to use Sophia as a bartering chip in an already questionable arrangement. It was as if, Lady Claybourne mused, in his becoming accustomed to the treatment of slaves, the buying and selling of humans, that his own family, his daughters, had ceased to be individuals he cared for and about. Now he merely saw them as tools of his trade. Either a liability to be cut—as Victoria had been. Or an asset to be used to his advantage—Sophia.

"In my letter I told the duke everything that had transpired and was transpiring between the viscount and your father. I begged him to interfere, to stop both the merger and your wedding. Imagine my relief when he agreed. I received but one, curt note from him, assuring me he would take care of both in a manner I was certain to find satisfactory, though he did not advise me of his plans. He promised me that no harm would come to you, Sophia, which is more than I might have hoped for had I given you over to the care of Lord Newsome."

Lady Claybourne sighed deeply, wearily, sadly. She had but one daughter left and vowed she would do better by Olivia. She would protect her and see that her path was easier, less fraught with danger and the dramatic—beginning tonight, when she sent Olivia home with her cousin and then off to the country tomorrow to stay with a distant relation, where her father could not gain access to her easily.

The time of courtship and marriage ought to be a happy one. Yet for herself and two of her daughters, that had not been true. Though at least Victoria had married for love and had one year with a husband who doted on her.

With a last pat to the lump on the bed, Lady Claybourne stood. She walked to the wardrobe and opened it, though she already knew it was empty. Earlier, after the duke had trusted her enough to tell her that Sophia would be leaving with him tonight, Lady Claybourne had seen to it that the servants, except for Sophia's maid, were all busy with tasks that removed them far from this hall and the back stairs. It had turned out even better than Lady Claybourne had hoped. An hour ago, when the housekeeper reported she could not find Mrs. Shelby anywhere, Lady Claybourne realized that she had gone too. And her husband and son. They would look out for Sophia. She would not be truly alone.

Heavy footsteps sounded in the hall. Lady Claybourne closed the wardrobe and rushed to the door, letting herself out quietly and holding a finger to her lips as her husband approached.

"Shh. Sophie has only been asleep for a little while. The poor thing is exhausted. She was so very distraught."

"Hmph." Lord Claybourne looked past his wife to the door behind her. "I'll talk to her. All she has to do is leave with Newsome tomorrow morning before the duke arrives. Once they're married, there won't be anything he can do about it. There will be another scandal of course, given his announcement this evening. But that'll be more on him. I've half a mind to send her off right now."

Lady Claybourne placed a gentle hand on her husband's arm. "Let her wait a few more hours. She's cried herself to sleep and needs rest. You don't want her in hysterics for the viscount, do you? She's too upset to think clearly about marrying anyone right now."

Her husband's mouth twisted, as if actually considering her words—a rarity.

"I suppose a few more hours won't hurt. I'll go down and tell Newsome he'll have to wait. But don't worry. I've taken care of everything."

"Thank you, dear." Lady Claybourne forced a smile. Because of him, *she'd* had to take care of everything. And she had. It was a most satisfactory feeling.

Eight

"Lucy!" Miss Claybourne's voice carried into the carriage seconds before her head appeared. "There is *no* other vehicle. Your husband and son are not here."

Mrs. Shelby's hands flew to her mouth as she made to rise from her seat.

"Nonsense." Graham sent the maid a quelling look, more than a little irritated that she would mistrust him now, after all he had done to prove himself to this point.

"If it's the other carriage you're wanting, Miss," the footman called from outside, "it has just arrived. Though it was parked in front on the street earlier, it changed places as soon as we set off. The carriage carrying His Grace always leads out."

"You might have mentioned that." Miss Claybourne sent Graham an icy glare. She withdrew from the doorway once more and was gone several minutes this time, presumably speaking with the occupants of the other carriage.

She returned with a considerably subdued countenance but did not avoid Graham or go to the opposite corner to pout, as he'd suspected she would. Instead, once she had seated herself directly across from him, and he had reattached the lantern to the hook in the ceiling, she looked him square in the eye.

"I apologize for doubting you, Your Grace." She turned to Mrs. Shelby. "Your husband and son are indeed in the carriage behind us—along with a great deal of your belongings and mine, it would seem. They are both well and enjoying the journey in such a fine vehicle."

"Thank you, Miss." The maid offered a weak smile, then leaned her head back against the seat once more.

Graham suspected she was not enjoying the ride nearly as much as her family. If what Miss Claybourne had said was true about her maid increasing again, that made the feat Mrs. Shelby had pulled off this evening even more spectacular. His brow creased with concern as he looked at her. She had likely lifted more than she ought tonight and done much more than a woman in her condition should. He had placed great responsibility and burden on her the past week, and she had not once complained but had, in fact, done everything he'd asked of her—and done it better than he had hoped.

He'd always found it perplexing that pregnancy could render a woman of the ton completely helpless for the better part of a year, while women of lower class toiled long hours and did all that was required of them, throughout their confinements.

He had little knowledge of such affairs but guessed that the proper behavior lay somewhere in between. Cautious and caring for oneself and unborn child, yet not acting as if upon death's doorstep.

Though some were.

He sent a surreptitious glance at Miss Claybourne, wondering her thoughts on the matter, as her sister had died in childbirth. That Miss Claybourne had spoken of Mrs. Shelby's condition at all had surprised him, as it was not a proper topic of conversation for a young, unmarried woman. He was starting to suspect that she did not care much for what was proper and what was not, and that made him like her all the more.

"Miss Claybourne, would you be so good as to stand for a moment," Graham asked. Though the door had been shut behind her, the carriage had not yet started out again. "There are blankets and pillows in the compartment beneath your seat. If you would agree to sit on my side, we might allow Mrs. Shelby to recline on the opposite seat. She has done a great deal of hard work this week, and especially tonight, and I believe rest would do her good."

"Of course." Miss Claybourne's wide-eyed expression of disbelief stayed with her as she stood as much as possible in the confined space and pressed herself against the window on the far side.

Graham lifted the seat top and withdrew two wool tartans and two feather pillows. He handed one each to the women, then closed the bench. "Mrs. Shelby—" He held his hand out, indicating that she should move.

She glanced from him to Miss Claybourne. "I don't have to sleep. I can stay awake."

"All will be well," Miss Claybourne assured her as she wrapped the blanket he had given her around her shoulders. "Take your rest if you can. The duke, for all his wicked reputation, does not seem intent on preying upon us tonight."

Once Mrs. Shelby was settled comfortably, or as comfortably as one might be in a carriage, Graham tapped on the roof, and their journey resumed.

Miss Claybourne sat as far from him on their seat as she might, her brows furrowed and lips pursed as she studied him openly. "That was kind of you," she said after a few minutes had passed.

"You find that strange, considering my reputation," he guessed.

She nodded.

"I suppose I should take care not to ruin what I have so

prudently curated. It would not do to have Society thinking me anything other than the rogue I am." His voice dripped with sarcasm which, he suspected, was lost on her. He had no care what Society did or did not think of him. He shouldn't care what Miss Claybourne thought of him either, yet a small part of him was beginning to.

"Did you kill two Englishmen on Saint Kitts?" Her hands fisted on the edges of the blanket wrapped around her, her intense gaze practically begging him to say otherwise.

He could not.

"I did." He focused on the blank wall of the carriage across from him as the events of that horrid day came to mind again, a day he would never forget, though he wished dearly he could. His gaze flitted to Miss Claybourne. He'd hoped to avoid this particular conversation for a while, but it appeared he was not to be granted that luxury.

"Was it self-defense? Were they attacking you and—"

"No." Graham cut her off before she could further embellish whatever rumor she might have heard. "*I* was in no danger." Not entirely true, perhaps. But firing that shot and throwing that axe hadn't had anything to do with *his* safety.

"Are you at least sorry you did it?" she demanded. "Have you any regrets?"

"I regret that I did not do it sooner." If he had taken passage on an earlier ship, if they hadn't run into storms, if he had arrived sooner, he might have spared—

"No kindness can make up for taking two lives." Miss Claybourne's back stiffened, and though her voice held reproach, in the soft light of the carriage, he glimpsed fear in her eyes.

"I suppose not," Graham replied in a clipped tone. He hoped she was done asking questions. There was much he needed to tell her, a lot of explanations to give, but it was too soon. *Too much.* On this night when she'd first fled from her home.

"I will *never* marry you." The icy glare was back.

"That decision is yours to make." He would not force her, but neither could he allow her to return to her father's house and be wed to Newsome, if he would even have her now, considering that Miss Claybourne's reputation had essentially been ruined the moment she set foot inside this carriage, with only her maid as a chaperone.

Graham suspected that Newsome might be willing to overlook that and marry her anyway. Certainly her father would champion that cause if Miss Claybourne returned home anytime soon. At all costs, Graham knew he must not allow her to do that. "That does not change the fact that I am still in need of a governess, and you are still in need of a place safe from your father and the viscount."

"I can be a governess anywhere," she tossed at him, her chin raised defiantly.

"I'll pay you more than a fair wage." Graham kept his tone casual, as if retaining her did not matter a great deal at all. What else could he offer? What else might entice her to come with him, when she was obviously not of a mind to care about his title or wealth, as other young ladies might have? He had misjudged her earlier this evening. He was not dealing with a typical socialite, and for that he was most grateful.

He recalled his conversation with Lord Brockhurst, one of her former suitors, a few days earlier.

"She was so pleasant with her rejection, it was impossible to be angry," Brockhurst had explained, or attempted to. "Miss Claybourne is the antithesis of her father. Like her sister before her, she doesn't care about money or a title. She is either unaware of or cares little about her beauty. She is the least vain woman I have ever known. Unfortunately, the things she does care about are not available to her."

"What would those be?" Graham had asked, sensing potential leverage for future bargaining with Miss Claybourne.

"An education. And a career. She loves to debate. She'd make an excellent lawyer, if you ask me."

He couldn't offer her a career—other than as a governess. *But an education . . .*

"Additionally, in exchange for four hours a day with the children, you may pursue your own education for four hours each day," he offered.

Her arms folded across her lap as she turned to face him once more. "How do you propose I do that? Am I to don men's clothing and pretend to be your nephew so I might attend Oxford?"

Graham turned away so she would not see his mouth twitch. No doubt she had entertained such an idea previously. He wondered that she'd not considered disguising herself as a man during her escape tonight. "Unfortunately my home is nowhere near either Oxford or Cambridge. However, I do have the means to hire tutors on any subject you might wish to study."

The carriage rocked as they hit a rough patch of road, dislodging Miss Claybourne's tightly tucked arms. She reached for the side, hanging on as the blanket slipped from her shoulders, displaying once again the all-too-revealing gown she wore. Graham looked away, displeased he had even noticed. Being attracted to Miss Claybourne was in no way a part of his plans.

The jostling lessened, and she drew the blanket around her once more. "*Any* subject?" She cast a glance at him, and he read the unmistakable interest in her eyes.

He would have to thank Brockhurst later. Graham

nodded. "Make your requests, and I shall send inquiries at our next stop."

"Law. I wish to study the law—how it works, how laws are created, which ones are currently in effect and which are proposed. I wish to form a complete understanding of how the House of Lords and House of Commons function and what each member's responsibilities are there. I want to understand the processes of a court of law—how arguments are made, how representation works."

Graham considered those he knew who were qualified and might be willing to teach Miss Claybourne—or at least those who might be willing to come to his home for a teaching position. He might have to lure them there under false pretenses. Not many would—at first—be willing to take on a female student. William might do for a start. While not a professor or a lawyer, he had studied to become the latter and was familiar with both Houses and England's legal system. "Very well. I have a few ideas for an instructor of law."

"Truly?" Her face brightened, a fleeting smile bringing to mind the one she'd given him across the dinner table earlier. Most ladies wanted gowns and jewels. She wanted to expand her mind. Graham found it a refreshing change.

He nodded. "What else do you wish to learn?"

"Geography—and I don't mean just places on a map. I know most of those already. I want to know what those places are like. I want to learn of the peoples and cultures, the plants and animals, the climates and—"

"Done." He knew just the man for that task. There wasn't a continent Harold McTavish hadn't traversed, and he was always eager to share his adventures and discoveries with anyone who would listen. It would be a match made in heaven. Graham studied Miss Claybourne's pleasing profile. On second thought, maybe Harold wasn't the best choice.

"Mathematics," she continued. "And science. And I should also like to learn—"

"*Four* hours a day," Graham reminded her. "The other four I expect you to teach my niece and nephew. Let's start with law and geography—two hours per each subject per day, Monday through Friday. If, after a month, you feel you would like to split that time further and add an additional subject, we can discuss it then."

"Very well." Miss Claybourne clasped her hands in her lap and sat prim and proper. She turned to him suddenly. "It would be excessively cruel of you to jest about this."

"I will do no such thing," he assured her. "Have we not already established that I am kind?" He inclined his head toward her sleeping maid.

"And a murderous blackguard," Miss Claybourne returned, squinting at him as if attempting to discern his true character. "Have you plans to kill anyone else?"

"No. But then I had no plans to on the previous occasion either. Should a situation arise that demands action, I will do as my conscience dictates."

"Hmmm." She brought a hand to her chin as she continued her perusal. "So you say. But what sort of conscience has a man like you?"

"A better one than your father." Graham regretted the words the second they left his mouth. He was not usually so careless. Something about Miss Claybourne's accusations bothered him and so he had spoken words he knew would hurt.

Her eyes darkened and she looked down at her lap. "That is little comfort," she said quietly. "I fear he has no conscience at all." She turned from him to look out at the dark night. "I think I shall attempt to sleep now."

SOPHIE SIGHED WITH CONTENTMENT AS the last vestiges of a splendid dream—in which she was at Oxford attending a law class taught by a most handsome professor with stormy gray eyes—left her mind. She tugged the covers tighter against the chill in the room, but instead of the soft sheets she was accustomed to, scratchy wool rubbed against her cheek.

Odd. She pressed a hand to the mattress to sit up and discover what was amiss and felt the edge of the plush seat cushion instead of her bed. "Oh no!" Sophie's eyes flew open, and she bolted upright, sending the wool tartan sliding to the carriage floor.

"Are you all right, Miss?" Shelby bent to pick up the blanket.

"Where are we?" Sophie turned her head, taking in the fine carriage, and Shelby, seated across from her, a needle in her hand and mending on her lap. The lantern overhead had been extinguished, but a sliver of sunlight shone through the parted curtain on her side of the carriage. Men's voices, amid horses' neighing and clip-clopping, carried from outside. "Where is—the duke?"

"We've stopped to change and rest the horses again. The duke takes great care with his animals—a good sign, to be sure," Shelby added cheerfully. "And you've no need to worry about him just now. He left in the night—back to London. He'd told your father he intended to call on you today, and the duke thought it best he keep that appointment to avoid suspicion."

"It's true, then." Sophie brought a hand to her head as the events of the previous night came tumbling forth. The stranger's warning, the viscount's obnoxious behavior at dinner, the absurd announcement from the stranger—who turned out to be the Duke of Warwick. Fleeing her home and landing in his carriage, of all places. The promises he'd made to her . . . She groaned.

"I fear I have made a bargain with the devil."

"How so?" Shelby rose from her seat to tuck the blanket around Sophie's shoulders.

"I think I agreed to be a governess to the duke's niece and nephew, in exchange for lessons in geography and law." Sophie turned forlorn eyes upon her maid. "I am no better than Father. It is just a different kind of greed that has driven me to agree to such."

"You are a great deal better than your father, and you are much better off here than you would be with Lord Newsome." Shelby shuddered. She leaned closer, lowering her voice to a whisper. "I would not speak of such things, but you must know—he accosted more than one of the maids, catching them unawares and forcing himself upon them. He is foul and loathsome and—"

"You, Lucy?" Sophie's own troubles fled as she looked at her distraught maid. "Did he hurt you?"

"No, Miss. He tried. But my Adam was near at hand, fortunately. The viscount threatened to get us both dismissed from our positions. 'Tis what made our decision to accept the duke's offer easier."

"What offer?" Sophie asked. "Tell me exactly what transpired between you and the duke right up to the moment I entered his carriage last night."

"Of course, Miss." Shelby settled herself in her seat again, across from Sophie, but did not take up her mending. "Sunday last Adam and I were requested to join him at his London residence. Can you imagine the likes of me, receiving an invitation from a duke?" She clasped her hands together, not entirely hiding the excitement she must have felt. "We were to tell no one, least of all anyone in the family."

"You went?" Sophie asked. Sundays were a day off for most of the servants, including her maid in the afternoon after services had concluded.

"Aye. We walked to the street he'd instructed us to, then a carriage picked us up and drove us the rest of the way. It was not a fine carriage like this, mind you. But it was still pleasant riding through town."

"What happened when you got there?" Sophie glanced at the door, wondering how long they had until they started off again and if she ought to leave now while she could. Where would she go? And how would she seek employment without risking being found by her father?

"He asked us to come work for him at his estate. Adam as gatekeeper, and I as your maid. His Grace told us about Newsome and the danger you were in if you stayed in your father's home. I—" Shelby looked down at her lap, as if uncertain or ashamed. "I believed every word he said because it matched much of what I already knew. Servants hear things."

"I am not upset with you." Sophie reached out, placing a hand on Shelby's arm.

If anything, she felt grateful—for Shelby's company and for being miles from home and her troubles there. Last night had been a bit of an adventure—something she'd longed for, though maybe not exactly as it had unfolded. But here she was, unharmed, and the duke not even around to prevent her leaving. Did he trust her that much to keep their bargain? Was she a fool to even consider keeping it, to remain in his carriage and see how this adventure continued to play out? Though it sounded like the wrong choice, somehow it felt right. The duke intrigued her, and she found that she wanted to stay, to see him again and to see if he would truly provide her the opportunities he'd promised. This might be her only chance to further her education.

Or it might be the worst decision of her life.

"How do you suppose the duke knew about the arrangement between Lord Newsome and my father?"

"I can't say for certain, but I—we, the servants—think your mother told him. She sent a letter, you see . . ."

Sophie leaned back against her seat, hand to her chin as she thought on this. Mother, of course, would be thrilled to have one of her daughters married to a duke, but to be so bold as to write to one? And *this* one?

We are not *going to be married.* Sophie glanced at the sun peeking through the drawn curtains. She had spent the whole of a night with the Duke of Warwick, in his carriage. *If I don't marry him, I shall never marry.* Because her reputation was now ruined. No one would ever want her now. *No one. No more offers.* No more running from one conversation to another, never lingering more than a few minutes for fear a man might show interest in her. There would be no more conversations at all. *Father will lock me away—if he even allows me back into his house.*

She felt a pang of regret for Olivia. With two sisters who had now brought scandal upon their family, Livie's prospects would be dim indeed. And she was one who would care.

Whereas . . . Sophie dropped her hand, let out a great sigh, and smiled.

"I'm free!"

Nine

"Thank you, Collins." Graham dismissed his valet and took a moment longer to study his reflection in the mirror. His eyes were shadowed, but not more than usual. He rarely slept well, so last night's activities shouldn't have altered his appearance too much. If anything, the brisk night ride back to London, followed by a few hours of rest and a morning bath, had left him feeling invigorated. A fresh change of clothes and he was out the door on his errands shortly after eleven.

A slight movement in the yard across the street caught his attention, though he gave no reaction. Only when he was settled inside the carriage did he carefully glance out the window and note more fully the man standing in the shadow of his neighbor's elm.

They are following me already. He doubted the man had been there at four o'clock this morning when he had returned home. Even if he had, it was not uncommon for a gentleman to return home early in the morning hours, after indulging in ungentlemanly behavior. His father had excelled at that.

Graham leaned back against the seat, closing his eyes for a few minutes as the driver guided the carriage toward Garrard's, where he intended to purchase an engagement ring. Though he and Miss Claybourne had come to an arrangement other than marriage, he still needed to continue the charade with her family. After selecting a ring he would stop at a florist before calling at the Claybourne residence—the last place he wished to visit but where he felt he must, particularly since it appeared he was already a suspect in her disappearance.

One hour and twelve minutes later, he stood in the foyer of the Claybourne townhome and waited as the somewhat flustered butler had requested. In the hours since he'd left the house, it seemed to have erupted in chaos, with servants running to and fro, lots of yelling in the background, and even the distinct sound of a woman crying.

Graham stiffened, squeezing the bouquet clutched in his hands. Was it Lady Claybourne that he heard? Or her youngest daughter? A servant being scolded? It didn't much matter to him who it was or what the woman's rank. Only that a female was in possible distress. Alarm rang through his mind, along with the overwhelming feeling that he needed to step in and help. He reached out to a servant rushing past.

"Who is crying?"

"Dunno." The boy bobbed and scurried away before Graham could detain him further.

"I'm sure you did," he muttered.

The butler returned then, his overly solemn demeanor nearly laughable. He stopped a foot in front of Graham and delivered his message stiffly. "Miss Claybourne is not at home."

"It took you a rather long time to come up with that excuse," Graham said, feigning exasperation at having been left waiting for several minutes. "I know the lady is in residence. Whatever her current indisposition, I request at least a brief audience. We have a matter of some importance to discuss, and her father should have been expecting me. Please tell him that I will not be put off that easily. I assume they have seen the papers this morning, announcing our betrothal?"

The butler grimaced. No doubt he'd seen them too.

"Your Grace." He stumbled over the title, as if it pained him. "Miss Claybourne truly is not home."

"Then I should like to speak with Lord Claybourne."

"The family is not accepting callers this morning."

Lord Newsome's raised voice carried to them from somewhere deeper in the house.

Graham arched a brow at the butler. "Not accepting callers? Or just not accepting *me*? They cannot think that declining my attentions will matter now, not when the whole of London has read of it."

A door slammed, and a few seconds later Lady Claybourne appeared. "Grayson, have the carriage readied. I shall be—" Upon seeing Graham she stopped midstride and midsentence. "Oh. Your Grace." She sank into a curtsy. "We were not expecting you."

"Your husband was. I advised him last night that I would be calling on your daughter this afternoon."

Confusion and concern clouded Lady Claybourne's already red-rimmed eyes. "Sophia is not at home."

"Where is she?" Graham asked, glancing at his watch as if he did not know the time. "It is barely past noon. Had I known she was such an early riser, I would have called earlier."

"Where is she, indeed?" Swinging both arms, with hands fisted, Lord Newsome marched into the foyer, which was beginning to feel rather crowded. "What have you done with her and her sister, you blackguard?"

Olivia is gone too? "Is that the best insult you can come up with today?" Graham *tsk*ed. "I expected worse from a scoundrel such as yourself. Though we are in the presence of a lady, and perhaps you have finally acquired some manners." He turned from Newsome to Lady Claybourne, silently applauding her foresight in removing Olivia from her husband's reach as well. He had suggested as much to her during their brief interaction last night. "I assure you, milady, that I have done absolutely nothing to your daughters." Beyond insisting

Sophia remain in the carriage long enough to hear him out last night, he had not done a blessed thing to or with her. She had acted entirely of her own will. "Am I to understand that you are not certain of their whereabouts?"

Lady Claybourne nodded. "Sophia and Olivia were not in their beds this morning. And all of their belongings are gone as well."

Graham's eyes narrowed as he turned to face Newsome. "Given your poor treatment of Miss Claybourne during dinner last night, what do *you* know of the girls' disappearance?"

"Me?" The veins on Newsome's neck bulged, and his face turned a mottled reddish-purple. Graham supposed it was too much to hope the man might be struck with a fit of apoplexy right here.

"I have done nothing," Newsome spluttered. "It was you who stole her—"

"Raymond! Is that you?"

Graham held in a sigh and instead looked past Lord Newsome and Lady Claybourne to her husband, bent forward and stampeding toward them as if he were a bull about to charge.

Olé! Graham forced his lips downward when they would have turned up. This was turning out to be rather more entertaining than he had anticipated. But he must not appear amused. Instead, he thought of how he really would feel, were Miss Claybourne truly missing. He recalled their conversation last night, the way her eyes had lit up beneath the lantern's glow as she rattled off the things she wished to learn. She'd been so excited, positively alight with hope and enthusiasm. The thought of anyone dimming that or hurting her in any way brought forth a surge of anger, the madman in him at the ready.

He stared down Lord Claybourne. "I have come to call on your daughter, as I told you I would last night."

"Well, you're too late!" Lord Claybourne spat. "She's far from here, where you won't be able to touch her."

Lady Claybourne gasped. "But you said—"

"Quiet!" Lord Claybourne snapped at his wife.

"I don't know what game you are playing at," Graham said, his voice soft yet menacing as he looked from Claybourne to Newsome and back again. "But I don't care for it. And when I don't care for something, I remove it from my path. Take care that you do not get in my way, gentlemen."

He turned to Lady Claybourne, his gaze fixed on hers as he handed her the flowers. He inclined his head in the barest nod, attempting to let her know all was well. "I trust you will enjoy these in your daughters' absence." He left the bouquet in her hands and took a step back. "Until we meet again."

Ten

"Good morning, ladies." Three days into their journey the duke poked his head through the door and smiled pleasantly, making it impossible for Sophie to do otherwise.

She appreciated the solicitous way he had treated them thus far, so she pushed aside the blanket she'd been curled up in and returned his greeting. "Good morning, Your Grace."

He had met up with them the evening before, after his hasty trip to London, where he had confronted her father. According to the duke, his purposes had been easily accomplished. Though Shelby had privately suggested it could not have been that enjoyable riding all those miles back and forth at breakneck speed, with an argument with Sophie's father sandwiched between.

"May I join you?" the duke asked, as if this were not his own carriage.

"Of course." Sophie scooted to the far side to allow him space on the seat beside her, Shelby being somewhat slower to rise.

He climbed inside, and the door was closed behind him. A moment later the carriage rocked slightly as it started out again.

From the corner of her eye, Sophie observed him, looking almost as perfectly groomed as he had the night of the dinner party. "You seem rather well rested for having spent the night riding outside." Last night he had insisted that both Sophie and Shelby be able to stretch out on the seats to sleep—inasmuch as possible—while he rode up top with the driver. It had been a gallant gesture, and one—after two days traveling without his presence—Sophie had been most grateful for. She hadn't known him well before, and when he'd reappeared last night, she'd felt awkward and unsure.

"I took a few minutes to refresh during our stop this morning," he confessed. "We'll be arriving at Gretna Green midday, and I feel it important we look the part we are playing."

"Ah." Sophie nodded, then moved to the opposite seat so Shelby could fix her hair. Sophie's lips pressed into a thin line of worry. Couples went to Gretna Green to marry, yet she and the duke had decided otherwise. He had given his word that he would not force that upon her. He had shared that they were headed, not to one of his English estates, but to a smaller holding he owned in Scotland, and thus would be traveling through Gretna Green. But dare she trust this, while still knowing so little of him?

The next two hours passed amiably enough, as they spoke of the history and geography of the borderlands. He seemed surprised at her knowledge of the Roman Empire, and they enjoyed a spirited discussion about Hadrian's Wall.

"It resides entirely in England and was never part of a border between Scotland and England," the duke informed her.

She knew this, of course. "Obviously, since it predates both of those empires. But people—who don't read—assume as much. It was also primarily used to prevent the crossing of raiders, those who would steal livestock or other valuables and then take them back to the barbarian wilderness."

"Barbarian?" He arched a brow at her use of the term.

"And yes, I am familiar with raiders. It is still a problem today, though not nearly as much as in centuries past."

"Might we be able to stop and see the wall?" Sophie asked. What a thrill that would be to see and touch something created so long ago.

But the duke frowned. "We shouldn't delay . . ."

"Oh." She turned from him, hiding her disappointment, and stared out the window, hoping she might at least see a portion of the historic wall from the road.

"Though I suppose a few minutes would be all right."

Sophie swung back around toward him, her smile true this time. "*Thank you.*"

GRAHAM HAD NEVER IMAGINED ANYONE could be so ecstatic about visiting a pile of ancient stone. But Miss Claybourne proved, yet again, that she was a most unusual female.

Her maid had chosen to wait near the carriages, so Graham walked alongside Miss Claybourne, witnessing her joyous discovery of everything she had read about the wall—and she had read a lot.

He had never considered the effort such an undertaking had to have been—where all the stones had come from, how long it had taken to move and place them, how many men were employed in the task, and precisely why it had been constructed.

"Vanity," Miss Claybourne pronounced when they had walked the allotted distance. "Men are so vain, so prideful."

"Excuse me?" Graham asked, confused and somewhat affronted that he was being accused of such.

"The true reason the wall was built," she explained. "Yes, it prevented raiders from easily crossing, and it marked the northernmost border of the Roman Empire, but was it really necessary? Was there a significant threat along that border?" She shook her head, answering her own question. "No. It was simply Hadrian's vanity that demanded it."

"I suppose the Great Wall of China is the same," Graham replied sarcastically, secretly amused at her ramblings that had at least some truth to them.

"China." Miss Claybourne breathed the word out almost reverently. "What a wonder it would be to travel there." She glanced back at him, a dreamy smile lighting her face. "My father would *never* find me."

Graham laughed, the sound and feel of it catching him by surprise. He'd not had cause to laugh or even smile for a very long time. And even then, those occasions had been few and far between. The Christmas he'd spent on Saint Kitts with his sister was the only memory that came to mind.

But Miss Claybourne elicited smiles, and now laughter. Being around her was like breathing in the fresh air of the country after being trapped in London for too long.

She frowned. "You find me amusing?" She looked at him sideways as they walked.

"Refreshing," Graham corrected. "I enjoy your company." He admitted what he'd been feeling since their first conversation.

"And I—enjoy yours," she replied rather stiffly.

Graham stifled another laugh, coughing into his hand instead. "You tolerate it."

"That too."

He caught her half grin and felt his spirits lift further. "I am afraid you are going to have to tolerate a bit more this afternoon."

"What do you mean?" Her steps faltered, and she turned to fully look at him.

Graham stopped and reached into his pocket, retrieving the parcel he had brought back with him from London. "In Gretna Green we need to pretend as if we have been recently married. We should be seen walking around the town and dining together." He unwrapped the pouch, opened it, and withdrew the betrothal ring he had purchased at Garrard's.

Miss Claybourne gasped and backed away, shaking her head. "I cannot—"

"Cannot marry me? I am aware of that and am still in strong favor of our earlier bargain. However, it would be most prudent for us to continue the pretense that we *have* married, until we have you safely hidden away."

"Why? Why here?"

He looked at her pointedly. "You are an intelligent woman. Surely you understand that we must play the part convincingly, knowing that sooner or later word of our presence and state will get back to your father. He will most certainly send someone to Gretna Green, where so many elope, to inquire after you. If he and Viscount Newsome believe you are a married woman, it is far more likely that they will desist in their plans and pursuit."

Miss Claybourne's shoulders sagged, but her eyes met his, and she nodded. "Very well." After a few seconds hesitation she removed her glove and held her hand out to him.

Graham took it in his own and gently slid the ring, a ruby surrounded by tiny diamonds embedded in a band of gold, onto the third finger of her left hand, surprised to find his own trembling slightly. He had never thought to have a moment like this in his life—real or pretend. "There now."

Her fingers curled into her hand, and he kept his over hers another few seconds, suddenly reluctant to release her. "That wasn't so terrible, was it."

She gave a quick shake of her head. "We haven't just participated in some sort of Scottish handfast, have we?"

His laughter returned. "No. You are perfectly safe from the likes of me. It is only a ring. We are just pretending." He held his arm out to her. "Shall we practice how we are to stroll about the town on our way back to the carriage?"

Relief evident on her face, Miss Claybourne placed her hand upon his arm with the barest touch as they retraced their steps along the wall.

Eleven

SOPHIE PAUSED AS SHE ALIGHTED from the carriage, her gaze sweeping the landscape before her. "So this is the infamous Gretna Green." "Green" was certainly appropriate, given the lush hillsides and towering pines framing the village. White-washed buildings made a lovely contrast to the vibrant background, with barrels of flowers and ivy-entwined sign posts creating a quaint and picturesque scene. Were she inclined toward the romantic, she could see the allure this place held for those in love.

Along with the more practical side of things—here, a young couple, where both were not yet twenty-one years of age, might marry without their parents' consent. She fit that category nicely, and the part of her that still did not completely trust the duke worried that he had brought her here under false pretenses. What if there were no niece and nephew needing a governess? What if he intended to force her to marry him so he might partner with her father on the plantation instead of Viscount Newsome?

What if everything he has told me thus far has been a lie?

She had considered, several times over the course of the two days that he had not been there to travel with them, leaving his carriage and running away on her own to be a governess as she had first planned.

Until she'd learned that his driver, Griggs, and the footmen had been instructed to allow her to leave and even arrange transportation for her, should she so desire. Had the duke *wished* her to leave? Was this a test to see if she would remain true to their late-night agreement? Or was he allowing her freedom, so she would do precisely the opposite and *not* run from him? Her head had spun with trying to figure it— figure *him*—out. And the worst was that she found doing just that to be a rather enticing proposition. For the first time in her life, here was a man who intrigued her, whom she wished to know better, to understand. And he was safe—so long as he spoke the truth about not wishing to marry.

Or have I been played the ultimate fool?

There was only one way to find out if he had deceived her. Taking in a breath for courage, Sophie stepped down onto the cobbled street. As if on cue, a piper launched into a jaunty tune. She turned, searching for him, and saw a young couple exiting the blacksmith shop, their hands entwined and smiles of utter joy lighting their faces.

Torie. A vicious beat of sorrow, like the sharpest arrow, pierced Sophie's heart. The first time she had witnessed such happiness had been at her sister's wedding. *And look how brief that joy lasted.* The last time she had seen such joy had been only six months later, during the most wonderful summer of her life, when she and Livie had stayed with Torie and Jonathan—before Father's return and his cruel actions that ultimately cost Torie her life. What was Jonathan doing now? How had he endured first having his reputation ruined and his business destroyed, and then losing both his wife and child? Sophie said a silent prayer for him as she watched the happy couple lean into each other as they stopped to listen to the piper's song.

"Miss Claybourne?" The duke's hand at her elbow pulled her from the scene before her and her memories—both happy and melancholy. "Will you walk with me?"

"Of course." He must think her daft to have forgotten their plan already. They were to behave as a newlywed couple, first out for a stroll and then enjoying a meal at one of the inns in town. She hoped the stroll would not be too long, as she hadn't eaten since early this morning—and then only a day-old bun—and was already famished. He had provided food enough for them each day of their journey, but instead of the schedule she was used to, their meals came at sporadic times, and the offerings were not always the best.

Sophie's hand curved over the duke's extended arm, and they started forward. The sound of the bagpipes followed them, its tune mournful now, as if it had sensed the weight in her heart. Her eyes darted to the bump on her finger beneath her glove, then briefly up to the duke's as he watched her.

"Relax." He patted her hand. "We are just play-acting."

She nodded, swallowed, breathed. *Just pretending marriage. It's not real.* She had not spoken vows. She wasn't trapped. He didn't own her. He'd slipped the ring onto her finger only as a precaution, as proof of their claim to anyone who asked or might be watching. It felt strange there, out of place. On the hand of a girl who had never wished for a ring or a beau.

I have neither. A thought that should have cheered her but did not. She would never know the joy of the couple outside the blacksmith's shop. Never experience the heady feelings of love. She would never have someone around whom her entire life revolved or be at the center of another's universe.

She'd always scoffed at such notions—until Torie met Jonathan. Watching the two of them together, it had been impossible to refute that such powerful emotions existed. Love was real, after all.

And rare. *And fleeting.* If one did not fall out of it of his own accord, it was snatched away when it had barely started to bloom.

Sophie wished someone would snatch away her melancholy. She was usually good at keeping it tucked away—far away, where it could not hurt her. But since meeting the duke, thoughts of her sister had crept into her mind more frequently. She wasn't certain why but attempted again to wrestle them to the back of her mind, where the past hurts she could do nothing about dwelt. She forced a smile to her lips and nodded to a couple walking past them in the other direction. The duke squeezed her hand gently, as if to encourage her efforts.

"Should we not be having a conversation?" Sophie asked when they were several steps past the other couple.

"We should. What do you wish to discuss today? The topography of the land, the types of vegetation growing here, the current population, or the lax Scottish laws that make coming here to wed so enticing to many?"

"I think I should prefer to know what is on the menu for our midday meal and how much longer I must wait for it." Her empty stomach grumbled its agreement.

A low chuckle came from the duke. "You are refreshingly direct for—"

"A young lady of my age," she finished with an eye roll. "And you, Your Grace, are terribly prejudiced against young ladies my age."

"That is a strong word, but perhaps it is deserving." He glanced down at her, his brow furrowed thoughtfully. "I will endeavor to be less so. Though in my defense, excepting my sister, you are unlike every other young lady your age I have been acquainted with. And I must say I am well pleased that you are."

"So much so that you will feed me soon?" Sophie queried, only half-jesting. She was beginning to feel a bit faint.

He laughed out loud then, just as another couple strode past them. "Right now, dear wife. Come with me this way."

THE FOOD AT GRETNA HALL was better than any they had eaten thus far on their journey. They had consumed three scones with clotted cream apiece before the meat pie was brought out. Miss Claybourne's eyes widened when it was delivered to their table, and Graham read her error in them—she had believed that all they were to have was the scones. He could not blame her, given the infrequent and somewhat sparse meals they'd had up to this point in their hasty travels.

Pretending not to notice her concern, he cut a generous slice for each of them and tucked into the delicious meat, vegetables, and pastry.

Miss Claybourne ate slowly, her eyes roaming about the room, ever alert and aware. Graham guessed that if he asked her she could tell him about everyone there. Was her overly observant nature due to her recent past, being sought after and pursued by the various men her father had courted for his business ventures? Or was she merely avoiding looking at him?

"You are very quiet for a new bride," he said when another minute had passed in which she did not speak but continued looking past him, taking in details he could not see from his vantage point.

"Perhaps I am shy."

He snorted. "That is one word I would never use to describe you." From the moment she had set foot inside his carriage she had been vocal with both her opinions and requests.

She put down her fork and focused her attention on him. "How *would* you describe me?"

"You are direct. And honest to a fault. From our first meeting you did not deign to hide your displeasure at your situation and the bothersome gentlemen vying for your attention." Graham smiled, remembering that conversation and his instant delight as he'd realized that Miss Claybourne had not been flirting. "You own up to your mistakes, as well. I was rather astonished at your ready apology that first night when you discovered that I had been truthful about the other carriage."

She did not share his smile. "Mmm. So romantic. You make me sound like every man's dream—a direct, honest woman who admits to her frequent mistakes."

"I did not say they were frequent." But he was beginning to see that she could indeed be every man's dream—or, at least, most men's. There were some, like himself, who were not permitted to dream. It was not safe. But if he were . . .

It was not her beauty that made Miss Claybourne desirable, though that was not insignificant. Nor was it her grace, though she was equally blessed with that. It was her wit and her company that he had found unexpectedly enjoyable. Given her parentage, he had not known what to expect, but her intelligent conversations had made the passing hours in the stuffy carriage almost pleasant. When he had given his word to her mother, he had envisioned saving Miss Claybourne from marriage to a despicable specimen of a man and alternately providing her his name and title, and then setting her up somewhere safe—and far from him. He had vowed never to marry, but marrying her and setting her aside—never or rarely to be seen again—would not have been like a real marriage at all.

He would not have been able to repeat the repugnant history that was his heritage.

Or so he told himself. But now he feared otherwise. If she were truly his wife, he would not want to send her away. He would desire her company, which could lead to devastating consequences. For them both.

Miss Claybourne glanced down at the ring on her left hand, then held it up, admiring the gem with a look opposite the one of revulsion she'd given him when he had slipped it on her finger earlier. "I believe we may have been followed somehow," she said quietly. "There are two men observing us. They were on the opposite side of the street when we left the carriage, and they have been with us ever since." She lifted her gaze to his with a smile even more dazzling than the one she'd bestowed on him the night of the dinner party.

Graham felt his breath stutter, as if for a second his body had forgotten the mechanisms behind breathing. *Ridiculous.* He wasn't fearful or even surprised at her news. He'd seen the men too, and even before that had half expected they would be followed. Her father had remained suspicious during his last visit, and it was only logical that he would send someone to Gretna Green just in case his daughter ended up here. *Or maybe they followed me.* Perhaps the decoy carriage he had sent from London to his estate in Derbyshire had not been such a decoy after all.

So what was wrong with him now? Why did he feel so unsettled? Certainly Miss Claybourne's smile did not affect him in any way, particularly when he knew it to be false. "Along with your previously listed qualities, you are a good actress as well." He lifted her hand and brought it slowly to his lips, then placed a lingering kiss over the finger wearing the ring.

Her skin was soft and smooth, cooler than his, and tasted sweet. He found himself reluctant to release her. But he did and described from memory the men he'd seen earlier.

"Yes. Those are the same two watching us now, from a table on the other side of the room." She kept her voice low, though it wouldn't have carried far. The tavern was full this afternoon—mostly with other couples like them—plentiful with the chatter of voices and the clattering of dishes.

Graham stood and moved his chair around the table, then set it next to hers. He sat beside her, placed an arm around her shoulders, and leaned close. "Can't have my back to them now, can I?"

"Of course not."

Her voice sounded slightly unsteady, causing Graham to wonder if his familiarity and closeness disturbed her, or if she was worried about the men who were watching them.

She turned to him, their faces close together, near enough that it would be only too easy to kiss her.

Maybe he should. *To convince anyone in the room that we are married.*

Miss Claybourne's gaze lifted to his, her eyes wide, as if she had read his thoughts.

For a long second he found himself lost in their depths, blue oceans of possibility he had never imagined. He dipped his head closer, tempted. She blinked, breaking the spell and returning him to his senses. He should not be contemplating anything to do with Miss Claybourne, other than to install her in his home as a governess to his niece and nephew and to stay as far away from her as possible. Imagining any other future with her was foolishness.

Graham swallowed, then spoke. "If you are finished eating, we should go upstairs. There we can discuss what is to be done next."

"Done?" Miss Claybourne's voice rose slightly as a pretty blush stained her cheeks.

"About those men." What had she thought he meant? Graham shifted his eyes to the other side of the room, to the two still lingering over their meal. "I've arranged for a pair of rooms, thinking you might enjoy a respite after four days of hard travel."

"Oh, yes." Miss Claybourne nodded, then picked up her pewter mug and took a sip, as if to conceal any concerns or anxiety she felt about accompanying him upstairs. Thus far on their journey, he had not been present when they'd stopped at an inn for the night. Yesterday, after he had rejoined them, they had continued driving through the night, and Graham had ridden with the driver, allowing Miss Claybourne and her maid some privacy as they slept inside the carriage.

He'd been looking forward to a nap this afternoon. That hope fled now. Miss Claybourne might be afforded that luxury—for a short while, perhaps—but he would not rest with a threat to her safety so nearby. They would need to be off, without being noticed, as soon as possible.

"What if they try to take me?" she asked quietly, only the barest hint of fear in her voice.

"I will not allow it. You are safe. I promise." He gave her shoulder a gentle squeeze as if to reassure her and felt an overwhelming surge of protectiveness. "I gave my word to your mother that no harm would come to you. I am many things—several of which are not worth mentioning—but when I give my word, I keep it." *At all costs.*

Their eyes met once more, hers filled with gratitude instead of fear.

"Thank you for bringing me with you."

"Mutual interests," he reminded her—himself as well. He'd brought her here for no other reason than to prevent the merger. "We are the business partners now. Preventing further harm to those on Saint Kitts."

She nodded and gave him a true smile. "I like the sound of that."

They finished their meal, and he rose and pulled her chair out for her. The casual intimacy of the inn pleased him much more than the stuffy ballrooms and dining rooms of London, where servants hovered and ridiculous rules dictated one's every action.

Graham placed his hand at the small of her back as he guided her across the room toward the stairs. He'd requested the rooms farthest from the stairs, hoping to get a few hours of decent sleep, but now he second-guessed that decision. It was a longer walk, with many doors to pass—doors that might harbor someone they did not wish to encounter—when it came time to take their leave.

Not that there weren't other ways to quickly exit a building.

He leaned down to whisper in her ear as they passed close to the two men she had described. "You're doing well."

In response, Miss Claybourne's grasp on his arm tightened, and she leaned into him, tipping her face up to his with another glowing smile.

This time he steeled himself against its effects.

They ascended the stairs and hurried their steps toward the door at the end of the hall. He unlocked it, and they went inside, closing it behind them and locking it once more. Graham looked around approvingly. Miss Claybourne's trunk had already been delivered, and a tub stood at the foot of the bed. He had guessed she might enjoy a bath as well as a few hours to relax. But he doubted if either of those were still a possibility.

He reached for his gun then felt her hand, still devoid of its glove, on his.

"I don't want anyone to die because of me."

"What do you think will happen if you are returned to your father and that merger goes through?" He spoke quietly, listening for any activity outside in the hall—any footsteps or doors opening or closing. But all remained quiet. He checked his weapon, reassuring himself that it was loaded. Since the incident at Saint Kitts he had been fastidious, if not a little paranoid, about always having two loaded guns as well as a knife on his person at all times.

Miss Claybourne had not answered his question, so he answered it for her.

"If your father and Newsome join their plantations people will die—more than those already dying there. There will be more slaves and more treated poorly—abused and overworked. Women violated. Children taken from their mother's arms. Fathers hanged or whipped to death in front of their families. *That* is what we are attempting to prevent here—the continuation and growth of slavery on Saint Kitts." Graham paused, listening once more for any activity in the hall. He opened the door a crack, peered into the empty corridor, then closed and locked the door once more. He turned back to Miss Claybourne.

"I don't intend to kill anyone today, but if necessary I will—to stop them from taking you back to your father and the viscount who commit such atrocities and who will only be empowered to commit more if they join forces."

Miss Claybourne's severe, almost scolding expression softened, the lines of worry around her eyes changing to one of solemn understanding and resignation. She gave a single nod, then spoke in low tones. "What do you need me to do?"

He could have kissed her for her accepting words, her simple faith—in him. For the second time in the last quarter hour he *wanted* to kiss her, to act the part of the married couple they were pretending to be. It was good that at least she remained sensible about their situation. He must too. He could ponder these moments alone together later—the way she defied the odds of her sex, facing fear head on and leaving the swooning and hysterics for others.

He pulled her away from the door. "I need you to stay here, in this room, with the door locked."

Her mouth opened in protest, but he held up a hand. "I'm going back downstairs to request that water for a bath be brought up. I'll also send a message to Griggs, and we'll have help here in no time."

"If you're just going downstairs to send a message, then you've no need for *that*." She inclined her hand toward his gun and held her own hand out expectantly. "I'll keep it safe for you here."

He frowned. "I don't think that's a good idea."

"Why?" she asked, hands on hips. "Because I'm a woman?"

Well, yes. What business did she have with his gun? Maybe she didn't actually trust him and intended to use it against him. It wouldn't be the first time a female had turned on a man. But then, he'd given her ample opportunity to leave over the past few days, and she hadn't. That had to mean something, didn't it? And it wasn't as if he didn't have a second weapon. He wouldn't be going downstairs defenseless. *Trust her, as she has trusted you.* It seemed the only fair and right thing to do.

"All right." He handed it to her reluctantly. "Do you even know how to—"

"Yes." She held it as he would have, her finger well away from the trigger. "I'm not a helpless female. I won't shoot myself."

"Good." He nodded and reached for the doorknob, eager to have his errand done and be returned once more in sight of her room and in possession of his weapon. "I'll be back in a few minutes. Keep the door locked." He stepped into the empty hall and started toward the stairs, already composing the message to Griggs in his mind.

Trouble here. Come at once. Leave the others to bring the carriages round. That will mean two of them. Three of us. He liked those odds better than the current ones.

Twelve

SOPHIE LOCKED THE DOOR BEHIND the duke, then leaned against it, eyes closed, heart still beating rapidly. *You're a good actress,* he had said. She hoped it was true and that she'd been able to conceal her unruly emotions while being so near to him. Men always unsettled her, but not like this. Not like he did. Before, she'd always found herself repulsed or wanting to run away. But with His Grace . . .

I want to stay near. To indulge in the new and intriguing reactions taking place within her. Heaven help her, but this afternoon she'd even imagined kissing him. *In public.* If she wasn't careful, she'd soon be acting as smitten as Torie had. Only it would be worse, because she did not love the duke. She wasn't even certain whether or not she liked him yet. So she most certainly should not be imagining what it might feel like if he kissed her.

"Good gracious." Sophie pushed off the door and walked to the washstand. She looked down and was relieved to see water in the pitcher. Perhaps she was just warm and weary from their travels. She set the duke's gun on the stand and poured water into the bowl, then splashed some onto her flushed face. Looking up into the oval mirror, she scolded herself. "You are to be a governess. You must stop reacting to him."

A noise from the hall gave her pause. Could the duke be

returned so soon? Perhaps he had forgotten something? But what? The only belongings in the room appeared to be hers.

The doorknob slowly turned, then stopped as it caught on the lock—the lock he had told her to fasten. So surely he wouldn't be trying to enter. *He would knock.*

The knob jiggled again, then was still. Sophie held her breath as she walked to the door then crouched, peering beneath it. A pair of dusty boots most definitely not belonging to the duke stood just outside. She straightened quickly.

The doorknob, though still now, continued to click, as if the person on the opposite side were picking it.

On tiptoe Sophie dashed toward the washstand. She grabbed the pitcher in one hand and the gun in the other. She would only shoot if given no other choice.

A final, louder click signaled that the lock had been breached. Sophie's heart pounded as she raised the pitcher high and stepped behind the door. It swung open, and a man stepped inside, his attention directed toward the center of the room as Sophie brought the pitcher smashing down onto the back of his head.

THE TWO MEN WHO'D BEEN watching them were nowhere to be found on the main floor of the noisy tavern. Not eager for their return, but certain they would be back, Graham had requested the water for a bath as promised, though he doubted there would be time for Miss Claybourne to enjoy such leisure. Then he'd scrawled a hasty note to Griggs.

"Lad." Graham beckoned to a boy sweeping the floor. When he came closer, Graham lowered his voice and spoke. "I need you to take a message." He whispered a description of Griggs and where he might be found, along with his request, then dug a few shillings from his pocket and placed them in the boy's free hand. With a quick bob of his head, the lad was off.

Errand done, Graham started toward the stairs once more, both reluctant and longing to return. He'd ridden up top last night, not only as a courtesy to Miss Claybourne and her maid but as a way to distance himself from them. That first night, as Miss Claybourne had slept on the seat beside him, it had been all he could do to keep from watching her, so impressed was he with their first interactions. Her honesty and intelligence had won him over to helping her already, and he longed to witness more of her rare spirit.

He was attracted to her, and it concerned him. Though she was not to be his wife, she was to reside in the same household. He would have to put as much distance between them there as he had with his sister's children. He could not afford to feel anything toward Miss Claybourne or the niece and nephew entrusted to his care. To do so was to risk not only their safety but his ruin.

Two maids hauling buckets of steaming water started up the stairs ahead of Graham, and he paused, wondering if he ought to wait and allow Miss Claybourne at least time alone to refresh herself. As for himself . . . *Perhaps a quick dram.* Another temptation in which he shouldn't indulge. Another vice of his heritage he longed to avoid—but just now a wee dram could be the very thing to take the edge off the tension thrumming through him, after a morning spent fighting his growing attraction.

A gunshot rattled the bottles on the wall. A woman's piercing scream followed.

Miss Claybourne! Graham bolted to the stairs, taking them two at a time. Water met him halfway down the hall, spilling from one of the buckets the maids had been carrying and dropped. Still running, he darted to the side to avoid slipping, then caught sight of the open door of the last room. Both maids were pressed up against the wall on either side, peering down at a booted foot sticking out of the doorway.

Graham withdrew his pistol, leapt over the largest puddle, and landed directly in front of the foot and the man attached to it, lying sprawled face down on the floor. Graham flung the door open the rest of the way. A second man slumped against the wall near the window, clutching his shredded hand as blood oozed from it across the front of his shirt.

"He w-was under the bed." Miss Claybourne stood amidst a sea of broken porcelain, gun clasped in her outstretched, trembling hands.

"You're all right?" *If I hadn't left her my gun . . .* But thankfully he had. Relief flooded his senses. He checked the injured man for any weapons and found none, aside from a knife on the ground a few feet away. Graham snatched it, barely resisted the urge to kick the man senseless, and hurried to Miss Claybourne's side.

"You can set the gun down. It's all right now," he said soothingly as he took the weapon from her. He kept his own drawn, pointed at the man she had shot. With his free hand he drew Miss Claybourne close, pulling her into his embrace. Her face had drained of color, and she swayed slightly.

"You're safe now." He meant to comfort her but felt comforted himself, feeling her securely in his arms.

She is well. All is well. It wasn't though, and he wrestled with a need to do something about that, to act—to punish those who had sought to hurt her.

"He broke into the room first." She lifted a shaking finger and pointed at the unconscious form sprawled in the doorway. "I hit him over the head with the pitcher. Then I heard something behind me, and *he*—" she pointed to the man slumped beneath the window— "was coming out from beneath the bed—with a knife pointed at me. He said I wouldn't get hurt if I came with him. I told him to stop where he was, but he wouldn't. He was in here—the whole time. And I had to—" She pushed away from Graham and whirled toward the basin. She leaned over it, barely in time as she began to retch.

"You there, in the hall," Graham called to the maids still hovering outside the room. "Come help my wife."

One of the maids ventured in, her face a mask of terror as she picked her way over the inert man and around jagged pieces of porcelain. She reached Miss Claybourne and put an arm around her as she sagged against the washstand.

More footsteps pounded down the hall, and the innkeeper and his wife rushed into the room. His wife swore when she caught sight of the broken pitcher. "There'll be charges for that."

"My wife was *attacked*," Graham said, put off by the woman's obvious lack of concern for Miss Claybourne's welfare. "If not for her quick thinking, she might be *dead*." Anger surged as he thought of what might have happened. *I can prevent it from ever happening again. At least with these two.* His lip curled as he stared at the prone man and the one nursing his hand.

"That man—" Graham jerked his head in the direction of the window— "was hiding beneath the bed, and the other—the one who had the pitcher smashed over his head—broke into our room."

"Not the first time something like this has happened," the innkeeper's wife muttered. "No doubt they were sent to stop her being ruined. I'd wager you didn't have her father's permission and ran off with her." She wagged a finger at him. "We've a nice establishment here, but one of these days fellows like you are going to ruin it."

"*Molly*," her husband warned, darting an apologetic glance toward Graham.

"I am sorry to have broken your pitcher, and I shall certainly pay for it." Miss Claybourne turned from the washstand, though she kept her hands braced against it. Her face was even more drained of color. "I don't know either of these men, and I was only defending myself."

The innkeeper's wife snorted. "An' your father was likely only tryin' to defend your virtue." One hand went to her ample hip. "Does *he* know that you're here?"

"My father is the one who arranged my betrothal," Miss Claybourne replied, looking the other woman squarely in the eye. "He is the *reason* I am here. And my mother was most influential in bringing about this match."

Graham silently applauded her entirely true, yet evasive reply. But though her words were strong, Miss Claybourne swayed, her knuckles white where they gripped the edge of the washstand. *She's going to swoon.* He moved toward her while speaking to the innkeeper. "I trust you're able to restrain these men until the constable arrives." *Or I'll do it for you.* If Miss Claybourne was not present, he'd already be rearranging their faces.

The innkeeper nodded. "Lottie, go fetch Irvin and his brother."

The maid helping Miss Claybourne nodded, then hurried off.

"I'll settle with you before we leave—which will be presently." Graham wrapped his arm around Miss Claybourne, ready to catch her if she fell. "The *duchess* and I will seek other, more appropriate lodging. She had longed to experience the romance of Gretna Green she has heard so much about, and your establishment came highly recommended, but I believe we have seen enough."

Graham knew a moment of satisfaction as the innkeeper's wife opened and closed her mouth once, twice, three times before managing to squeak out, "Beg pardon, Your Grace."

"Let's get you out of here, darling." Graham spoke the endearment for the benefit of the others in the room, but it did not feel as foreign as it should have. Nor did sweeping Miss Claybourne up into his arms and carrying her from the room.

"I'm sorry," she murmured, closing her eyes and laying her head against his chest as they walked.

"You have nothing to apologize for." Graham navigated the slippery floor in the hall and then the stairs, concerned with what—or who—he might find at the bottom. But in the roomful of patrons, Griggs was the only familiar face. The man held the door open to Graham, and though his eyes held questions, he spoke none aloud.

A footman waited by the carriage. Graham stepped through the doorway and settled Miss Claybourne on the seat. She murmured her gratitude and leaned against the window, eyes still closed.

He stepped outside and gave instructions for the retrieval of her trunk and the second carriage that was to follow as soon as the Shelbys—who had been given the afternoon off—could be located. Griggs returned to the inn and came back with a jug of water, some clean cloths, and a pail for Miss Claybourne, should she be sick again. After a quick look up and down the street, Graham climbed into the carriage and settled on the seat beside her, placing the items for her on the seat opposite. The door closed, and they were off.

Graham put his arm around her and pulled her into his side. When she did not object or try to move away, he leaned close, resting his head lightly on top of hers. "I am sorry we must travel when you feel so ill."

"I am all right. I am," she repeated, as if to convince herself.

"I should not have left you alone in that room. If I'd had any notion that those men—"

"They weren't those who followed us earlier." She tipped her face back to look up at him.

"I know," he said gravely, then pressed a quick kiss to her forehead. "Rest now. I have a plan to lose all of them."

She nodded and snuggled into his side as her head dropped and her eyes closed.

Graham's arm tightened around her, as if holding her close might protect her. He'd wanted to get her settled then circle back to the inn on his own to take care of matters satisfactorily. But perhaps that was not to be if she wished to be held like this.

But something would need to be done. This was a more serious game than he had realized. More at stake for Newsome and her father than he had calculated. *Or Newsome is just a sore loser. A bully who doesn't like to be beaten.* He could still merge his interests with her father's without Miss Claybourne. Nothing was stopping the two, and Graham half expected they would do it just to spite him.

But not until they'd exhausted every effort to get Miss Claybourne back.

Thirteen

SOPHIE BLINKED AND STRETCHED, SURPRISED to find herself alone on the carriage seat, a blanket tucked around her. The only other occupant watched her from the seat opposite, a wary, uncertain expression on his face.

"How do you feel?" the duke asked.

She closed her eyes and reviewed the events of the past hours, from her vomiting in front of him to having to be carried out of the inn, to allowing him to hold her as they traveled—very much alone. *Oh, dear.*

"Exceedingly embarrassed," she said, struggling to sit up.

"Excellent." His boyish grin took years off his face.

She frowned. "You enjoy my discomfort?"

He shook his head. "On the contrary. But if you are feeling well enough to be embarrassed then I know you are on the way to recovery. You had me quite worried. For a lady I thought the least likely to ever swoon, you came remarkably close to doing just that."

"I remember." Sophie pressed a hand to her stomach, worried that the same, uncontrollable lightheadedness and nausea would return. "I'd never shot anyone before. He startled me and came at me with his knife, and I felt I had no choice." She suppressed a shudder, recalling those awful moments. "It was terrible—the noise, his expression, the blood. And I was frightened the other two men might come in the room at any moment."

"I think," the duke said gravely, "that given the circumstances, we can excuse your temporary weakness."

"Magnanimous of you," Sophie muttered, secretly grateful for his return to sparring and the distance—both physical and emotional—that he'd put back in place between them. Yet earlier she hadn't imagined—

He called me darling. She knew it had been an act, as much as stating she was his duchess had been. *But still . . .* The tenderness with which he'd spoken and the way he'd swept her into his arms and carried her . . . *He is a good actor too.* She'd do well to remember that. If she didn't, if she wasn't careful, she was going to start being a romantic like Torie. *And look where that got her.* The somber thought banished any notions that her relationship with the duke would ever be anything other than a business arrangement.

I am to be a governess, and that is all. She'd turned down his offer of marriage, and he did not seem wont to suggest it again. No doubt her practical side had relieved him of any gallant notion he'd originally felt he must make. She had been relieved as well. So why, now, did she feel so forlorn?

"I was not entirely weak." She lifted her chin as she stared at the duke, challenging him to engage with her in one of their previous, not quite disagreeable but definitely not in-agreement dialogues. "I hit my intended target."

"You did?" Surprise and disbelief tinged his voice. "You mean to say that you aimed for his hand?"

Sophie nodded. "Jonathan said that if one did not wish to kill a man but merely stop him for a short period—say, enough to get away from said individual—that hitting the middle of his hand, particularly if you are able to hit the one holding a weapon, would disable him quicker than shooting him in the leg. Having studied the anatomy of the hand, I agree. There are twenty-seven small, delicate bones in the hand, in addition to numerous ligaments and tendons. The arteries and veins within the hand provide blood flow and, when compromised, will bleed profusely. The nerves centered there ensure that a great deal of pain results from a gunshot wound. The hand is both an intricate and intimate part of the body and therefore a logical choice for wounding someone when you wish to stop his assault."

The duke's mouth opened, as if he wished to say something, but then closed again without a word.

"Jonathan gave an additional suggestion for bringing a man to his knees, but I—" She broke off as warmth flooded her cheeks.

"You preferred leaving the man still capable of producing children," the duke concluded.

Sophie nodded, embarrassed once more, only this time she did not have an excuse for her poor behavior. What must he think of her for knowing such things?

"And who is this Jonathan who imparted to you such details of the human body?"

"Oh, it wasn't Jonathan who taught me anatomy. I read a book in my cousin's library. I don't think I was supposed to discover it, but I did and read it in my room at night during our visit. It was quite fascinating. Though seeing a real hand in pieces after being shot was—not. It was horrifying." The roiling feeling in her stomach threatened to return, so she steered their conversation elsewhere. "Jonathan is—was—my brother-in-law." Another piercing sorrow struck, bringing a literal physical ache to her chest and a lump to her throat. She'd never had a brother, but Jonathan had been exactly what she would have hoped for in one. They had all loved him—everyone except Father.

And now . . . Did he hate them all? She couldn't blame him if he did. She had no claim to his friendship, though she very much would have liked it. But he would not welcome anyone from her family and probably hoped with all his heart never to see or hear from any of them again. "He taught my sisters and me to shoot and to defend ourselves."

"It appears that he taught you well—and I am thankful for that." The duke's voice dipped low, and he cleared his throat. "Hitting a man's hand as you did, dead center, and when it was likely moving, required some skill, even at close range. He won't die, but it will require a talented surgeon and considerable attention for him to keep that hand."

"If he loses it, he will be furious." Sophie closed her eyes, recalling all too well the flash of steel from the raised knife and the look in the man's eyes when he had come at her.

The duke nodded. "It might have been better if you'd aimed for his heart. If there is a next time—which I deeply hope there is not—I would encourage you to shoot to kill."

"I didn't think I could," Sophie said. "I—what does it feel like to kill a man?" She bit her lip, regretful the second the question left her mouth.

The scowl the duke had been courting for some minutes took over his face. "When the man is evil, it feels like relief."

Sophie wished he would elaborate but chose not to ask more when he did not. He turned away from her, staring out the window, giving her opportunity to study his scar again. How had he come by it? Was it related in any way to the incident where he had killed two men?

"I am sorry that I upset you," she said instead of asking further questions. "I am too curious and forget myself sometimes."

He shrugged and looked back at her. "I should probably be grateful you haven't shot me in the hand—or elsewhere—yet. Given that you know me to be a murderer."

She met his gaze. "Murder is a strong word. I cannot

reconcile it with the man I have spent the past five days traveling with. There is a story there—whether you wish to share it or not. But I can no longer believe the worst of you. Your hand—and other parts—are quite safe from me."

He gave a bark of laughter and shook his head. Sophie felt her face heat, though she didn't mind if her bluntness and blunders were the cost for pulling him from such a somber mood.

His laughter died, and his gray eyes darkened, intensified, as they studied hers. "You have impressed me as well, Miss Claybourne, and continue to surprise. You say I am safe from you, yet I worry I still have reason to fear."

Fourteen

AT SIX O'CLOCK THE NEXT morning, Graham rapped on Miss Claybourne's door at the inn. He'd given her notice five minutes ago that they needed to be off. Yesterday's events still had him on edge, and he did not wish for a repeat today, though he'd done everything he could think of, short of permanently silencing the men they'd encountered yesterday—something both the law and Miss Claybourne would have frowned upon—to avoid being followed from Gretna Green. They had taken the carriages marked with his crest a good three hours on the road toward Newcastle Upon Tyne. Then, during a stop to rest and water the horses, all five of them—Miss Claybourne, the Shelbys, and himself—had transferred, unnoticed, to a plain conveyance, heading north while his carriages continued on to his English estate.

The new carriage had been cramped and uncomfortable, particularly with the shades drawn the entire afternoon. It should have been an entirely miserable ride, but thanks to Miss Claybourne it had been almost pleasant. She had surprised him yet again when she'd removed *A History of England from the First Invasion by the Romans to the End of the Reign of George III* from among several books in the bag she always kept close at hand.

"For the children's education," she had explained in a very governess-like tone. "But the topics make for interesting conversation as well."

And so they had. She read aloud to all of them, stopping frequently for open debate about everything from war tactics to the various monarchs that had ruled England over the centuries. He had learned even more about her as they conversed. She treated the Shelbys as equals and valued their friendship over their service to her, and, in turn, they felt comfortable joining in the conversation and sharing their opinions.

Miss Claybourne loved history and was a veritable well of dates and names and facts. She also considered everything thoroughly and examined both sides of any situation. For a while he'd thought she was determined to oppose him on every topic, but he soon realized that it wasn't opposition at all. She merely looked at the world through a wide lens that encompassed everything and everyone, and she felt all should be equally represented.

It boded well for her as a governess for his niece and nephew. He had not told her that there was to be a trial period for the position, and if she failed he would dismiss her outright. In such a circumstance he would still offer her his protection, but she would have to be sent elsewhere, where his sisters' children were not.

When they'd finally reached their lodging shortly before midnight, though he felt cramped and stiff from sitting so many hours on the uncomfortable seats, he'd almost been sorry to see the evening come to an end. *All the more reason it was good that it had.* He enjoyed Miss Claybourne's company more each day when he should not allow himself to enjoy it at all.

Graham knocked on her door again, giving in to the urge to be grumpy with her for taking so long this morning. Whatever she was lacking in sleep, he'd had less by half, after taking turns with Mr. Shelby staying up to guard the women's door throughout the night.

Having come this far and put this much effort into her rescue and foiling her father's plans, Graham intended to see success. *To see her safe.* "We need to be going," he called through the door.

It opened slightly, and Miss Claybourne poked her head out a second later. "Shelby is ill. She cannot leave yet."

If the stench coming from the room was not enough to confirm her words, the sound of retching from within was.

"Is it her bairn—child?" Graham amended, but not before receiving a strange look from Miss Claybourne, who appeared unusual herself, her long, honey-colored hair unbound and falling well past her shoulders.

"Nothing is amiss," Mrs. Shelby called in a raspy voice. "'Tis sometimes the way of things when a woman is—" Another bout overtook her before she could finish her sentence.

Graham motioned to Miss Claybourne to join him in the hall. With a quick glance back into the room, she followed him, closing the door behind her.

"Does she require a physician?" Graham asked, concern for the young maid and her family temporarily overriding his desire to put more distance between them and the men they'd encountered yesterday. If something happened to the Shelbys it would be his fault. They were his responsibility now, as he had convinced them to leave their home and employ on his behalf.

Miss Claybourne bit her lip. "I do not think so, though I am uncertain, being inexperienced in these matters." A pretty blush stained her cheeks, but she did not look away.

Graham brought a hand to the back of his neck, considering this latest hiccup in his plans. "I'll pay the innkeeper to lodge Mrs. Shelby until she is well enough to travel. Her husband and son will stay with her, of course, and I'll leave the funds with them for a physician, if necessary."

"That is very generous of you," Miss Claybourne said. "I can look after her, as well," she offered.

Graham shook his head. "That would not be wise."

A frown marred Miss Claybourne's otherwise lovely face. She folded her arms across her middle in what he'd come to recognize as her look of defiance. Already he'd learned that she did not care for being told what she could or could not do.

"Have you forgotten that your father has men scouring the countryside for you? If they find you here, they will take you back to London—and the viscount."

"Did your deception yesterday not send them searching in another direction?"

"That was the intent, but I have no assurance that it worked. I will not feel you are secure until we have reached my home and the protection offered there."

Her frown softened into lines of concern. "I am worried for Shelby—Lucy. She is more than a maid to me. We have been friends for many years, and I cannot abandon her in her time of need."

"Will you not be abandoning her if you are forced to return to your father's home? She and her husband have left their positions there and no doubt would not be welcomed back. You would be parted from her permanently."

Miss Claybourne was silent for a long moment, hand to her chin, one finger absently tapping the side of her face. "You are right. I just wish there was another option—aside from leaving her here."

"She will not be alone," he reminded her.

"How much farther have we to go?" she asked.

"Two days by carriage. Were we riding, it could be accomplished in one. A man on a horse is able to travel much faster than a coach and four." What would he do if she refused to come? Unmarried as they were, if they were found now it would go bad for both of them—he would be tried for abduction, and Miss Claybourne would find herself still subject to her father's will and with a reputation left in tatters.

"We'll leave the carriage here for the Shelbys," she announced quite suddenly. "Unless you don't think a *woman* on horseback can travel equally as fast as a man." She turned back toward her room without waiting for a response.

"It will be a long, hard day," Graham said, feeling the need to warn her, though the prospect of continuing on horseback was heartening. "And you will not have any sort of chaperone. It will be the two of us alone—even more so than yesterday."

She looked over her shoulder at him. "I trust that you shall find it within yourself to act as a gentleman during all portions of our adventure."

"So long as I must only *act* as one and not truly be one, you have my word." He gave a slight bow and felt an easing in his chest. *A day of fresh air and space between us instead of being so close together in that carriage for miles on end.* And at the speed they would need to ride, there would be little opportunity to speak. A little distance, in preparation for the distance he planned to give her once they reached his home, could only be a good thing.

"And you have my word to behave as a lady." Instead of returning his bow with a curtsy she grasped the knob and opened the door to her room. "Give me but a moment to speak with Lucy and gather my belongings."

"I THOUGHT YOU PROMISED TO behave as a lady." The duke looked at Sophie pointedly as she sat astride the horse she'd been given.

Was that teasing she heard in his voice? *Doubtful.* He'd been so somber and serious for much of their entire journey.

Whether he was teasing or not, she wasn't going to let it bother her. It was too fine a day to have it spoiled by a grumpy duke or anyone else. The pretty, chestnut mare seemed as pleased as Sophie felt about the pairing and turned easily to face the duke and his mount. She pulled up alongside him, both aware of and unconcerned about the impropriety of her position.

"My riding boots were not in my trunk this morning, and I did not think it prudent to take time to look through all the other luggage the Shelbys packed in order to find them. Furthermore, we are not going for a jaunt in the park but are attempting to outrun men my father has hired to come after me. Riding sidesaddle is not practical in this situation, so I requested the saddle be switched. If my ankles offend you, feel free to ride out front." She had donned her longest riding skirt, but the fabric still bunched when split, revealing her stockinged ankles above her low boots. It was a miracle—and entirely thanks to Shelby—that she even had a habit and any boots with her.

"No offense taken," the duke said, his eyes darkening as his gaze passed over her.

Sophie turned the mare away once more, worried suddenly about *his* word to be a gentleman. The look he'd given her just now wasn't like those she'd suffered from Lord Newsome, but more one of appreciation. She could not afford to have the Duke of Warwick appreciating anything about her. Just as she should not have noticed how fine he looked atop his black stallion in his fitted breeches and shirtsleeves. *A dark horse for the man with a wicked reputation.* She would do well to remember that.

After a few parting instructions to his coachmen, the duke guided his mount alongside hers. "Let us be off. You set the pace."

Sophie nodded, pleased at this and even more pleased a few minutes later as they galloped along the road, the wind whipping her hair back. Lucy had been too ill to pin it up this morning, and Sophie had not wanted to take the time to bother with it on her own. Freedom flowed through her veins with every stride. This was vastly preferable to riding in the carriage.

The countryside around them consisted of deep green, gently rolling hills and fields of tiny yellow wildflowers, interspersed with purple Scottish thistle—so much prettier than anything that could be found in London. After a short while, the duke took the lead, guiding them off the side of the road until they were nearly perpendicular to it and then had left it behind altogether. They rode on at a steady pace the entire morning, speaking little, allowing Sophie's mind to wander where it would.

A week ago she'd been confined to a stuffy townhome. She'd rarely gone out, for fear of encountering one of the gentlemen she had previously refused or any that were currently pursuing her. She understood now why there had been so many seeking her hand. She wasn't a great beauty. She didn't flirt or encourage any gentlemen's attention. More often than not men were annoyed with her intelligence, but she'd never attempted to disguise it or her true self, or her intent to make no match at all.

But her father had completely disregarded her wishes and cared so little for her that he'd offered her up as collateral for his business dealings. Little wonder so many men she'd never previously heard of had taken interest. A large dowry was one thing; the promise of joint ownership of a successful plantation on Saint Kitts was so much worse.

Sophie held in a sigh and tried not to worry about the future.

For a short while after the scandal that resulted from Victoria marrying a merchant—an utterly ridiculous thing to cause a scandal—Sophie had felt certain her marriage prospects were slim, given the stain on her family's name. Instead of upsetting her, this had brought great relief. But then father's brusque and brutal handling of the whole affair had somehow brought him back into society's good graces.

Why couldn't people simply keep their noses in their own business? It was vexing that others took such interest in who married whom. Torie had been so happy—until their father had set out to wring every bit of joy from her and Jonathan. Father had caused Jonathan's business to fail by spreading rumors about him and undermining his network and supply chain. He'd gone so far as to hire thugs to damage the goods in one of Jonathan's warehouses—an act Father saw as justified, as Jonathan had *stolen* his eldest daughter.

What will Father do to the duke for stealing me? Jonathan hadn't stolen Victoria at all. Mother had approved of the match, though he wasn't titled. There had been little else she could do after Torie had threatened to run away with him if Mother didn't give her blessing. So Jonathan's proposal had been accepted and banns posted. Torie and Jonathan had married in the small country church near their summer estate. All of this while Father had been away conducting business in Saint Kitts. His fury upon his return—at both Mother for allowing the wedding to happen, and at Victoria and Jonathan—had been instant and severe. Though Father had been gone nearly two years, he had not expected anyone to make such decisions in his absence. Furthermore, he'd had other plans for Torie's future.

Just as he had plans for mine. He would be even more furious and vengeful this time. Sophie had no doubt of that, as she had made her bold decision of defiance right under his nose. She could only hope the duke had more resources to withstand whatever her father attempted against him.

But for now, for today, at least—this hour, this very minute—she felt freer than she ever had, riding across fields of wildflowers on a hillside in Scotland. She finally had the chance to go somewhere and see someplace new, albeit still on the same continent. But it was a start. The sun warmed her back, the breeze cooled her face, and the magnificent horse seemed to carry her with ease. The knowledge that she had escaped a terrible fate and was now in charge of her own life was intoxicating. Gradually, by degrees as the minutes and hours and distance passed, Sophie's heart grew lighter until she could rarely recall feeling as much joy and possibility as she did today.

They continued riding, the duke looking over at her frequently, as if to ascertain if she was well, and each time Sophie smiled and nodded to him to continue. Thankfully her lapse into weakness yesterday had been short-lived. This morning she was alive and strong. She didn't ever want this wonderful day to end. Yet the hours passed. All too soon the sun was directly overhead, and they stopped to rest.

The duke dismounted and hobbled his horse to a tree near a slow-moving stream. He turned, as if to assist her, but Sophie had already dismounted, having taken the moment his back was turned to swing her leg over the side and slide down. He might have seen her ankles today, but he need not view anything else. She smoothed her skirts and handed him the reins.

He took them from her and tied her horse beside his, in a plentiful patch of grass and near the water so the animals could drink freely. "You ride very well."

"As do you," Sophie said, brushing aside his compliment. In her experience, compliments never led to anything good.

"Where are we?" she asked, taking in the idyllic meadows beneath the partially cloudy sky.

"This is a tributary for the Annan River, which, oddly enough, is near the town of Annan." The duke peeled off his gloves, then crouched beside the water and scooped a handful onto his face before refilling the water pouch he'd brought with them and which they had shared throughout the morning. "It's about halfway on our journey today—unless you need to stop sooner."

Sophie shook her head. She *was* sore and tired—more noticeably now that they'd stopped; no doubt she'd pay for this ride tomorrow and even for a few days after, but she was ready and willing to ride much longer. "I'll keep going as long as I need to if it means I'll not be found."

"I think there is little danger of that now. We are far from the road, and few travel this way."

"Yet you know it." Sophie wandered along the bank, attempting to walk the stiffness from her legs. She removed her gloves, and the ring still on her finger sparkled in the sunlight. She had twice attempted returning it to the duke, and each time he had asked her to continue wearing it—just in case— until their journey was complete. She would be glad when it was in his possession again. She didn't usually care much for jewelry, but the ring was the most beautiful she had ever seen, and after only one day it was beginning to feel familiar.

She bent to touch the water, skimming her fingertips over the cool surface. She supposed she ought to feel afraid, alone with the duke in a place foreign to her, but she no longer found him threatening. Five days traveling together had proved he was much more a gentleman than he claimed.

She glanced at him now as he checked each of the horses' hooves carefully, wondering how it was he did not appear in the least exhausted. She felt the strain of their hastened journey, and she'd had far more rest than he. Stopping at another inn last night, so she and Shelby might get a few hours' sleep, had been very considerate of him. Though a tiny part of her wished that they had continued traveling and instead she had been able to lean her head against his shoulder as she slept.

The unexpected thought had disturbed her at first, but then she reasoned that it had likely come to mind simply because of their interactions earlier in the day. They'd sat so close at the inn, and then he'd been beside her in the carriage, encouraging her to lean against him as she slept. It had been surprisingly pleasant being close to him like that, and she hadn't worried that he was pursuing her in any way. After her ordeal he'd simply offered comfort, both emotional and physical, and she had been grateful.

From the very beginning he had told her that he was not looking for a wife, and he had not once suggested they marry when they were in Gretna Green. Since she was not looking for a husband, that left them free to simply be. *Friends, perhaps?* Another unusual thing for her to be contemplating. Could an unattached female be friends, and friends only, with an equally unattached male? The possibility intrigued her. She enjoyed talking to the duke, sparring and debating with him, and enjoyed the way he spoke to her as an equal.

"My mother's ancestral home is half a day's ride from here," he said, pulling her from her musings. "We'll stop for luncheon first, in Annan, after we've watered the horses." He stood and stretched, as if working out sore muscles of his own.

Maybe she wasn't the only one unaccustomed to long rides. She eyed the water again, thinking how good it would feel. Now that they had stopped, and there was no longer a breeze against her face, she felt sticky and hot.

"Would you like a few minutes of privacy?" the duke asked, looking upstream as he spoke.

Sophie suspected he wished to get in the cool water as well.

"Yes, please." She eyed the stream with eagerness.

"Very well. I'll stay within shouting distance, should you need anything."

"I'll be fine." Sophie watched his retreating form until he had disappeared. Confident that she was alone, she walked over to her horse and placed a hand on its withers for balance. Her other hand reached down, beneath the hem of her skirt, to grasp first her boot and then her stocking. With considerable maneuvering she was soon free of both, then lifted her skirt and stepped into the stream.

"Oh!" Freezing water that felt like a thousand needles against her feet and ankles made her gasp. Sophie hopped from one foot to the other, forcing herself to stay in the water, though her senses shouted at her to get out.

After a minute or so of her awkward dance, the shock to her feet began to subside, replaced by the refreshing sensation she had sought. Gathering her skirts in one hand, she bent low and cupped the other in the water, splashed some on her face and neck, and felt even better.

After that, she wandered up and down a small section of the stream, enjoying the feeling of the slippery rocks and pebbled sand beneath her bare feet. It had been years since she'd enjoyed such a luxury, and even as a girl, the removal of her shoes and stockings had almost always landed her in trouble with her nannies or governess. *I shall not be that kind of governess.* If there were streams near the duke's estate, she would encourage her pupils to play in them.

Sophie closed her eyes and lifted her face to the sky, enjoying the contrast of the warmth above and the cold below. The melodic sounds of the moving water soothed away her worries, and the sweet fragrance of the grasses and ferns, the bluebells and primrose growing along the bank and in the meadows beyond restored her grieving soul in a way nothing else had since her sister's passing. Torie had loved the outdoors as much as Sophie, and they had shared many childhood adventures in the fields surrounding their country estate. Those had been blissful days before Father's business interest in Saint Kitts had escalated, and his temper and unfeeling manner along with it. Before the requisite London Seasons, before Sophie had learned all that her tutors could or were willing to teach her. Before life had become both stagnant and stressful.

"Miss Claybourne?" The duke's voice carried to her, sounding nearly as far away as her thoughts had been. "Are you ready to resume our journey?"

She imagined him cupping his hands about his mouth and calling to her, and she experienced the peculiar, unsettled reaction she'd come to associate with being in his presence.

This morning, when she'd stepped outside of her room to speak with him, the feeling had been particularly strong—not unpleasant, but a sensation, nevertheless, that threw her off balance and made her feel not quite in control. She'd decided it was because the duke was unpredictable. He did not act as other men did—for which she was mostly grateful.

This morning his obvious worry for Lucy had both surprised and touched Sophie. In her experience, most men of rank did not concern themselves with their servants' conditions, outside of their abilities to perform their assigned duties. Then, while she was still deciphering his acceptance of Lucy's illness and his generous plans to accommodate it, he had readily agreed with her idea to ride on horseback instead of in the carriage.

A man listened to and agreed with me. He took my suggestion.

She'd been both baffled and elated. But revealing either of those emotions had not seemed prudent, so she had thrown out the reminder that he must act as the gentleman. Which, of course, he had. With each passing day, she doubted more and more that he actually deserved the reputation assigned to him. Yet the fact remained that he had killed two men and felt no remorse.

"I suppose we can go," Sophie called back. "If we must," she added to herself. She didn't want to rush one moment of this day. Soon enough she would be stuck inside again, teaching young students who were probably less eager than she to be in a classroom. Though she would also be able to learn once more, and that possibility excited her. Even more than lingering in this delightful stream.

Reluctantly, she turned toward the shore and the spot by the horses where she'd left her shoes. She waded toward them and, when she was close, paused to lift her right foot from the water. She gathered her skirts higher as she looked down, circling her foot about, trying to shake the remaining drops from it so it would be easier to put on her stockings. Foot still in the air, she leaned forward to reach for her shoes, but they were gone.

Fifteen

"LOOKING FOR THESE?" GRAHAM, WORKING hard to keep his mouth from twitching, held up the pair of dainty boots, complete with stockings poking out from the top.

Miss Claybourne's foot plunged back down into the stream, and her hands, including the one holding up her skirt, flew to her pink cheeks. The hem of her skirt floated on top of the water in a graceful circle about her, though Miss Claybourne looked anything but graceful at the moment, standing awkwardly in the middle of the stream as she thrust out her hands to him.

"Give me those. Please," she amended, then added, "Your Grace," as if the proper form of address might somehow fix her predicament.

But Graham was too amused to return her shoes so quickly. Instead, he set them on the shore, out of reach unless she were to exit the water altogether. He ignored her gasp of protest and the severity of her frown as he crouched to remove his own shoes and roll up his trousers. Once this was done, he stepped into the stream beside her.

The initial cold should not have surprised him—he'd played in enough lochs and burns in his childhood to know how freezing the water could be, especially in spring—but he felt the shock of it all the same.

"You've a strong constitution if you're able to withstand

this temperature." He glanced at her with admiration and gritted his teeth against the cold.

Her eyes were wide as she watched him. He'd given her no indication on their journey thus far that he was anything other than serious. With the exception of their afternoon in Gretna Green, he'd rushed them through meals and in and out of inns as quickly as possible, always giving orders, always tense, always on the lookout for her father or anyone else who might be after her. It was a feeling all too similar to the one he'd experienced in Saint Kitts, and he did not wish for a replay or anything close to the events he'd experienced there.

But this afternoon felt a bit lighter. They were nowhere near the road, nowhere near any place her father was likely to look. They could afford a bit of time to refresh both body and soul. Indulging in her company for a few minutes would not hurt anything. As soon as they reached Caerlanwood, they would scarcely see each other. *It will be better that way.*

But just now . . .

Miss Claybourne stopped frowning and offered a suggestion. "It helps if you hop around a bit at first." She hugged her arms to herself and looked at him warily. "Once you're used to the water, it feels wonderful."

Graham took her advice, though he felt ridiculous hopping about in the stream. She was right; it did help. And even better, his actions elicited a smile. If his playing the fool put her at ease, then so much the better.

When his feet had grown accustomed to the chill, he stopped moving and came to stand a short distance from her. "Your gown may be wet all afternoon."

Miss Claybourne shrugged as she glanced down at the hem of her skirt, no longer floating on top of the water, but sunk below it and clinging to her legs. "No matter. The wind will dry it, and until then it will help me remain cool."

"Was the heat what drove you to walk in the stream?" When he'd left a quarter of an hour ago to give her privacy, he'd never imagined he would find her in the water upon his return.

"Partially. I have fond memories of running about barefoot as a child. They were few and far between, but I enjoyed it. Today the stream beckoned me to revisit those days."

"And have you?" he asked, imagining Miss Claybourne as a precocious child.

"I have." She nodded. "I was remembering and thinking of times with my elder sister when you called to me."

"I am sorry to have interrupted," Graham said, knowing what he did of her sister's fate. "Would you like me to leave you alone? I believe we can spare a few minutes more." He started to turn away, but Miss Claybourne shook her head and reached out as if to touch him. He paused, her hand dropped, and he found himself disappointed.

"Don't go," she said. "The water is refreshing, and it was kind of you to join me—to overlook my very unladylike behavior."

"Perhaps more ladies should think and act as you." What a different world this might be. He might feel more at ease in it, enjoy it more were the ton to concern itself less with appearances and ridiculous rules of behavior and more with simply living and enjoying life, as Miss Claybourne appeared to be this morning.

Her eyes narrowed slightly. "Are you mocking me, Your Grace?"

"Not at all." He shook his head. "You don't allow Society or anyone or anything else to govern you. You see a situation or a problem, and you assess it quickly. Then, instead of lamenting the outcome or bemoaning and accepting your fate, you take action. You were warm today, and the water looked inviting, so you took the steps to enjoy it. Your father arranged a marriage to a most unsuitable man, so you left home to avoid that marriage."

Her mouth twisted in a half smile. "Actually, you were the one who acted to prevent that most unsuitable match—for which I was grateful. But I then had to act to avoid being stuck with you."

"Hmm." Graham brought a hand to his chin. "How is that going?"

"Not well! Not well at all." She laughed.

He stepped back as if affronted, but her laughter went straight to his heart, dislodging a bit more of the heaviness that had been there for so long. "In that case, I shall—"

"Truthfully, it is going very well," Miss Claybourne said, her smile remaining, but the teasing glint leaving her eyes. "You see, the Duke of Warwick is not at all what I expected. In fact, he is not like any other gentleman I have ever met."

"As I have assured you repeatedly, he is no gentleman," Graham scoffed, then scooped water at her to prove his point.

She jumped out of the way, as if she had anticipated such a move. The way she'd seemed to sense what he was about intrigued him. How would it be to have someone who truly knew him and his heart? And who accepted both?

William was as close as any to that juncture, but even he did not fully understand the agonies and demons Graham wrestled with. Not that he wished William or, especially, Miss Claybourne to be burdened with those things, but it was nice to imagine sometimes that he had someone to talk to and counsel with, a confidant who understood him and the reasons for the things he had done and might still be called upon to do in the future.

"Society may have judged him harshly in that regard," Miss Claybourne said, speaking of him again as if he were not present. "But he is more a gentleman than any other I have met. And I am grateful it was he who rescued me from a life of certain misery with Viscount Newsome." She looked up at Graham boldly, much as she had done that first night in the carriage when she had discovered she was wrong and had apologized for doubting him.

Graham's insides twisted at the thought of her in Newsome's clutches. He pushed aside the murderous thoughts that followed, focusing instead on her honesty and candor. "Do you know what I admire most about you?"

Her face clouded. "I would prefer you admire nothing about me. We, you and I—" she gestured back and forth between them— "are friends. Or I should like us to be. But it has been my unfortunate experience that when a man begins to admire a woman, friendship is not possible."

"Then I shall have to prove you wrong, as I both admire you and wish to count you as a friend." He held back a grimace, appalled at the dandy words coming from his mouth as much as at his admission. Was he no better than her other gawking suitors? And they should *not* be friends once this journey ended, but merely employer and employee. "I shall change my wording to *appreciate*. I appreciate your honesty, Miss Claybourne. And your bravery in standing up for and saying what you feel. It is a refreshing change from my interactions with other ladies in your position."

She looked down at the stream and her feet beneath the water. "I very much doubt there are any other ladies in my position at present."

Graham chuckled. "You are likely correct." He glanced at the sky and the gathering clouds, knowing they ought to be going but reluctant to leave this spot and the tranquility he had discovered here. "As averse as I am to changing that, we should probably go." He hoped they would have sunshine the remainder of their ride, but it was late spring in Scotland, so rain was likely. And her clothes were already partially wet. He held out a hand to her. "Will you allow me to assist you from the stream—though, as you got in here on your own, you are, no doubt, entirely capable of getting out on your own as well."

After a few seconds hesitation, Miss Claybourne shook her head. "I will wait until you have exited the stream and turned your back to me before I get out. It would not do for you to see both my ankles *and* my toes today."

He had seen both already but did not wish to make her uncomfortable again. "Very well." Graham dropped his hand, turned from her, and sloshed toward the shore, wincing as his foot encountered a sharp rock. "This has been refreshing, but I much prefer sand beneath my feet instead of these stones."

"Sand?"

At the hopeful note in her voice, he looked over his shoulder. "Not here, of course, though Scotland does have some walkable shoreline. But I was referring to Saint Kitts. When I visited my sister there we often spent the evenings walking on the beach. The water is warm and blue, yet translucent. And there is something to be said for the feeling of bare feet upon the sand."

Miss Claybourne's head tilted slightly, and she looked at him with something akin to wonder. "It sounds lovely," she said quietly.

"It was," Graham said. "The whole island might be, if not for the curse of slavery upon it."

The rapture in her gaze faded, replaced by a troubled expression. "I hope my leaving home will have some slight impact for good."

"That remains to be seen. Your father and Lord Newsome may yet merge their plantations. But for now, I believe we have stalled their plans." Graham turned from her once more and left the stream to retrieve his shoes. When he had donned them, he moved hers closer to the water's edge, then went to stand on the other side of the horses. A few minutes later, Miss Claybourne joined him, her shoes and stockings in place and her skirt still dripping.

She looked up at him, her gaze considerably less cautious than it had been when they had started out this morning. "Thank you for this reprieve and for not making me feel the fool for my actions."

"There is nothing to feel foolish about." Except perhaps the way his heart had begun pounding at her nearness. "I find your actions as refreshing as the cool water."

"THE BLUE BELL INN." SOPHIE leaned back to stare up at the large, blue ship's bell and the lettering above the doorway to the red brick building before her. "An original name." She didn't particularly care what the establishment was called, so long as it served food—any food. They'd ridden another hour past the stream—long enough for her stomach to realize she'd missed both the morning and midday meals—and she couldn't remember ever being this hungry.

At the duke's light touch on her back, she hurried forward, uncomfortable with the familiarity of his touch and the flutter of strange feelings that accompanied it. For the past hour, since he'd so casually spoken of walking on the sandy beach on Saint Kitts, she'd been reeling internally, at first convinced that he'd somehow overheard her conversation with Lord Newsome and then certain that he had not. How could the duke have possibly heard her, seated at the opposite end of the table as he had been? She'd been facing away from him when she'd spoken those scandalous words about walking barefoot on a beach.

That he had not heard but had spoken of such to her caused a riot of confusing, conflicted thoughts. The first—delight! Here was a man who appreciated the opportunities presented to him and made good use of the situations he encountered. He was not too stuffy or proper to remove his shoes and walk in a mountain stream or on a sandy beach. Such a simple thing; so trivial. But somehow it felt vastly important. She *admired* him for it, and that frightened her, as did his hand at her back now, because it was not unpleasant at all.

The duke leaned forward to grasp the doorknob and whisper in her ear. "Remember, we are betrothed. We must pretend such until we are alone again."

Sophie nodded. Yesterday they had pretended to be married. But here, where they were unlikely to be discovered by her father, but might possibly run into the duke's acquaintances, he had suggested that pretending to be betrothed was preferable.

Honesty would be preferable, but she could not deny that their charade had been almost pleasant. She rather enjoyed the duke's solicitous attention when he was pretending to be her husband. Dissimilar to the other men who had pursued her, he did not repulse her. Nor did she feel the clammy spike of panic whenever he was near. *Because we are just pretending.* Had there been any sincerity to his actions, she would have been terrified. But knowing that he was not seeking a wife—not intent on capturing her—allowed her to enjoy his care and courtesy.

Mostly. His hand at her elbow, as he assisted her over the uneven stone threshold, caused a spike of an entirely different nature, bringing a blush to her cheeks and making her step light, as if she might float away.

The door closed behind them, and the aroma of fried

fish—usually not her favorite—assaulted her. Her stomach grumbled as if anticipating such fare. Sophie squinted as her eyes adjusted to the low light. A long, wood counter ran along the left side of the pub, with tables scattered around the right side of the room. Behind the last, a set of steep, narrow stairs were visible until they disappeared into the floor above.

"Graham? Is that you, lad?" a raspy voice called from the bar side of the room.

"Aye. 'Tis the wee beastie come home at long last," the duke returned in a jovial brogue, startling Sophie almost as much as he'd startled her when he'd stepped into the stream. He guided her farther into the room.

"Canna' be Graham Murray," another voice said. "Not with a bonny lass at his side."

At this, laughter erupted, followed by chairs scraping against the wood floor and footsteps shuffling toward them.

"Murray?" Sophie whispered, glancing up at him.

"My mother's name. And what I am known by here."

A gaggle of elderly men surrounded them, calling out good-natured greetings to the duke as they stared, wide-eyed, at her.

"And who be this, Graham? And how is it she's agreed to stand so close to ye?" a white-haired, white-bearded man asked. "Have ye finally taken to bathing more regular now?"

Another set of guffaws followed, but instead of taking offense at this, the duke smiled broadly as he reached out to clap the nearest man on the back. "That I have lads, though it doesna seem the lot of ye have followed suit." He wrinkled his nose, as if his senses were offended.

The unfamiliar brogue slid easily off his tongue, and Sophie watched the cares of the world—or his dukedom, at least—seem to slip from his shoulders as well. This was a side of him she had not seen before. Less formal, more friendly. *Comfortable. Happy.*

"Gentlemen, may I present Miss Sophia Claybourne, my fiancée."

Gasps and then silence followed this announcement—absolute, deafening silence that went on and on. Sophie darted a glance up at Graham, still grinning broadly. If he was bothered by the less-than-enthusiastic reaction, he didn't show it. The men gathered around them continued to gape, disbelief evident in their wide eyes.

At last the one who had asked the question snorted, then broke into laughter. The others followed, their belly laughs echoing around the room. When this had gone on for a full half minute, she could take no more.

"What is so amusing?" Sophie demanded, stepping forward.

"It is true. His Grace and I—"

Graham's hand pressed against her back.

"Graham and I," Sophie amended, supposing that a true fiancée would not refer to her betrothed so formally, "are engaged to be married." It was no worse a lie than the one he had told at her parents' dinner party. And for a worthy cause, as well. Who were these men to mock him? Why should they doubt his ability to procure a fiancée? He was a duke, after all. Not to mention handsome as well. And in their short time together, she'd found him to be the antithesis of his ill reputation. Any woman who wouldn't give him a chance did not deserve his attention.

At her announcement the laughter ceased and the slack-jawed expressions returned.

"An *English* lass?" A balding, stooped man straightened as best he could to look the duke in the eye.

"Aye," the duke said, not sounding nearly as relaxed and comfortable as he had. "Sophie is English."

Sophie. Her head spun as she glanced up at him. How had

he known to call her that? Only her sisters and friends referred to her by that name.

The duke's arm wrapped around her waist protectively, pulling her close to his side. He looked at her with a smile she felt was meant to reassure her that she was safe. Until a moment ago, she had not considered that she might not be, because of the country of her birth.

"Look at them, lads," the white-haired man spoke once more. "I believe it's true. 'Tis easy to see they're besotted with each other."

Sophie pulled her gaze from the duke's and felt a blush heating her cheeks. *I am not besotted.* And the duke most certainly wasn't.

One of the men slid the cap from his head and slapped it against his leg. "Well, I'll be. We've seen everything now, lads."

"Two moons be shining in the sky somewhere," another said.

"We can go to our graves having witnessed a miracle."

"Two of them," the stooped man agreed. "Graham has broken his vow to never wed, and he'll be takin' an Englishwoman to his bed."

More laughter followed this poetic decree. Sophie felt as if her face was practically on fire, and the duke's flushed red too. But her discomfort was soon forgotten as the men came forward, hands outstretched to greet her. Some shook her hand heartily. The stooped man bent over it and kissed it with much exaggeration, exclaiming that she was perhaps the only English lass who tasted sweet. The white-haired man engulfed her in a most unexpected hug when the duke was turned away accepting congratulations from the others.

"Name's Cameron," he said, pulling back but still keeping hold of her shoulders. "Been friends to Graham since he was a wee-un barely above my knee." He released her and held his hand low to indicate the height of a small child. "I've no notion how you've done it, given Graham's distaste for all things English and his strong aversion to marriage, but know that you've caught a good one. See that you take care with his heart." Cameron thumped a fist over his chest. "Graham's no' had an easy time of it, and I suspect he needs love more'n most."

"I will," Sophie said, stunned from both his hug and everything he'd just shared. She glanced sideways at the duke, currently engaged in a conversation with another man. *Graham. His name is Graham Murray.* She hadn't even known that before they entered the inn. Had not known him a full week. Everywhere they'd been people had addressed him as Your Grace. She knew practically nothing about him, yet she had just promised to take care with his heart and had lied to a man who'd been a friend to him since childhood.

I will take care with the duke's heart, she vowed silently, amid a surge of unexpected tenderness toward him. He turned to her, a smile on his face that Sophie easily matched. He had saved her from Lord Newsome, had shown her more care and consideration than her own father. He had not harmed her but escorted her to safety, offered her employment, and even promised her the education she so desired. The least she could do was take care with his heart.

But for the first time in her life, she began to fear for hers.

Sixteen

"THIS MAY BE THE BEST thing I've ever eaten." A smile of bliss upon her face, Miss Claybourne closed her eyes and licked her fingers after taking another bite of the battered, fried fish the Blue Bell Inn was known for.

"The sea is nearby. The fish are caught and delivered daily," Graham explained, pleased that she was enjoying their meal so much and pleased at her easy adaptation to their surroundings. If anything, she seemed more at home here than she had in her father's dining room.

"But I do not even particularly *like* fish," she said. "Or I didn't used to."

"Eddie's fish and tatties are different," Graham said, thinking of the times he had eaten similar meals elsewhere and come away disappointed. He had eaten at the Blue Bell Inn more times than he could count and enjoyed each one, but none more so than today with Miss Claybourne at his side and Eddie, Cameron, Ian, and the others continuously popping over to give their congratulations.

If not for Miss Claybourne's bold affirmation, they never would have believed that he was betrothed. He had detected her ire at their disbelief. She'd been incensed at their laughter and had spoken up. *For me.* Something precious few had done in his lifetime. Her actions had startled him and they had touched him more than he dared admit. He admired her even more than he had an hour ago, but as she had so bluntly pointed out earlier, nothing good could come of his admiration. Yet he could not seem to help it.

Graham leaned back in his chair and observed her now, conversing easily with Eddie, answering his questions and asking her own. Miss Claybourne—Sophie, as he wished to think of her now—exhibited the same grace and ease here, in a humble inn in Scotland, that she had displayed with the guests during their first meeting a week ago. There, he had learned she was only play-acting. But here, though they had both lied about being betrothed, he sensed sincerity in her communication. She was friendly and outgoing, curious, and interested in learning about others.

A zest for life practically radiated from her, creating a magnetic pull to anyone in the vicinity. Graham had thought the number of suitors vying for her hand was due to the absurd terms of her dowry that her father had heavily advertised, following his eldest daughter's unfortunate marriage. But having spent a week in Sophie's company, he was beginning to think otherwise. Her vibrant and pleasant personality, her enthusiasm and optimism acted as beacons, particularly to a male population burdened with an overabundance of husband-seeking debutantes. That Miss Claybourne did not wish to marry had likely only made her more attractive, and it was to her great credit that she had managed to reach the age of twenty without being ensnared in a betrothal.

Until now. Unease stirred within him. The last thing he wished to do was crush her bold spirit and her quest for freedom and knowledge. He would never force her to marry him, yet what choice would she ultimately have, given the way he had so utterly destroyed her reputation? Even finding employment as a governess would be difficult if she wished to move on after teaching his niece and nephew.

Graham pushed those troubling thoughts from his mind and glanced out the window at the darkening sky. There were already troubles aplenty awaiting him at home. Two, in particular, that required his immediate attention, though he wasn't at all certain how to go about giving it to them. It was entirely possible that what had seemed a brilliant solution—hiring Miss Claybourne to be their governess—would be a complete disaster. And then where would he be? He could not contemplate that now. One problem at a time, and the first was the threat of rain in the clouds above.

"We should be off if we're to arrive at Caerlanwood before dark and without being entirely soaked," Graham said. "Have you had enough to eat, Sophie?"

At the use of her name, she looked up at him, an unreadable expression on her face. Having spoken her name once and heard his own from her lips, he felt reluctant to return to their previous formality. And in this situation of pretending, they should not.

"I am not certain I could ever have enough of these delicious fried fish and potatoes." She gestured to her near-empty plate. "Thank you for a most satisfying meal." She directed her smile at Eddie, the one responsible for their feast.

"Ye must come to us again soon," he gushed as he rose from his chair and reached for their plates. "And Graham, you'd best be inviting us all to yer nuptials. Will ye be wed in the village kirk?"

Graham shook his head. "Among other repairs, I'm restoring the chapel at Caerlanwood. When it is complete, we'll be married there. In the meantime, I've invited my friend William Fitzgerald and his wife to join us and act as chaperones."

"If ye would have asked me yesterday if I'd ever believe ye'd need chaperoning around an English lass . . ." Eddie shook his head. "I woulda said never, that you'd stay as far away as possible all on yer own. But now . . ." He winked at Sophie. "I like her fine, and as she seems to like you fine, I think your chaperone is a good idea. Just don't take too long restoring that chapel."

Graham pulled Sophie's chair out for her, and she placed her hand on his arm as they turned toward the door.

Cameron shuffled toward them. "Surely you dinna intend to start out now?" His gaze drifted toward the window and the darkening skies beyond.

"Aye, we do. I've been gone from home long enough." *Too long and not nearly long enough.* How was it that his heart could both soar and squeeze at the thought of Caerlanwood? He yearned for it and dreaded it in the same breath. "Sophie is an accomplished rider. Another four hours should see us safely there."

She glanced up at him, a surprised smile lighting her face. He placed his hand over hers on his arm and squeezed gently. He'd been impressed with her skill this morning, and he was happy to let her know it, happy to compliment her as he might. *For another few hours, at least.* Once they were home the pretending would have to be over. In every way.

"Ye havena been home for a spell, ye say?" Cameron chewed his lip. "Then you'll not know that the bridge washed out a month past. It's not yet repaired." His gaze drifted to Sophie. "She'd best be able to fly, if you're thinkin' to be home tonight."

That cursed bridge. Graham closed his eyes in frustration. "I didn't know." It shouldn't have surprised him. How many times had it flooded before, leaving Caerlanwood cut off, except by travel through the dense forest surrounding it?

"It's settled, then." The tension left Cameron's face. "Eddie will find you some rooms upstairs, and you can join us for the cèilidh tonight. We've got a new fiddler in town, and he plays a right good tune."

"What is a cèilidh?" Sophie asked.

"A celebration of life," Cameron answered before Graham

could. "It's song and dance and drink and friendship—the Scottish way to have a good time."

"It sounds lovely," Sophie exclaimed.

Graham had a brief vision of Sophie, skirts flying, laughter on her lips as she danced the circle. He imagined catching her arm and holding her close, claiming her for himself as the tune slowed.

"I love my lassie, my bonnie lassie . . ." From the bar, Ian sang the first words of the familiar ballad.

"My bonnie lassie," the others joined in, raising their glasses.

"We'll see if those English feet of yours can keep up with us," Cameron said with a wink.

"No," Graham said, louder than he'd intended, but it shut the lot of them up, their impromptu song ending abruptly. "We need to be home tonight. Especially now that I know the bridge is out and the road's been closed. I need to see how everyone is faring." It wasn't as if they weren't used to this sort of thing practically every year. They had plenty of supplies stockpiled, but this was the first time with the children there. What if one of them had been ill or hurt? Maime had come with them from Saint Kitts, and she was a fine healer, but still—if anything serious had befallen anyone . . .

"I wouldna advise it." Rory lifted his cane and tapped his leg with it. "Knee's been botherin' me all morning. It's bound to be a bad storm. Not likely you'll reach Caerlanwood before it hits. You wouldna want the lass to be caught in it."

The others in the room nodded and murmured their agreement, as if Rory's knee were the ultimate predictor of the weather.

Graham scoffed. "I'll place my bets that we can outride it." He continued toward the door, but not before noting the disappointment in Sophie's eyes.

Guilt niggled at him. It was a risk they were taking, but

what of the risk if they stayed the night here and he danced with her? They'd been close enough this week to wreak havoc on his normally disciplined actions and principles. All this pretending was getting the better of him, giving him ideas that were all too real. And he *couldn't* entertain those. A little rain would harm her far less than a possible true attachment to him.

Grumbling ensued behind them.

"Still the same pig-headed lad," someone mumbled.

"Too good for the likes of us, now that he's all grown up," another said.

Graham halted before the door and turned to face the room once again. "Lads, none of that be true. I've a reason for wanting to get home."

"Aye, so ye can have the lass all to yourself!" Ian called.

Graham frowned and shook his head, reminding himself that their jesting was good-natured and he oughtn't to ruin things with his temper. He held up a hand, silencing the room.

"I've been away too long now. My neglect has been great, and I intend to make amends—to both Caerlanwood as a whole and to those who've served her faithfully these many years. It was a promise I made to my mother, and one that until now I've failed to keep."

"God bless her and rest her soul," Rory said, head bent over his cane.

"Aye." The others nodded in agreement.

"Never a sweeter woman, other than your sister, perhaps, to walk these shores," Cameron said.

"And now Miss Sophie here to fill their shoes." Eddie paused wiping a table to beam at them. "You've chosen well, Graham. Ride hard and get her safely home tonight."

Seventeen

ONCE OUTSIDE, GRAHAM EXPECTED SOPHIE to release his arm and step away from him, but she didn't as they hurried down the street to collect their horses.

"I imagine word will get around town rather quickly," she said, as if to explain why their arms were still linked.

"Aye," Graham said. "Don't let it worry you. Folks will forget soon enough if we don't come around. And it is doubtful anyone from England will follow us here. Only William knows of my home at Caerlanwood. I am careful whom I share it with."

"Yet you intend to share it with me?" She glanced up at him, question in her gaze.

He nodded, unwilling to chance saying something else that would make him sound far too much like one of her suitors. He was sharing his home with her out of necessity. Caerlanwood had been a safe haven for him and could be for the children and Sophie as well. That was his reasoning at the start of this journey, anyway. Now he wished to share it with her because it was a part of him. It was special and sacred, and he'd come to trust her enough that he wanted her to see it.

Once mounted—Sophie with a tight expression of discomfort, though she did not voice any complaint—they left Annan the opposite way they had entered, riding slower this time, though they ought to be hurrying.

"That first night in the carriage when you told me you were not in the market for a wife, I was not certain that I believed you. But this afternoon that truth was more than confirmed." She turned to him. "Why did you vow never to marry? And would you have truly broken that vow for me? Or to prevent the merger on Saint Kitts?"

"Marriage has never appealed to me," Graham admitted. "My parents' marriage was miserable. I've never wanted to repeat history."

"I could say the same of my parents' marriage. Perhaps that is why I have been so averse to the institution as well." She tilted her head slightly, as if just now considering that possibility.

"When I suggested that we wed, I was not thinking of marriage in the traditional sense," Graham explained. "It was a way to offer you an escape from Viscount Newsome and your father, as well as a way to prevent the merger of their plantations. I did not foresee any emotional or physical attachment or entanglements between us. You would be free to live your life and I mine. I did not imagine that we would reside together or even in the same country, perhaps. That was one of the reasons I hired your maid and her husband to join us. Wherever I sent you, I did not wish for you to be truly alone."

"You would have sent me to the continent?" Instead of dismay, he heard yearning in her voice.

"I had considered it, yes. I wanted you to be safe from your father and Newsome." *And me.* "So somewhere far away seemed a good idea. But then you mentioned being a governess..."

"In other words, our marriage would have been a business transaction and nothing more," Sophie summarized.

"Aye." He gave her a look of apology, though he wasn't entirely certain what he was apologizing for. She hadn't wanted the union either, yet he felt he had dishonored her somehow by suggesting such an arrangement. A great deal of marriages—the majority of those among the ton—were nothing more than business, though the couples had to suffer one another's company. It was as his parents' marriage had been and precisely what he intended to avoid. It was a blessing Sophie had felt the same. Another young lady might have insisted on a hasty marriage at Gretna Green and objected to being sent far away.

"Then why the pretense of being betrothed today—here, where you find it unlikely anyone will follow us? Why not simply tell your friends that I am to be the governess for your sister's children?"

"Because they do not know of the children." He hadn't told a soul—other than those at Caerlanwood, and Sophie and her maid now—of the children's existence. "Losing their parents was traumatic, and I wished them time to recover before being faced with visitors or anyone else. Let's see how they do getting used to you before we consider introducing them into society."

"*We?*" She glanced at him, one brow arched. "You are their guardian. I believe decisions of that type lie with you."

"Perhaps, but I have no experience with children." *Nor will I ever.* "I will leave their education and all else to you once we are at Caerlanwood."

Sophie gave a single nod. "Very well. If that is what you wish."

"It is."

Graham gave an inward sigh of relief, grateful to have that matter cleared up. Now to explain to her that they would see very little of each other once they were home. She would lead her life with the children, and he would lead his. *Alone.*

"And what of your aversion to Englishwomen?" she

asked, interrupting the melancholy direction of his thoughts. "I think your friends' shock at my birthplace was possibly even greater than the news that you were to marry."

Graham contemplated how to explain his feelings without offending her or revealing even more of his past. "My father was English and my mother Scottish. Like oil and water." His father had been slick and slimy. Mother had been like a fountain of pure water, cascading over the rocks of life, blessing all she came in contact with. "They did not mix well."

"And you feared marriage to an Englishwoman would be the same?"

Graham shrugged. "Something like that. My father earned the disrespect of everyone in the village. He was a foul man. A selfish man. A—"

"A lot like my father?" she said, a frown marring her pretty face.

"Worse."

She flashed him a look of sympathy, then nodded as if she understood, but she couldn't possibly. Not the half of it, and he didn't wish to spoil the day by telling her.

As if brought on by the direction of his thoughts and their conversation, the day changed rapidly all on its own. A clap of thunder shook the distant skies as the first raindrops fell, splashing down on their faces.

"No chance of my skirt drying before our arrival now," Sophie mused. "Oh well, at least I shall have an excuse for it. Shall we ride faster?" she asked, glancing over at him once more.

Graham nodded, only too happy to leave their conversation behind.

"How fast can you safely ride?" he called to her through the now rapidly falling rain.

"Fast," she assured him. "You lead. I'll keep up."

He nodded and set out, riding hard. They weren't going to outrun the storm, but at least they could be out in it a shorter amount of time. True to her word, Sophie kept up. He looked over his shoulder frequently, each time to see her bent forward over her horse, her hands clenched on the reins, eyes tightly focused on following him.

She was an excellent rider, better than some of the men he knew. He'd been amused this morning when he'd discovered her sitting astride her horse, what had to have been a frequent practice based on what he was seeing now.

Miss Sophia Claybourne was nothing like he had imagined and, if he was not very careful, might turn out to be everything he had ever dreamed.

THEY LEFT THE ROAD AND entered the forest well before dark, though the light did little to help them. Graham navigated the wood by memory alone, as the path seemed nonexistent. It had been years since he and Katherine had traversed it, and new foliage had long grown over what had once been a somewhat marked trail.

Of necessity their pace slowed as they picked their way over fallen logs and around boulders and clusters of trees. They hadn't spoken in hours, and when he glanced back at Sophie, she appeared to be bent lower over the mare each time.

Finally, when he could see her face no longer, he guided his horse to the side and to a halt, waiting for her to catch up.

"Are you all right?" he called through the gale.

She pulled up next to him and sat up slowly. Strands of wet hair lay plastered against her face, so much so that he could hardly see her, but she made no attempt to brush them aside.

"Ha-have we arrived?" She didn't bother turning her

head to take in their surroundings, but he noted the shiver ripple up her back, visibly shaking her arms above their viselike grip on the reins.

Her knuckles were white, nearly blue, as were her lips. Her mouth pressed into a thin line, but not before he glimpsed her teeth chattering.

"Caerlanwood is still a distance away," he said regretfully. *Too far.* What would have been four hours on the road might be five or six through the wood, but with the rain . . . *Seven— or more?* He should have heeded Rory's knee. Then they might have still been in town, warm and dry. But no, this was temporary discomfort. The cèilidh would have been far more dangerous. *To both of us.* Pretending to care for her had been one thing, but he could not play-act much longer, not without all pretense falling away and this growing attraction he felt for her becoming a real problem.

"We've another hour or two, at least," he said, gentling his tone because what he could view of Sophie's face suddenly appeared distraught, her lip quivering and the one eye he could view filling with tears. "The road is far more direct. Had the bridge not been washed out, we might have been home already. Traveling through the wood and in the rain adds quite a bit of time."

He hadn't minded so much as a child. The forest had offered protection from his father on those rare occasions he came to visit them during the summer. The servants or his mother had always sounded the warning, and then he and Katherine were off, running through the forest—where they would not be followed or found—to the safety of any number of town folk who would take them in temporarily. While his mother stayed behind to face the wrath of their father.

"Come with us," he'd begged the summer he was nine. He knew his father would hurt her if she stayed behind. One of the servants would always send word when he had left and it was safe to come home again, and he and Katherine would return to find their mother bruised and beaten.

"I cannot leave Caerlanwood." She'd knelt in front of him, taking his hands in hers. "It is my ancestors' home—yours too, now. I fear your father would destroy it—more than he has already—if I were not here when he came."

"But he hurts you," Graham had argued. "I don't want him to hurt you anymore."

"It would hurt me more if he destroyed our home." Mother stood and looked around the garden she so loved. "Where would we escape to every summer if that happened? You wouldn't wish to spend the summer in England, would you?"

"No." Graham shook his head. "I wish we could stay here always."

"Me too. But I am grateful we have our summers, at least." She stood and hugged him, holding him close a long moment before bidding him to find his sister and hurry through the forest to town.

It was the last time he had stayed away. After that, he had escorted Katherine to safety, then returned to Caerlanwood to spare his mother what he might. Any blow he took from his father was one less delivered to her.

"Is there no place we can stop for the night?"

Sophie's forlorn question brought him back to the present and their predicament. That she had made such a request bespoke the depth of her misery.

Graham shook his head, second-guessing his decision yet again. "The trees will be closer together soon, and that should offer some protection from the rain." Rain that had turned to icy sleet.

She nodded even as she shivered. He didn't have so much

as a jacket to offer her. The only thing they could do was to keep going.

"Think of the roaring fire and warm bowl of soup that will be awaiting us." He attempted an encouraging smile, though no doubt it came off as more of a grimace. He was miserable too.

They started off again, as fast as he dared. He looked back frequently, checking to see that she still followed. Darkness fell, and the trees closed in around them. He slowed their pace even more, picking his way carefully, trusting his horse to step wisely, and trusting himself to remember enough to go the right way and not add hours to their journey. He could no longer see Sophie when he looked back, so he stopped, waited for her, and then attached a rope to her lead, to ensure they didn't become separated. As he finished tying the knot, a tiny sob escaped her. Graham paused and leaned closer.

"What is it?" He brushed some of the hair from her face and was alarmed to see tears sliding down her cheeks along with the rain.

"I ca—can't feel my fingers. I don't think I can hold on much longer. I'm afraid I'm going to fall. And I hate that I'm so weak."

Graham silently cursed himself and the weather—and everything else that had led to his poor decision. *My father. His father before him.* No doubt if he had a normal heritage he would have stayed in town, grateful for the opportunity to dance with Miss Claybourne and extend their journey one more night. Instead he'd risked their lives traveling through the forest at night in terrible weather, all because he feared growing any closer to her. He needed to get home, to the vast halls of Caerlanwood, where he wouldn't interact with her each day and could avoid her altogether if he wished.

His intentions had been good. He'd wanted to avoid

dancing with her because it wasn't safe, but now . . . *This is going to be much worse than a simple dance.*

He held in a resigned sigh. "You don't have to hold on any longer. You can ride with me the rest of the way. I'll keep you safe."

"So-some horsewoman I turned out to be. Not so ac-accomplished as you thought."

"You're very accomplished. It's my pig-headed nature that is to blame for our predicament." Graham reached for her hand, alarmed at its iciness. He pried her grip from the reins and took a minute to rub her fingers briskly, trying to restore feeling, though he knew that would bring a pain of its own.

He repeated his ministrations with her other hand, then began the awkward transition of getting her onto his horse. Had she not been so cold and stiff and their situation so dire, it might have been laughable. Certainly he would have seen far more than her comely ankles had it been light out, but at the moment neither was concerned with propriety.

At last he had her settled in front of him. He did his best to pull her skirts lower, apologizing as his hand skimmed her bare leg.

She leaned back against him, and he wrapped one arm securely around her waist. Oh, that he could simply dance with her now instead of being in this predicament, holding her in his arms for the next couple of hours. *God is testing me.* Or maybe he should consider it a blessing—this last bit of time being close to her before they reached Caerlanwood and he put the necessary distance between them.

She sighed and scooted backward so that his thighs pressed close on either side of her. "Th-thank you for rescuing m-me again."

Graham swallowed and willed his pounding heart to slow. "You're welcome." *Heaven help me.*

Eighteen

IT WAS WITH MUCH RELIEF that Graham guided them onto the road a few miles before the entrance to his property, well past the washed-out bridge. Sometime in the last hour the sleet had turned to snow, and a layer of white coated them both. They couldn't get inside soon enough. Graham tightened his grip around Sophie's waist and increased their gait.

A while later when they approached the stone wall—or what was left of it—he shook her gently. "Sophie, we're almost home. This is the border of Caerlanwood."

Dusted with snow, and silent in the night, save for the clopping of the horses' hooves, the scene felt serene and beautiful, despite years of neglect and its many shortcomings. The tall iron gate hung open, secured only by one hinge, and the lanterns on either side were no more. Even their pedestals had crumbled. But the stately pines still stood tall and proud, and the gatekeeper's cottage was visible just beyond the remains of the wall. The road curved from there, disappearing into another grove of trees on either side. Beyond them he knew the twists and turns it would take as it meandered through the wood until it finally opened up to the great drive and house beyond.

A thrill of excitement flickered within him, a rare spark of good memory from his childhood. He remembered stopping here countless times with his mother and sister. They would always disembark from the carriage. Mother said it was because she wished to walk the rest of the way, but really it had been because his father's driver was under strict instructions not to set so much as a wheel of the carriage onto Caerlanwood's drive.

"It's a cursed place, and you don't want to go there."

Graham had been eight when he'd overheard his father's words to the driver.

"Drop them off at the gate and take your leave as quickly as you can."

Caerlanwood was decidedly *not* cursed—excepting those few days his father chose to visit each summer—and Graham had later deduced that his father hadn't wished anyone to realize the true treasure that lay at the end of the road. *Fine by me.* To this day William was the only other Englishman who'd visited and knew of it.

But William didn't know it as Graham had, before his father had pilfered the gems and art and weapons and antiques, before his temper had splintered doors, broken windows, and marred walls. Before his utter neglect and refusal to allot any money for its upkeep had left the main house and outbuildings and land in a state of disrepair.

His father had hated Caerlanwood, hated that because of it and the wealth generated there, he had been forced by his own, cruel father to abandon the woman he loved and instead marry for money that was needed to support the flagging Raymond and Warwick estates. Caerlanwood represented everything his father had not wanted—a Scottish wife, Scottish wealth, and his dependence upon both to survive.

That they were allowed to visit Caerlanwood at all was no small miracle but, rather, foresight on the part of Graham's maternal grandfather, who had written the yearly trips into the marriage contract. If his daughter was not allowed a long holiday at home in Scotland each summer, then the allotted year's allowance would not be released to her husband.

Grandfather was wise, Graham mused as they plodded along the snowy path and he thought of the house beyond it. Would that he had known the man better—a good man, someone he might have looked up to as a boy ought to be able to look up to his father. But at least his grandfather had seen to it that they had summers at Caerlanwood and that his father had not been able to waste his wife's fortune in one fell swoop. Instead he'd been forced to make investments and live somewhat wisely. He'd become shrewd with his business dealings and made his own fortune.

All while letting Caerlanwood go.

As they passed the sagging gate, Graham frowned and moved it to the top of his repair list. If the Shelbys were going to live in the cottage and be gatekeepers, there ought to be a gate to keep. And while he felt confident that Sophie was safe here, there was always the slim chance that her father or Newsome could learn of her whereabouts and come after her. A proper fence and gate would at least deter unwanted visitors and provide time enough to get her safely away if need be. His English estates didn't matter nearly as much as Caerlanwood, and it was time he showed some love to the only place he'd ever considered home. When he'd brought the children here, he'd made sure that at least part of the house was mostly livable again, but it could be so much more—grand as it used to be. *A place of happiness?* Perhaps, with Miss Claybourne and Ayla and Matthew within its walls.

He would not be a participant in that happiness, but he might at least have his sense of peace restored—something he'd not had since his mother's and sister's deaths. Rescuing his niece and nephew from Saint Kitts had not helped, and he most definitely did not feel at peace now, with Sophie asleep in his arms.

No peace, but possibility...

He lowered his head, resting his cheek next to hers briefly, allowing himself a second of indulgence to imagine he was free to pursue their friendship as a man interested in a woman might.

Her frozen skin ended that fantasy abruptly. She'd not warmed at all since joining him—if anything, she seemed colder. Alarmed, he sat up and gave her a quick shake. "Sophie. You need to wake now."

She flopped forward, unresponsive.

Graham pulled on the reins and stopped the horse. "Sophie," he repeated, rubbing her arms a moment until she stirred.

"Miss Claybourne." He shook her once more.

She moaned, and a deep shiver wracked her body. Graham touched her hands—like ice, though they had been tucked close. *Literally freezing. Lethargic. Slipping in and out of consciousness.* He glanced toward the road, weighing their options. At the pace they were traveling, the house was another twenty minutes away. Going any faster was not an option, with the mare trailing behind and Miss Claybourne unable to support herself. Dare he keep going any farther? *If something happens to her...*

I can't risk it. She needed to get warm now.

Keeping one hand on her arm, he slid quickly from the horse, then reached up to her. "Lean forward. I'll catch you."

She leaned, or rather fell toward him, and he caught her and pulled her away from the horse. He lowered her to the ground, and her legs buckled.

Of course she couldn't walk. At least she was breathing. He swept her into his arms, and her head lolled back, her face tilted upward toward the still-falling snow. Awkwardly, Graham leaned back and to the side, maneuvering until her face pressed safely against his shirt.

She jostled as they moved, and he concentrated all his effort on keeping her still as he hurried toward the gatekeeper's house. *Let there be wood for a fire inside. Let there be blankets. Please let her be all right.*

Graham jiggled the handle on the cottage and nudged the door with his knee. The weathered wood swung open easily, creaking in its frame, another reminder of the poor state of affairs at Caerlanwood.

The morning he'd returned to London—under the guise of calling on Miss Claybourne—he had sent a letter, instructing Caerlanwood's staff to tend to the cottage and ready it for the Shelbys. But with the bridge washed out and the road impassable, there was little chance the letter had been delivered. Even if it had made it here somehow, the staff had likely not had the time to even assess the cottage's deficiencies.

But at least the door had opened. *At least the Shelbys are coming. Eventually.* Who knew how many days they'd be delayed, with the bridge washed out. All of tonight's rain certainly hadn't helped that situation. But he had hired them and, tomorrow, would begin to work on hiring others, mostly tenants on his land who wished for extra income, until Caerlanwood was fully staffed once more.

Graham stepped over the dark threshold and made for the fireplace. He deposited Sophie on the floor near the empty hearth, then knelt and searched in the dark for flint, kindling, and logs. He found a few of the latter already in the grate, and he groped blindly among the shelves until he located a book whose pages could be used to ignite the fire quickly.

Outside, Miss Claybourne's mare whinnied pitifully. No doubt it wished to come inside from the snow as well.

"Be patient, girl," he called as he worked, wondering if the old shed out back still stood. If so, was it safe enough to house two horses overnight?

After a few minutes more fumbling about, the fire caught. A soft glow lit the room, and Graham turned back to Sophie, lying where he had left her, unmoving.

"Miss Claybourne." He crouched beside her and patted her white, frosty cheeks. "You need to get out of your wet clothes."

Her eyes opened at this, staring at him with a wild, bewildered expression.

"You're soaked, and you'll become very ill if we don't get you dry." He grasped her arms and pulled her to a sitting position, then picked her up and placed her in the nearest chair. "Take off your riding habit, and I'll bring you a blanket to cover up in."

Her expression slid to blank, but her hands moved, slowly rising to the front of her jacket to begin on the row of buttons there.

Graham stood and went to the bedroom, fumbling around in the dark again until he located the bed and—gratefully—a quilt on top. He pulled it free and returned to the other room to find Sophie slumped sideways and shivering, with only one button on her jacket unfastened.

I am truly cursed, or God has a wicked sense of humor. "If you cannot undress yourself, I will have to do it for you," he said sternly.

She didn't respond. Not a rebuke about his reputation or even a feeble protest that she was too cold or tired. No wide-eyed gaze. Nothing. Graham gave her a little shake and received only a groan in return.

"*Sophie*," he pled. "You must sit up and get out of these wet clothes, or I will take them off of you."

Nothing.

What is wrong with her? His own fingers shook as he began unfastening the buttons along the front of her jacket.

The wet wool didn't budge easily, and it was all he could do not to pull the two sides and rip them apart. But this was the only clothing Miss Claybourne had with her, and it wasn't likely that her trunk would be arriving anytime soon.

When at last he undid the final button, Graham pulled her forward. She flopped against him, unmoving as he worked to free her arms from the sleeves. Her shirtwaist beneath the jacket was equally soaked. He removed that as well, then leaned her toward him, her head resting on his shoulder as he unlaced the stays of her corset.

If she lived through this, she was going to kill him, and rightly so. He'd never undressed a woman before—never planned to. Especially like this. But there was no help for it. She was wet and beyond cold. He had to warm her.

He spoke as he worked, telling her exactly what he was doing and hoping against hope that she would wake up, slap him, and finish undressing by herself.

"These are ridiculous contraptions." He not-so-patiently pulled one of the long ribbons through yet another loop. "Reason enough to be grateful I'm a man. Why females wear such apparatus is beyond me." He gave a final tug on the second ribbon, and the wood busks sprang free. Sophie's chest expanded, and she expelled a breath.

"Feel free to desist of such unhealthy practices while you're at Caerlanwood," Graham muttered, then tossed the offending item aside.

He started on her soaked boots and stockings next. "I'm going to see more than your ankles if you don't wake up." His taunt brought no response. He hurried his fingers, tossing her boots and stockings aside. Her skirt and petticoats followed, all while she remained limp as a rag doll. Graham found himself too worried over her condition to find any pleasure in the task. His hands at her waist ought to have affected him greatly, especially since he'd dreaded even the little contact that would have happened if they'd danced together. But all he could think of was getting her warm and awake.

"Why do women wear so many ridiculous layers? And how are they all so inefficient at keeping one warm?" he grumbled.

Her shift was the only thing left between him and her bare skin. He reasoned that it was only damp, and that she would personally shoot him—and not in the hand—if he took that from her. Leaving it in place, he picked her up and carried her to the sofa, where he bundled her like a mother might her baby. Satisfied that she was as cocooned as possible, he pushed aside the chairs and moved the sofa closer to the fire.

He added another log, then searched the house for more wood. Finding none, he broke a chair—and nearly broke his hand doing it—then stacked the pieces on the hearth. He tossed in a couple additional books to build the fire and stacked a few more of those on the hearth as well.

A pity. His mother would highly disapprove. But then she would have disapproved more of his kidnapping a lady from her home in London, dragging her all the way here, and nearly killing her off in the process.

Sophie is not going to die. Or get pneumonia or anything else. And he hadn't truly kidnapped her. Excepting those first few hours in his carriage, she had been willing—eager, even—for this adventure, since he had promised her lessons and tutors. *And freedom.* He'd seen how she craved it and how well it suited her, especially this morning—yesterday morning now—as she'd ridden with her hair streaming behind her and a smile stretched across her face. She didn't belong in a stuffy London drawing room.

Nor does she belong here. Shivering uncontrollably in a dark, long-abandoned cottage.

Satisfied that the fire was supplied for some time to come, Graham moved to Sophie's side. He unwrapped the blanket enough to place the back of his hand to hers, then to her arm, her cheek, her forehead. *Still far too cold.*

He brushed his palms against his pants to remove any lingering wood shavings, then took one of her hands in both of his and began alternately rubbing and blowing warm breath onto her fingers.

It was going to be a long night.

Nineteen

FLICKERS OF ORANGE SHONE IN her peripheral vision, through an otherwise black night. *Where am I?* Sophie blinked twice and turned her head, only to have the orange disappear, covered by—a blanket? Her nose brushed against the musty cloth pressed close to her face. She moved her head back to its previous position, and the flicker returned.

She tried reaching up to remove the covering and found her hands tucked in tightly at her sides, also cumbered. She raised her head and gave it a shake. *Ouch.* Stars swam before her eyes, as an all-encompassing swell of pain shot across her forehead. She didn't remember sustaining an injury, but her head pounded. Her eyes squeezed tight against the pain, and she lay still, waiting for it to pass.

After a minute the throbbing retreated to a dull ache. Hesitantly she opened one eye and then the other to find that whatever had blocked her vision had fallen away, revealing a shadowed room.

Being careful not to move too much or too quickly, Sophie worked at freeing her hands as her eyes adjusted to the low light. Shapes formed before her, hazy at first, and then clearer. She was in a sitting room of some sort—not large. A door, presumably one that led outside, was only a few feet away. Wind whistled through its cracks, evidence of the continuing storm outside.

She was lying on a sofa, wrapped in a thick quilt—no, *two* quilts. With her free hand, she peeled the first away and sat up, instantly feeling the chill of the room. A short distance in front of her a fire burned low, and on the floor before it, unmoving—

"Your Grace!" The words came out as little more than a whisper, so parched was her throat. He did not respond.

Sophie struggled to push aside the blankets in her haste to get up. *What has happened? Where are we?* They'd been riding. It was bitter cold. She'd felt as if she was going to fall. *He held me . . .* Snatches of memory—or had it been a dream?—came back to her. They were no longer on the horse, but he was just as close to her, talking to her, begging her to wake and protest his removal of—*my clothing!*

Her gaze landed on the two chairs on either side of the fireplace—the first with her shirtwaist and riding habit draped over it, as if put there to dry. The second chair held her stockings, corset, and petticoat. A man's shirt hung off the side. Sophie's heart hammered as she pressed a hand to her chest beneath the blanket and felt the soft fabric of her shift. *Not entirely undressed, then—just* mostly. She leaned back against the sofa with a sigh that was equal parts relief and exasperation.

Wicked reputation, indeed. How dare the man take such liberties? Her gaze slid to the duke, where he lay on the floor, shirtless, his back to her. The slight, rhythmic rise and fall of his side told her he was breathing. The way his arms wrapped around his torso told her he was cold.

Her initial shock and anger melted into a puddle of gratitude as the misery of the previous hours hit her full force. Tears stung her eyes, then slipped down her face. She'd been certain she was going to die—she'd been so very cold. And then *so* tired. She'd given in and simply fallen asleep. *Never to awaken again.* Another death on her father's head. After all, it was his actions that had driven her to this desperate journey. Poor Livie would be the only sister left. Those had been Sophie's last clear thoughts, though in retrospect she'd likely not been thinking clearly at all.

But the duke hadn't let her give in so easily. She remembered that now—some of it, at least. He'd lifted her from the horse and carried her inside. He'd tried to rouse her and get her to undress herself, but her fingers were too frozen, and she was so exhausted. She couldn't keep her eyes open, couldn't force her stiff hands to move.

So he'd done it for her. He'd talked her through all of it, asking her repeatedly to wake, telling her that he was touching her only to get her warm, wrapping her in a blanket and holding her in his arms before the fire. And now here she was—alive and mostly warm and dry on a sofa, wrapped in two blankets, with even a pillow for her head. While he slept on the hard floor without anything to warm him. Sophie's throat constricted. Perhaps it was that she had almost died. More likely it was that she'd never known someone like Graham Murray, someone who would show such kindness and selflessness. *To me.*

She wiped her streaming eyes, swung her legs over the side of the sofa, and stood, curling her toes against the cold that stole into the bottoms of her feet when they hit the floor. She finished unwrapping the outer blanket from around her, picked up the pillow, and took a shaky step, her legs and back protesting and reminding her of the hours she'd spent on a horse. With less-than-graceful movements, she made her way over to the duke. She draped the blanket gently over his back, then stepped around him and knelt in front of him, intending to pull the quilt across his front and tuck it in.

The firelight was brighter here, casting a glow across the duke's muscular chest. Sophie paused, her hands in midair, holding the blanket aloft as she admired him. She'd never seen a man without his shirt on before—except in her cousin's anatomy book.

Nothing good will come of reading that. Her mother's reprimand rang through Sophie's mind, and she recalled Mother's horrified expression when she'd discovered Sophie with the book.

If by *nothing good*, her mother had implied that Sophie's curiosity would be made all the stronger because of her reading, she was right. Just now she felt an almost overwhelming desire to touch the duke's torso, to run her fingers along his arms, to place her palm against his chest and feel the heart beating within.

Your behavior is appalling. Mother's voice again.

If she could see my thoughts now...

Noting the gooseflesh that had sprung up along the duke's arms and across his chest, Sophie lowered the blanket over him, closing the window on her curiosity. *He's freezing, and here I am gawking at him as if he is a statue in a museum.* Shame and mortification rushed to her cheeks. She tucked the blanket in around him, then carefully lifted his head and gently slid the pillow beneath.

Sophie turned away before her curiosity could engage yet again.

Trying her best to forget the duke's fine figure and the way his hair curled across his forehead, Sophie set about building up the fire and was surprised to find that the logs were pieces of a chair. Had the duke broken the chair, or had it already been thus when they arrived? She'd never laid a fire before and did her best, piling what pieces she could find haphazardly on top of each other and those already there, hoping the flame would catch again. It didn't seem to want to, so she wedged another piece onto the top and was maneuvering it to reach the embers when at once the whole thing crumbled, sending the half-burned wood toward her in a *whoosh* of spark and ash.

"What are you doing?" A hand grasped her wrist and jerked her away from the hearth.

Sophie fell backward, practically into the duke's lap. "Trying to build up the fire. You were cold." She turned her head and found her face perilously close to his. His eyes were wild, startled, as if he'd just been rudely awakened—which he had. His hair was tousled, and he mussed it further as he brought a hand up and shoved it through the thick, dark mass.

He pushed the blanket behind him and scooted past her, using one of the broken chair legs to sweep the cinders and stray pieces back to the hearth. "I thought maybe you intended to set the place on fire and burn it down with me in it because I—" He broke off, his eyes straying to the still-intact chair beside them, over which half of her clothing draped.

Sophie shook her head slowly even as she felt her face warm. "I had no malicious intent. You were cold. I was only trying to show you a kindness—as you did for me." Her words were quiet, but her eyes met his boldly. "You've saved my life twice now."

"Twice?" His brow furrowed.

She nodded. "First, by rescuing me from Lord Nuisance. I would have either died of boredom in his company or been sent to prison for murdering him."

The duke's mouth twitched.

"And last night . . ." Sophie drew in a deep breath. "I would have frozen. I think I almost did. I was so cold I didn't care if I lived or died."

"You frightened me," he said. "You wouldn't wake." He faced away from her and with one hand began reassembling the fire so that the chair pieces formed a crude square that supported each other. Sophie tried to focus on this instead of the smooth, muscled back he'd presented to her. When he'd finished stacking the pieces of wood, he tore the pages from a book on the hearth and stuffed these inside the square on top of the glowing embers.

Sophie watched as the pages slowly caught fire, then were gobbled up by the growing flame. Apparently satisfied with their progress, the duke sat on the floor, arms resting on his bent knees as he settled between the chair and sofa and faced her once again.

Sophie pulled her gaze from the flames to him, careful to keep her eyes focused on his face.

"You've been crying." He reached up and brushed moisture from her cheek. "Are you unwell? You were shaking so badly before—" His hand covered her arm, sliding up and down from shoulder to wrist, as if to assure himself of her wellbeing.

The familiarity of his touch startled her and then quickly lit a flame of its own, making her feel both extremely well and a little faint at the same time. "They were tears of gratitude. I was surprised to find myself still alive. And it became apparent that it was thanks to you." Her eyes drifted to her riding habit, draped over the back of the chair. "I was warm and safe, while you were lying there cold, on the ground, without so much as a blanket. You ought to have used one of those you gave to me."

He shrugged. "You needed it more. It took hours to get you to stop shivering. There was another quilt in the bedroom I also might have used, but the horses needed to be rubbed down. As it is, they're spending the night in a leaky shed out back." He inclined his head toward the side of the room opposite the door.

"Will they be all right?" Was he telling her he'd done no more for her than he had for the horses?

"Hopefully well enough until the morning, when they can be properly stabled and cared for—much like ourselves. I apologize for placing you in this situation."

The growing fire flickered behind him, casting light upon his disheveled hair. Seeing it so out of place and him so—less than proper—did something strange to her heart.

"I hope I am not to be stabled when this is over," she teased. "And this *isn't* your fault. You cannot control the weather." There was no reason for him to feel badly about anything.

"I should have listened to Rory and stayed in town."

"You were concerned about getting home—to your niece and nephew, I presume—to make certain everything was well with them, since the bridge is washed out."

"Aye." He shoved his fingers through his hair again. "It will be washed out even longer, given this storm." He tilted his head slightly, angling it toward the door and the steady pitter-patter coming from the other side. "It's raining again. I suppose that's good—warmer than snow. It was a bit much for this time of year. We don't typically get a lot here. Too coastal."

Sophie watched him closely, perplexed at his odd, less-than-confident behavior. Clearly something was bothering him. Perhaps *he* was upset at their compromised situation. Perhaps . . . *Does he think I'll demand that we marry?*

The idea made her heartbeat escalate in the same sort of way his hand at her back had yesterday and his hand on her arm had just now. She could only imagine how she might have felt if she'd had her full faculties about her as they rode together on the same horse. It was likely a blessing she'd lost consciousness for much of their ride.

"Your Grace." She reached out, placing her hand on top of his for a brief second. "I am grateful to you for saving my life. I do not blame you for any of your actions and hold no claim over you for our—unusual—circumstances. No one need know. We can move forward tomorrow as if this never happened." She would always remember this night and his tender care, but allowing him to believe otherwise might ease his mind.

He stared at her, his eyes haunted. "When I could not get you to wake, I feared the worst. I didn't know if you would make it up to the main house, so I stopped here."

"Here?"

"The gatekeeper's cottage. Though it has not been used for some time." His eyes slid from her face briefly.

Sophie looked down and saw that the blanket had fallen from her shoulder, leaving it bare, save for her shift. He had seen almost as much of her shoulder the first night they met, in the evening gown she'd been wearing. Still, they were alone now, and she ought to be covered as much as possible. With her free hand she tugged at the blanket, pulling it up and tightly around her once more.

"This is where I intend the Shelbys to live." The duke looked around the room, as if assessing it.

"Lucy will love this." Sophie took in the small cottage, now that the light from the fire was a bit brighter. It was still difficult to see much, but she sensed the room's coziness and charm. "She'll love having a home of her own. It is very generous of you."

"It will be good to have a gatekeeper again. And a gate." He muttered the last beneath his breath. He turned from her, added the last two pieces of wood, then tossed what remained of the book into the fire, grimacing as he did. "There wasn't any kindling and very little firewood to be found here."

"So you broke a chair and burned books so I could get warm." She was touched by his sacrifice, that he'd so willingly given of his property—no matter how insignificant—to help her.

"I would do it again, though my mother would turn in her grave if she knew about the books. She treasured the library at Caerlanwood. No doubt the volumes I found here are from the big house."

"Books *are* meant to enlighten," Sophie teased, trying again to alleviate the somber feeling in the room, though the thought of the volumes that had been fed to the fire saddened her as well. The flames blurred as her eyes filled once more. She looked down, but not before he'd noticed.

"You *are* upset with me."

Sophie shook her head. "More good tears. Grateful tears. You've given me a great kindness."

He snorted. "Some kindness. Nearly killing a woman and then ruining her."

Sophie searched out his gaze and held it. "We both know my reputation was destroyed several days ago. This night does not do any further damage. So let us speak of it no more." She rose to her feet and, keeping the blanket wrapped around her, stepped toward the sofa. In spite of the proximity to the fire, sitting on the floor was much colder, and the pounding in her head was increasing again. She longed for a drink of water but doubted such a thing was possible right now.

"You are quite remarkable, you know."

Sophie glanced over her shoulder at the duke and read the unmistakable relief in his expression.

He leaned back, bracing his hands on the floor behind him, then winced and straightened at once, holding his hands in front of him, examining them.

Sophie hoped he hadn't picked up a splinter from the mini avalanche she'd caused over the hearth.

"*Any* other female," the duke began, "would have awakened and started screaming when she realized her circumstances. Or she might have bashed me over the head with a chair leg. Or, at the least, insisted that we marry."

"The night isn't over yet," Sophie teased.

"The chair legs are all gone. And I believe you are almost as averse to marriage as I."

There was her confident, surly duke. It was a relief to have the personality she'd become familiar with back in place.

"My throat is too parched for screaming, so I suppose you are safe, after all." Sophie sank onto the sofa, relishing the warmth it promised. If she could just get herself cocooned as she'd been before, she might be comfortable enough to sleep. But the chill in the room pressed in, and she unsuccessfully attempted to suppress a shiver.

"You are still cold." The duke stood and moved about the room. "There are no more books or chairs—or, at least, those I feel I could break without injuring my hand worse than it already is." He held his left hand aloft, examining it. "The previous chair and I had a bit of an altercation."

"I can see that." Even from here and in the dim light, Sophie could see his hand was swelling. "Come here and let me look at it."

To her surprise, he complied with her request, picking up the other blanket and the pillow and carrying them with him to the sofa. He sat beside her, and she reached for his hand.

Sophie probed it gently, feeling first for the metacarpal bones beneath the surface, following their lines. He sat still, eyes closed, his manner rigid as she proceeded with her examination.

"The carpal bones of the wrist are where things really get complicated," Sophie explained, moving on to gingerly probe his wrist. "There are eight bones clustered closely together that allow for the various movements the wrist performs, as well as to support the incredible tasks required of this part of our bodies. But without an obvious break—of which there is no sign—it will be quite impossible for me to tell if your trapezium, trapezoid, capitate, hamate, scaphoid, lunate, triquetral, or pisiform bones have a small fracture or chip or are otherwise broken."

"My wrist does not hurt. Only my hand," the duke said.

"Even exempting the bones, there is much that can be affected there."

"I recall that," he said drily. "That anatomy book has served you well."

"My mother would disagree." Sophie grimaced.

"Because . . . you are as knowledgeable about the other parts of the body?"

Her face warmed. "Not *as* knowledgeable. I learned more about the hand because of Jonathan's self-defense lessons. This hand," she lifted his gently, "ought to be wrapped." She peered around the room, studying her choices and settling on her petticoat. A few strips from the bottom ought to work well—if it was dry.

"There is nothing suitable—or dry—to wrap it with," the duke said, gently tugging it from her grasp. "But if I leave my hand alone, it mostly leaves me alone as well."

"You must stay on the sofa, then," Sophie said, though she did not relish sleeping on the floor or sitting up all night. "Put the pillow behind you and lie back, then rest your hand on your stomach. I'll tuck the blanket in around you."

"If I do that, where will you sleep?"

"On the floor, as you did." The quilts had probably come from a bed in the other room, but it would be too far from the fire to stay warm.

He shook his head. "I agreed to act the part of a gentleman on this journey, and I plan to keep my word—inasmuch as I have not already broken it." His frown and furrowed brow and overall look of consternation were such that Sophie could not help the laugh that bubbled to the surface.

"You look every part the gentleman, barefoot, with your

hair mussed, your shirt off—" The heat returned to her face, and she averted her gaze quickly, turning to stare at the fire instead of his chest.

"You're one to talk. You should see yourself," the duke groused. "Your hair has taken on a life of its own. I've no idea how you'll ever get a comb through it again. And when I removed your corset, you gave a great hiccup."

"I did not!" Sophie clapped a hand over her mouth, horrified.

"You did not," he confirmed, a true grin on his face now. "You did take in a deep breath, however."

"You try having your lungs compressed all day." She narrowed her eyes at him. "And telling me how awful I look was most *un*gentlemanly of you." She fingered her tangled curls. "Even if it is true."

"My apologies." He held up his hands as if in surrender, then winced and drew his left back to his chest. "It would seem we are at a stalemate, so let us assess the situation."

Sophie folded her arms across her middle and turned to face him, giving a curt nod. "Go on."

"We've one sofa, two blankets, the fire as it is now, with no additional wood, and at least a few hours more until dawn. It is still storming outside, and I'm not willing to risk you freezing again by taking you out in the rain, so we are stuck here. The only thing that makes sense is to pool our resources—we won't count your wild hair as one of them."

She harrumphed and turned away, though this more lighthearted, teasing side of him was growing on her.

"Let us both sit on the sofa for the remainder of the night. We can each wrap in our own blankets to preserve our modesty—or what we've left of it—but we will also sit close to preserve warmth."

It was a sensible solution, but it stirred up that new, not-altogether-unpleasant feeling in Sophie's middle. "Very well. Allow me to wrap your blanket around you, as your hand is not functioning properly."

"It's functioning fine. It just hurts." He took up both sides of the blanket and pulled them around himself, as if to prove his point.

Sophie settled her own around her, then leaned back on the sofa and closed her eyes, doubting very much that she would get any sleep with the duke in such close proximity.

"You'll get a crook in your neck that way. Lean against me instead." He scooted closer to her, and warmth worked its way up her right side where their bodies touched.

"Thank you, Your Grace." Sophie angled her head slightly so that it barely touched his shoulder, then closed her eyes in surrender—not to sleep but to the feelings stirring through her, this awareness of and attraction to everything about him. Dangerous though it was to indulge.

"Graham."

She did not respond, uncertain whether or not he had actually spoken or if she had been merely thinking his name. She hadn't spoken it out loud—had she?

"Given our—unusual circumstances—I think we are beyond *Your Grace* and *Miss Claybourne*. Unless you feel otherwise?"

"No." *Graham*. She loved his name, and, snuggled up on a sofa together like this, she could almost imagine coming to love the man himself. Were she inclined to things of that nature.

"At Caerlanwood we are somewhat less formal," he continued. "Considerably less so than those of the ton. Many of the servants have known me since I was a young boy, so they, too, call me by name—either first or last. I answer to both Graham and Murray. Everyone at Caerlanwood has work to do, including myself, and all are equally valued, from the boy who brings in the firewood to the head housekeeper. I am not fond of servants hovering about waiting upon me—I am quite capable of dressing myself and spooning my own soup into a bowl. They are efficient at their jobs, and I am grateful, but they need not bow and scrape before me. Were you to address me as Your Grace in their company, they would likely think it odd."

How peculiar that all sounded. *How delightful.* She had long struggled with calling Lucy by her last name as her mother had instructed she must the day fifteen-year-old Lucy—with whom Sophie had formed a secret friendship some years before—had been assigned as her maid. How she had hated the fear that came to the servants' eyes at times when her father was home. How she hated that Viscount Newsome had felt he could command them to do as he ordered, simply because they were servants. It wasn't right. Just as slavery was not right. And she admired the duke—Graham—for thinking so too.

"I do not wish your servants to find me odd—or, at least, any more so than they shall already find me, especially considering that I shall at first be appearing in this state, with sodden clothing and hair that has taken on a life of its own."

"I should not have said that." His tone was light, amused, and he raised his hand and gave her tangles a gentle tug.

"You do not sound the least repentant," Sophie scolded, tipping her face up to him and willing her heart to calm. His eyes darkened as his hand fell away. Sophie drew in a breath—hopefully not as loud as the one she'd drawn after he'd removed her corset. *He* removed *my corset.* But she was finding it difficult to breathe just now. His nearness and touch were wreaking havoc on her.

Their banter was different tonight—more personal.

There was no one else around, no need to pretend conversation or that they were fond of one another. *We are not play-acting.* Whatever this was that was happening between them was real. And new and thrilling. Never had a man made her so curious, so comfortable, so . . . alive and aware of her every sense.

Sophie closed her eyes and leaned against him once more, willing her senses to quiet, praying she would fall asleep.

"Here. Use this." He pulled away slightly and stuffed the pillow in the space between her head and his shoulder. "That should be more comfortable."

"What about you? How will you sleep?"

"Most likely I will not." He cleared his throat, as if something was stuck in there, bothering him. He probably wished for water as well. "I've too many things to think about now that I'm home. Caerlanwood has long been neglected, and I am eager to make amends. My mind is full of all that needs to be done and how to best accomplish those tasks."

"I am sure you will succeed," Sophie murmured and tried not to feel hurt that her nearness was obviously not affecting him as it was her. She had only imagined this new closeness between them. It was just their circumstances. Nothing more. And tomorrow she would simply be one of his many employees, albeit one treated better than any in her father's household. She would be foolish to read any more into this than that. After all, Graham had all but told her he'd cared for the horses in the same manner he had cared for her tonight. She ought to feel grateful he'd seen to her needs first.

She adjusted the pillow and relaxed into his side, finding that easier now that she'd realized her feelings had all been imagined nonsense. Disappointment she could deal with, whereas those other emotions could cause a great deal of trouble. "Thank you, again, for your kindness, Graham. You've truly been a gentleman and do not deserve your reputation as the Black Duke."

He stiffened at her last words, and Sophie wished she could recall them. She wanted to sit up and look at him, to see if she might read in his expression his feelings about his uncalled-for reputation. But she forced herself to stay as she was. She had meant to compliment, not to offend.

"The Black Duke was what they called my father—a well-deserved moniker. I inherited that name, along with his title."

"But it is not deserved." Again, she stayed as she was, sensing his vulnerability and that he did not wish her to look at him in this moment. "Your heart is kind and generous. Just this night alone, you have saved a life, cared for me—even cared for your horses, at detriment to your own health. There is nothing sinister about you."

"Nothing that you have seen . . . yet."

The word was spoken with finality, as if it were a foregone conclusion that she would witness such behavior from him at some point. "I do not believe that. Those with the true black hearts we left behind in London. Lord Newsome, for example."

"I wanted to kill him that night."

"That makes two of us," Sophie said. She felt Graham shift beside her.

"No. You misunderstand. I *truly* wanted to kill him for the way he treated you. And in Gretna Green, at the inn, had you not required my assistance getting to the carriage, I would have attacked the men who had thought to hurt you. I cannot abide a man who mistreats a woman or child. And so I have no qualms about hurting or even killing one who would do so. *That* is why my reputation is deserved."

"Because you are willing to defend the less fortunate?"

"It is more than defending. I want to rid the world of those who would bring harm to the defenseless. I have little regard for or faith in the law to right this world's wrongs. It has been my experience that the law encourages the opposite more often than not."

She had no answer for this and so made none. Her mind returned to one of their early conversations, when she had asked him if he was sorry he had killed a man—men?—on Saint Kitts. His answer that he was not had shocked her then, but this perhaps explained a bit more. He had said it was not self-defense. But had he acted defending another?

There was much she wished to ask him and did not dare. Perhaps someone at Caerlanwood could tell her. But even if she never knew what had happened, she trusted Graham. He was a far better man than he gave himself credit for. A far better man than most.

Twenty

HE HAD LIED TO SOPHIE. Not about being unable to sleep for the remainder of the night—that much was true. But it wasn't thinking about repairs at Caerlanwood or even concerns about his niece and nephew that occupied Graham's mind. It was her. *Sophie.* The woman presently curled up against his side, her lovely hair in disarray, her eyes closed in slumber, and completely trusting in him. *Believing me to be a better man than I am.*

Around her he *was* better. He had failed his mother and sister, but he had not failed Sophia Claybourne. He *would not* fail her—nor his niece or nephew, nor any other female or child entrusted into his care.

Is that what Sophie is? Entrusted to my care? Her mother's letter had all but asked that of him, asked that he intervene and prevent the marriage of her daughter to Lord Newsome. *Lord Nuisance*, Sophie called him. But he was far more than that. *Dangerous. And I saved her from him. And from the men at the inn at Gretna Green, from the freezing storm tonight.* Though the latter two he had caused her to be in danger of in the first place. But still . . .

Warmth and the strong conviction of finally having done something good—something right—filled his heart. In saving Sophie, he felt the slightest bit redeemed. It would never be enough to make up for failing his mother and sister, but it was something, and he reveled in it, the sensation of, for once, having done good. *The right thing.* Somehow, despite his unconventional methods of rescue, he felt his mother would have approved. And she would have loved Sophie.

They were all but home, and he had hope that, for the first time in a long time, Caerlanwood might begin to feel like such a place again, with the force that was Miss Sophia Claybourne in residence.

After his mother's death he had stayed away—with both Mother and Katherine gone the house was nothing but a reminder of his father's destruction. But it had seemed the safest place to bring the children, the place that might afford them the most privacy and peace. He believed they might be happy there.

As for himself, he would be content as an onlooker. It was much more than he'd ever expected to have—the opportunity to restore the only place that had ever felt like home, and to have children there and a delightful woman to care for them. It was as close as he'd ever get to having a family of his own, and he would be grateful for that. He would move heaven and earth to protect them from everyone and everything. *Including myself.*

He was ever wary of his tendency to violence and anger. How easy it would be to lose his temper with Sophie or the children, with the household staff, with a neighbor or friend. As the Raymond dukes before him had.

His only memory of his paternal grandfather was of the man throwing a chair and then striking Graham's father before turning his anger on Graham's mother, cowering in the corner with Graham hiding behind her skirts, blaming her for her husband's gambling habits.

Mother had told Graham that his father hadn't been violent with her when they first married, though he hadn't loved her or wanted the marriage and had made that clear from the beginning. Gradually, however, his temper had sharpened and he'd become as his father before him had been—bitter, angry, abusive. It seemed a family trait that could not be avoided, some inbred mental deficiency.

His father had pointed as much out to him the day Graham had finally fought back.

"You've some Raymond in you, after all." A full twenty minutes after Graham had hit him, sending him slamming into the corner of a wall and rendering him unconscious, his father had staggered into the study, his grin savage, his split lip still bleeding.

Graham had looked up from his father's desk, where he'd been rifling through drawers, searching for the funds necessary to get himself and his mother and sister safely to Scotland. Instead of feeling afraid of his father as he had for so many years, he'd felt only a burning anger. Hatred. *I wish I'd killed him.*

"And here I thought I'd raised a coward, that your mother's influence had softened you too much, but I see now that when the time comes you'll do."

Graham had threatened to kill him, then, if he ever came near his mother or sister again.

The smirk twisting his father's mouth only seemed to grow. "I don't doubt that. I have killed before, as did my father before me. You have it in you too, boy. I see it in your eyes. There's no denying it once unleashed. It's a part of you." His father had thumped his chest. "You're a Raymond through and through." His bloodshot eyes had grown large and wild as his nostrils flared. "Savage. Like the rest of us."

Savage. Graham stared down at his hands, his heart heavy.

The only way to prevent repeating history was to avoid

marriage altogether. But now Sophie would be here. The children too. *Near me.* If need be, he would leave Caerlanwood so Sophie, Ayla, and Matthew would be guaranteed a peaceful and safe existence.

Sophie sighed in her sleep and snuggled closer against him. What remained of Graham's good feelings slipped away as he considered, realistically, the hardship that living in the same house with her would be. While it wasn't likely they would be alone like this again, neither was Caerlanwood so cavernous that he wouldn't see or hear Sophie or the children, at least occasionally. Beyond that, he would know they were there. Just knowing she was asleep in the carriage below him or in the room next to his, the past few nights had intruded upon his thoughts more than it should have. He enjoyed her company and longed to be close to her, as much to spar with her and see her smile and the light of intelligence in her eyes as to feel her beside him as he did right now. After tonight, he could not do any of that but would have to studiously avoid her. Rory's knee wasn't the only thing that had been correct yesterday. Cameron had been right as well. *I* am *besotted with Sophie.*

For a normal man that would have been a welcome prospect. For him—*for them*—it was dangerous.

Graham told himself to be thankful for the week he'd had with her. Again, it was more than he'd ever expected to have with a woman in his lifetime. These feelings he'd developed, the memory of this unexpected affection for her, if guarded carefully and not spoiled by some future action of his, could last a lifetime. It would have to.

A rush of tenderness and gratitude for Sophie overwhelmed him, and he leaned down, pressing a kiss to her forehead. She stirred at the contact and tilted her face up to his, eyes flickering open, drowsy with invitation.

He answered without thinking, his mouth continuing downward, skipping her forehead this time and landing softly upon her lips.

There they lingered, joined innocently but a second before an explosion of glory and utter chaos erupted inside of him. Sophie's response was nearly as instantaneous. She pressed her lips more firmly against his as she turned toward him. The blanket slipped from her shoulder as she lifted one hand to his chest. The other found its way around the back of his neck, pulling him closer. Their lips moved together, hungry and searching. He moaned, surprised at her fervor, delighted by it. Sophie's mouth parted slightly with further invitation, and then his arms were around her, their connection setting them both ablaze.

She belonged in his arms. Everything about this moment, their tangled limbs and roaming lips, felt right. *I saved her. She is mine.* The possessive word set off an alarm somewhere in the recesses of his brain. *Mine* meant permanency and commitment—two things he must not engage in.

Drawing in a ragged breath, Graham pulled back. "What are we doing?"

"Kissing one another with wild abandon," Sophie said joyously, her full lips curving in a tempting smile.

"Have you kissed many men with such abandon?" Graham asked, suddenly suspicious.

"*No.*" She drew back from him, mouth turned down, her expression wounded. "Why would you think that?"

"Most women—particularly those who are inexperienced—do not kiss like that. They are rather timid and—reserved."

"Are you certain?" Sophie withdrew her arm from around him and folded it across her middle. "My sister was not timid and reserved. Torie kissed Jonathan quite often, and I—being curious, of course—watched them. From the very beginning they held nothing back in their affection for one another. I supposed that was how it was to be done." Sophie looked up at him, her brow wrinkled with concern, and doubt in her eyes. "Was I wrong?"

"No." He touched her chin, caressing it tenderly. "I was just surprised. That's all. I did not expect—" *Did not plan to ... Did not think.*

"I've wanted to kiss you since that day in Gretna Green," she confessed.

She wanted to kiss me. He need never worry about pretense with Sophie, so unabashedly direct and honest. He could love a woman like that. *I could love her.* Graham swallowed and looked away, past her to the dying fire. If he kept gazing into her eyes, he was certain to succumb again. Instead he bent his forehead to hers so they were touching. "We should not be here alone, half-clothed, and we should definitely not be kissing."

She sighed. "I suppose you are right. This is most inappropriate behavior if I am to be a governess in your home. But I wonder ... I was dreaming just now, or thinking in my sleep—something like that. What if I was too hasty in dismissing your suggestion of marriage? If we are able to kiss one another like this, then perhaps ..."

Graham's breath caught, and something—everything—clenched inside of him. He could never marry her now and send her away. And he certainly could not marry her and stay with her. Kissing had been a very bad idea.

Slowly he leaned back, breaking their contact. When she leaned forward, as if to follow him, as if to lean against him as she had earlier, he braced his hands on her arms and held her away. "It is too late for that now. We cannot ever marry. I need you to care for my sister's children."

"I could do both. Surely you feel this"—she waved her hand in the space between them—"these feelings too. Whatever it is that happens when we are together. I think we might suit well. I had never thought to marry, never wished for it, but—"

"No." He pressed a finger to her lips, then withdrew it quickly. "We would both be sorry later. I am certain of it. We will keep to our original agreement. You will be a governess for Ayla and Matthew, and in return I will protect you from Lord Newsome and your father, and you shall have the opportunity to continue your education."

He rose from the sofa before she could say anything else. "I apologize for my actions tonight. They were not in keeping with those of an employer. It shall not happen again." Graham strode across the room and removed his damp shirt from the chair. "I'm going to see to the horses." He left the cottage, stepping out into the rain.

Twenty-One

As soon as the sun began peeking in through the dusty windows of the cottage, Sophie wrestled herself into yesterday's clothing as best she could, her mind churning—as it had the past few hours after Graham had left—with what she must do to right the mess she'd made. *I have to fix this.* It would not do to start out her first day as a governess at odds with her employer. Even worse, she feared that the friendship that had developed between them was threatened because of her careless words and actions. And she very much wished that friendship to continue.

For the first time in her life, she desired the companionship of a man. The past week had been exhilarating, from the moment he'd spoken to her behind the palm trees in her father's drawing room, to their near-constant conversations while traveling, to their kiss last night. He was perhaps the truest friend she had ever had, and she did not intend to lose that. *I cannot.*

Sophie fastened the buttons of her still-damp jacket as she turned for a last look around the little cottage. *Magic happened here.* She would forever cherish it, those stolen moments that should never have been, but that had somehow happened anyway. When two newly minted friends, who had never wished to marry or been inclined to romance at all, had kissed one another *with wild abandon.* Sophie closed her eyes, cringing at all she had said and done last night. She had sensed that Graham was concerned she would demand marriage, given their compromised situation, so she had assured him that she would not. And then, only a short while later, she'd all but suggested that very thing. *Because of a foolish kiss.*

She wished she could take those moments back, but at the same time she was fairly certain she would do the same again, given the opportunity. She'd never daydreamed of her first kiss, as many young ladies did. Instead, she'd concerned herself with avoiding such an event.

But now . . .

Sophie closed her eyes. She had felt alive as she never had before. The world had seemed to tilt off its axis and, at the same time, feel more solid and sure, full of joy and possibility she'd never considered. *I should not have considered it.* Even now she could scarcely keep thoughts of Graham and the way he'd held her, the warmth of his lips upon hers, from her mind. The entirely new and delicious sensations were all too easy to linger in and dwell upon. *To revel in.*

Is this what Torie felt? If only her sister were still alive, to seek advice from and confide in. Perhaps Torie, too, would have enjoyed that—would have appreciated having a sister to talk to about such things. Before, whenever Torie had tried talking to her about matters of love, Sophie had scoffed, stating she had no interest in affairs of the heart and instead wished she might pursue her love of learning.

But now . . .

A soft knock sounded on the cottage door, and Sophie squared her shoulders and did her best to clear her mind as she faced it.

"Come in."

The door swung open, and the duke filled the doorway.

The dark circles beneath his eyes, along with his tousled hair, made him appear as weary as she felt. She hadn't slept at all after he'd left. He couldn't have had an easy time of it out with the horses. Yet he had stayed outside. *Because he dared not remain in the same room with me.*

"I'm sorry," Sophie blurted. "My behavior last night was reprehensible, and I—"

"Think no more on it. It is forgotten." Graham stepped aside, braced his back against the open door, and held his hand out, indicating she should exit ahead of him.

Forgotten? The word stole her breath, and not in a good way. Did he really mean that? *Forgiven,* she might have understood—and appreciated. But the idea that he could forget their kiss hurt deeply. She felt certain she would never, ever forget it.

Head held high, though inside she was reeling, Sophie walked stiffly past him, determined to hide her feelings and the fact that her legs could scarcely move this morning.

The horses stood tethered outside the cottage, happily nibbling the wet, overgrown grass. Sophie felt hungry enough that it was tempting to kneel down and join them—had she been able. At present she found the rudimentary task of putting one foot in front of the other challenging, after so many hours in a saddle yesterday.

"I thought we might leave the horses here, and I'll send a groom back for them—assuming you would prefer to walk, rather than ride once more," Graham said, eyeing her as if he guessed her discomfort.

She nodded and stepped onto the path leading away from the cottage. *Forgotten.* The word echoed through her, spreading a pain she could not have imagined, one she had never experienced before. Was this what her suitors had felt when she rejected them? *Not likely.* She had never spent close to the amount of time with any of them that she had spent with Graham. She'd never confided in any other man, nor he in her, the way she and Graham had during their long hours in the carriage and yesterday. She'd never kissed any other man.

Forgotten. She tried to banish her anguish at his easy dismissal but could not seem to.

"Sophie." His hand on her arm stopped her.

She turned to him questioningly, even as heat from his touch spread to her shoulder and beyond.

"I have called your name three times. Are you not speaking to me now?"

"No." She shook her head. "I mean, of course I am speaking to you. I did not hear you before. I must have been lost in thought." *Or just lost.* "I apologize."

His brow furrowed, and he removed his hand from her arm. "And *I* apologize for my earlier words. I can see they've hurt you, and I'm sorry."

"Think no more on it. *They* are forgotten." She started to turn away, but he spoke again.

"What I meant to say—what I should have said first—is that I was in the wrong, not you. We should not have been alone in the cottage last night. And I *never* should have kissed you. I take full responsibility. After all, you were half asleep."

She might have been at first, but she had most definitely been awake by the end of their rather lengthy kiss. *Would it be considered one long kiss, or several short ones?* Sophie sighed. What did it matter now, when he had already forgotten it?

"I will not hold it against you. And if we are speaking of who is at fault, well then, I never should have climbed into your carriage last week." A pang of anxiety struck at the possibility that she could have missed this entire adventure. And knowing Graham. *And that kiss.* "Or at the least, I ought to have left when you returned to London. It is what any proper young lady would have done. But, of course, we have long ago established that I seldom behave as most proper young ladies." She waved a hand dismissively to show him she was not bothered by that.

"May I inquire as to why you did not leave?" Graham asked, his head tilted slightly.

Sophie shrugged. "Many reasons. You were kind to Lucy. And, in spite of your rather obvious and ridiculous prejudices against females, you spoke to me almost as an equal. I appreciated that. It is something no other man has ever done."

Graham's stance relaxed slightly, and a corner of his mouth lifted. "So it was not just the promise of lessons that led you here?"

She shook her head, then too late realized she'd done it again—said too much, revealed too much of herself when she ought to have remained aloof, ought to have shown him that his kiss was forgotten already too. But that would have been lying, and she'd never been any good at that. Neither was she any good at the coy games she'd seen other women play.

Lifting her chin, Sophie met his gaze. "The lessons, while appealing, are not the only reason I stayed." *I was intrigued by you from that very first night.*

At her honest answer, something flashed in his eyes. A spark of hope, perhaps, followed immediately by deep pain. He cleared his throat. "Still, you shall have your lessons, beginning within a fortnight, I hope." He held out his arm to her. "Shall we go? A twenty-minute walk is all that separates us from both a hot bath and a breakfast tray."

Sophie nodded and placed her hand gently upon his arm, at once affected by even that slight contact. It was as if that kiss had awakened something in her. Feelings she hadn't even known existed. Was Graham truly so unaffected? Or was it possible he was merely trying to mask his own feelings? She did not know, nor did she know how she would continue on, without hoping and wishing that he would someday kiss her again.

"I LOVE THE MORNING AFTER a good rain." Sophie tilted her head back, inhaling deeply. "The air is so fresh and crisp."

"Aye," Graham agreed and sucked in a lungful himself. He could do with some of that fresh air to clear his head, to clear out thoughts of her. They had walked in companionable silence a good five minutes, allowing his mind to wander too frequently into thoughts of what might have been.

In comparison, Sophie's mood appeared to have lifted as they traversed the path to the house. Her steps weren't quite as stiff now, and the walk from the gatehouse to the manor was a pleasant one, shaded with ancient trees and bordered by wildflowers on either side.

Sophie wrinkled her nose in an adorable expression he'd not seen before. "It also smells of the sea here. Is it very close?" She turned to him, hope in her eyes. He was happy to see it, given the wounded look that had been there only a few minutes earlier.

"It is," he said vaguely, wondering if she would be pleased at Caerlanwood's proximity to the ocean.

"How lovely." She smiled. "Perhaps one day this summer we might take the children there on a picnic."

"*You* might," he corrected. "I shall have work to do. The children will be your responsibility."

"Yes, but surely you spend time with your niece and nephew. Though if you would prefer it to be when I am not with them, that is fine—"

"I'm about as useful as an uncle as I would be as a husband."

"How can you know how useful you would be, unless you've tried it?"

He noted her vagueness and the way she had avoided specific referral either to marriage or to his role as guardian and uncle. "*I know.*"

She did not reply, and they continued walking through the wood toward the house.

"Do you intend to stay at Caerlanwood permanently? You have at least two residences in England, do you not?"

"Three," he said, wishing he had none and none of the burden that came with his inheritance. "I am undecided. Much depends on Ayla and Matthew. I must do what is best for them. For now I believe that to be here, in Scotland."

The path ahead widened, and the trees lining their way gave way to a recently trimmed, and somewhat butchered, hedge that circled the back garden. *Paden.* The old gardener's eyes must be getting worse. It used to be he just missed things here or there, but the poor hedge was so bald as to be seen through in some places. Graham held in a sigh and wondered how he might go about getting some help for Paden without insulting him.

As they left the trees, he led Miss Claybourne to the right, glancing at her at the exact second the house came into view.

"Oh . . . my." She stopped walking and craned her head back, taking in all three floors of gray stone, topped by numerous chimneys and the steeply pitched roof. Graham tried to imagine what it must be like seeing Caerlanwood for the first time and what her impressions might be.

Ancient. The stone was centuries old and looked it, thanks to years of weathering and soot from the fireplaces.

Immense. The height was impressive enough, but the length stretched even farther, extending sideways into two seldom-used wings. They'd been closed off as long as he could remember, at least since his childhood, when his grandda had died and left the place to his mother. She'd never felt much like having any cèilidhean.

Intimidating. Nothing about the house or the neglected yard seemed welcoming, and for the first time Graham wondered if bringing the children here had been the right thing to do. He'd always viewed Caerlanwood as a place of safety and seclusion. But suddenly he could see how it might seem the opposite to others.

Beside him Miss Claybourne stood perfectly still, her head tipped back, eyes closed, a half-smile curving lips that looked all too kissable again. Graham wished very much to know what she was thinking. Perhaps she was praying, asking God to save her from the dreadful fate of living with a mad duke and two orphaned children in this wild, abandoned tomb of a house perched on a cliff above the sea.

"Listen." She shushed him, though all he'd done was shuffle his feet a bit. "If you're quiet you can hear the sea."

Had she seen the house at all? If so, it didn't seem to have affected her. "Keep your eyes closed, and follow me." Graham placed his hand over hers on his arm and guided her toward the right wing of the house, around the side, and to the opposite edge of the back garden.

He led her a dozen steps more, through an arbor—still intact, thankfully—onto a crumbling stone path. Another dozen steps, and he stopped. "Open your eyes."

She did, slowly at first until they grew wide with astonishment as she looked out at the ocean and then down at the surf crashing onto the shore below.

"Oh, Graham." She clasped her hands over her heart. "You live *here*? Right by the sea? I must be dreaming." She turned a slow circle, taking in the butchered hedge and the imposing stone, as if they were the Taj Mahal. Her gaze drifted to the veranda they stood on and the low wall, overlooking the sea gate and beach below and the ocean beyond. Each turn widened her smile and sent a jolt of memory to his heart. How many times had he and Katherine raced each other to this very spot at the beginning of summer and paused with delight at the view before them?

"Your room will have this view as well." He tipped his head back, looking up at the second floor. He would give her his room, the master suite and one with the best view, and move to one of the unused wings—as far away from her and the children as possible. Effectively banishing himself in his own home. "If you leave your window open you can hear the waves cresting on the shore."

"Thank you." She looked happier than he'd ever seen her, excepting perhaps last night when he had foolishly asked her what they were doing. Hearing her answer—*Kissing one another with wild abandon*—he'd wanted nothing so much as to crush her against him and never let go. *What a rare jewel you are, Sophie.* Was it wrong of him to hide her away from the world here? Though she had agreed to it, he suspected she hadn't thought it a difficulty then. But in the past week she had discovered some things about herself. With those realizations, might she find happiness with another man?

"You'll have plenty of time later to enjoy the view. For now, let's get inside where we can get truly dry, eat something, and get some rest."

"That all sounds wonderful too."

Graham did not take her hand this time but led her around to the other side of the house, where the hedge and all else appeared not to have been trimmed for a very long time. The foliage was so thick around the front that it seemed to be devouring the house, already in shadow at this time of morning, lending it an even more frightening appearance.

"Welcome to Caerlanwood," Graham said bitterly, angry with himself as much as anyone that he had allowed the neglect to go so far. "Do you see now why I think no one will find you here? It is difficult to get to, particularly when the bridge is washed out, and it's practically uninhabitable."

"It's practically a castle," she clarified, her neck craned back as she stared up at the monstrosity he had once called home. "Complete with towers, ivy climbing the walls, and even a bridge." Her gaze strayed behind her to the old stone bridge arching over the wee burn that ran along the front of the property. "It's straight out of a fairy tale."

"A rather dark one," Graham muttered. But perhaps the happy ending was in sight—at least for the house itself. "I am in the process—the very beginning stages—of restoring Caerlanwood."

"What happened to it? And to the ground in front of it?" She gestured to the muddy swathe before them that looked as if it had been plowed by giants.

Graham's muscles tensed as he followed her gaze. "My father. The last time he hurt my mother it was very bad—she nearly died. I threatened to kill him if he ever came near her or my sister again. We left him and came here. He followed about a month later and in a drunk fit did this—among other things—attempting to make it so we could never leave."

Sophie's gaze clouded as she stared at the destruction. Then she turned from it and faced the house, shoulders squared. "And now we must endeavor to make it a place you always *wish* to stay."

Twenty-Two

GRAHAM HELD SOPHIE'S ELBOW AS she picked her way across the uneven ground—a task made more difficult by last night's rain and the drizzle that had started a few minutes ago.

"I'll hire a crew from the tenants, and we'll start on this as soon as possible," he promised. "Until then, use the door from the kitchen when you want to go outside."

Sophie glanced at him from the corner of her eye. His face was still set in a grim expression, caught somewhere between anger and embarrassment. She set out to put him at ease.

"It does not matter to me what your garden, or even your house looks like. That you have the sea as your neighbor is the most delightful thing I can imagine." She meant every word but wasn't sure he believed her.

A set of enormous front doors creaked open just before they reached them. But instead of a butler, they were greeted by two young children, the smallest of which barreled straight toward them in a blur of movement, skidding to a stop just short of Graham.

"You came back!"

"I did."

Sophie peered down at a head of dark curls.

"I promised you that I would," the duke said, his tone gentle and patient, if not affectionate as the child had likely hoped. "And I brought someone with me."

The child, a little boy dressed in short pants and sensible shoes, turned his attention to Sophie. He tilted his face back to look up, and she looked down into large brown eyes—and at equally brown skin. Sophie stifled her shock and glanced quickly to the other child, a girl, standing aloof just inside the doorway. Her skin was lighter, though not nearly as light as Sophie's or Graham's.

"Are you going to be my mother?" the little boy asked.

A pang of sympathy pierced Sophie's heart at the pleading in his voice. Ignoring her stiffness, she crouched in front of him as her mind scrambled for the right response. "No one can replace your mother, but I should very much like to be your friend."

"I would like a friend." Two little arms flung outward, then wrapped around her in a hug so fierce it nearly toppled her.

She caught herself and fell forward onto her knees as the child clung to her. Instinctively she wrapped her arms around him in return. Rain continued pelting them both, but she refused to let go—not until he did, at least. *If he needs a hug this badly.*

Graham reached down to ruffle the boy's curls. "Let's go inside, Matthew."

The fierceness she'd witnessed earlier was gone now, replaced by weariness in both Graham's tone and rounded shoulders. She felt the same, yet somehow invigorated by such a welcome greeting.

"Will you introduce me to your sister?" she asked Matthew.

He nodded against her shoulder, then pulled away at last, a shy smile on his face that melted her heart. He put his small hand in hers, and she stood. He led the trio inside, where his sister hovered in a vast, dark hall.

Sophie turned to her. "Hello."

"Ayla this is Sophie Claybourne," Graham said. "She's come to be your governess."

Ayla said nothing but regarded Sophie with narrowed eyes.

"I'm so sorry, Graham! I must've overslept. I didna mean to let the bairns loose." A woman who looked too old to be tending children shuffled toward them, a lantern held aloft in her hand.

"It's all right, Finella," he said to the flustered woman. "I was just introducing the children to their new governess, Miss Sophia Claybourne."

"Praise be to God," Finella exclaimed. "I'm pleased tae make your acquaintance." She held a hand out to Sophie. "'Tis pure barry."

"Yes," Sophie agreed, though she wasn't certain with what. "The pleasure is mine." It *was* good to meet another woman who lived here too. Sophie's hand was pumped up and down heartily, causing her to reassess her initial thoughts on Finella's capabilities.

"Why isn't Maime watching the children?" Graham asked, looking around as if expecting another woman to appear.

Finella waved a hand. "A bairn's on the way down at the cottages, and Maime's off tending to the mother. She doesna have time to chase after the weeuns with her skills as healer so in demand."

Graham gave a grunt of understanding, if not approval. "Why are there no candles lit? And why has nothing been done in the garden—save for Paden's butcher job on the hedge out back?"

"Bah." Finella batted her hand in the air again. "Lazy bams, the lot of 'em. Canna get more'n a half day out of any. Though now that you're home I s'pect that will change."

"And the candles?" he asked, peering around the dark room.

"I havena lit any yet. A body like me can only take so much, and I'm plumb wore out by these two—" She inclined her head toward the children. "We'd another round of night terrors last night."

"Aye, well you'll have some assistance now. Miss Claybourne will be responsible for the children four hours a day."

"Just four?" Matthew's lip jutted out as he looked up at Sophie.

She bit back a laugh. "We'll see."

Ayla stood still as a statue, hiding whatever reaction—good or bad—she had to this news.

"Goodness!" Finella's eyes widened as she held the lantern higher and actually took in the sight of them. "You're all drookit. And ye must be knackered as well. Ye look like something the cat dragged in."

"Thank you," Graham said drily. At Sophie's confused expression, he translated. "We're all wet and tired and not looking our best at present."

How could they look any other way, given what it had taken to get here, plus this morning's rain? Sophie glanced down at the skirts clinging to her and at her muddy boots. She could only imagine the state of her hair.

"Finella, if you'd be so kind as to find something dry for Sophie to change into, and see that a bath is drawn for her. I'll find Cook and see what she has that we can eat before retiring. It has been a long, exhausting week, particularly the last day. As the bridge is washed out again, we came by horse and got caught in the storm last night. We are indeed drookit and knackered."

But not embarrassed. Sophie gratefully noted his omission of their stop at the cottage.

"Sophie is to have the room across from the children's," Graham continued. "I'll be moving to the east wing. She is to rest today and begin her duties on the morrow." With that, and without so much as a glance at Sophie, he turned and started off down another long, dark corridor, leaving her alone with Finella and the children. A similar pang to that which she'd felt earlier, when he had told her their kiss was forgotten, accosted her once more. She watched his retreating figure, quickly lost in the dark vastness of the hall, and felt suddenly vulnerable. *I've become too used to him protecting me.*

Sophie gave herself a mental shake. *Depend on no man.* None before had been worthy of her time and trust, and while she'd believed Graham to be different, she suddenly was not so certain.

She turned back toward Finella and found Ayla watching her.

"Come along, then," Finella said, sounding more chipper than when she'd first come into the hall. "Since you'll be in the room across from the children, I'm guessing I'll be free to move back downstairs, and that suits me fine. I'm long past needing some peace and quiet, thank ye very much."

"Shouldn't a governess sleep downstairs as well?" Sophie asked, still holding onto Matthew's hand as she followed Finella and the bobbing lantern.

"You'll be nanny as much as governess, so it's best you stay close. They're young yet." Finella swung her head toward the children.

Sophie did not care for the way she spoke of them as if they were not present, just as Graham had done to her a moment earlier, but she let the matter go—for now. She would bring it up with him later. She was not averse to being near the children, but she also wished to be treated as any other governess was, and that meant her quarters should not be near those of the family.

She followed Finella and the children this way and that, down one dark corridor after another and up a flight of ancient stairs, feeling more than discouraged as they made their way to the heart of the castle. It wasn't much of a heart; no warmth. Not a home. Just an aging pile of stone, though she had tried to see it as more than that—from the outside, at least.

Graham was right. No one would think to look for her here, because no one would believe anyone could actually live here. Sophie thought wistfully of the cottage near the gate and wished, small though it was, that they might have lodged there.

"Here we are, lass." Finella stopped before a heavy wood door. "The children's room is across the way, yours here. Nothing else much worth showin' ye, but on the morrow I will anyway, if ye'd like."

"Thank you," Sophie said.

Finella reached past her and pushed the door open, then stepped through and crossed the dark room and pulled open a long set of drapes, revealing the overcast sky.

"Like the rest of the house, this room needs attention," Finella said. "But it's cleaned regularly, and you'll not find a better view."

Sophie took in the dark furnishings and thick rug. It wasn't to her taste, but it was a well-appointed room that, no doubt, at one time had been decorated to the height of fashion. *Perhaps a hundred years ago.*

Her gaze shifted to the four-poster bed, and her eyelids and limbs drooped with sudden exhaustion.

"Ayla, dear, run downstairs and tell them we'll need water for a bath." Finella reached her hands out, as if to usher both children from the room.

"Will a bath get rid of her stink?" Matthew asked, his small nose wrinkling adorably.

"Haud yer weesht," Finella scolded. Turning back to

Sophie, she grimaced. "My apologies. The lad has a tendency to speak his mind."

Sophie used the last of her energy to muster a smile for the children. "You're right. I do smell terrible." Maybe that was why Graham had departed from her in such haste. She dipped her chin to her riding jacket and made a face. "Wet wool stinks terribly. I'm surprised you allowed me inside at all."

Matthew grinned, apparently happy that she had not scolded him as well or found fault with his blunt assessment. Ayla did not return Sophie's smile or say anything, but for a few seconds her eyes—a startling, brilliant blue—met Sophie's in challenge before she allowed Finella to lead her away.

Twenty-Three

NEAR EIGHT O'CLOCK IN THE evening a slight shadow darkened the surface of Graham's desk, making the current missive in his bandaged hand difficult to read in the already-too-dark room. Apparently ordering candles and oil needed to be a priority. One he saw to, instead of the overworked Finella.

Graham looked up to find that Miss Claybourne— Sophie; why had he thought it a good idea to use each other's given names?—had entered his study without his notice. Without being invited. Reason enough for him to be even more agitated than he had been since their arrival this morning, when the burden of caring for his sister's children weighed upon him once more and he'd seen all too well, through Sophie's eyes and his own, the dismal state of Caerlanwood. He'd expected more to have been accomplished in his month-long absence. At the least, the front drive could have been filled in by now and the steps repaired. But the whole place was as run-down as ever, nearly driven into complete and utter ruin. Thanks to his father.

Oh, the irony. His mother's money had been used to shore up the Raymond estates in England. His father had done well with that money, multiplying it several times over. And now those properties could rot, for all Graham cared. His father's money would be used here, to not only repair the damage he had done but to restore Caerlanwood to its former glory. To the place of beauty his mother had loved.

Sophie cleared her throat softly, as if to remind him of her presence.

As if he could forget. After this past week, and especially last night, he would never forget her, even if she left tomorrow—likely what she'd come to tell him she intended to do.

He couldn't allow it. They'd outrun and outmaneuvered anyone searching for her, but to what end? He had no authority, no permanent protection for her as giving her his name would have offered. Still, her best hope of safety from Viscount Newsome and her father was here, no matter how wretched *here* happened to be at present.

He looked up once more, met her gaze, and felt oddly calmed. After so many days spent together, their separation today had unsettled him. He told himself it was only because he had become used to looking after her.

It is only my concern for her safety. When she was out of his sight, he felt uneasy, imagining her father or Newsome had snatched her away. *Ridiculous.* She was safe enough here, as were those living on the plantation in Saint Kitts, for now, so long as Newsome and her father did not merge their powers there. *I have accomplished what I set out to do.* He need only steady the course now.

Apparently tired of waiting for him to welcome her in, Sophie took a step closer to the desk. "You might have told me," she said, her tone clipped.

The children or Caerlanwood? Graham wasn't sure if she referred to his niece and nephew's race or to the unfathomable condition of his home. She had every right to be upset about both.

"I would have been better prepared to greet them."

Ah. The children. The censure in her voice made her topic clear.

"I might have told you—" He paused, taking in her appearance. The hem of a yellowed gown peeked out beneath a plaid that could likely wrap around her several times. Her hair appeared to have been washed and brushed and now hung in a long braid draped over her shoulder. He could only imagine the effort it had taken to tame all those tangles.

Her eyes were bright, sparking passionately, though not as they had last night. Pursed lips and crossed arms gave away her anger. And certainly she had plenty to be upset about. Any other young lady would have been having a fit or lying in bed crying her eyes out after being dragged miles from home by a man with a dire reputation, and taken to a fortress—decaying though it was—in the wilds of Scotland. Any other young lady, but not Sophie. Graham wasn't certain whether he was more amused or impressed. Or worried.

"Then why did you not tell me about them?" she demanded, her shadow creeping ever closer. "You told me they were your sister's children. As such, I expected them to look—"

"Sit," Graham ordered, tossing aside the letter he had been attempting to read.

Instead of obeying she held her ground, arms folded across her middle as she stared him down from the opposite side of the desk.

Graham met her gaze and held it. "I did not tell you about their skin color because I needed to witness your reaction, to judge for myself whether you were inclined to any sort of prejudice. If you were, I could not allow you to be around them. Ayla, in particular, has been through much already and needs to be treated with extra kindness."

"Ayla has put *me* through much today," Sophie retorted. "I believe she is inclined to prejudice against *me*."

Graham winced. He should have warned Sophie about Ayla—not her race, but her propensity for mischief and taking matters into her own hands.

"I don't know how she snuck in and did it, but there was a dead *rat* in my bath with me. Then, when I lay down on the bed to rest, I discovered the mattress drenched in icy water. The first gown Finella lent to me had some sort of burr or pokey flower embedded in the bodice—"

"Scottish thistle," Graham supplied—unhelpfully, he realized quickly.

"I am fearful to see what she has done when I return to my room." Sophie sank into one of the chairs and slumped against the back.

Graham resisted the urge to come around the desk and offer comfort. "Ayla *is* a difficult child, but she has cause, or believes she does. During the first seven years of her life she has experienced the loss of first her birth mother and then my sister. And she was taken from the only home she has ever known, to this place." Graham waved his hand about the dismal room. "She does not trust anyone. You will need to show a great deal of patience." A matter which he had been struggling with, when it came to Ayla.

"If I were prejudiced against her you would send me back to my father's house?"

Graham shook his head and frowned. *Maybe she does want to leave.* "After the great deal of trouble I went to bringing you here? I think not. I would not have had you be the children's governess though."

"Nor your wife either, I should hope." Sophie straightened in her chair. "What if I had not been averse to your offer of marriage, and we had wed? And then you had discovered me prejudiced?"

"Then I should have sent you away somewhere the children are not." He would have sent her away regardless.

To his surprise, she nodded. "Good. Ayla and Matthew must be your priority over all else—even above your goal of freeing slaves on Saint Kitts."

"Thank you for the lecture." Graham pinched his lips together and shook his head, astounded at her temerity and somewhat confused by their conversation. Was she upset with Ayla, and therefore him—or not? "I know where my priorities lie. And I hope yours align as well. I'll not tolerate mistreatment of any kind, no matter what Ayla does. However, I will speak with her tomorrow about her behavior."

"Good." Sophie gave a firm nod, emphasizing her agreement.

Graham's frown grew as he leaned forward over the desk. "You dislike the children, then?"

"No!" She straightened in her chair. "I like them very much. Or Matthew, at least, for now. Though Ayla intrigues me. I will be patient with her. I only meant that *you* must take more care with them. It was a great risk you took, not knowing me and bringing me here, when you did not know how I would react to the children."

Speechless for several seconds, Graham stared at her as he processed the dressing down she'd just given him. "Aye, well, I am a good judge of character and pleased that I did not misjudge how you would receive them."

"You did not," she said in that same prim tone. "I am eager to begin teaching them and have little care for what color their skin is. It is my hope that you will show more concern for them going forward. Matthew, in particular, longs for your attention and affection."

"It is motherly affection they are seeking. I am neither experienced at giving such attention nor equipped to do so. They are better off without my company. I am sorry if this removes me from your good graces." If he was there now—doubtful after the kiss debacle.

Sophie shrugged. "It is too soon for me to complete my entire assessment of your character."

Graham suppressed a smile, while at the same time feeling somewhat disgruntled. She was very good at turning the tables. What she thought of him was not relevant—at least, not for this conversation. It was he who had been judging her worthiness to be around the children. *My children. Katherine's.* All that he had left of her. He just didn't know what to do with them. He leaned back in his chair. "As for *my* assessment of your actions . . . You have passed muster. I found your initial interactions with the children both refreshing and hopeful. Though you should consider the next month a trial period. If either you or the children are unhappy with this arrangement, we shall have to consider other alternatives."

Sophie relaxed ever so slightly, her shoulders softening and her hands unclenching. "There is a great deal of work to be done, and I am not speaking of their education—not yet, at least. I have spent the last two hours in the nursery with them. I have much hope regarding Matthew. He is quick to love and only wishes for the same in return. But I fear Ayla will require considerable time to trust me. She has been deeply wounded, I think." Sophie placed her hands on the edge of the desk as eagerness and interest sparked in those eyes that revealed so much intelligence. "Will you tell me their story?"

Graham glanced at the clock on the wall and then back to the pile of correspondence awaiting his attention. "Meet me in the library at nine o'clock. That will give me time to finish what I must here."

The library was more neutral ground than his study. Already, he would have to contend with this memory of her here. He need not have any others to complicate his plans to distance himself from her.

Twenty-Four

SOPHIE ENTERED THE LIBRARY JUST as the tall clock beside the door chimed the hour. She had left her room fifteen minutes earlier, after dismissing the maid who had come to help her, declining further assistance with styling her hair or putting on any of the fancier but outdated dresses that had been provided. She was a governess, not a guest, so it did not matter in the least how she looked, so long as she was clean and respectable.

The bath had been lovely, and fresh clothing—even the simple, borrowed dress—a luxury Sophie had not fully appreciated before. But she doubted most governesses enjoyed the services of a lady's maid. She did not want the duke making exceptions for her because of her former position. She was his employee now and fully intended to behave as such.

Their days of travel and close proximity were over. That he had both truly forgotten their kiss and did not miss her company had become quickly apparent by his absence today. She'd not seen him once until she'd sought out his company on her own. And even then he had put her off, citing more important matters than telling her the background of the children she was to care for. Sophie doubted that she would see him much at all after this. He hadn't been exaggerating when he'd said Caerlanwood was in great need of repairs, but surely he could see that his niece and nephew were in even graver need—of love and affection.

But now that he had returned home, he seemed more intent on righting all that was wrong with the edifice, perhaps more so than the people inside of it.

Their journey here and arrival at this otherworldly place truly had been like a fairy tale—but she was uncertain of a happy ending.

It is the ending I *wanted,* she reminded herself. She had yearned for independence and to avoid marriage. To continue her education. All of which were in her grasp now. So why did she feel so forlorn?

Sophie forced her mind to the positives. *I am to live in a castle perched on a sea cliff.* For being in such a state of neglect, Caerlanwood was still impressive, vast, and even grand—or there was evidence that it had been. Though the walls held mostly bare spots where paintings and tapestries had once hung, and many of the rooms she had glimpsed were either bare or decorated with furnishings and fabrics from another time, she could still imagine what this place had been.

Long ago. Much of Caerlanwood seemed dusty and in disarray. Sheets covered many of the furnishings, and some of the rooms she'd peeked in during her quest to find the library looked as if no one had stepped inside them for years. Even the floors carried a thick layer of dust, and nothing was where it should be, with large crates and trunks scattered here and there throughout the great hall, as if a number of people had recently arrived and nothing had been unpacked.

The library, however, was different from the rest of the house. Sophie stood just inside its double doors, her mouth curving into a smile as she took in the high shelves encircling the room and the many volumes crammed there. A large, plush rug covered the floor, framed by the polished parquet on each side, and comfortable sofas and chairs filled much of the space, with a round mahogany table near the center of the room. Instead of the customary flower arrangement, a beautiful globe stood in the middle, gleaming in the fire's glow.

Sophie crossed to a chair near the fireplace that looked particularly comfortable. She sat, then slipped off her shoes and tucked her feet beneath her. She was beyond tired and would have gone to bed already, if not for her need to understand the children she was to be teaching. *More than teaching.* Healing *is what they need.* She could not hope to accomplish that without some knowledge of what they had been through. Beyond the fact that they were orphans and would likely face prejudice during their lifetimes, she knew little.

Sophie sighed, concern for their fates already weighing on her. Little Matthew had hardly let her out of his sight all afternoon. And this evening he'd refused to leave her lap as she'd told the children bedtime stories—one after another for the better part of an hour, until both her voice and memory began to fail her.

This was not at all how she had envisioned her first day here. *It was much better.* She had not imagined that her pupils, one of them at least, would show such affection toward her. Instead she had imagined mischievous children who might play pranks on her or refuse to do their lessons. Much as she had been and done. *Much as Ayla is.*

Lessons. How was she to teach two children of such different ages and needs? She supposed she ought to begin planning her second day as a governess at once, starting with where to hold lessons.

She glanced around the cozy room again, relieved that it did not in any way mirror the neglect found in the rest of the house.

The children's room was clean and furnished with the necessities, but it was void of all else—no pictures, no art, or tapestries. Not even curtains at the tall windows. No toys or books. In contrast, this room felt warm and inviting, from the fire in the grate to the comfortable sofas and chairs to the volumes lining the shelves. While not exactly a schoolroom, it did have a table the children could work at. It would do. This was where they would have their lessons.

That decision made, Sophie smiled, sank deeper into the chair, and leaned her head against the back.

"Already feeling at home here, I see."

She sat up but refused to feel self-conscious as Graham entered the room. "We have traveled together for the better part of one week. You have seen me with my shoes off before." He'd seen much more than that. "If it offends you now, that is unfortunate." She shrugged, unconcerned.

"On the contrary. I am glad you are settling in. I believe you'll find that we do not worry as much about propriety here at Caerlanwood." He strode toward her, making a detour to a waist-high cart that held a decanter and two glasses. The latter he turned over. "The tale I have to relate is a long and difficult one." He held a glass up to her. "Would you care for a drink? It is strong Scottish whisky, but I can have something milder brought as well."

"No, thank you." Sophie wrinkled her nose and watched as he used his unwrapped hand to pour himself a liberal glassful from a crystal decanter.

"I don't usually drink like this at night, but what I am about to share requires fortification."

Sophie nodded and decided to reserve judgment for later. Though, in her experience, alcohol never did anything good for a man. Her father was always at his worst whenever he was into his cups.

Graham replaced the stopper in the decanter, took up his glass, and crossed the room. While waiting for him to speak, she continued to study the details of the library, particularly the titles of the books closest to her, which appeared to be a series of volumes having to do with Caerlanwood and the family that had lived here over the centuries.

Who else sat here in this room? What did it look like then?

Green damask wallpaper covered the one wall without bookcases, and matching curtains with their tasseled ties hung at the windows. Similar cushions backed the sofas. It was not a feminine room, but she guessed that at some time it had had a feminine touch.

"You are welcome in the library whenever you would like. You may read anything and borrow any volumes you wish."

"Thank you. I would like to teach the children lessons here."

Graham nodded his approval. "This was my mother's favorite room, and it still speaks of her."

Was that why it had been cared for in his absence—preserved as some sort of shrine to his mother?

His fingers brushed the top of a pillow as he made his way to the chair across from Sophie's. "She used to curl up on the sofa and read at night, and during the day she could oft be found in one of the window seats, an open book on her lap. Reading was her escape."

"Escape from what?" This was not the story she had come to hear, but if he wished to tell another, she would not complain. The more she learned about the man before her, the better she might hope to understand him. In the week she had known Graham she'd felt, at times, as if she were clinging to a giant pendulum that swung back and forth from one extreme to the other. She'd gone from believing he was the vicious madman society labeled him as, to realizing that he was a good man, concerned with righting the wrongs in this world. But she did not pretend to understand everything about him yet. Was he an aloof duke, or the ordinary man who had visited with old friends yesterday and then held her in his arms and kissed her passionately last night?

"Reading was Mother's escape from my father and then—life as a whole, I believe."

Graham's words brought her back to the present. He sipped his drink and stared past Sophie, as if remembering previous events in this very room.

"She was not here with us, was not the mother of my childhood, during the last several years of her life. I like to think that she was still able to escape to her other worlds then, but I am not certain even those were open to her. She had suffered one too many *accidents*, and her mind was never right again after the last."

"Accidents?" Was he saying that some misfortune had befallen his mother, or that someone had hurt her? Sophie tucked her feet in tighter and held her breath, afraid of his answer.

"My father was not a good man. He deserved his reputation as the Black Duke. Anyone who knew him knew he kept company with the devil."

"He was unkind to your mother," Sophie clarified, trying to piece together the things Graham was not telling her directly.

His face grew hard with a look of hatred that would have frightened Sophie, were it directed at her. But his gaze was still distant, his mind in the past.

"*Unkind* is too generous a word. From the day of their marriage, he set out to prove how much he disliked her. He had wished to marry another, but my mother's money was needed to maintain his English estates, so his parents forced the match. He held that against my mother for the rest of her life, as if it were her fault they had wed, when she had not desired it either. *Her* father had deemed the match to an Englishman—particularly one set to inherit a dukedom—necessary, to ensure Caerlanwood's future during a time, as with many periods in our history, when Scotland was not favored by the throne and many Scottish holdings had been seized, or even destroyed. Little did my grandfather realize he was handing his daughter and the estate over to the devil himself."

"Did your father hurt you too?" Sophie searched Graham's face and glimpsed not the enigma of a man she had come to know the past several days, but a vulnerable boy, afraid of his own father and worried for his mother.

"Aye." Graham nodded. "Until I was thirteen—the day he hurt Mother for the last time. He knocked her down a flight of stairs at our townhome in London. My sister and I ran to her, and he ordered us to leave her be. My sister refused. But I stood as he had asked and came to him. I marched up the steps to my father and hit him so hard that he fell backward and struck his head. For a few, magnificent seconds, I thought I had killed him. But we were not so fortunate, and he recovered quickly. Mother did not."

Sophie suppressed a shudder at the anger simmering in Graham's eyes and the words he had spoken. *He felt* magnificent, *believing he had killed his father.* "He never hit her again?"

Graham shook his head. "Never. I had proved to him that I was his son and capable of violence as well. He left us all alone. My addled mother, my sister, and I came here to live, while he remained in England. Had Mother only been well again, those might have been the best years of my life."

"I am sorry that they were not, that your father—"

"Was a poor excuse for a human, as yours is?" Graham

said. "My father was a feeble-minded bully. His selfishness and greed and stupidity cost him his life in the end. He died in a fight in a club." Graham held up a hand, his palm facing her. "And do not tell me you are sorry, because I am not. I wished him dead from a very young age. Learning of his death was the first time I felt God had answered a prayer."

That Graham found his father's death an answer to prayer seemed even worse. Yet Sophie could not deny the way she had felt those times her father had been away for months, visiting his plantation. It had been pleasant at the house without him, the air lighter, all of them happier. On more than one occasion she had wished he would never return home. Was that feeling so much different from what Graham had just so honestly expressed?

"Continue your story," she said quietly. A quarter of an hour had passed already, and he had yet to tell her anything of the children. She would not hurry him along. Though their conversation was not of pleasant things, she savored the time with him, fearing it might be the last conversation they enjoyed alone. In the future when they talked, it was likely that Ayla and Matthew, or others in the household, would be present as well.

"My sister Katherine was four years older than I and an almost exact replica of our mother—in her fate too, unfortunately." Graham set his half-empty glass on a table beside him, then stood and walked to the mantel. He removed a miniature and studied it a moment, a sad smile upon his face, before handing it to Sophie.

Sophie stared at the tiny portrait. Dark ringlets framed a delicate face, the hint of a smile curving the lips upward. "She is very beautiful."

"She was. To her detriment." He began pacing before the fire.

"Katherine's beauty caught the attention of a cruel marquess, Jack Kempton, and she was forced into a marriage that our father arranged. Lord Kempton was as cruel as he, and Katherine suffered greatly at his hands—and as with our mother, I could do little to help her. She married when I was fifteen years old, some twelve years ago—another lifetime."

Graham is twenty-seven. Seven years my senior. Not the more than twenty that Lord Newsome had been.

Sophie watched Graham from the corner of her eye as he continued pacing. His hand was still swollen and had been bandaged, but aside from that he looked perfect. From his dark hair and stormy eyes all the way down his trim figure to his polished boots, he was the sort of man women swooned over. *Myself included?* She remembered the feel of his bare skin beneath her hand last night, the warmth of his body beside hers. She felt a flush sweep across her cheeks and reined her thoughts back to the present and the serious topic at hand.

"A few years after Katherine married, she traveled with Lord Kempton to Saint Kitts, to live on his plantation. She wrote frequent letters to me, describing in vivid detail her life there and that of the slaves on their plantation. Her husband treated them even worse than he treated her, and in return she made it her mission to secretly help them in any way she could."

"Would that not risk his wrath?" Sophie asked, liking Katherine already, imagining that had she been Torie's mother she would have stood up to her husband or, at the least, secretly helped her daughter.

"Aye." Graham nodded solemnly. He ceased pacing and stopped to stare into the fire. "But Katherine did not care. She had found her cause and threw herself wholeheartedly into it. The plight of many that she shared in her letters nearly broke my heart. I had not thought much about slavery before, but reading her letters I could no longer ignore it.

"I wanted to visit Katherine, to help with her endeavors, but I could not leave our mother—still clinging to life in that half-existence she had been in for many years."

"Did Katherine and her husband have any children?" Sophie leaned forward, sensing that Graham was coming closer to sharing how Matthew and Ayla came to claim Katherine as their mother.

"They were not blessed with any children—something that both saddened Katherine and simultaneously made her grateful. She had been with child once, but a blow from her husband caused her to miscarry. She never conceived after that and, though she longed to be a mother, felt it better that she was not, as she would have feared for her children's safety. I wrote to her, promising that if she did find herself with child again, I would come to Saint Kitts and rescue her. But that never happened."

"Then how—"

"A mulatto slave girl was born on the plantation—not an uncommon occurrence," Graham said with a frown of disgust. "The white overseers often forced themselves on the slaves. But this infant looked remarkably like Lord Kempton. When he deemed that the child's mother was to be sold—and was not to be allowed to take her one-year-old daughter with her—Katherine intervened and tried to get him to change his mind. She was badly beaten for it, and the mother was carted away, her screams and cries for her daughter carrying into the house where Katherine lay on the bedroom floor, beaten and bloody. Though she could barely move, she crawled to the room where she hid the money she used to help the slaves. She removed a generous sum and then half-scooted, half-crawled down the stairs to get to the front door and outside, where she was able to call for help. Because the slaves knew and trusted her, they were willing to risk helping her, and she arranged for the little girl to be hidden in a cottage an hour's walk away and a woman paid to look after her."

"You sent Katherine money," Sophie guessed, wondering if that had contributed to Caerlanwood being in such disrepair. Was Graham's money still going to aid in Saint Kitts?

He gave a quick nod, as if it were of no consequence, then continued. "Katherine feared what her husband would do, as he had threatened upon his return to kill the child. So at great risk to her own health—she nearly died from her injuries that day—after she had arranged for the child's safety, she was helped back upstairs, all while in excruciating pain.

"When Lord Kempton returned he found her upstairs in the same position on the floor that he had left her. As he'd gone earlier, he had forbidden anyone from coming to her aid. When he found her again, as she had been, he believed that his orders had been followed. Katherine could not move at all and was slipping in and out of consciousness."

It was then she died? But that could not be. It did not account for young Matthew.

"At last Lord Kempton relented and called a physician to attend to her. She had a concussion, a broken arm, several cracked ribs, and damage to her spleen. Only a miracle of God spared her."

"Did the physician not note Katherine's injuries? Was there no one to stand up for her?" Sophie asked, her ire rising with every breath. But there had been no one to stand up against her father when he had turned against his own daughter. Why should she think anything would be different on the islands, where there were even fewer freedoms?

Graham shook his head. "Who might have spoken up for or defended her? Other, equally vile, plantation owners? Certainly not the slaves, who would have been whipped or shot or hanged—or, worse, had similar done to their families if they intervened."

Sophie pressed her lips together, saddened and sickened at such injustice and imagining her father partaking in it all too well.

"The only good thing about the severity of Katherine's injuries was that they made it seemingly impossible for her to have had anything to do with Ayla's disappearance. Her husband never suspected Katherine was responsible, and he had his hands full seeing that his wife lived. His threat to kill the child was mostly forgotten, or at least overshadowed by his current predicament—without Katherine to run the estate, things did not go well. The house slaves were not inclined to serve him but were loyal to Katherine, and so they thwarted his efforts and mismanaged everything they could in her absence. Oh, what joy their antics brought to Katherine." A sad smile lit Graham's face.

"She wrote to me tales of burnt dinners, insects discovered in her husband's trousers and drinks, and how one evening when he lit his pipe it burst into flame, singeing his beard and burning the tip of his nose and his cheeks—one of the slaves had packed some gunpowder in beneath the tobacco."

Sophie grinned. "That was quite a risk."

Graham nodded, and his voice grew somber again. "More than one slave paid for it, unfortunately."

"And Ayla? She was safe?" Sophie asked.

He nodded. "As soon as Katherine was well enough to make the walk to see Ayla, she went, if not every day, at least several times a week—as often as she could slip away unnoticed. Most visits were only a few minutes, just long enough to check on Ayla and make sure she was well and to deliver food and supplies. Then Katherine had to hurry home, so as to not be missed."

Graham's gaze was far away again, and a sad smile curved

his lips. "How Katherine loved her, and through her letters telling of Ayla's growth and doings, so did I." He turned to Sophie. "About the time Ayla grew old enough that it became difficult to keep her hidden, Katherine's husband contracted yellow fever and died."

Another blessing. The unbidden thought should have made Sophie feel guilty, but it did not. Any man as cruel as Lord Kempton didn't deserve to live. "Katherine became the owner of the plantation." Sophie recalled her amazement the first time she had heard this.

"She did, and one of her first acts as owner was to collect Ayla to come live with her. Katherine tried to get the old woman who had cared for Ayla to come too, but she refused and told Katherine that no good would come of it and that the plantation was not a safe place for Ayla."

"Because she was the daughter of a slave?" Sophie asked.

The duke shrugged. "Possibly. Though given what I know now, I think her prediction had more to do with her abilities as a soothsayer."

Sophie arched her brow. "Truly? Do you believe in such?"

"I did not used to, but now . . . I'm not certain."

Sophie wanted to ask him more about this woman and what she had told Katherine but held her tongue, not wishing to disrupt his tale of the children. The hour was already late, and she feared he would stop at any minute, leaving her to hear the rest later. Which would not do. She needed to know the children's stories tonight, before the new day, when she would begin teaching them. *Caring for them.* They seemed to need that more than anything else.

"Katherine did not heed the old woman's warning but instead brought Ayla up to the big house to live with her. They still visited the old woman regularly, but Ayla lived at the big house now. Katherine fixed up a beautiful bedroom for her, right beside her own. Then Katherine set about trying to find Ayla's mother. It took her a couple of months, but at last she did. She went to her owner and asked to buy Ayla's mother—for a generous sum. But the man would not agree to the sale. Ayla's mother, a mulatto herself, was very beautiful, and her beauty cost her too."

Sophie wrung her hands in her lap, frustrated by such unfairness. "What did your sister do?"

"The only thing she could. She told Ayla's mother that her daughter was alive and well. The woman begged Katherine to keep the child and raise her as her own. Katherine promised that she would, and then she went home and did just that. She loved Ayla as her own, lavishing her with everything from dolls and dresses to time and love. I sent presents from London, everything that Katherine asked for and more. It was the first time Katherine's letters were truly happy."

"And the plantation? The slaves working there? What became of them?" Sophie asked, eager to hear how a woman had managed on her own.

"Katherine always had a good head for numbers, and she figured out how to free the slaves, pay them a wage, and still make enough to keep the plantation afloat. Everyone had to work hard—herself included—but she made a small profit that first year, largely due to the help of her foreman, Daniel, a former slave himself.

"Conditions improved. Spirits rose. Her letters were filled with their joint accomplishments and joys. I could practically feel the happiness seeping through her words."

Graham returned to the chair across from Sophie, a smile not quite reaching his eyes. "At Christmas the next year, 1827, she held a big party for all on the plantation—black or white. There were presents and plenty of food. They had music and dancing... Katherine danced. With Daniel. I was there, as our mother had passed away that October. I danced with little Ayla. It was the best Christmas either of us—Katherine or I—had ever had." He leaned back in his chair, more relaxed than Sophie had seen him all evening.

"Katherine and Daniel fell in love?" Sophie guessed how at least part of this story might unfold.

"They were already in love, long before that dance," Graham said. "They worked so closely together, and they had mutual respect for each other. Katherine had spoken of him frequently in her letters. But though Daniel was a free man, marrying Katherine was not an option—or was it?"

"It was?" Sophie asked hopefully. She thought of Torie and the happiness she'd experienced before her death. It was comforting that her sister had known true love. She hoped that Graham had that same comfort when he thought of his sister.

"They had found a minister willing to marry them and were wed a few months before I visited. Katherine hadn't told me in her letters because she was uncertain of what my reaction would be."

"Much as you were uncertain what mine would be today," Sophie said.

Graham nodded. "I was simply happy to see her joy. Daniel was a good man. And another miracle—Katherine was already carrying his child, Matthew, that Christmas. It was shortly after that the trouble began."

Graham picked up his glass and drained the rest of it. He leaned forward, elbows braced on his knees, hands clasped together, as if in prayer.

Sophie waited quietly, hating the mounting tension in the room and the feeling of dread enveloping her.

After a long moment, he continued softly. "At first it was just harassment. Shunning by the other white people, including women who had been Katherine's friends. Then there were threats. Daniel was to leave, to move out of the house—or he would pay." Graham lifted his head, his sorrowful eyes finding Sophie's. "Then there was a mob. Nearly a year to the day of that Christmas party, they were both murdered. Little Matthew was barely six months old. He would likely have been killed too, if not for Ayla's quick actions. She took him, ran into the cane fields, and hid, watching as her parents were dragged into the yard."

Sophie covered her mouth. Tears stung her eyes as she thought of the beautiful, silent girl upstairs. "How old was she?"

"Five. Can you imagine?"

She shook her head. "No." She didn't want to imagine.

"Slave children grow up fast, and though Ayla had never been treated as a slave, she was about to become one. Her childhood ended that day."

Sophie wanted to argue against this, to tell him that age seven was still a child—that there could still be dolls and tea parties, and laughter and joy and running barefoot outdoors in Ayla's life. But she wondered if that was possible.

"Ayla carried Matthew all the way to the cabin and the old woman who had cared for her. Ayla left the baby with her and returned to the house, hoping to help.

"What she found was Daniel swinging from a tree, and her mother—Katherine—lying on the ground beneath him barely clinging to life. She—she died a few hours later. It was—"

"Shh." Sophie was out of her chair and kneeling on the rug in front of Graham before the first hoarse sob left his throat. "You don't need to tell me *any* more." She wrapped her hands over his that were cradling his head.

"Katherine was so good," Graham managed. "And they killed her."

Sophie wondered who *they* was, but she didn't ask. She wasn't ever going to ask him to relate anything this painful again and was sorry she had. Seeing him hunched over with grief, his heart laid bare and tender, she wondered how anyone could have thought him evil. Her father had never shed tears like this. *Jonathan did.* And he was a good man, a man who had loved dearly and paid for it just as dearly.

Graham Murray Raymond is a good man too. The best she had ever known. Seeing him hurt like this brought her own grief at losing Torie to the surface, but instead of pushing that pain away, Sophie let it encompass her. For once she wanted to feel every overwhelming sorrow, so she could understand at least a part of what Graham felt.

She wanted to understand and even absorb his pain—to take it away. Her own heart swelled with empathy and a desire to make him whole again, if such a thing was possible.

After several minutes he spoke. "You see why you must be patient—with Ayla."

Sophie squeezed her hands gently around his. "I will," she promised. *I will help her. Somehow. I will help you.*

"There is more—"

Sophie pressed her lips together, holding back a demand that he not say whatever it was. She didn't want to know any more. The images his words had already brought to mind were disturbing enough.

"Katherine's plantation was taken over by some of those in the mob. The people living and working there were no longer free, Ayla included. She was made to work hard and was punished frequently. The day I came for her she had been whipped—for stealing milk to bring to Matthew, who was still hidden."

"Whipped—a child that young?" Sophie shifted off her knees as her hands fell away from Graham's. One pressed to her stomach, and she felt suddenly that she might be sick.

He nodded solemnly. "I don't know the extent of all that Ayla has experienced. She has not spoken since the day Katherine died. Maime told me all that I know, all that I have shared with you."

"Maime?" Still fighting a swell of nausea, Sophie looked up at him.

"One of the other slaves on Katherine's plantation. When I came for Matthew and Ayla, I offered any who wished to leave with me the opportunity. Most chose to stay, but there were a few who accepted my offer and joined us. They are employed here now but are free to leave at any time." Graham stood and reached a hand down to her.

Sophie accepted it and allowed him to pull her up, grateful when he did not release her immediately. They stood facing one another, her hand clasped in his. "And the others?" she asked. "Those who chose to stay on Saint Kitts?"

"Are free once more. I pay a steward handsomely to run the plantation. He keeps me apprised of affairs on the island, and as I am able, I have slowly been purchasing other, smaller plantations and freeing those who work there."

"But my father and Lord Newsome have threatened to put an end to that?" As she looked up at Graham she tried to remember every snippet of conversation she'd heard between the two. It wasn't much, as mostly she had avoided being anywhere near either of them.

"They proposed a law to the governor that no one on Saint Kitts be allowed to free their slaves. It sounds ludicrous, but it is likely to pass, as most of the plantation owners see the economy as dependent upon slavery. Newsome and your father promote that idea, and the merger of their plantations will give them additional sway and power when it comes time to vote."

"But your sister managed without slaves."

Graham nodded. "She did, though hers was not a great profit. Katherine had what she needed, but no more—no wealth was to follow her decision."

"I see." Sophie did—so much more than she had a week ago, or even a day ago. He'd opened her eyes to the violence and atrocities happening on the islands. She swallowed uneasily and squeezed her eyes shut, wishing she didn't know, that she could go back to her former ignorance. *The coward's way.*

She looked up at him again and took a deep breath. "There are so many wrongs in this world. I have always wanted to right those against women, but now that feels childish—selfish. What is being deprived of an education when there are children being whipped for taking a cup of milk? Mothers being taken from their babies, people being killed because of whom they love?"

Graham took her other hand and looked down at her, his eyes somber and filled with renewed grief. "If you can right one wrong, can help two orphaned children, that will be more than enough for me—for them."

"I can. I will," Sophie vowed. There was not an *I do* in her future, but this—these children—were important and perhaps the best way she could take care with Graham's heart.

Sophie gently tugged her hands from his and twisted the ring he'd given her three days ago from her finger. "Governesses do not require wedding rings." She smiled as she placed it in the palm of his hand, though she didn't feel the relief at having removed it that she'd expected. Instead, she felt almost—sad.

Twenty-Five

SOPHIE JERKED AWAKE, SITTING UP and throwing the covers aside in practically one motion. *Ayla.* For the third night in a row, the girl had awakened her with a night terror. Sophie leaned toward the end of the bed, reaching for her wrap, then paused, realizing she didn't hear screaming. Instead, rain lashed against the panes of her window. She sat perfectly still, ears straining to hear any sounds that might be coming from the other room, but all was silent save for the storm.

Perhaps it is too early yet. She had little hope that Ayla would sleep peacefully through the night. On Sophie's first day here Finella had told her that the girl carried on like a *caoineag*—a type of specter who keened of death—every single night. Finella had applied poultices to Ayla's pillow, and Maime had given Ayla herbal tea before bed. She'd tried singing lullabies to Ayla as she fell asleep and Finella had even had the priest out to bless her.

"Nae a thing helps the poor lass," Finella had said. "An' the wee lad, nae much more than a bairn himself, wakes with her each night. I said to Graham that they must be separated, but he didna agree. Says they're all the other has and must stay together. But how's the lad to grow, with his sleep interrupted night after night? Isna' right, so I've done the only thing I could—when the lass takes to screaming and carrying on, straight away I take the pitcher to her."

"The pitcher?" Sophie had asked, appalled at any number of things this might mean.

"Aye. A dose of cold water wakes her." Finella gave a resolute nod, as if pleased with her solution.

"That seems a bit—harsh," Sophie said, though she was at least grateful to know the woman wasn't using the pitcher any other way. She suppressed a shudder, remembering the man at Gretna Green over whom she had smashed a pitcher.

"Isna' harsh at all," Finella had said, sounding a bit affronted. "Would it not be worse to let the lass linger in her terror? The cold water wakes her at once. Then I'm quick to help her into a dry shift, and we can all get back to sleep. Works a fair sight better than anything else I've tried. But awake or asleep, the lass is a difficult one. I tell ye."

Finella had a great many other things to tell Sophie, and she was thankful for them, for the only source of information she had here, as Graham had not spoken to her since their conversation in the library her first night. She'd glimpsed him only twice—once unpacking crates in the great hall and the other time outside, in front of the house, as he spoke with the elderly gardener. No doubt he had a great many responsibilities, but still—she'd hoped he might inquire about her progress with the children, at least. Or perhaps Finella had already reported to him that thus far there had been little.

Wide awake now, with her thoughts once more centered around the man who had brought her here, Sophie slid from the bed and hurried across the cold floor to the window seat. She knelt there and peered outside, hoping to glimpse the moon and estimate the hour, but it was not to be seen, blockaded by thick fog, clouds, and storm.

After a brief respite, the rain had started again in earnest, relentless the past three days in its determination to keep her indoors, when since their arrival she'd wanted nothing so much as to traverse the long stone steps down to the beach.

At the least, she wished she might leave her window open to hear the sounds of the surf cresting on the shore, as Graham had promised she would from her bedroom. *His bedroom.* That he had given up for her, so she might have one of the few decently kept and furnished rooms in the house. *And so I might be near Ayla to comfort her in the night.*

After three interrupted nights, Sophie wasn't certain if his gesture had been gallant or a punishment. Regardless, she felt a little desperate for a good night's sleep.

Caring for three-year-old Matthew, who rarely stopped talking, and seven-year-old Ayla, who had yet to utter a word to her, had proven more exhausting than Sophie had believed possible. What was supposed to have been a four-hour-per-day position had turned into eight—or more, as Matthew refused to leave her side unless forcefully shooed away, so she could perform basic, personal necessities. She hadn't the heart to turn him away at other times, though she longed for a bit of quiet, a few minutes alone to contemplate all that had happened in the past week and a half or to get lost in one of the many books in the library that beckoned her.

But that, and her promised lessons, and even the arrival of the Shelbys and her trunk, had to wait, so long as this storm raged and the bridge was still washed out.

As eager as she was for her belongings to arrive, she was most looking forward to having her books again, particularly those she might share with the children. As it was now, she had little to work with for such young students. Matthew was eager to learn the letters and their sounds, to attempt to write his name, and to listen to her read—though he interrupted frequently, asking dozens of questions. Without the proper teaching materials, there was only so much she could do each day. So they had filled the hours with activities other than learning.

Finella had given them a tour of the house, or the part they lived in, at least. The main tower house was the original building, and the wings had been added in later centuries. Sophie's room and the children's, the library, the great hall, and the dining room were all in the tower house. She had no idea what was in the other parts of the house, as those appeared to be blocked off—though Graham had to be getting in and out of at least one of them somehow.

As for the tower house—it needed restoring as well. The great hall was currently filled with crates and boxes, many of which were partially unpacked and revealed artwork and other treasures.

As they had walked by the open double doors, Sophie had glimpsed Graham hefting a large painting from a crate and wondered out loud at the number of similarly sized boxes filling the hall.

"They're all filled with something that belongs here at Caerlanwood, pilfered by Graham's father when he was alive," Finella explained. "Since his father's death, Graham has spent considerable time and expense locating as many of the missing belongings as he can. Some were at the duke's estates in England, but many he'd sold."

"That explains the empty rooms and walls." Sophie stood to the side of the doors and watched as Graham carefully unwrapped a portrait of a woman wearing clothing from the Tudor period. *A Murray family member?*

"He wanted to restore the house before his mother passed on but wasna able to, given the care she required, his many responsibilities in England, and then his travels to Saint Kitts and having the bairns to look after." Finella sighed. "Isna' like to be complete anytime soon."

"Coming to rescue me has put him further behind," Sophie mused, the gratitude she already felt increasing.

She could only imagine what a task that must be, and how bitterly Graham must feel towards his father—not only for lost treasures but for the lives of his mother and sister. *Is he lonely as well?* She wished he would include her, and even the children, in his quest to restore Caerlanwood. She could unpack boxes, paint walls, or tend a garden. *I could listen. I would try to understand.*

After the way he'd held her hands and spoken to her that night in the library, she'd thought—had hoped—that he was to remain cordial to her. Or, at the least, that he might wish to know how she was getting on with the children. Instead, it seemed he was taking pains to avoid them all.

He hadn't joined them once for breakfast or dinner, had not summoned her, had not come to visit the children. Which left Sophie with only little Matthew to talk to, and occasionally Finella, when the woman wasn't busy with her multitude of household responsibilities.

Loneliness was not a new feeling, precisely, but it was the first time Sophie had been bothered by it. *The first time I've longed for a man's company.*

How was it possible that ten days had changed her so completely, from a woman who wanted *nothing* to do with men, to one who could not stop thinking about one particular man?

Would the passage of time change her back to how she had been? Did she want it to? Or— *What might I do to change Graham's mind about us?*

The thought caught her off guard, but she couldn't deny its allure. She missed Graham—missed speaking with him, being near him. *Kissing him.*

Sophie tucked her knees to her chest as she revisited those moments in his arms. The fluttering in her stomach hadn't lessened any over the past days. If anything, it seemed to be getting worse. A glimpse of him was all it took to start it up again. And when she went an entire day without seeing him . . .

The realization that she was pining for a man did not sit well. Perhaps when the roads cleared and her tutors arrived and her lessons began, then she would forget this strange obsession that had come over her. *I'll forget him. I* must *forget him.*

Sophie tipped her head against the cold glass, as if that might shock her mind from its new, unsatisfied state. *I have what I've always wanted. Freedom. The possibility of an education. A challenge.*

She peered through the window again, barely able to make out shapes in the garden below. The view of the beach was obscured by the fog, but she knew the ocean was there, and it sent a lovely thrill of anticipation through her.

I live with a mysterious duke, in an ancient Scottish castle, perched on a cliff near the sea. A shudder of pure delight rippled down her spine. It was all so gothic—so *romantic.* And, apparently, she *was* given to that sort of thing.

For now she left the two children out of her thoughts. They rather deflated the vision her mind was conjuring of herself traipsing down the stone steps to the sea gate, then walking through it and wandering, barefoot, along the sandy beach. She'd be staring out at the deep blue of the ocean, contemplating all the places it might carry her away to, when Graham, also barefoot, would come up behind her, take her in his arms, and—

A piercing scream from the other room jolted Sophie from her musing. Just in time. *I really must cease thinking of that kiss.*

She jumped from the seat and ran to her door, grabbing her wrap on the way. Shoving her arms through the sleeves as she moved, she hurried across the hall and into the children's room. Matthew was just sitting up, rubbing sleep from his eyes.

"She scared again," he said solemnly, holding his arms out to Sophie.

"I know." She tied her wrap, then scooped him up on her way to Ayla's bed.

Eyes opened wide, but not truly seeing, Ayla thrashed about, her mouth open in a long, piercing wail of terror.

"Shh," Sophie murmured, though it would do little good. She winced, her ears hurting already as she settled herself beside Ayla on the bed, then tucked Matthew in next to her, half on top of her with her arm around him. "Ready?"

He nodded, his curly head brushing against her shoulder. Together they began singing the lullaby Matthew had taught her.

He lasted through two verses before he nodded off again. Ayla's screams had turned to whimpering. *She's calming more quickly than last night.* Sophie continued singing, using her free hand to brush the damp hair from Ayla's forehead. *Poor child.*

It was good that Graham had told her of the children's past. No doubt that knowledge stretched her patience, as she waited to earn Ayla's trust. It wasn't the girl's fault she had these terrors. Anyone who had witnessed and endured the things she had could experience the same. *I must find a way to help her forget. Or, at least, to overcome.*

She needed to forget about Graham and focus on Ayla and Matthew. She needed to get through to Ayla, to reach her somehow, to help her experience things beyond the horrors she had endured on Saint Kitts. To show her that the world was a beautiful place with many possibilities. That there was hope, even for a girl with her challenges.

There is hope. Sophie wanted to feel that too. She didn't

have time to flounder here. She had a task to do—a few of them, maybe. Perhaps in reaching Ayla's heart, she would begin to reach Graham's. *If I can help his sister's children . . .* Maybe that would help him too.

Twenty-Six

GRAHAM LOOKED UP FROM THE documents spread across his desk, the latest report from Katherine's plantation, as a sense that something was off niggled at the back of his mind. A quick glance at the clock showed it was a little after midnight. Time for him to leave his desk and retire to the sofa in the library. There were beds aplenty in the east wing, but there hadn't been time to air any out yet, not when the staff was busy readying additional rooms in the main house for William and his wife, as well as preparing the gatekeeper's cottage for his hopefully soon-to-arrive gatekeeper.

If the rain ever ceases. Graham recalled summers past when he and Katherine had lain on the library carpet, facing one another and making bets in hushed tones about how long a storm might last. The loser always had to snitch a biscuit for the other from the kitchen—not such a difficult feat, given the way the staff indulged them. Graham wondered idly if those working in the kitchen now were as indulgent with Ayla and Matthew.

Ayla. He stood abruptly, a sense of foreboding crashing over him. He'd heard her cry out briefly, but within just a few minutes her screaming had ceased. Graham snatched the candle from his desk and strode from the room. Ayla never stopped carrying on after such a short period. Even when Finella doused the lass with water—a practice he wasn't particularly fond of—there had still been crying and the commotion of getting her and her bedding changed. Why, then, was he hearing nothing now?

Had Sophie lost patience and done something drastic? He'd seen them traipsing about together earlier today, Matthew clinging to Sophie's hand and chattering nonstop, while Ayla trailed behind, a petulant expression on her face. Sophie had looked—exhausted. He'd recognized her tiredness at once, having suffered that himself for months on end when getting up at night with Ayla. His conscience prickled. He ought to have made other arrangements for tonight, so Sophie could get a good night's sleep.

Graham took the stairs two at a time. At the top, he turned down the hall toward his previous room and what had become the nursery since Ayla and Matthew had taken up residence. Both doors stood ajar; he strode toward the children's but stopped just short of entering as the melody of a familiar song carried to him.

"Oh, kind hearts were dwelling there, and bairns full o' glee. And wild rose and the

jasmine still hang upon the water. How many cherished memories do these sweet flowers recall?"

He peered inside the dark room, feeling five again, his mother singing him to sleep as she brushed the hair from his forehead. Much as Sophie was presently singing to Ayla and stroking her hair, while Matthew slept snuggled against Sophie's other side.

How . . . Graham stepped farther into the room, candle held aloft, uncertain of what he was actually seeing.

Sophie looked up at him, her voice trailing off. She returned her gaze to Ayla for several long seconds before carefully moving her arm and attempting to sit up.

"Will you put Matthew back in bed?" she whispered.

Graham set the candle on the bureau, then stepped forward and took Matthew from her. The child turned his face toward Graham's chest, as if noting Sophie's absence and seeking a replacement. Graham held Matthew a little closer, relishing his sweet scent. Sophie must have insisted upon a bath before bed. Graham carried Matthew to the other bed and tucked him in as Sophie, clutching her wrap tightly around her, tiptoed past them to the hall.

Graham took the candle and followed, catching up to her and reaching for her arm before she could disappear into her room. "Where did you learn that song?" The words came out more gruff than he'd intended.

She turned back to him, her expression wary. "From Matthew. Is there something wrong with it?"

"No." Graham shook his head as he released her. "I was simply surprised to hear you singing it. I haven't heard it, haven't thought of it in years. My mother used to sing the same to me."

"And to Katherine?" Sophie looked up at him, her wariness melting to a look filled with compassion.

"Aye." The previous tension fled Graham's body, replaced at once by a swell of sadness. *Mother and Katherine. Both gone.* How he missed them, and how difficult it was to be at Caerlanwood without them. He could imagine Katherine peeking around every corner, inviting him to get up to some mischief with her. And Mother . . . healthy, happy at the peak of their summer holiday. How often she'd gone about singing then. But by summer's end the songs had always ceased. Evidence of the years of hardship returned to the lines of her face, and she'd be stooped and sorrowful as the time drew near for them to return to England.

"I believe Katherine also sang that to Ayla, and she, in turn, sang to Matthew."

"And tonight, you sang to calm Ayla?" Graham glanced toward the children's bedroom, as if not quite believing what he had just witnessed. Ayla's night terrors had gone on for months with no relief, no improvement, no matter what he and Finella attempted. Sophie hadn't even been here a week yet, and already she had made progress.

Sophie shrugged and stifled a yawn. "Since it's a Scottish tune, I assumed that Ayla must have learned it from Katherine, rather than anyone from Saint Kitts. And since Ayla is calling out for Katherine when she cries at night—"

"She is?" Graham frowned as he tried to recollect whether he'd been able to distinguish any specific words among Ayla's wailings.

Sophie nodded. "The first two nights I followed Finella's lead in trying to quiet Ayla as quickly as possible. But last night I listened to her instead. She was difficult to understand at first—and painful." Sophie lifted her hands to her ears, as if recalling their discomfort. "But after a few minutes I was able to decipher at least some of her words—enough to realize that she was crying out for her mother."

"But she knows Katherine is gone," Graham said.

"It may be that her mind hasn't truly accepted that," Sophie suggested quietly, her concerned gaze flitting to the children's door. She lowered her voice. "You haven't many books on the mind in your library, or none that I've found very helpful yet. But I recall some time ago reading about something called our subconscious, that it holds our deepest desires and fears—and it controls much of what we do during our conscious hours. These nightmares that Ayla endures night after night indicate that her mind has not yet accepted the reality that her mother is gone."

"I don't see the connection to the lullaby," Graham admitted. Finella had sung to Ayla at bedtime with little success.

"I am not certain there is one," Sophie admitted. "It was only an idea I had. Without her telling us, we cannot know exactly what Ayla may be experiencing in her dreams every night. She might be witnessing Katherine's death once more, or it might be that someone or something is hurting Ayla or frightening her, and she is calling out to Katherine for help and comfort. But either way, it is Katherine she is pining for. And as Katherine is the one who sang that song to her, I hoped that if Ayla heard it when she was in the throes of her nightmare it might bring comfort, might soothe her, as it likely did when she was very young."

Ayla was still very young, yet wise beyond her years. Much like the woman standing before him. Amazed and impressed by her yet again, Graham stared down at Sophie, who looked very fetching in her wrap, with bare feet peeking out beneath and with her long braid spilling over her shoulder. She was yawning and practically asleep again already. A gentleman wouldn't be noticing or admiring things like her bare feet, nor would he detain her in the hall in the middle of the night. But Graham couldn't let her go without a compliment. "That was incredibly clever of you." Brilliant, really. "Why didn't I think of it?" Graham shook his head as his mouth twisted in a wry smile.

Sophie's lips turned up in response, and his gaze drifted there, to her mouth, to soft lips that his own had covered, caressed . . .

He snapped his gaze from her mouth to her eyes and found hers wide with realization. *She knows my thoughts.* He barely knew them, could barely control them, and at this moment in the middle of the night, he didn't much care. He only knew that he was tired and lonely—tired of this life he was condemned to live on his own. Sophie seemed the solution to both, to everything. He had only to take her in his arms and kiss her again.

He took a step forward, and she took one back. "Why didn't you think of it?" She repeated his question, her voice husky with far more than sleep. Candlelight danced in her eyes, mesmerizing Graham. "Probably because you are a *man*." She turned from him and practically fled to her room, closing the door behind her and clicking the lock.

Graham stared at the solid wood barring him from Sophie and thanked God for it, even as disappointment washed over him. He closed his eyes and let out a low groan of frustration—with himself, mostly. Thank goodness she had kept her head. *I should never have come upstairs.* Tonight he would sleep in the east wing even if it meant sleeping on the floor. He needed to stay away from Sophie Claybourne, from her cleverness and charm and the increasing temptation he felt to sweep her into his arms and never let go—his curse be damned.

Twenty-Seven

"Good morning." Sophie entered the dining room sounding especially rested and cheerful, and looking...

Graham blinked several times, attempting to clear his vision, certain he had to be seeing incorrectly. But, no, there it was again, there *she* was in the most hideous garment he'd ever seen.

He lowered the week-old paper he'd been reading, which had arrived yesterday with the Shelbys, and took a moment to wipe his mouth with his napkin as he tried to formulate a tactful way to inquire about her... gown. It was a dirty gray with faint, wide stripes that ran vertically along the skirt and horizontally across the bodice. There was no lace or adornment of any kind, but a high neck that came practically to her chin. All of that was distasteful enough on its own, but the texture of the fabric exponentially increased the horror. It appeared to be a stiff canvas that stood out at odd angles. He had no doubt that were she not in the dress, it would stand up just fine on its own. He had never seen anything so ugly. After a week and a half of wearing borrowed clothing from what could be found here, Sophie now had full access to her trunks and belongings. So why was she clad in this atrocity?

After a few seconds of her standing in front of him, a paper clutched in her hands, Graham finally gave up any hope of tact.

"What are you wearing?" he managed to choke out, reaching for his glass and taking a drink to mask the worst of his revulsion.

"A governess dress." Miss Claybourne held out one side of the stiff garment and turned a slow circle. The side she had held remained stuck outward even after she released the fabric. "I made it myself. The modiste gave this fabric to me absolutely free. The other, finer, more delicate fabrics came wrapped in it when they were shipped from the continent. I have a brown one that matches."

Brown. Heaven help him. She would look like a patterned mud puddle. "She should have paid you to take that fabric *from* her shop," Graham said. "You'll need to change. You'll terrify the children in that."

Sophie's mouth turned down, not in a look of hurt but rather one of irritation. She folded her arms across her middle. "I'll do no such thing—neither terrify the children *nor* change. Besides, they have already seen me in this and paid it not the least attention." She stepped forward and placed a list on the table beside Graham's plate.

"These are the things I require immediately for Ayla and Matthew. There will be more later, of course, but these are what I need to get started."

Graham waved to the chair closest to him. "Please join me for breakfast."

"I've already eaten with the children." She stepped farther back from the table. "A governess does not take her meals with her employer. However, if you were to invite the children to dine with you on occasion, at least, that would be of benefit to them."

Graham scowled, displeased with this assessment, accurate though it was, and her suggestion regarding the children. He'd eaten his meals alone for many years now, but the idea of company this morning had appealed to him, though conversing with her while she wore that dress hurt his eyes.

As for inviting the children to join him . . . He had to make Sophie realize that it was better if he did not encourage their affections, if he distanced himself from all of them as much as possible. A problem, as he continually found himself drawn to Sophie—apparently even when she dressed in wrapping canvas.

"Do you have any questions about the list?" she asked, her gaze fixed on the paper in front of him.

Graham picked it up and began reading. Along with the expected chalk and primers, she'd requested round hoops, balls, a custom-made doll—one with skin tones like Ayla's—wood blocks for building castles, a rocking horse, a rope for jumping, and nets for catching insects.

"That is quite the list of playthings," he remarked, silently adding to it himself. There were a few other things the children might enjoy, including a new toy he'd seen in a shop in London last year.

He'd been so concerned with the children's safety that anything beyond that, aside from the basics of food, clothing, and shelter, had not occurred to him. Until now. Unfortunately, he could not acquire all of these items *immediately*, as she had requested. Had she forgotten that they were miles from any sort of town or city where one might make purchases of this sort? The bridge might be open again, but that did not mean that anything traveled here quickly.

"Children's play is an important part of their learning," Sophie said succinctly, hands clasped in front of her. "And Ayla and Matthew don't have the first notion *how* to play. I believe Ayla must have known at some point—with Katherine as her mother—but the fear and darkness she has lived through has made her forget. The children must be shown that there is good in this world before we can expect them to fully engage their minds for learning. If a child cannot imagine, how is she to believe that letters can be matched with sounds? Why should she desire to know her alphabet and read books—stories of far-off places and adventures?" Sophie shook her head. "She won't. Unless we help her. I believe Ayla is still somewhat in a state of denial and fear. So much has happened to her. We must first lift her from that place of darkness before she can begin to learn to read and write and study languages or mathematics."

"And Matthew?" Graham asked.

"Is blessedly young." Sophie's face blossomed with a smile, which somehow made the hideous dress less so, though only just. "Too young to remember much of his early life, if we are fortunate."

Graham felt disconcerted at the way she kept saying *we*, as if they were a partnership in this endeavor. The less he was involved, the better.

"Do not worry," Sophie continued. "I shall also be teaching mathematics, literature, and geography—to begin with. Oh, and please add a large map to that list." Having declined joining him at the table, she paced back and forth alongside it, her dress making an awkward sort of rustling as she walked. "I should like to show them how very tiny Saint Kitts is on the map in comparison to the entire earth. Perhaps that will help Ayla to know that, similarly, her experiences there were but a tiny part of her whole life. That there is a big, beautiful world with much goodness in it." Sophie stretched her hands wide. "It is up to us to help her discover it."

"That is a lofty goal and most positive outlook." Graham took his last bite of bannock and pushed back from the table, intent on writing a letter to go along with her list and sending a messenger off with it posthaste.

"Is positive not how we should be?" she queried, her hands out, palms upward. "I generally find that the best way to tackle problems."

"Are the children a problem?"

"*No.* Not at all." She shook her head vehemently. "It is only that, thus far in their lives, they have not been allowed to be children. It is this I wish to teach them first."

He nodded in wholehearted agreement. A vague but similar thought had occurred to him before, but he'd never taken the time to ponder it and consider how that might be accomplished. That Sophie *had* pleased him immensely. Thus far she was turning out to be a very fine governess. She did not seem displeased with their arrangement, either, so why did he feel as if he was doing her wrong by it?

Work of any type was below her station, but was looking after two young children not preferable to marrying a man who acted like one? *One known to react poorly, to throw a tantrum or seek revenge, when he does not get what he wants.* At the very least Newsome would have been a nuisance, but likely Sophie would have found him much more than annoying.

Though they had enjoyed nearly two weeks of peace here, Graham had not been lulled into thinking that all was truly well and that Sophie would live happily ever after here. That they would eventually face difficulties from her father or Newsome seemed likely.

But for now she seemed content, even happy interacting with the children—or with Matthew, at least. Once the weather had cleared, Sophie had taken to spending time with them outside, even moving their lessons from the library to the lawn, and Graham had taken to watching them from the windows. Their smiles and laughter lifted his own spirits and gave him renewed hope for a future of peace, if not complete happiness.

It had been a long time since Caerlanwood had hosted any happy events, since there had been laughter here. Since it had been a safe haven. Those weeks of summers here had always been fleeting, and always there had been the underlying threat of his father's unexpected arrival. So it was with Sophie. Eventually her whereabouts might be discovered. And so long as she remained Sophie Claybourne, he could not truly safeguard her. She needed the protection of his name, of the law on their side. *I will have to marry her.* While the idea now appealed to him, it was also still a distressing thought. If he did pledge himself to her, he would also have to leave her.

"Your Grace—Graham?" Sophie questioned, her brow furrowed as she studied him, likely perplexed by his prolonged silence.

"Very well." Graham cleared his throat as he stood, reining his focus back to the children, even as he met her concerned gaze. "I will acquire the items on your list as quickly as possible. In the meantime, may I suggest that if you wish Ayla and Matthew to see the beauty of the world, you change from that dress and *never* wear it again."

Sophie lifted her chin, eyes sparking and an almost smug expression twisting her lips. "I have no intention of changing. It is a practical dress."

"Practically the worst thing I have ever seen," Graham muttered.

Sophie turned from him and moved toward the double doors. "That was the idea."

"What did you just say?" Graham asked, starting after her.

"Nothing." She continued on her way.

"It was not *nothing*." He followed.

Sophie paused at the doors, one hand on the knob as she glanced back at him. "A governess dress such as this is intended to aid the wearer in *remaining* a governess and nothing else.

In other words, it is to dissuade interest from those of the opposite sex, namely the master of the house."

Graham's mouth fell open slightly at her blunt explanation. Of course she would have researched being a governess before hatching her plan to run away and become one, and of course she would have been concerned at keeping any men in the house she worked in at bay, given her previous experience avoiding suitors. But was she concerned now? Here? With him? "You say you made it before you came?"

She nodded. "Plain, ugly, overly modest clothing was advised in Lady Georgiana Stevens's *Guide to Being a Governess*—as a measure to protect one's virtue."

Graham brought a hand to his mouth and coughed. "And are you concerned with that here? With *me*?" There had been that night in the cottage, of course. But he'd only undressed her to keep her from freezing. He'd thought she understood that. And for all his thinking about her day and night, he hadn't touched her again. "After all, it was you who once confessed to kissing me with *wild abandon* and even divulged that you had wished me to kiss you previously."

Her eyes narrowed. "A gentleman would not have brought that up. Besides, you said it was forgotten."

"Perhaps not entirely," he admitted, enjoying the rush of color that had come to her cheeks. He ought not to jest with her or flirt with—or even talk to—her. Especially not remind her of that kiss that continued to haunt him. But after a solid week of only glimpsing Sophie here and there, he could not seem to help himself this morning. He missed her company. And he had most definitely lied when he had told her that their kiss was forgotten. "Besides, I am no—"

"Gentleman. I know." She waved away whatever else he might have said. "Yet I feel perfectly safe here. But as you previously pointed out, now that we are at Caerlanwood, things are different. You are my employer and nothing more."

Her words hit their mark, whether she'd intended to target his heart or not, and he felt wounded by them. "Are we not friends as well?" he queried, playing with fire, with her emotions and his own, as he'd sworn not to. It would be better if they were not friends. But he wished for her friendship all the same.

She bit her lip. "I am uncertain. Before we arrived, I had thought that, but now . . . You are a duke with multiple estates to run. I am the woman you've hired to care for your niece and nephew. It seems that our respective positions do not allow for friendship."

Her hand on the knob visibly tightened, and Graham wondered that she hadn't yanked the door open and fled, to avoid this rather tricky and uncomfortable conversation. But that wasn't Sophie's way. She did not shy from awkward conversations or anything else. *Just one of the many reasons I find her so appealing.*

He sighed and squeezed his eyes shut for several long seconds, wishing fervently that he did not feel so drawn to her and searching for the mental armor to surround himself and keep Sophie safely away.

"If the sight of this dress, of me, pains you so, then it is serving its purpose," she said quietly.

"Aye." Seeing her was painful and getting more so each time, as yearning for what he could never have only seemed to be building. He nodded, opened his eyes, and looked at her briefly, long enough to know that she had misinterpreted his agreement and it hurt her.

"Good day, Your Grace." Her formal tone ended their conversation as much as her exit. She turned from him once more and opened the door.

"Good day." He watched as she left the room, the stiff, striped garment marching along with her, and couldn't help the pull of his lips upward. There was nothing in the way of an ugly gown that was going to stay his attraction. If anything, he admired her all the more for trying. One point for her.

Well done, Sophie.

Twenty-Eight

GRAHAM STOOD AT THE WINDOW in his study, another of his increasingly frequent smiles tugging at the corners of his mouth as he watched the scene outside. Sophie, holding Matthew by one hand and the Shelbys' little boy by the other, moved across the lawn with exaggerated motion, lifting one leg slowly and giving a slight hop before setting it down and following with the other. Ayla walked along beside her. It had taken Graham a minute to realize that Sophie was teaching the children how to skip—or trying to. The toddler was hopeless, but Ayla seemed to be catching on, while Matthew simply jumped up and down while simultaneously attempting to jerk Sophie's arm from her body.

Graham wondered if most children needed to be taught how to skip. From his childhood memories and what limited experience he'd had around young children, it seemed a natural progression of things. First one crawled, then walked, ran, jumped, skipped, and climbed. His niece was expert at running; from a very young age she'd had to run as if her life depended on it—and it had—to meet her master's demands and to stay clear of his hands and the whip they yielded.

Skipping was a happy movement to which these children were unaccustomed. It equated with being carefree, something neither his niece nor his nephew had experienced while living on Saint Kitts. *And since they've been here...* Graham was all too aware of his shortcomings as an uncle and guardian. After their arrival in Scotland, he'd left the children largely to Finella's care, excepting the nights during which he was in residence and had attempted to calm Ayla. *To calm, but not comfort.* Sophie had taken a different approach, and it was yielding results.

As were her other tactics, based on Matthew's laughter that carried to Graham through the open window. He watched as she joined their clasped hands in a circle where they half-skipped, half-hopped around and around until they collapsed on the ground in a pile of flailing limbs and skirts, including the abhorrent brown garment Sophie wore today. Even somber Ayla appeared to be almost smiling. Matthew climbed up into Sophie's lap, and she hugged him tight, ducking her head to rest on top of his.

Something stirred deep in Graham's chest as he watched the exchange. A sudden tightness, then a loosening. A rush of warmth. Before he had a chance to ponder those feelings, the door to his study opened.

"Lord and Lady Fitzgerald have arrived, Your Grace," his butler announced in a rare show of formality and a comical English accent.

"No need to worry about all that nonsense, Boyce," Graham assured him, his gaze still focused on Sophie and the children tumbling about on the grass. "William and Elizabeth know me well enough for who I really am—a reluctant duke who was unfortunate enough to inherit the unwanted title, and became no more a gentleman for it."

"Aye, but the half of ye that's Scottish more'n makes up for that terrible bit o' luck," Boyce said, sounding more like himself. "Come along then, ye lot."

"Perhaps a little less informal than that," Graham grumbled good-naturedly. Like many of Caerlanwood's staff, Boyce was elderly and more an aging resident here than an actual employee. He'd have nowhere to go if Graham replaced him, and Boyce was too stubborn Scottish proud to remain at Caerlanwood if he was not working—in some regard, no matter how unorthodox. He could still open a door, so that counted for something.

"When Sophie and the children return to the house, will you please ask them to come and meet our guests?" Graham wondered if Boyce could remember an instruction that long.

"Aye. Send the wee beasties tae see ye."

The sounds of Boyce's shuffling steps faded away, replaced by the swishing of a lady's skirt and two sets of footsteps across the parquet floor.

"Welcome. Come in." Graham waved them over, his attention still on the lawn below, where Sophie was bent over walking behind Matthew, rolling him sideways down the hill.

"What has you so raptly engaged that you cannot properly greet my wife?" William chided.

"My apologies." Graham tore his gaze from the window, bowed, took Elizabeth's hand, and kissed the back of it.

"Your Grace." She dipped into a curtsy. "Thank you for inviting us to stay."

"Ordering us to come is more like it," William said. "Though I can't think of a more pleasant place to pass the summer—even with the current renovations and restorations underway."

"Your rooms, at least, are ready," Graham assured them, hoping he was correct and Finella had used the extra week afforded them to do all that he had asked. With the rain passed, the men he'd hired before his departure to London had returned, too, and a flurry of repairs and improvements were in progress, both inside and out.

William came to stand beside him and gazed out the window. "I see what had your attention so riveted."

Graham nodded, watching as Matthew reached the bottom of the hill and stood—or tried to. It was apparent he was dizzy. But Sophie was right there to catch him, and he latched onto her with a hug Graham could tell was fierce, even from this distance. *The lad is smitten with her.* But then it seemed he had been from the moment of their introduction, when he had all but knocked Sophie to the ground as he launched himself into her arms. And she had not hesitated to return his affection.

Just as she did not hesitate to return mine. Graham forced the unwanted thought aside and looked at Matthew once more. To anyone watching it would seem that he and Sophie had a bond between them already. "Tell me, William, do you believe in love at first sight?"

William's brows rose as he looked at his wife. "Possibly. Though Elizabeth would tell you that at our first acquaintance, *love* was perhaps the last thing on her mind. Why do you ask?"

"I think you're looking at it," Graham said, his nose practically pressed to the glass as the group outside moved into the shadow of the trees and out of his view.

"I would not have pegged you as a romantic, Your Grace," Elizabeth said, studying him. "But I believe you are right."

"I am not speaking of romance," Graham said. "But pure, unadulterated love. The children—my nephew, in particular—are enamored with Sophie. It happened so quickly with him and appears to go beyond simple adoration."

"There is nothing simple about adoration," Elizabeth said, as a look of warmth passed between her and William.

"Miss Claybourne appears to be equally taken with them," William observed.

Graham nodded, dealing with another unexpected and surprising surge of emotion. He wasn't usually concerned with matters like this and did not give much thought to love or relationships beyond those he had enjoyed as a child. But given what these children had meant to his sister and what they had been through, to see them laughing, to see little Matthew being held and cherished—already—in Sophie's arms, filled him with an almost overwhelming sense of gratitude and relief. Ayla and Matthew were going to be all right. Sophie was going to heal their many wounds.

"It is the most beautiful and extraordinary thing I have ever seen," he said in a voice that sounded strangely choked. He cleared it quickly, then turned from the window and crossed the room to his desk, where a maid had just deposited a tea tray and poured out. He handed a teacup to Elizabeth first and then one to William. "I think this is going to turn out far better than I dared hope."

Elizabeth sat in one of the chairs arranged before his desk. "I think you are right about that as well. You have chosen the perfect mother for your niece and nephew."

"She is not to be their mother," Graham said, suppressing a wince at his swift and almost harsh reply. "Sophie did not wish to marry me, but she was quite amenable to the idea of being the children's governess. In return, I am to provide tutors for her continued education, as well as protection from her father and Lord Newsome."

"Protection?" William set his cup down swiftly. "How do you propose to do that if she is not your wife? Her father could arrive here at any moment, take her away, and force her to marry Lord Newsome. And you would have no recourse but to allow it. Without giving her your name, you have merely postponed the inevitable—that she will be taken from you, and you may be prosecuted by the law for abduction. Not ideal when you are already under scrutiny for that business in Saint Kitts."

Graham sank into the chair behind his desk with a weary sigh. "Remind me why I invited you to come visit?"

Elizabeth laughed. "You cannot blame William for the way he views things. He cannot help himself—always practical and precise to the letter of the law."

"Pity that you inherited a title too," Graham said. "All that schooling for naught when you would have made a fine lawyer."

Grief flashed in William's eyes, and Graham brought a hand to his forehead, regretful of his words. "I am sorry. I did not mean to make light. You *would* have been brilliant in court, but more than that, I know you mourn the loss of your brother."

"As you still mourn your sister," William said soberly. "Do you intend to continue your commitment to her work freeing the slaves on Saint Kitts?"

"I do," Graham said.

"Then those are the exact words you must say—and soon." William set his cup and saucer on the tray and placed his palms on the desk, leaning forward over it. "You *do* realize you will have to marry Miss Claybourne?"

"If, for nothing else, to save her. In bringing her here, you have ruined her reputation beyond that which may be repaired," Elizabeth said, stating the very thought Graham had been trying to dismiss for the past three weeks, from the minute Sophie had stepped into his carriage.

"I am aware that has been added to the list of my many sins." He scowled, hating that this one actually bothered him. Because it involved Sophie. He didn't care what people thought of him, and while he knew Sophie had no concern for Society either, the ramifications for her were still potentially catastrophic. If she returned unwed now, after three weeks with him, she would be utterly shunned. *Which might actually please her.* Regardless, he had to consider her protection. William was correct in that.

"I do not wish to do anything to make Sophie's life more difficult than it has been to this point. If she does not wish to marry, I will not force her to."

"Perhaps Elizabeth can persuade her to that course," William suggested.

"I am confident that I can," Elizabeth said demurely. "I saw the two of you talking the night of the dinner party, and I saw her reaction when you announced your betrothal. Perhaps it was not love at first sight, but there was definitely something between you." Elizabeth directed her attention to Graham. "She was intrigued by you, whether she wished it or not. I daresay that fascination has only grown since I last saw you together."

Graham worked to keep his face impassive as memories of Sophie over the last three weeks accosted him . . . Fascination was too mild a word for what he felt. He wasn't entirely certain Sophie's feelings were reciprocal, but they had been the night they'd spent together in the cottage. *When she'd brought up marriage.*

Elizabeth *would* have success convincing Sophie that they must marry. *And then what?*

"If we marry, I will have to leave," Graham said quietly. His heart hurt just thinking of it. But he couldn't send Sophie away, not when the children were already so attached to her. Caerlanwood was the best place, the safest place, for all of them. He would have to be the one to go.

"Why?" Elizabeth asked. "I can tell you from personal experience that most wives wish to have their husbands around—at least, at the start of their marriage," she added, shooting a playful grin at William. "I have not grown tired of him yet, and we have been wed nearly a year."

"Indeed," Graham said, attempting a smile while inwardly discomfited at the flirting occurring on the other side of his desk.

William took Elizabeth's hand and kissed it.

"You are fortunate in William," Graham said. "You have married a good man who will always treat you well, one who is not laboring under a curse sure to destroy himself and all in his path."

Elizabeth and William both turned to him at the same time.

"You cannot still believe that," William said, his tone uncertain. "Whatever your father told you was not true. It was just one of his many cruelties and an attempt to hurt you. Surely you know that, by now."

Graham shrugged. "What is there to believe, when it is truth? The past three generations of Warwick men have gone mad with it—with anger and violence ruling their lives and ruining all they came in contact with."

Elizabeth's face paled slightly as she glanced at her husband. "I do not know of what you speak, Your Grace."

Graham's mouth twisted. "There is nothing *graceful* about the Warwick dukedom. The men on my father's side are a cursed lot—or they bring the curse upon themselves, acting out in anger and violence, abuse and even murder until, eventually, someone ends their reign of terror—until the next generation comes along. That is me." Graham touched his chest—not a proud gesture, but one of mourning. "I cannot be trusted not to hurt those close to me. I never wished to marry or father children because of this. And now fate has placed before me the ultimate temptation—two beautiful children, and a woman that I have come to care deeply for." His feelings for Sophie strengthened suddenly, as if made all the more certain by the easy admission that rolled off his tongue.

He turned to Elizabeth. "You are not wrong in your assumption that our interest in one another has only increased over the past weeks. Much like Matthew, I adore Sophie. I respect and admire her. In truth, the thought of claiming her as mine is exhilarating. I can think of nothing I should like better. There *is* something between us, and it is only growing. But so, too, is my sickness. I wanted to kill—and could have—the men who tried to harm her on our way here. If she were my wife, I would be terrified to allow her to go anywhere, and that would smother Sophie. I fear it would lead to her unhappiness. To possible arguments. And eventually . . . to violence." Graham shook his head, disgusted with himself already. "It is the legacy I inherited along with the title, and it is one I must end. If I must marry Sophie to give her my name and protect her from others, then I shall have to leave to protect her from myself."

Elizabeth's mouth opened partway, as if she wished to say something but could not find the words.

"I don't believe that of you," William said, his voice low and insistent. "I *won't* believe it. You are not your father. You've got to quit blaming yourself for your mother's suffering. His sins are his own."

"As mine are *my* own," Graham said. "Let us not forget that I have killed two men already."

Twenty-Nine

"Oh, my. We are a mess, aren't we." Sophie stopped the children on the stairs outside. "Shoes off, everyone. And let's brush the sand and grass from our clothes." After playing at the beach, rolling down the hills, and then running across the lawn and through the trees, it seemed not a speck of either of the boys was clean. Ayla looked a little better, having passed on rolling down the hills. But it had been a good day—well worth the mess and the necessity of baths for all this evening. *Thank goodness for the ocean and the beach and the trees and garden.* The grounds of Caerlanwood were truly glorious. It seemed each day that they discovered something new.

Today she had spied a gazebo in the distance, its white columns a stark contrast to the lush green of the surrounding garden. Sophie thought it would be a perfect stage, and her mind was already filtering through possibilities for recitations and simple plays that she and the children might perform there. They would have no audience, but still she thought it might be an enchanting place in which to further engage the children.

The first step to showing them that the world was a beautiful place was to help them experience the beauty of *this* place.

Sand and all. She laughed at the stream flowing from Matthew's overturned shoe. "Goodness, Matthew. Did you leave any sand at the beach for next time?"

"Uh-huh." His curls bobbed as he nodded, and Sophie couldn't help but reach down to ruffle them, sending more grains flying. *Definitely baths tonight.*

Ayla waited by the door, pouting with impatience. She'd been exceptionally obedient to Graham's edict that she stay with Sophie during the days—mostly, Sophie believed, because Ayla wished to keep Matthew safe. *And she does not yet trust me.* Who could blame her when there had been precious few white people in Ayla's life who'd proven trustworthy?

"Come along now," Sophie said, not wishing to try the girl's patience further. "We'll go upstairs and get cleaned up. Then I'll read to you after dinner." She reached for the door handle, as had become her custom to let herself and the children in and out as desired, but it opened before her. Boyce stood on the other side, stiff and straight, almost looking like a real butler.

Sophie's startled gasp nearly morphed into a laugh as Boyce looked down his nose at her, his mouth twitching as if he was trying very hard to appear somber. She mightn't have found his attempt so amusing had she not witnessed him crawling on his hands and knees under a table while playing hide and seek with the boys this morning.

"His Grace would like you and the children to come and meet his guests."

His Grace. "Guests?" Sophie glanced down at her ugly dress, made worse by a large grass stain running across the front of her skirt. Who knew what the back looked like after today's escapades?

"He wishes us to come right *now*?" Who had come to call? Someone important, obviously, as Boyce was pretending to be an actual butler.

He nodded. "Dinna worry yerselves, though. Nice folk. Friends of Graham's."

"Oh." Sophie sighed with relief, then smiled, wondering if any were friends from the Blue Bell Inn, where they had eaten that delicious meal. Everyone there had been so kind and friendly—after they had recovered from the shock that Graham was engaged to an Englishwoman.

Engaged. Was she going to have to pretend again? It had been awkward before, but

now, when she was already fighting the attraction she felt, it would be torture. Her relief of a few minutes before turned to dread as she and the children marched into the hall.

Finella appeared. "Lucy said to fetch her bairn when you returned." She scooped the toddler into her arms. "She also said to tell ye she'd be down at the gatehouse if ye need anything."

Sophie nodded absentmindedly, doubtful that Finella or Lucy or anyone else could help her with what she needed. *Graham.* She frowned, once more displeased with her errant thoughts. What she needed was distance from him, since they were not destined to be more than friendly business partners. *I am safe and unwed. The slaves on Saint Kitts have a better chance at becoming free.* That seemed a highly successful partnership, if ever there was one. So why did she wish for more? Why couldn't her usually logical brain take control of things?

Sophie led the children toward Graham's study—after two weeks in the house, she knew well enough where everything was. Voices from the partially opened door carried to them as they came closer.

"You admit to killing two men?" a rather alarmed-sounding female voice asked.

"I have never denied it," Graham said. "I am possibly the only white man to spend time on that island who has killed *only* two—and those both of the same race as myself." Sarcasm laced his words.

Sophie felt alarmed as well, hearing him speak so casually of ending life.

"Had you not acted that day, would you be here now? Would Ayla and Matthew be here?" a male voice Sophie did not recognize asked insistently.

"Not likely," Graham muttered. "The way he was whipping Ayla might have killed her." His voice was serious now, upset. "When I think of it, I want to shoot him again."

Sophie slowed her steps and glanced at the children. Matthew was distracted, busy running his fingers up and down the wallpaper, following its pattern, but Ayla's head was downcast. Sophie felt suddenly queasy, and her heart ached for Ayla, for the scene Graham's words brought to mind. Sophie stopped walking altogether, wondering if they ought to come back later.

"Your actions were not premeditated murder, but self-defense," the other man said. "Of yourself and a child entrusted to you. You're fortunate to have come away at all, let alone with only a scar to show for it. Had that shovel struck but a little higher, you'd have lost an eye. A little more to the side, and it would have killed you."

A shovel caused his scar? The ghastly image sent a shudder down Sophie's spine.

"It is not the fact that I killed two men that is the problem," Graham said.

"It isn't?" the female voice asked, sounding stronger now.

"*No*," Graham practically shouted. "It is how I feel about it. Sophie asked me that once, and I told her that killing them felt like relief—and it did."

"Of course it did," the other man said. "You were privy to Higgins' many sins, including those against your sister. Any sane man would have wanted him dead."

"But I shouldn't have felt so good about it. Killing him

brought more than relief. It brought satisfaction. I was and still am *glad* that I did it. Does that sound like the emotion of a normal man—a sane one?"

Oh, Graham. Sophie's heart ached at the anguish in his voice.

"Perhaps it might have been, or I might have rationalized that it was," he continued when no one answered. "But those feelings haven't gone away. At the inn at Gretna Green two men tried to hurt Sophie, and it was all I could do not to strangle them right there in front of her. I was so angry—it pulsed through me. A need. An obsession." Graham's voice quieted. "To kill."

"But you didn't hurt anyone there, did you?" the woman asked, her voice timid once more.

"No," Graham choked out. "But I wanted to. Oh, how I wanted to."

Sophie imagined him hunched over his desk, his body sagging with emotion. She had to go to him, had to help. Whoever these people were, they needed to know that he wasn't a bad person. More than that, Graham needed to know.

She hurried to the room, practically running until she burst through the door. Graham and a couple on the other side of his desk all turned to look at her.

"He didn't hurt anyone," Sophie said. "*I* shot one of the intruders, and I smashed a pitcher over the head of another. You," she directed her attention to Graham and softened her voice, "showed remarkable self-control."

She glanced briefly at the others, a gentleman dressed in fine clothing who looked vaguely familiar and the woman seated beside him, hair coiffed perfectly, back straight, gloved hands folded demurely in her lap, resting over the delicate pattern of her gown.

"Pardon me for interrupting—and eavesdropping,"

Sophie said, belatedly realizing she might have only made things worse for Graham. "The door was open, and your voices carried into the hall." She pursed her lips, awaiting certain retribution—if not from Graham, then from his guests. *Could I have made a worse impression?* But what was she to have done? She was the one who'd been there, who had been the recipient of Graham's tender concern—all during which he had supposedly been entertaining murderous thoughts? She couldn't believe it. And even if he had felt that way, he hadn't acted on those feelings.

Behind her Ayla and Matthew shuffled into the room. Matthew latched onto her and held tight, as if sensing the tension. Sophie wished she had someone to hold onto too. *Graham.* Her eyes flitted to his, and she tried to discern if he was upset with her.

"Miss Claybourne." The gentleman rose from his chair and faced her. "It is good to see you again. It seems you have had many adventures since we last met at your home in London."

Graham's voice was haggard when he spoke. "Sophie, may I present Lord and Lady Fitzgerald—William and Elizabeth, my good friends. At my invitation, they have come from England to spend the summer with us."

Sophie dropped into a curtsy, a feat made difficult by both the stiffness of her dress and Matthew, clinging to her with his face buried in her skirt.

"Ayla, Matthew, these are my friends."

Ayla gave the slightest curtsy, though her face remained blank. Matthew peeked out from behind Sophie briefly, sharing one of his heartwarming smiles.

"It's a pleasure to meet you all," Elizabeth said.

"Thank you," Sophie replied, internally cringing at the state she and the children were in as she noted how pretty

Elizabeth was, how English her accent, and how fine her gown. "It is our pleasure, as well. If you would be so kind to excuse us—the children and I have been playing out of doors all day and need to tidy up."

"We shall look forward to becoming better acquainted at dinner," Lord Fitzgerald said.

"I—" Sophie cast a pleading look toward Graham, hoping for his aid explaining her position in the house. But if he caught her plea, it did not register, as he stood much as she had imagined—before his desk, with a jaw set tight with worry.

If the Fitzgeralds were to be here for the summer, it was best they knew the truth. She couldn't possibly pretend engagement that long. "I don't suppose that Graham has explained that I am the children's governess. That arrangement worked out best for all."

"She's mine," Matthew piped up loudly, releasing his grip on her leg enough to swing out to her side for his proclamation.

"Aren't you so fortunate," Elizabeth said, smiling at him.

"As such," Sophie began, "I do not take dinner with—"

"I would like you and the children to join us," Graham said suddenly, more than surprising her with the invitation.

Her gaze shifted to him. "I will see that the children are ready, but I shall take my meal with the staff below stairs."

"And leave me the only female with these two?" Elizabeth said, gesturing to the two men. "Please don't do that to me, Miss Claybourne."

"Please, call me Sophie." She smiled warmly, hoping Elizabeth would not think her even more rude. "Ayla will be there," Sophie said, hopefully. She did not believe that Graham really wished her to join them. Other than yesterday morning, when he had invited her to take breakfast with him—out of a sense of obligation, no doubt—he had never requested her presence for any meal since their arrival.

"Please come," he said quietly, as if he had heard her thoughts.

"Please," Matthew echoed, swinging out from her leg again.

Sophie looked down at him helplessly. He could probably ask her to go to the moon for him, and she'd try. She found him impossible to resist. "Very well," she said at last. "We will all join you."

"Marvelous," Elizabeth exclaimed, clasping her hands together. "It will be the perfect start to our summer."

Thirty

FOR THE FIRST TIME THAT Graham could recall, six people dined at the table at Caerlanwood, with two servants attending throughout the meal. Considering that those servants hadn't performed any sort of similar function in decades, the evening went fairly well. He had taken his place at the head of the table, with William and his wife at his right. On his left, Sophie sat between Ayla and Matthew, the latter of whom required her attention nearly every minute.

With extreme patience Sophie had told him when to use which utensils and how to place his napkin. She'd reminded him not to slurp from his spoon or chew with his mouth open. To Ayla Sophie had given no instruction, only encouraging smiles from time to time, but Graham had noted Ayla observing and following the directives given to her brother.

Grudgingly, he realized that Sophie was right—he ought to have the children dine with him, at least a few times a week, if he wished them to learn how to function in polite society. On Saint Kitts, they had eaten their meals on the floor, in the corner of a dirt hovel. Getting enough to eat had been of primary concern. Silverware had not been available or even a thought.

With Sophie busy attending to the children's needs, Graham had attempted to carry the conversation at the table. It had been somewhat stilted and confined to topics such as the Fitzgeralds' journey from England and the various repairs he was making to the estate. *Safe topics.* He supposed they were all a little on edge from his earlier, foolish confession. But William's insistence—*his irrefutable logic*—that Sophie and Graham must marry had forced the issue that had been going around in his mind. The right thing was to marry her and then leave.

A prospect he found increasingly unpleasant. *Each hour,* if he were being honest with himself. It was no longer the marrying part, but the leaving he found fault with. Because he wanted to be with Sophie.

Finella arrived to take the children up to bed, and the four adults adjourned to the library, as the drawing room was not yet fit for visitors.

Sophie and Elizabeth settled on the sofa, while Graham and William took the chairs near the fireplace.

Graham observed the women's profiles as they talked, Elizabeth chatting animatedly while Sophie listened. She looked much as she had the first night he'd met her. Her ice-blue gown complemented her eyes, and matching teardrop earrings sparkled from her ears, along with the jewels woven through her hair. A few tendrils trailed down from the pile of regal curls, coming to rest near her neck.

Her neck. Graham looked again, closer this time, and noted the red rash creeping up from the neckline of her gown. How had he missed that at dinner? Probably because he'd been doing his best to pay William and Elizabeth the proper attention, hoping to keep them from leaving first thing tomorrow morning, given his outburst this afternoon.

But now . . . "Excuse me," Graham said to William and rose from his chair. He strode nearer the sofa and looked down at Sophie. "What has happened to your neck?"

Sophie brought a hand up and brushed her fingers lightly

across the inflamed skin. "It is nothing. A little reaction to the grass today."

"Did you purposely rub it all over yourself at that particular spot?" Graham asked. Did she take him for that much of a fool? A quick glance at her hands and arms showed a similar rash along parts of her arms and especially at her wrists, but her hands were completely clear. "Does it not seem odd that your hands are unaffected? It would seem those would have had the most contact with the grass."

"Yes. Very odd," Sophie said dismissively, then shrugged and turned her attention back to Elizabeth, who was watching their exchange with rapt attention.

"I think it is not the grass at all," Graham said, "but that infernal dress you were wearing earlier that caused the irritation. It did seem as if it were about to strangle you."

Sophie gave an impatient sigh, then turned toward him. "I would not have to wear such a dress if your eyes did not wander." She bestowed upon him a falsely bright smile that did not come close to reaching her eyes, then turned back to Elizabeth. "As you were saying—"

"My gaze has never wandered anywhere near the vicinity of your neck or anything close thereof," Graham said, affronted by her accusations.

"No?" Sophie queried, her glance up at him suggesting otherwise.

"Never," Graham insisted. William and Elizabeth would think him not only a murderer but lecherous as well. "Perhaps you are confusing me with your former suitor, Viscount Newsome."

Sophie sucked in a breath at the mention of Newsome. Her spine straightened, but she did not look up again.

"The worst *I* have done is to notice your bare feet on occasion."

Elizabeth gave a quiet gasp.

"I apologize for those instances," Graham continued. "I do not wish you to feel that you must dress as an impoverished nun around me. I will redouble my efforts to stay out of your sight so you may wear gowns that are more comfortable and less—canvas." He gave a slight bow, pivoted, and returned to his chair. William gazed at him with sympathy and a tinge of amusement.

"It's not my fault she has attractive ankles," Graham muttered, low enough that only William could hear—or so he thought.

"The ankle is *not* part of the foot," Sophie said. "It is the joint *above* it that connects the leg to the foot. You see," she nodded in Elizabeth's direction, "his eyes did wander."

"I suppose you learned that from your stolen anatomy book," Graham said, giving up all pretense of acting the gentleman. He had only meant to point out that she need not wear that fortress of a gown, and now he was being attacked on all sides.

Sophie's cheeks colored, but her reply was pert. "It was not stolen. I borrowed it from my cousin. And there is nothing wrong with reading a book and increasing one's knowledge. Better to read a book than spend one's time staring at another's ankles and feet."

William's lips twitched at their highly inappropriate conversation, while Elizabeth's eyes had grown so wide Graham feared she might swoon.

He shrugged. "I only looked because you removed your shoes and stockings."

"When you were not around," Sophie declared. "And which you then took from me!" She jumped to her feet, hands fisted at her sides as she glared at him.

William looked between the two of them, then gave an

overexaggerated yawn and stood. "It has been a long day. I do believe Elizabeth and I shall retire early."

"We shall?" Elizabeth said, sounding both surprised and disappointed. "Oh, yes. We shall. We are most tired." Her pretend yawn was even worse than William's, but she stood and took his arm, allowing him to accompany her from the room, though not without several furtive glances back, as if to ascertain that Sophie would be safe.

Of course she would worry, given what I told them today.

"Good night," Sophie said, her voice soft and almost repentant.

"Tomorrow will be better," Graham gave the half promise under his breath.

"Will it?" Sophie asked as the Fitzgeralds disappeared into the hall. Her fists had unclenched into hands that hung limply at her sides. "I am sorry. I should not have said what I did."

"Nor I." Graham ran a hand through his hair. "I simply wish you to take those two dresses and burn them. This rash is just further proof that you ought not to wear them. If you are that worried about my actions, I will make it a point not to be near you at all."

"It isn't you I'm worried about," she said quietly and with an air of defeat.

Graham's head snapped up at this. He met Sophie's gaze—honest, and more vulnerable than he had ever seen. "Certainly you aren't concerned about Paden or Boyce? Neither can hardly see anything anymore, you know." Currently they were the only two manservants employed full time at Caerlanwood.

"I know." Sophie's lips turned up slightly at his attempt at levity. She sighed, then drew in another breath. "It is myself I am afraid of."

Graham's brow arched. "Tell me," he said quietly, then

took her hand and drew her toward the chair William had vacated. He sat in the one across from it and waited.

Sophie's hands clasped and unclasped a time or two in her lap. Then she looked up at him. "Ever since we kissed—"

Graham's heart sped at the mere mention of that night. "Yes," he encouraged.

"Since then, when we have been near each other, particularly at night, and then again the other morning, I have felt—have imagined—that you wished to kiss me again. And so I have begun to yearn for it. Which is both maddening and utter foolishness. I am *not* my romantic sister. I am *not* like the other women my age in the ton who are always pining after men and swooning. Marriage has never been my goal. And neither, most certainly, has kissing been. I promised you it would never happen again, and I wish to keep my word. And so I must stay as far away from you as possible. I supposed that if I looked particularly dreadful that would be easier. *That* is why I have been wearing those awful dresses—to keep myself safe from me, not from you."

She feels this pull as much as I. Graham sat back in his chair, stunned as his heart soared and ached at the same time. He had never meant for this to happen. Never dreamed that it could. *It can't. I cannot let it.*

"First," he began, scrambling to organize his thoughts and take care not to say anything to hurt Sophie. He loved her honesty and the way she always laid everything bare. *The way she trusts me.* "There is nothing in the way of any dress or other garment that could make you look dreadful. You are a beautiful woman, Sophie. And I would have to be blind not to notice."

"Thank you." She looked down at her lap, and Graham guessed that she hated the color flooding her cheeks again.

"Second . . ." He paused, gathering the courage to be

honest himself, all the while wondering if it was wise. "You have not been imagining anything. I *have* wished to kiss you again on those occasions you spoke of. That desire has tormented me day and night."

She looked at him again, her eyes wide and mouth partly open in surprise.

"But like you, I wish to keep my promise that it not happen again. You overheard at least part of my conversation with William and Elizabeth this afternoon. It began because William wondered why you are a governess and not my wife. I attempted to explain to him that it is for your protection."

Graham leaned forward, elbows braced on his knees as he looked at her. "Sophie, if we were to marry I would have no reason not to kiss you or touch you or do any number of other delightful things with you. But it would not be safe—not wise. The men I descend from on my father's side have all had a sickness, a madness that makes them dangerous and violent— even and especially to those they care for. I sense that in myself, and so I vowed not to marry or bear children.

"In accepting responsibility for Ayla and Matthew, I knew I put them at risk, yet I had no choice. I was their only hope for a better life. I have purposely stayed away from them so there will be no attachment between us. If the day comes that I must leave for *their* safety, I do not wish to make it more difficult than it will already be.

"In answering your mother's plea to save you from marriage to Viscount Newsome, I realized it would likely change my vow never to marry. But if we had married right away, we would have gone our separate ways. Now, however, I do not trust that I can do that. If you were mine, I would never want to let you go. I never want to take you from the children now, either. If we marry, it will be I who leaves. And I don't trust myself to have the strength to do that."

"So we cannot ever marry," Sophie said bluntly.

"Not until the time comes that we must for your safety. Your father could force you to return home now. If you were my wife, he could not."

"But then you would leave?" Sophie's voice echoed his own anguish.

He nodded. "I would. To protect you and Ayla and Matthew."

"And you are certain? About this madness? Because I have not seen it in you. Killing the men who were hurting Ayla and trying to hurt you does not seem like a crime or the act of a madman."

"Perhaps not, but as I attempted to explain to William, it is the way I feel about it, as much as or more than my actions, that reveals the madness. I cannot trust myself."

"I see." Sophie stood suddenly, giving Graham the impression that she did not see, did not understand at all.

"It is not something I can avoid or control," he said, attempting to explain again.

"I am sorry for that, Graham. Sorry that I wasn't wrong about there never being true love and happy endings."

THE SOUND OF FOOTSTEPS APPROACHING the library doors jolted Elizabeth from her many thoughts and sent her scrambling. Holding tight to William's hand, she half tiptoed and half ran toward the nearest door. She grabbed the knob, opened the door, and tugged her husband inside after her. And not a second too late. From behind the half-open door she watched as Sophie hurried past.

"That was close," William whispered. "It would serve us right to be caught. When I suggested we go to bed, I didn't mean linger in the hall. I meant to give them privacy to hash out whatever it was going on between them tonight."

Elizabeth shut the door to the room, enveloping them in darkness, save for the shafts of moonlight shining through the tall windows. "What is going on between them is that they've fallen in love with one another. And they aren't going to hash it out, not while His Grace is harboring that absurd notion that he's on his way to becoming a common murderer."

"It may not be as absurd as you think," William said grimly. "Graham's father and his grandfather were the worst sort of men—abusive and cruel. It's difficult to recall a time when Graham wasn't sporting bruises or bandages as a boy."

Elizabeth rubbed her hands up and down her arms, chilled at the thought of a child hurting like that. She looked around the room, ghostly in appearance, with sheets covering much of the furniture. A pianoforte peeked out beneath one in the far corner. This must have been a music room at some point. Or perhaps the sitting room doubled as such. "Didn't you say Graham hated his father?"

"*Hate* seems a mild word, but yes."

"Which makes Graham all the more likely *not* to be like him," Elizabeth insisted. "We have to help him—help them—realize it isn't hopeless. That Graham can overcome this and Sophie can help him."

"I don't know," William said reluctantly. "It's their affair, not ours."

"But you don't really believe him a danger, do you?" Elizabeth persisted. She touched his sleeve, and he turned toward her. "You would not have brought me here had you believed him any sort of threat."

"No," William agreed. "I would not, and I do not believe that Graham will echo the actions of the past. If so, he would have already begun. Yes, he has killed two men, but had he not been in a position of needing to rescue Ayla and Matthew, that never would have happened."

"I knew it." Elizabeth raised up on her toes and kissed him. "You have always been a good judge of character. Now, please. Say that you will help them. Or, at least, allow me to try."

"What do you intend to do?" William asked as his arms encircled her waist.

"I am not certain, exactly," she said. "But as you pointed out earlier, as Graham did just now, they must marry. Her life will be ruined one way or another if they don't. And we've no idea how much time we have, so we must act swiftly. We have to prove to them that love is worth the risk and that Graham is no monster. All before the real ones find her."

Thirty-One

"Twinkle, twinkle..." Sophie prompted, pointing to the gray-striped canvas star fastened to a stick that Matthew held.

"Little star," he shouted, waving the fabric star wildly as he danced about their impromptu stage.

"How I wonder what..." Sophie waited expectantly to see if he would remember the rhyme.

"You are." He grinned, apparently pleased with himself.

She nodded and returned his smile. "Up above the world..."

"So high!" He stood on tiptoes, raising the star as high as it would go.

"Like a diamond..."

"In sky," he finished proudly, unaware that the meter had been slightly off.

No matter. "Well done," Sophie exclaimed, clapping along with Elizabeth, Finella, and Ayla who was sharing one of her rare smiles with her little brother. Matthew was too young to learn to read, but learning rhymes was a step that would help him later—and Ayla now, if she would allow it to.

Sophie closed her volume of *Rhymes for the Nursery* and stood to face the other members of the small audience. "That concludes our recitations today. Thank you for joining us." She stepped aside and held a hand out to Matthew, who bowed gallantly, nearly striking Sophie with the star as he leaned forward. "We hope to have more to share with you soon." In the three and a half weeks since her arrival, Ayla still had not spoken to her—to anyone during that time, and long before, as well. Sophie kept trying new things, hoping something would work to get through to the girl.

"Come, children. It's time to get you cleaned up if you wish to dine with your uncle again tonight." Finella reached a hand out to Matthew and tugged him gently from the stage—the pavilion Sophie had discovered last week.

She had spent the days since then teaching the children nursery rhymes and today had given them the opportunity to perform for a small audience. Only Matthew had wished to do so, and both Graham and William had been too busy overseeing the installation of a new gate to join them. Or so Graham had said. Sophie thought it made a convenient excuse for not spending time with the children. Something she entirely disagreed with. If he wished to avoid her—fine. She had tried to make that easy for both of them since their talk last week when, yet again, she had said more than she ought. But the children were a different matter.

Protecting them. "Hmph," she grumped aloud as she set down her book and bent to gather the edges of the blanket.

"You are displeased," Elizabeth said, taking up the opposite end of the blanket.

"Not with the children," Sophie hurried to assure her. "Of course I wish Ayla would participate—would speak. But I do not fault her for her silence. It will take time for her mind to heal."

"And Matthew is such a darling." Elizabeth stepped toward Sophie, and they joined the edges of the blanket. "I am afraid I shall hold our own little one to that high standard of adorableness now." She ran a hand over her stomach.

"I am certain that he or she shall be perfection," Sophie

said. In the past week, Elizabeth had taken to spending most of her time with Sophie and the children, citing the impending arrival of her own child in the new year and her need for learning about children and how to care for them. Sophie had assured her that she was no expert, but Elizabeth seemed to think otherwise.

"If not about the children, what was your harrumph of dissatisfaction regarding?" Elizabeth pressed.

"It was about Graham declining to join us today. I realize he has much to do here, restoring his estate, but I feel that rebuilding these children is even more important."

"I overheard him telling William that he will feel better about your safety once the fence is mended and a proper gate is in place again," Elizabeth said.

"Be that as it may," Sophie said, feeling only slightly mollified, "they yearn for his attention."

"I thought he did not wish to spend time with them so as to make his inevitable departure from them less painful for all."

Sophie folded the blanket once more before looking up at her new friend. "I don't recall sharing that with you." But perhaps Graham had said as much to both Fitzgeralds.

"You didn't." Elizabeth looked away, but not before a guilty flush crept across her cheeks. "I overheard it."

"You listened to our conversation in the library." Sophie cringed as she recalled all else she and Graham had discussed. *Kissing, among other things.*

"I did," Elizabeth confessed. "Please don't be angry."

"You know I cannot be, not when I did the same to your conversation earlier." Sophie waved a hand dismissively, wishing to move on to another topic before details from either dialogue could be discussed. "It is of no consequence."

"I eavesdropped only because I feared for you, given

what His Grace had told us earlier that day. I did not wish to leave you alone with a madman."

"Graham is not mad." Sophie picked up the book again and stacked it atop the blanket in her arms. "Though I find his avoidance of the children maddening."

"Only his avoidance of the children? What about his neglect of you?"

"That is not neglect, but a mutual understanding. And better for both of us." It did not feel better. "That is the way we must proceed, since he believes himself a danger to me."

"But he is not," Elizabeth said. "I see that now that I have been around him. But our first day here . . . I was not certain, particularly after his impassioned speech about what happened on Saint Kitts."

"He believes the worst of himself." Sophie began walking toward the house, crossing a field of soft grass and wildflowers. The grounds at Caerlanwood came more alive, became more beautiful, each day. She could no longer fault the rain that had made for a late spring, as she was enjoying the fruits of that rain so much. This garden where the gazebo stood had become one of her favorite places.

Elizabeth fell into step beside her. "William has told me of Graham's past now, of the many abuses he suffered at his father's hand, and all that he has had to overcome."

"Does William find him a threat?" Sophie asked, curious what Graham's best friend truly thought of him.

"He does not believe him to be dangerous. And William is a very good judge of character."

"Obviously. As he married you." Sophie smiled at her new friend, grateful for the ready camaraderie Elizabeth had offered. It had eased Sophie's loneliness a bit, though watching Elizabeth and William interacting with one another—their gentle touches and secret looks and the way he was so attentive to her—seemed to bring that loneliness rushing back.

Also maddening. She did not need a man. She did not wish to spend her days pining for one. And, until recently, she used to think it the greatest of blessings to be left alone by all members of the male species.

Elizabeth grinned, linking her arm through Sophie's. "William would not have brought me here if he believed there to be any sort of threat."

"Aside from the bed frame that was not set up properly or the stair that crumbled beneath his foot?" Sophie said.

"Aside from those." Elizabeth winced. "The bed incident, in particular, was a misadventure I shall never forget."

The two laughed, recalling the first night of Elizabeth's stay and the ensuing commotion when the bed had collapsed beneath her and William in the middle of the night.

"Poor Graham," Sophie said. "He needs some better help—some servants who are younger than seventy and can still see."

Elizabeth nodded. Then her laughter quieted, and she turned to Sophie. "He needs a wife. He needs *you*."

Sophie shook her head. "If you heard that conversation, you know he would leave if we married, and that would only make things worse. Caerlanwood is his home. He belongs here. It is his best chance at the healing and happiness he needs as well."

"You are his best chance," Elizabeth said, then forged on. "He cares for you, and I know you love him."

"I do not." Sophie stopped walking and looked sternly at her friend. "What I feel for Graham is most decidedly *not* love. He intrigues me. I enjoy his company. And yes, I even enjoyed it when we kissed." *Too much.* "But none of those things equates love. If anything, he unsettles me. I feel as if I hardly know myself sometimes when I am around him. The things I thought mattered most somehow fade away when he is there, and he is all I can see before me—past, present, and future."

"But that *is* love." Elizabeth turned to face her. "When everything else in your life takes on secondary importance to that one, wonderful person, when you act on his behalf rather than your own—"

"I don't do that," Sophie said. "I did not stop wearing those dresses because he asked it of me, but because they truly were giving me a rash."

"You *do* act on his behalf," Elizabeth insisted. "I knew you loved him the moment you burst into his study and defended him, proclaiming him innocent of any wrongdoing at Gretna Green. You took no thought for what we all might think of you, attired as you were and having been so obviously eavesdropping. You didn't even have a care for the children in that moment and what they might hear. All you knew was that Graham was hurting, and so you acted."

Sophie made no reply. What could she say? She *had* been thinking only of Graham in that moment.

"The way you looked at him showed how much you loved him. It was not dissimilar to the look you gave him after he announced your betrothal—a look filled with utter adoration."

"I did not even know him then," Sophie protested, feeling off balance once again, her mind a dizzying whirlwind centered around one word. *Love.* A strong word, and one not common in her vocabulary, at least not when it came to people. *I love books and learning, not—*

"Do you know what Graham asked us when we first arrived?"

Sophie shook her head. "I'm sure I do not. I don't listen to *every* conversation."

"I wish you would have heard that one," Elizabeth said. "Because he asked if we believed in love at first sight. And he asked as he was watching you playing with the children outside. He was so transfixed by you that he did not even turn to greet us when we entered the room."

"He does not follow conventions," Sophie said, as if that wouldn't have become apparent to Elizabeth by now, after a few days in Graham's company.

"There you go again." Elizabeth smiled kindly. "Standing up for him."

"I wasn't—" But she had been. She hadn't wanted Elizabeth to think poorly of Graham. She had wanted Graham to be understood. *The way I understand him.* "Oh, dear." Sophie hugged the blanket and book to her chest and glanced helplessly at Elizabeth, who nodded.

"You love him."

"I can't," Sophie whispered helplessly. But that he haunted her dreams, and the way she always found herself searching for him throughout her days, hoping for a glimpse of him, dictated that she had *some* feelings for him. *Too many feelings.* Complicated ones. But it couldn't be love, could it? Torie had seemed so happy when she was in love. Jonathan had doted on her, day and night. They had been inseparable.

If Graham acted the same toward me . . .

She probably would have hit him over the head with one of the children's primers. She didn't want to be smothered with affection. *But a kiss once in a while.* Or a good debate like those they had shared in the carriage on the journey here. She would like that. She missed that.

I have felt so lonely. She wished for *his* company. She longed for something other than the opportunity for an education. She missed Graham's friendship. *I miss him. Because I love him?*

"What am I to do?" she asked. It was such an odd thing for her to say. Whenever she wished to learn about something she simply found a book on the subject and read until she understood. *But this . . .* The ending would be worthy of a Shakespeare tragedy. "Even if I did love Graham and convinced him to marry me, he would leave. He'll never stay with me, never allow himself to love me in return so long as he believes he is a danger to me."

"Precisely," Elizabeth said. "You are going to have to change his mind."

"About being a danger to me, or that he cares for me—or both?"

"About his perceived curse. He already loves you," Elizabeth assured her. "Why else would he be willing to marry you?"

"To stop the merger on Saint Kitts," Sophie said, then wondered if Elizabeth even knew about that.

She was already shaking her head. "He would marry you to protect you, even knowing it would mean his leaving Caerlanwood—the place where his only good childhood memories reside. Do those sound like the actions of a man who isn't in love?"

"I don't know," Sophie said. "But they certainly don't sound like the actions of a madman."

"Of course not, because he isn't," Elizabeth said. "And it's up to us—to you, with my help—to convince him of that."

Thirty-Two

"It's good to feel I've a purpose again," Lucy said as she wove strands of golden filigree through Sophie's hair. "I don't mind the other tasks His Grace had set me to, but being a lady's maid—your maid—is what feels right and where I can give my best service."

"You are a genius with hair and fashion," Sophie concurred. "And I missed you dearly when we were apart. But don't you think this is too much?" She studied her reflection in the mirror. The white diaphanous gown with gold embroidery and trim was the most exquisite piece in her wardrobe, and Lucy had already spent over an hour fixing her hair, having unwound a delicate necklace to use as ornamentation among her curls. "It won't seem obvious that I'm trying to catch the duke's attention?"

Lucy shook her head. "He'll be caught, all right." She looped another piece of the golden chain. "But it won't be obvious that you've set out with that purpose. Lady Fitzgerald is wearing her finery as well. And don't forget, there is an additional guest dining with you tonight. With any luck, the duke will think you've set out to impress your new teacher."

"I had forgotten he was coming," Sophie said. That she had done so was even more telling of her uncharacteristic state of mind. The start of her own lessons tomorrow, and the arrival of her teacher of geography, was a momentous occasion—which she had entirely forgotten, focused as she was on one objective, since her conversation with Elizabeth a few days previous. They had devised a plan—of sorts. It began with Sophie being with Graham as much as possible. As such, last night she had arrived in the dining room with the children, contrary to her habit of eating alone or with the staff in the days since she and Graham had last spoken in the library.

"I insisted that Sophie join us tonight," Elizabeth had stated before Graham could even attempt to hide his surprise. "One can only take so much male company, and as Sophie and I only have a few weeks together, I simply must have her to talk with at dinner."

"Of course," Graham had said with hardly a glance in Sophie's direction.

But by the end of the meal, she had become aware that Elizabeth was correct—in one thing, at least. Graham watched her almost constantly when he thought she was not looking.

The actions of a man who is interested in you, Elizabeth had said and also shared with Sophie that Graham, too, took every opportunity to look for her throughout each day, particularly when she was out of doors and Graham could see her from his study windows.

Interest did not equal love, but it perhaps hinted that he missed their friendship as well.

"There, now." Lucy stepped back as her hands fell away from Sophie's hair. "If you don't look just like a princess."

"You're just pleased I'm finally amenable to dressing up and letting you do those fancy hairstyles you're so good at."

"True." Lucy grinned. "I have to confess that when we left London, I was a bit sad to be leaving Miss Olivia and her hair behind. She always appreciated my efforts."

Sophie spun in her chair to face Lucy. "I am sorry that I did not. But tonight . . ." She glanced at her reflection once more. "Tonight they are perfect."

Harold McTavish was a veritable well of information on just about every continent and country on the earth. Not only that, but he was entertaining—charming. *The perfect gentleman*, Graham thought with a scowl. Harold probably never scowled. Instead, it seemed he had that congenial smile plastered permanently across his ruddy face.

Already, Sophie had fallen under his trance, hardly taking her eyes off of him during dinner and plying him with question after question until Graham had jokingly insisted that she save some for her first lesson tomorrow.

She had not found his question amusing. Though Elizabeth had, so much so it sent her into a fit of giggles.

"It's her condition," William had whispered by way of explanation for his wife's hysterics.

They retired to the library—the drawing room still wasn't fit for company. Though the gate and stonework at Caerlanwood's entrance had been repaired. *Far more important than a drawing room.* Graham leaned back in his favorite chair by the fireplace and allowed some of the tension to leave his body. Another week had passed, with no sign of Sophie's father or Newsome. Or anyone related to them. And with a gate and gatekeeper in place now, as well as the new groomsmen and groundskeeper he'd hired, he felt better than he had since taking Sophie from her home.

She is safe. Across the room, Sophie spun the globe with her eyes shut, then stopped it randomly with her finger. She opened her eyes and bent close. "New Guinea."

"Ah, a remarkable place." Harold held up one finger. "Had a close encounter with headhunters . . ."

Harold rambled on while Sophie hung on his every word.

Graham drummed his fingers impatiently on the arm of his chair. He'd known this was a bad idea, but what else was he to have done? He'd promised Sophie lessons in geography. She had been upholding her end of their deal magnificently; he had to uphold his. Besides, he wanted to. He wanted to make her happy.

Sophie clasped her hands together and laughed at something Harold said. *Maybe not this happy. Already.*

"You should tell her about Saint Kitts," William suggested.

Graham turned to him. "Why would I do that?"

"So she'll pay attention to you instead of Harold," Elizabeth chimed in.

"I don't need anyone to pay attention to me." *Least of all Sophie.* The less attention she paid him the better.

"You know," William began, leaning back in his chair and stretching his legs, "that could actually work in your favor." He inclined his head toward the couple bent over the globe, then lowered his voice. "McTavish could marry her, she'd be safe from her father, and you could stay at Caerlanwood. Problems solved." William brushed his hands together.

"Sophie *isn't* a problem," Graham said under his breath. "She's a—my responsibility."

"Exactly what every woman wishes to be thought of," Elizabeth said with a frown. She turned to William. "If I ever hear you referring to me that way—"

"Never, *my love.*" His smile turned seductive, and Graham looked away, disgusted. Though he supposed that, given the choice, he'd rather be around married couples who loved each other and showed it instead of those like his parents, who couldn't stand one another.

I wouldn't behave like either set. Nor would Sophie. It would be apparent to others that they enjoyed each other's company. Her sharp wit would keep him on his toes and entertain their guests, who would think him the luckiest man in the world.

Because I would be. Or Harold would be. It was he hanging on Sophie's every word now, following her movements a little too attentively, standing a little closer to her than he ought.

Graham jumped up from his chair and strode across the room. He stepped between them. "I think it's time I told you more about Saint Kitts."

"Another lovely place," Harold said, stepping nearer to Sophie on the other side of the globe, as if undeterred by Graham's interruption.

"I would like that very much." She looked up, meeting Graham's eyes, her own warm with appreciation. "But I think, perhaps, first I ought to see to the children. They won't go to sleep until I read to them."

"An excellent idea," Graham said. "I'll accompany you and bid them goodnight." William would understand and excuse his abrupt departure. Harold might not, but Graham didn't much care what he thought.

"Of course," she said smoothly, hiding any surprise she might have felt.

Graham bade their guests farewell and escorted Sophie from the room. Out in the hallway, he held his arm out to her. "In case any of the other steps decide to give way."

She placed her hand lightly upon his sleeve. "Thank you."

They started up the stairs in comfortable silence, Graham happy to have snatched her from Harold's grasp. But by the time they reached the second floor, discomfort had taken over in the form of acute awareness of everything about Sophie, from the floral scent surrounding her—*when did she start wearing perfume?*—to the slight brush of her body against his as they climbed the narrow staircase. He darted a glance at her and noticed the décolletage revealed by her low-cut gown. Maybe he should have encouraged her to keep the governess dresses. Little wonder Harold had been so engrossed in their conversation as they bent over the globe.

He's fired. I'll find her another teacher. A blind one. Graham looked quickly away, not wanting to be guilty, himself, of her previous accusations.

They reached the children's bedroom and went inside to find them waiting in their beds, as Sophie had predicted. Matthew beamed at him while Ayla studied him warily, as if he had come to be the bearer of bad news. Graham took a seat at the end of Matthew's bed and attempted to look non-threatening.

"I heard there were stories in here each night, so I've come to listen too."

"We're reading *The Swiss Family Robinson*." Sophie plucked the book from the top of the bureau and scooted one of the two candles closer.

He'd not heard of it. Unless— "Is that some variation of *Robinson Crusoe*?"

Sophie shook her head and smiled at him. "It's much better."

Graham scooted farther back on the bed and leaned against the wall. Sophie settled across from him, on Ayla's bed, opened the book, and began reading.

It did not take him long to see that she was right and to become engrossed in the story of a family salvaging what they could from a shipwreck and making discoveries on the island they had landed upon.

Graham closed his eyes and imagined himself on an island, free of all of the cares and worries of this world. In a way, Caerlanwood was that place for him, though at least some of his troubles followed him here. *Others I have brought.*

Sophie. But he wanted her here, wanted her on the island with him when his ship wrecked. *And it will.* Surely they were headed for disaster.

"Graham." Something soft touched his cheek. He reached for it and found himself grasping Sophie's hand as she stood over him. "You fell asleep." She glanced over her shoulder. "The children did too."

"Sorry," he mumbled but did not release her hand.

She took a few steps back and tugged him up along with her until they stood very close. *Too close.* And also not near enough.

"Thank you," he managed.

"Thank you for joining us tonight," she said. "It was a pleasant surprise. Will you consider making a habit of it? You could even read the story sometimes. It would mean a lot to the children."

"What about you?" he asked, though warnings rang through his mind again. *Don't do this. Don't. Don't.* "Would my being here mean anything to you?"

"You know it would." Their hands still entwined, she looked up at him, so honest, so innocent. So *his* if he wished it.

No. Not if I wish. She was exactly what he wanted, but that didn't matter. Sometimes—every time for him—a man just couldn't have his heart's desire.

Graham loosened his fingers from hers and tried to step back but bumped into the bed. Sophie moved aside, giving him room.

He took two steps toward the door, then stopped, knowing he had to say something before he left, especially after he'd asked her that question and she'd answered so honestly. He faced her once more, intending to tell her that he would come for stories again, just maybe not every night. He couldn't trust himself to be this close to her every day.

But instead, "You smell good tonight," came out of his mouth.

Her brow furrowed. "Do I usually have an unpleasant aroma—aside from the night of the wet-wool riding habit, that is?"

"No." He shook his head, as much to clear it from memories of that night as to express that she'd misunderstood. "What I meant is that whatever perfume you are wearing is pleasant."

She smiled. "It was a gift from Elizabeth."

"That was kind of her, but you should probably *cease* wearing it. You're beautiful enough already without adding anything else to tempt me. Like that gown you're wearing."

"You find fault with my gown?" Sophie arched a brow. "Would you prefer that I return to wearing my governess dresses?"

"Heavens, no," Graham said swiftly, deciding that he was terrible at compliments and at communication altogether. "What you're wearing now suits you much better. It's a beautiful gown—stunning on you."

"Thank you," she said, a lovely blush stealing across her cheeks.

He angled his head, studying her closely. "I just complimented you, just *admired* you, and you didn't run away."

"You're blocking the door," she pointed out.

He stepped aside.

Sophie didn't move. Her expression grew serious, and her lips rubbed together. Her eyes seemed to darken, to invite as they had the fateful night he'd kissed her. "I'm not going to run away."

"You should," he advised. "Isn't that what you've done in the past when a man began to admire you?"

"You're not the first man who has told me I am beautiful," Sophie stated.

"I imagine not," he said. "Considering the many marriage proposals you've had." Her simple statement rankled, though she was only referring to a compliment. He wanted to be her first everything. *And her last.*

"You aren't the first," she repeated. "But you are the first man I ever wished to think that of me, and to tell me." She moved closer to him.

"I don't give compliments lightly," Graham said, barely resisting the urge to take an additional step back. "I spoke the truth—even those ghastly governess dresses could not hide your beauty." His mouth quirked, remembering the way the stiff fabric had poked out at odd angles. "But you're so much *more* than your appearance, Sophie."

"As are you." She took another step closer to the door, to him. "What you've done for these children in bringing them here, what you're trying to do for other children and women and men on Saint Kitts, *that* is beautiful, and it's a reflection of who you truly are. Your soul is beautiful, Graham. I just wish you could see that too."

He shook his head. "You don't know my soul, but it's black and bleak. I do not wish you ever to view it. At all costs, I must not repeat the past. I do admire you, Sophie. For so many reasons." He reached out and brushed his fingers along the side of her face. "But it must be from afar if I am to remain at Caerlanwood."

His hand fell away, and he moved quickly toward the door, pulled it open, and hurried down the hall. *Running away.*

Thirty-Three

"It is most unfortunate that Mr. McTavish was called away so suddenly." Elizabeth set her embroidery aside as Sophie entered the library for her afternoon lesson on law.

"Most," William concurred, sounding amused as he looked up from the book he was reading. "Welcome, Miss Claybourne. Graham tells me that you wish to learn about Parliament and the law, or rather how laws come into effect."

"Yes to all of that." Sophie slid into the seat beside Elizabeth at the large, round table. "Let us hope that I do not frighten you off as quickly as I did Mr. McTavish."

"*You* didn't frighten him off," William said. "That was all Graham. Though, I wasn't the one to share that with you," he added hastily.

Sophie's mouth fell open. "Graham—you mean there wasn't a matter of urgency that called Mr. McTavish away?"

"Oh, it was urgent," William said, a smile in his voice.

"What happened?" Sophie turned to Elizabeth. "Tell me all of it, please."

Elizabeth launched into the story. "Mr. McTavish came into breakfast this morning, and the rest of us—His Grace, William, and I—were already there. His Grace was reading the paper and did not even lower it as he addressed Mr. McTavish."

"'I brought you here as an instructor of geography,'" Elizabeth said in a deep voice Sophie guessed was intended to mimic Graham's. "'*Not* to go exploring.'"

"'Aye. I ken that, Graham,'" William said, joining in and pretending to be McTavish. "'Dinna' fret. I'll stay long enough to satisfy the lassie's thirst for learning of the exotic.'"

"'Ye willna' stay past breakfast,'" Elizabeth said, her attempt at a male Scottish accent rather hilarious. Though Sophie did not laugh. There was nothing amusing about this situation, if Graham had indeed lost his temper with the man.

"'Ye were looking at her last night—looking at places ye ought not and, by so doing, dishonoring her.'"

Though Elizabeth was a poor imitator, Sophie could well imagine that very accusation rolling off of Graham's tongue.

"Graham lowered his paper then," William added. "He looked directly at McTavish—just a look, nothing more. Then McTavish stood, and said, 'I'll bid farewell to the lady and be on my way.'"

Elizabeth jumped in with her line, as if this was a well-rehearsed play. "'Bid her farewell, but if ye so much as look at her even once more, Scotland will be the last country ye ever see.'"

"He didn't look at me—he wouldn't," Sophie said. "He just stared at his shoes and mumbled his apologies about an urgent matter, and then he practically ran out of the house."

"Isn't it wonderful." Elizabeth clasped her hands together and lowered her voice. "His Grace was *jealous*."

Sophie frowned. "I do not wish to play coy games, particularly if they involve another's well-being. I only meant for *Graham* to notice me last night."

"I would consider that a definite success," William said. "He both noticed you *and* noticed Mr. McTavish doing the same." William closed the book.

"But you don't think Graham would have actually hurt him—do you?" Sophie bit her lip, her concern growing.

"That depends," William said. "If McTavish hurt you or

the children, then yes, I absolutely think Graham would have done him bodily harm. As a boy he witnessed his father hurt his mother and sister, and for many years Graham was too young and small to do anything about that. When he finally did fight back, it was too late. His father had already delivered the blow that rendered his mother senseless for the remainder of her life. Graham carries a tremendous amount of guilt because of that."

"And more because of his sister's death," Elizabeth added. "He feels that he failed them both because he did not act soon enough. Isn't that right, William?"

He nodded. "Graham is angry—at himself, more than at his father, which is where the real blame lies. But Graham doesn't see it that way. He feels that it was his duty to protect his family, and he didn't and, therefore, lost them. He feels it is *his* fault that they suffered and that they are gone."

"But it isn't his fault," Sophie exclaimed. "Not at all."

"I know that, and now you do as well—it's a conclusion any rational person would draw. But not Graham. And so he is always trying to make up for that, to atone for what he believes are his sins, to try to alleviate his guilt, and to right what wrongs he can." William sighed and drummed his fingers on top of the closed book.

"At school he was the champion of any underdog. Whenever someone was being bullied, he intervened and stopped it. If there is an elderly woman needing assistance into a building or carriage, if there is a child in the street who looks hungry, Graham will help every time. And when your mother wrote to him, asking him to prevent your marriage to Viscount Newsome, he did not hesitate to put a plan into motion that very day."

"Because he feels responsibility for the slaves on Saint Kitts," Sophie clarified.

William shook his head. "That is also true, but his first thought was that he could not allow a young woman to be forced into a marriage to the viscount, whose own despicable reputation is well earned. Graham had the means and ability to save you, and so he would."

"So he *did*," Elizabeth amended.

Sophie leaned back in her chair, her arms crossed as she pondered their conversation and Graham's actions. "So he has never hurt anyone, aside from the men on Saint Kitts that he—" She couldn't say it. She had before, had questioned him about it directly, but now that she knew him, it seemed impossible to put *Graham* and *killed two men* into the same sentence.

"He hurt plenty of people at school—those who were hurting others younger or smaller than themselves, and those Graham decided needed to be stopped."

"*He* decided?" Sophie repeated.

William nodded. "Therein lies the problem. Graham is a law unto himself. He answers only to his own conscience. It is fortunate that his reputation precedes him, elsewise he likely would have found himself in more trouble by now. Most, when faced with his wrath, as McTavish was this morning, are smart enough to go on their way and leave well enough alone."

"None of that explains why he believes he might hurt the children or me."

"It is because his father told him he would," William said.

"What? His father?" Sophie's brow furrowed. "Explain, please."

"When Graham finally stood up to his father, his father laughed. He pointed at Graham and said something to the effect that he'd known he had it in him, that he carried the family trait—the anger that fuels violence. Graham was his son, and there was no escaping it. Just as Graham's father was the son to his own abusive father before him. For the first time in his life, Graham's father told him that he was proud of him and the man he was becoming."

"He must have felt sick." Sophie felt ill just imagining such a scene.

"I'm sure he did. When he told me of it the next semester at school, it was with great concern—and even fear. He didn't want to turn into his father, but neither could he deny the feelings of anger that seemed, at times, to overwhelm him."

Elizabeth touched Sophie's arm. "You can help him overcome this. I know you can."

"I wish I had your confidence," Sophie said, unsettled by this latest information. She felt ill prepared for this challenge, and there was no text she might read on how to proceed. Helping the children was proving challenging enough, and she already felt as if she was maneuvering in the dark without a candle. Even so, she enjoyed that challenge and cared for the children greatly already—something she had not anticipated when considering taking on the role of a governess.

But the role of a wife . . . It was so much more. So permanent. The Sophie of a month ago would have been miles away already, fleeing that possibility. Instead she was purposely here and focused on how to get Graham to marry her. *And stay.* Even with his flaws, she wanted him. She wanted to help him. To love him and ease the burdens he carried.

Take care with his heart. She would take the greatest care. If she just knew where to begin, what to say and what to do. Wearing perfume and attractive gowns wasn't the answer. Neither was telling him that which was obvious to her and the Fitzgeralds—that Graham was not his father and was not on the path to becoming him either. *I have to show him.*

But how? And which thing was she to help him with first? Convincing Graham that they would make a good match and that he would be an excellent father to the children and that they needed him? Convincing him that she trusted him, that he would never hurt them? Or convincing him that she loved him?

I do love him. Sophie pressed a hand to her heart, amazed at the leap of joy and the ache of sorrow she felt simultaneously. *Love is complicated.* Complex. A challenge she'd never anticipated. The revelation that she loved Graham was still so new. Part of her wanted nothing so much as to sit on the beach, stare at the water, and savor these new feelings. But there was no time for savoring. She needed Graham to marry her so they would both be safe—she from her father and his plans, and Graham from any legal trouble he might face from abducting her. And then she needed him to stay. If he wouldn't, then they could not marry. She would rather risk having to do her father's bidding than driving Graham away from Caerlanwood.

That is *love.* It was just as Elizabeth had described—a willingness, a need and desire, to put the other person first. Surely Graham felt the same for her, if he was willing to marry her and then go. But how was she to convince him of the depth of their feelings when she'd barely realized them herself? How was she to convince him to stay?

"Are you all right?" Elizabeth's hand still rested on Sophie's arm, and she looked at her with concern.

"Yes," Sophie said. "Or rather I will be, once I've sorted this all out."

"Time," William said. "Though, unfortunately, we do not have much. Each day you wait to marry is another that brings your father closer. The only reason he hasn't found you yet is because Caerlanwood isn't known to many. Graham's father was so furious and ashamed at having to take a Scottish bride and Scottish money to fix his estates that he kept this place a secret. Graham continued that tradition because Caerlanwood is sacred to him."

"You know of it," Sophie said.

William nodded. "Graham and I have been friends for almost twenty years. We were neighbors in England first and then went to school together. Even then, it wasn't too many years ago that he finally told me about this place and invited me to stay."

Elizabeth turned to Sophie. "That he brought you here so soon would seem to be the greatest of compliments."

"He trusts you." William pushed his book aside. "But he won't trust me if I don't teach you something. Shall we begin our lesson, ladies?"

"Yes, of course," Sophie said, having nearly forgotten the reason for her visit to the library. She'd been so eager for her lessons, but now, somehow, they didn't seem as important. Her causes, her dreams and goals, while still enticing, held less appeal than they once had.

Instead of spending her time fretting and fuming over her inability to attend university, and scheming about ways to get there, she'd become consumed with helping Ayla and Matthew. The greatest learning she'd wished for lately was that which would tell her how to help them to heal. She wished the same for Graham. She wanted knowledge so she could help those she loved.

Geography and law were not likely to aid in that endeavor. She wasn't certain what *would* help. Her mind was still spinning with all that William and Elizabeth had just shared. She needed time to herself to think about everything.

"You two may begin." Elizabeth picked up her embroidery once more. "I shall endeavor not to fall asleep while listening."

William shook his head at his wife, his mouth twisted in a wry smile. "Let it be noted that husband and wife do not have to share all the same interests in order to be happily married."

"Just the *important* ones." Elizabeth glanced up at him beneath her lashes with a look meant only for him.

Sophie cringed inwardly. *Heaven help me if I ever behave like that.* Then again, maybe she already had, *kissing Graham with wild abandon.* There were moments, like this one, when she really wished to return to the woman she had been before meeting him.

"Parliament," she said, clearing her throat. Best to get this lesson over with so she could have at least a little time alone with her thoughts before readying the children for dinner.

"The British Parliament is the finest example of government to be found in the world," William began. "It is legislative supremacy, an example to numerous other countries and the envy of many."

"Especially those recently independent United States across the Atlantic?" Sophie asked.

Elizabeth giggled. "This may be more entertaining than I had realized."

William scoffed. "The colonies don't know how good they had it."

"Yet they seem to be doing fairly well on their own," Sophie mused.

"Time will tell. But we are not speaking of them today, but of the fine system employed here. Our parliament is bicameral, meaning—"

"It is made up of the House of Lords and the House of Commons. But there is also the sovereign, so really there are three parts, often described as the King-in-Parliament."

"Who is teaching this lesson?" William queried. "And are you certain that you actually need it?"

"I'm sorry." Sophie pressed her lips together. "I will listen. It is the process of drafting a law and getting it through Parliament that interests me. I already understand the governing bodies and their purposes. It is the intricacies of getting a new law formulated and voted upon that I am not entirely certain of."

William leaned forward, elbows on the table. "Why do you wish to learn this?"

"Because she wishes to change the laws regarding women's rights. Is that correct, Sophie?" Graham strode into the room, his expression serious instead of amused, as William's was.

"Yes," she admitted, wondering how he had known that. She had never said anything to him, to anyone, about this particular aspiration and dream. "Why should women not have the right to attend university? Why can we not be lawyers and politicians—or anything else we wish? Why can we not vote?"

"Splendid questions." Elizabeth clapped lopsidedly, as her embroidery was still in her hands. "Though I wouldn't have the faintest idea what to vote for."

"You would if you were given the same opportunities as your husband," Sophie argued. "If you were permitted to go to the same places, allowed to learn and gain knowledge as he is."

"Well said." Graham took the last chair at the table, the one on the other side of Sophie. He looked to William. "What have you taught her so far?"

"Nothing," William said. "She appears to know it all already. I realize you meant to save her from Newsome, but I suspect she could have taken him in hand."

"Do not mention his name," Graham said. "We do our best to keep the rats out at Caerlanwood."

Sophie cast him a grateful smile, then ceased abruptly, wondering if she looked like Elizabeth had a few minutes earlier.

"Go on," Graham encouraged, nodding at William.

"Perhaps you can teach me something as well, though I have little faith in the processes of the government, as it has never seemed to serve me."

"A fine pair of students you are," William muttered. "One cheeky and one a dunce."

Elizabeth giggled again.

"Sophie is not impertinent; she is brilliant," Graham said.

A flush of pleasure washed over Sophie at his praise, a compliment that meant far more than those he had given last night. He was the first man, the only man, to ever suggest that she was intelligent and to appreciate such.

"And remember that you are lodging at the dunce's house," Graham added. "It would be unfortunate were you to find yourself removed prematurely, as was Mr. McTavish."

"You admit to it, then," Sophie cried, turning on him. "The poor man would not even look at me this morning as he apologized for having to leave so abruptly—*on a matter of great urgency.*"

"Oh, it was most urgent," Graham assured her. "And most prudent of him not to risk looking at you again."

Sophie turned away from Graham with a huff. "I rather liked him and had been eager to hear about more of his travels. Please do go on." She waved a hand at William. "At this rate, and with our new pupil, it is doubtful we will cover much at all today."

Grinning broadly, William continued. "As is customary each parliamentary session, a bill is introduced pro forma in both houses. In the House of Lords it is the Select Vestries Bill, while in the House of Commons it is the Outlawries Bill. Neither ever becomes a law."

"They are merely ceremonial," Sophie said. "To demonstrate that each house has the power to debate independently of the Crown."

"That is correct," William said.

"A waste of time," Graham muttered. "But that is what the pompous fools do best."

"I cannot entirely disagree," William said. "After those bills are introduced, each house debates the content of the Speech from the Throne. This takes several days, and each house sends a response. Then, and only then, may legislative business commence, the last of which is the introduction of new measures or bills to be debated and voted upon."

Graham turned to Sophie. "Someone within Parliament would need to champion your cause. That individual, likely having joined forces with campaigners and men of influence outside of Parliament, would then present the bill."

"But the chances of getting anything substantial and revolutionary—and the changes you suggest are both—would be extremely small." William's mouth turned down in apology.

"I would say that the chance for that kind of change is non-existent." Graham placed a hand on Sophie's. "I know from experience. I have been working, with many others, on various forms of a bill to get slavery abolished. It is a cause I fear I may take to my grave without seeing it come to fruition."

"And because of Graham's reputation, he is unable to aid this cause publicly," William added.

"I would do more harm than good."

And with my reputation now . . . "So would I," Sophie concluded what they had not said directly. She had not cared that she was ruined, had not considered this ramification, that she would be listened to or taken seriously even less than she had been before. If such was possible. No one had ever considered her opinions—until Graham.

He squeezed her hand gently, and she looked over at him, grateful for the warmth of his touch and how the simple gesture lessened the sting of his words.

She sighed in resignation. "I am sorry for your own frustrations—for you. Your cause is far greater than mine."

"Yours is not without merit too." He turned her hand over, so it was palm up, and entwined their fingers. "Given what you have accomplished already in the little time that you have been here—Ayla waking for shorter and shorter periods each night, Matthew growing and maturing before my eyes—I've no doubt that were women allowed in Parliament much more would be accomplished in less time."

"Thank you," Sophie said, touched by his praise. "What you and William said is largely what I expected to hear, and it does not dissuade me—at least, not much. Perhaps what I really need to learn is who, within Parliament, might be persuaded to take up such a cause—presented by another, more upstanding female of course." She turned to Elizabeth.

"Me?" Elizabeth shook her head. "Oh no. I wouldn't have the faintest idea where to begin such a petition."

"But your husband would," Sophie said.

William chuckled. "I like your thinking. You may have just found a way to get Elizabeth to take an interest in my ramblings."

"Don't count on it, darling."

"Combined with my other powers of persuasion . . ." William winked at her.

"I've work to do," Graham announced abruptly. He released Sophie's hand and pushed back from the table. "I'll see you all at dinner." He strode from the room, leaving William and Elizabeth gaping.

"What just happened?" she asked. "He was here, and the two of you were—"

"That is Graham's way." Sophie stared at her hand that, a minute earlier, had been snug and warm in his. "It is wearying," she confessed. "All this back and forth. It is as if he is at war with himself, and I am caught in the crossfire."

"I'm so sorry," Elizabeth said.

"He *is* at war with himself," William said. "Because what he wants goes against everything he has ever believed he deserves. He is fighting his feelings with all he's got, while still indulging them a little as well."

Sophie smiled wistfully. "He is like Matthew at the beach this morning. He kept teasing the tide, walking out farther and farther to dip his toe in, then turning to run so the wave could not get any more of him wet."

"His Grace is afraid of getting wet," Elizabeth concluded. "He is afraid of drowning." She clasped her hands together. "If only he realized how lovely it is to drown in love."

"He's not afraid for himself." William's voice was somber. "He is afraid for Sophie. He does not want to pull her under with him."

Thirty-Four

GRAHAM POKED HIS HEAD INTO the nursery, or what had become such under Sophie's care. Though she'd had little to work with in the month she had been here, she had nonetheless transformed the room from bare to bright. Lines of seashells and polished rocks lined the windowsill and bureau top—treasures that Sophie and the children had collected during their almost daily walks on the beach.

The letters of the alphabet, with illustrations to go with each, which Sophie had drawn on the backs of his discarded correspondence, had been tacked up on the wall. Pretty pillowcases, sewn by Shelby and embroidered by Elizabeth with Ayla's and Matthew's names, adorned each bed, and piles of books were scattered around the room. It wasn't much, but the difference was still palpable. More than anything, it was Sophie's presence that had made such a profound difference.

My turn. Though it was midsummer, Graham felt a bit like Father Christmas as he snuck into the room with his crate filled with treasures. It was Sophie who had requested these items, or most of them, anyway, but he had seen to it that they arrived. It wasn't just the funds that he had spent; it had taken some sleuthing to acquire everything on her list. Ayla's doll would have been the most difficult of all to obtain, had it not been for his previous experience sending her an identical one, years earlier at his sister's request. That he'd recalled the dollmaker in Glasgow seemed like an achievement in and of itself.

Finding the nursery empty, Graham opened the door the rest of the way and went inside. Sophie and the children spent most of their mornings out of doors, either at the beach or at the gazebo, or simply out exploring the grounds and garden. Glimpsing them traipsing about here or there throughout the day always had a peculiar effect on him, a tightening in his chest followed by a comforting warmth that flooded his entire being. They were here. They were safe. His family, of sorts.

Not mine. He told himself that again as he set the crate down and began placing the items around the room. Primers and picture books at the end of each bed, a stack of blocks on the floor between. Slates and chalk beside the books, hoops and butterfly nets against the wall. He placed the kaleidoscopes he'd seen in London last year on the bureau and laid pretty ribbons in every color on the washstand near Ayla's brush. He rested the doll against her pillow.

Graham picked up the empty crate and stood back to admire his work. The room looked even better. The rocking horse he'd commissioned from a woodworker in town, and that ought to be completed soon. But this was a good start. He would have liked to see the children's reactions when they discovered their new treasures, but it was better that he didn't, that he faded into the background of their lives. Sophie may have lured him into reading with the children each night, but as soon as they had finished *The Swiss Family Robinson* he would return that task, that pleasure—reading to the children was definitely not a task—to Sophie.

"Uncle Graham!" the small, but mighty force that was Matthew knocked into the back of his legs.

"Whoa, there!" Graham set the crate down and picked up Matthew instead. The boy had grown friendly with him over their nights of reading together. Sophie had handed the book off to him after the first night he'd joined them. Then, a few days later, she'd made some excuse and left the room, leaving him alone with Ayla and Matthew. So he'd kept reading. That night and the one after and the one after that. Sophie rarely joined them anymore. Graham guessed it was her way of giving him time alone with the children. *Without her there to distract me.* It was a kindness he appreciated. Particularly when Matthew crawled out of bed and into his lap each night.

The first time it happened, Graham had sat almost frozen with fear. Who was he to be holding this little boy close? He shouldn't even be around the children by himself. Yet here he was, with Matthew snuggling into the crook of his arm. When the lad had tilted his head back, looking up at him expectantly, it had been all Graham could do to read a single word. Despite their differences in skin color, Matthew *looked* like his mother. His face was the same oval, his eyes the same, his smile similar. Looking at him was a little like looking at Katherine. How Graham had loved her. And now he loved her child.

And Sophie for helping me to make this connection. Though he warred within himself over this, as well. Being close to the children couldn't be wise, but as it was with Sophie, he couldn't seem to help himself anymore. The pain of separation would be that much greater when it came, but for now . . .

"What this?" Matthew wiggled out of Graham's arms and trundled toward the blocks.

"Those are for you," Graham said, grinning as Matthew squatted near the blocks and immediately began stacking them. Graham turned to look behind him and saw Ayla lingering in the doorway. "Come in," he beckoned. "There are things for you too. Sophie asked me to get them for you." Ayla had probably figured that out already, or she would have. In the months they'd lived under his roof before Sophie came,

Graham hadn't given the children any toys, anything at all beyond the basics of food, shelter, and clothing. But Sophie had seen the need for playthings at once.

Ayla stepped into the room, her eyes focused on her bed. She took another step forward, then another and another, each faster than the previous, until she reached her pillow and the doll resting there. She reached out to touch the porcelain face nearly the shade of her own. The doll's pink gown was long-sleeved and adorned with lace and frills. Brown hands peeked out at the bottom of each sleeve, and black shoes had been painted at the bottom of her pointed feet.

Ayla turned back to Graham, her eyes large and filled with more expression than he'd seen since the Christmas he had visited Katherine.

He nodded to Ayla. "She's yours. You can pick her up."

Ayla did, hesitantly at first. Then she clutched the doll to her chest, her head bent to the bonnet and curly hair.

"I see too," Matthew said, getting up from the floor, his hands held out toward the doll.

Graham shook his head. "That is Ayla's. She may show it to you later, but let her enjoy it a while first."

"Ayla sad." Matthew tugged on her arm, and Graham realized she was trembling.

He hurried over, took her by the shoulders, and gently turned her around to face him. Sobs shook her little body.

"What is it, Ayla? What's wrong?" He crouched on the ground to better see her face.

Instead of telling him, she cried louder, then— "Mama."

The word sounded foreign to Graham's ears. When had he last heard her speak, aside from her screaming during night terrors? He hadn't. She'd not said a word since he'd found her on Saint Kitts. Not to him, anyway. But Sophie had heard this same pleading cry from her in the night.

Graham reached out and pulled Ayla into his arms. "Your mama is gone," he said. "But I'm here, and so is your brother." He extended one arm, encircling Matthew as well. "I loved your mother too, and we're doing what she wished. We're together, and you're both safe."

"SOPHIE, YOU'RE NOT GOING TO believe—you have to see—" Lucy stood in the doorway to the library, trying to catch her breath.

"Are you unwell?" Sophie rose from the table, where she'd been having another lesson with William. They had moved on to court procedures now, as he'd already shared with her everything he knew about getting a bill drafted into a new law.

Sophie crossed the room to Lucy, who leaned forward, one hand braced on the wall.

"I am well enough." Lucy's hand went to her growing abdomen. "Just encumbered is all. But you must go. Upstairs. Quickly now." She took Sophie's hand and pulled her toward the hall.

"Is something wrong?" Elizabeth called, half-risen from the table herself.

"Do you require assistance?" William asked.

Lucy shook her head. "No. Miss Sophie needs to see something, is all. She'll return shortly."

Sophie allowed Lucy to pull her down the hall toward the stairs.

"Quiet-like, go up to the nursery."

"Why—"

"Just go." Lucy released her hand and made a shooing motion toward the staircase.

"Very well." Shaking her head, Sophie started up the spiral steps, careful where she placed her foot, lest any others give way. Graham had spoken of repairing the stairs, but first he was focused on the outside projects while the summer weather was good.

At the top of the stairs, she heard voices, one male, speaking in a soothing whisper, and another—a child's, high-pitched and quavering.

"Mama. Mama."

Ayla? Sophie hurried down the hall, stopping just short of the nursery when she heard Graham's voice.

"I miss her too. She was my sister, and I loved her *very* much." He sounded hoarse, as if he were having trouble speaking. "If I could, Ayla, I would trade places with her and have her be here with you."

Sophie peeked into the room. Graham knelt in the middle of the floor, facing away from her, one arm around Ayla and the other around Matthew. Matthew clung to Graham's neck and rested his head against his shoulder, but Ayla stood stiffly in his embrace, tears spilling from her eyes as her slender form shook with sobs and she repeated the only word Sophie had ever heard her say.

"Mama. Mama."

What had caused this sudden outburst? In the middle of the day, with Ayla fully awake and aware—Sophie had just left the children in the kitchen a short while ago, and nothing had been amiss then.

"*Mama—*"

Sophie's heart constricted, and she longed to offer comfort. *But Graham is—* That was as it should be. *He* was their guardian. *Not I.* He was still whispering soothing words and holding the children close. The tender scene brought a spark of joy, even amidst Ayla's sorrow.

Sophie stepped back from the doorway and tiptoed to her

room. She let herself in and closed the door softly behind her, then leaned against it, her heart alternately aching and soaring with hope. *Graham is comforting them. They are letting him be close to them. He is* choosing *to be close to them.* It was everything she'd hoped to accomplish when she'd turned reading to them at night over to him.

Surely he saw how much they needed him now. How could he not, with Matthew's so-eagerly-given love? And Ayla . . .

She spoke *to him.* Even if it was only one word. It was the middle of the day, not the night. Her mind was finally acknowledging the past and facing her pain. This could only be good. It could be the beginning of a positive future for Graham and the children.

And me? She wanted to be included in that circle too.

Sophie wrapped her arms tightly around herself, but the gesture brought no comfort. No longer was she the girl who wished to be left alone to her own devices and her books. Those were still lovely, but this—this caring for the children and Graham. *Loving them.* It was so much better than anything she had imagined for herself. *So much more.* She still relished learning, but helping others to learn, to heal, to feel loved . . . Those elicited feelings that she'd never dreamed of before. These were feelings she wanted to experience every day for the rest of her life.

The yearning she felt stole her breath. No one had ever told her love would feel this way, that it would overwhelm her so much she wanted to weep.

With joy—if she could belong to the three people in the other room. With sorrow if she could not. If her presence meant that Graham would leave, then she couldn't stay. The children needed him. Matthew, at least, was his flesh and blood. Graham needed them, whether he realized that fully yet or not.

Sophie wanted him to need her desperately, too, but maybe love didn't always work that way. Maybe some, like her mother, never knew it. Some experienced it for a little while, as Torie had. And maybe there were some like herself, who could give it but couldn't have it in return.

Thirty-Five

AT TEN-THIRTY, SOPHIE WALKED quietly down the hall to the nursery. She had stayed in her room all afternoon and evening, pleading a headache and missing dinner with Graham and the children, Elizabeth and William.

Her head had ached a little, though it was mostly her heart that felt heavy. She'd stayed away on purpose, wanting to give more time to Graham and the children to continue whatever bond had begun being forged between them in the nursery this afternoon. But she couldn't deny that she'd missed being included, and she couldn't go to sleep without at least checking on the children first.

"Ayla wasna weeping at dinner," Finella had reported to Sophie when she'd brought a tray up to her earlier. "But Matthew looked as if he might, when Graham told him he'd best eat every one of his peas, no matter that he'd already smashed them all."

Sophie smiled again at the image that evoked—Graham being fatherly, and Matthew poking around at the vegetable he found more entertaining to play with than to eat. Hearing that Graham had stepped in to direct the children in her absence was further evidence that she'd made the right decision in staying away this evening. But going forward, what was she to do? She was still their governess, and besides that, she enjoyed spending time with Ayla and Matthew, teaching them of the wonders of this world and what they must know to succeed in it, while allowing them the freedom to do and be all that she'd wished as a child.

The door to the nursery stood partially ajar, and Sophie pushed it the rest of the way open, leaving the candlelit hall for the darker room. Moonlight filtered through the partially open shutters, illuminating the space enough for her to walk safely—though there were a few more obstacles on the floor than had been there previously. A block tower reached nearly to the top of Matthew's mattress, and a pile of books and a new slate were stacked neatly near each bed.

At last. With their primers here, they would be able to begin real lessons. But they needn't change their habit of spending most of their days out of doors. Learning could be just as effective, if not more so, while sitting on a grassy slope or beneath a shady tree.

She tucked Matthew in first, pulling the quilt up to his chin, then leaning over to kiss his forehead. A half smile formed on his mouth as she did, and Sophie's lips curved upward in response. *Dear Matthew.* Had there ever been a sweeter child? He gave of his love freely, holding nothing back. *If only adults could do the same.* Her smile faded as she thought of Graham's stiff and distant behavior the past weeks. If it had always been that way between them, it would have been easier to bear. Instead, her mind recalled their many discussions, his considerate behavior toward her on their journey, the way he had cared for her after the scare at the inn, the way he had saved her life during the storm, and then . . . *That kiss.* And the almost ones since then, when the pull between them had weakened his resolve to forget that the first kiss had ever happened.

What if she had given in again? Would they be engaged in this same awkward dance of avoidance? Or would they be married and falling even more in love with each other?

Or would Graham have left her and the children already? Sophie squeezed her eyes shut briefly, attempting again to banish his image and the cherished memories from her mind. She was a governess. He was her employer. Even though her feelings on the matter of marriage had done an about-face since their first meeting, she feared he could never be hers. Not if marrying Graham meant depriving the sleeping child before her of an uncle he very much needed in his life.

Sophie took Matthew's limp hand in her own, then brought it to her cheek and held it there a moment, bolstering her resolve to do the right thing.

She turned to Ayla next and discovered her curled on her side, a doll clutched tightly to her chest. Graham had done well. The doll was nearly as beautiful as her owner. Sophie smoothed Ayla's coverlet, then lightly brushed the hair away from her forehead. Perhaps someday she would kiss her goodnight too, but not yet. Not until Ayla was ready.

"You're very good with them."

Sophie startled at the whisper, then looked over her shoulder at Graham, seated in the rocking chair in the corner of the room behind the door.

"You frightened me," she whispered back, a hand pressed to her pounding heart. Had he been there the entire time?

"My apologies. I only meant to sit here until they both slept. I was concerned about Ayla. She had a difficult day."

Was that censure in his tone? *Does he think* I *caused her midday crying spell?* "You are good with the children too," Sophie said cautiously, her tone softer as she returned his compliment. Seeing this new side of him, his tender concern for the children, had banished any last doubts she might have had about his character or the likelihood that he could ever hurt any of them.

"It does not come as naturally to me as it does to you. You'll make a fine mother someday."

But not to your children? And if not to his, then to no one's. She might be inexperienced in matters of the heart and hadn't initially recognized her own feelings as love, but she knew enough to realize that Graham was an exceptional man, and she would never find another to fill his place in her heart. Sorrow swept through her. She turned from the bed to face him. "I never imagined myself being a mother." She shrugged. "When one does not plan to marry, then the possibility of motherhood is nonexistent. But I am enjoying this time with Ayla and Matthew very much. I did not know I would feel this way, that I would care for them so much and so quickly." *That I would care for you even more.*

"They missed you tonight," Graham said with a slight hint of reprimand.

Ah. There it was. He was displeased by her absence this evening. "I wasn't feeling well." She hadn't been physically ill, but her emotions had been a mess. They still felt confused, especially when he was just a few feet away. What she wanted seemed so simple. Yet if she pursued it, pursued him, it would make things so complicated, and none of them would have a happy ending. But if she stayed away, at least Graham and the children might have one.

She walked toward the door. The best course of action was to return to her room as quickly as possible. "I'm sorry to have intruded. I'll bid you goodnight." She hurried into the hall, but he stood and followed, catching her sleeve as he had before in this very spot. At least this time she was still in her dress instead of in a nightgown.

"What is troubling you?" he asked, releasing her but still standing far too close.

You. Them. Us.

Standing so near to him, her senses flared to life, and she drew in a deep breath, attempting to calm them, but only made matters worse as she inhaled the scent that was so specifically his. He smelled as he always did now, as he had since their arrival, and possibly before that—a heady mixture of the pine forest mixed with the sea. It suited him perfectly. He was tall and strong as the trees, mighty and unwavering in his convictions—at times maddeningly so. But there was also a wild, unpredictable side to him, similar to the ocean and the storms it brought to their doorstep. At times the waves roared, and Graham did too. Other times, like today with Ayla, he was as gentle as a breeze. Always, no matter whether he was being as immovable as Caerlanwood's forest or as alluring as the ocean, Sophie felt drawn to him.

She closed her eyes, unable to look up and meet his— afraid of what she would see there. Rejection and dismissal would wound, but if his eyes held desire tonight they would surely lure her in. She'd withstood the need and yearning she'd seen in their depths before, but her will was only so strong. She couldn't let it slip, not if her giving in would lead to his leaving.

He belongs here. Not I. Ayla and Matthew need him. More than they need me. Those same circular thoughts had been churning through her mind and heart all afternoon, and she couldn't see a way to break free of their grasp and what they meant for her. She and Graham could not be together. Not unless, or until, his belief in who he was changed.

Sophie opened her eyes but did not look up at him. "I simply wanted to check on the children, as I do each night. Now that I know you are doing the same, I'll not—"

"You'll not give them attention because I am, is that it?"

Not exactly. "You are their guardian, and I am so pleased to see you finally acting like one. I do not wish to encroach upon your time together."

"*Finally?*" His voice came out as a low growl. "Did I not retrieve them from Saint Kitts, though doing so and seeing the place where my sister died nearly tore my heart out—not to mention nearly cost me my life?"

"So you admit it *was* self-defense," Sophie exclaimed, jubilant at having finally gotten such a confession from him, though that had not been her intent tonight.

He ignored her. "I brought them here. I have clothed and fed and sheltered them. I have provided for their every need."

"Except perhaps the greatest one," she argued. "Until recently, you have withheld your love. Much as you are withholding it from *me*." She pressed her traitorous lips together. Would she never learn to hold her tongue? She dared a glance up at his face and saw that it had hardened, his features turned to stone, save for the scar across his cheek, which seemed to have developed a tick.

A very angry, frustrated tick. Well, good. She was frustrated too.

"I am doing what I deem best for all of us." His eyes glittered, and his tone was harsh, reprimanding. "You know I cannot give you what you want. It will only lead to more hurt, for all parties involved, including the two children in there."

Sophie shook her head, though she had come to that very conclusion herself this afternoon. "I don't know that, and you don't either. One action does not have to lead to the other." *To your leaving.* "If you could just see the person you really are, who is nothing like his father. Did he ever comfort you as you did Ayla today? Did he read to you, bring you presents?"

"You don't understand. You didn't know him. You don't know me."

"I know enough," Sophie insisted. "But until you know yourself, that doesn't matter. So *I* will be certain to stay away, because you *cannot* leave Ayla and Matthew." Sophie turned from him. "Good night, Your Grace."

"I've asked you repeatedly *not* to call me that here." He spoke so loudly she feared he would wake the children.

"You are a duke, and it's *just* a title." She spoke without turning around.

"Not here, I'm not." Fury edged his words.

So much passion over a word. Because it linked him with his father, and especially here, he did not want the reminder, did not wish to be that man.

"It is difficult to remember when you are acting like a stuffy, old duke. Nevertheless, goodnight, *Graham.*" Why was she pushing him so? To see if he really would harm her? *No.* She knew he wouldn't. To prove to *him* that he wouldn't. No matter how angry she made him.

"Do not ignore the children again," he warned.

"I wasn't—"

"You were. Do not avoid them on my account. I will continue to read to them at night. You are to be with them during the day. I am too busy to be bothered with nursery games then."

"You weren't today," Sophie snapped, finally facing him once more. "And it isn't about games. *This* is not a game." She gestured between them. "And the two children in there"—she pointed to the door behind him—"*need* you. They want to be with you, to feel your hand on their shoulders, to see approval in your eyes, to hear from your lips that they are safe and loved and cherished."

If possible, Graham's features grew more rigid, and Sophie didn't see so much as a spark of recognition or softening in his eyes.

"My behavior today was an exception. See that yours was as well." He turned on his heel and strode in the opposite direction.

Sophie threw her head back in frustration, then marched off to her room. He would never harm her, but right about now giving *him* a good shake or even a swift punch would feel so very good.

Thirty-Six

WILLIAM STROLLED LEISURELY TOWARD THE small table on the back terrace where Graham sat, staring out toward the ocean. "I don't recall you being such an avid tea drinker prior to this summer."

"Tea? Is that what this is?" Graham glanced at the cup in his hand and aimlessly swished the liquid in it.

William took the seat across from him and peered into the teapot. "It's certainly not that fine Scottish whisky you have locked away in the cabinet."

Bemused, Graham arched a brow. "Was that perhaps the real reason you agreed so readily to stay the summer? You are welcome to it anytime. Just ask Finella. She has the key."

"I will." William took a scone from the plate beside the teapot. "The last time I was here, you didn't have the whisky locked up."

Graham shrugged, and his mood darkened slightly. "That was before I met Sophie."

"She drives you to drink already?" William *tsk*ed. "I've been told that usually doesn't occur until a few years into marriage. Personally, I've not encountered that phenomenon yet."

"*She* doesn't," Graham said. "Or it's not her fault, at least. It's fighting the attraction I feel for her and knowing all the while that she *could* be mine if circumstances were different."

William leaned forward, elbows braced on the small table. "Don't you mean that she *will* be yours? Shortly? Elizabeth and I are here only another two and a half weeks—and that's already extending our visit."

Graham looked out over the low wall to the cove below as the sound of laughter carried up to him. He stood and walked closer to the edge, a smile tugging at the corners of his mouth as he watched a barefoot and blindfolded Sophie stagger about the beach with her hands outstretched in front of her, trying to locate the children. Ayla stood silently in the same spot just a few feet to her right, but Matthew zig-zagged back and forth in front of and around her, laughing and then shrieking every time she drew close to catching her prey.

"Well?"

Graham turned to find William standing beside him. "Well, what?"

"When are you going to marry her?"

Graham released a weary sigh, and his delight at watching Sophie and the children seeped away. "I'm not going to."

"We discussed this." William placed a hand on his shoulder and turned Graham to face him when he would have looked away. "Let's review why you *must* marry Miss Claybourne." William dropped his hand, instead holding it in front of him to count off reasons. "One. She is not safe from Newsome until she bears your name. Two. You have compromised her reputation beyond repair. No decent man will ever have her. Three. London Society will shun her. Four, she'll never find another job as a governess with such a reputation. In other words—you have taken away any chance for her to have any kind of a happy future—outside of being with you, that is."

"At the moment she does not appear too distraught about any of those possibilities." Graham watched as Sophie finally caught Matthew and, laughing, swung him around, dragging his bare feet through the surf, eliciting shrieks of delight from the lad. Graham wrestled with an all-too-familiar and increasingly frequent desire to join them, to shed his boots, squish his own toes into the sand, and sweep Sophie off her feet and into his arms.

He gave a slight shake of his head and turned away, attempting to banish both the pleasant images and the desire from his mind. Neither left easily.

Sophie and the children looked so happy together. *So free.* Matthew and Ayla from a life of slavery, and Sophie from the society that was so filled with rules and regulations her spirit had been tied down, bound with invisible, yet also stifling restraints.

He didn't think she would care about never having another suitor of her father's choosing or even of her own from the ton. Nor would she be concerned about London Society casting her away, but he felt great remorse that she would never be able to be a governess again beyond this time with Matthew and Ayla. Nor would she be a mother, and that seemed the greatest loss.

He would see to it that she was supported financially the rest of her days, so that wasn't a concern. But since coming here she had blossomed before his eyes. Before, she had been strong-willed, independent, intelligent. Unabashedly honest, amusing, and rather good with a pistol. She was still all of those things, but she was also loving. Of her many talents and strengths that he had observed, it was her way with children that he saw as her greatest gift. She was marvelous with them, and it was a pity that she would never have a brood of her own.

"If she is not distraught," William said, intruding into his thoughts, "it is because she believes she has a future here with you."

Graham shook his head as he thought of their last meeting in the upstairs hall. "I don't think so. She knows my mind on the matter of marriage, and she has resigned herself to it as well."

"Which is what?"

"That I cannot marry her—is that not obvious?" Graham returned to the table and poured another unsatisfactory cup of tea. Whisky would have been far more preferable.

"The only thing obvious is that you are growing increasingly agitated and miserable with each passing day, and that this most idiotic decision you have arrived at requires your housekeeper to lock away the liquor so you don't drown your sorrows in a cup—or ten—each eve." William shook his head, as if disgusted.

"It is only precautionary." Graham sipped his tea, then set the cup in its saucer with more force than necessary. "The drink never did anything good for my father, and I don't trust myself to leave it alone right now. It *is* hard—especially at night—not to think of Sophie or give in to the temptation to claim her."

"You make it sound as if marrying her would be a sin," William grumbled. "While the things you may imagine doing with her might seem sinful, I promise that if you have spoken vows before God and are joined in a bond of love, intimacy with your wife is akin to a holy sacrament itself."

Graham held up a hand. "I do not wish to hear of the way you came to be approaching fatherhood. That would be enough for me to seek out Finella and the key to the cabinet, and she is under strict instructions *not* to give it to me, no matter what tale or excuse I ply her with."

"So that is it, then?" William threw up his hands. "You've truly no intention of marrying Sophie."

"None," Graham admitted, finally speaking out loud the

conclusion he had been coming to over the past several days. "I had considered it, had thought perhaps . . . But, no. Living this way, seeing her every day and wanting her as I do, is a burden—one at times I can barely live with. But I *can* live with it."

"It's your life to spend miserably," William said. "So much the more if the lady's father ever ventures here and finds that you have not married her. It would be within his rights to prosecute you for abduction. If he doesn't shoot you first."

"What is one more added to my already-long list of crimes?" Graham asked, unconcerned. This wasn't about him. It was about doing what was right. "I am trying to avoid more mistakes—the worst one of all. My decision has everything to do with what is best for Sophie and the children."

"Does she think it best that you do not marry?" William asked. "Have you asked or considered her feelings on the matter?"

"Considering either of our feelings is a luxury neither of us can afford. What we want is not pertinent. I can live with wanting her," Graham repeated. "But what I could not live with is hurting Sophie or the children. *That* would destroy me."

"Why do you believe you would hurt her or them if you married?" William pressed. "You are around her every day now and living in a state of constant vexation, as you deny yourself what you most want. If you are able to keep your temper in check in these circumstances, it would seem certain that it would be even easier to keep when you give yourself into a loving relationship."

"But if I did err—" Graham ran a hand through his hair in frustration. Why could no one understand the dilemma he faced? "If she was bound to me by the law and I hurt her—"

"You won't," William said, his voice sure and confident. "I have known you well over a dozen years, and never have you hurt another who was undeserving. Indeed, during that time you have prevented many others from being hurt. You have been a champion of right over wrong."

"As I am trying most earnestly to be now."

"I will leave you to it, then." William walked past the table and toward the door, then turned back suddenly. "If you are so certain you will never marry her, then why have you devoted so much time of late to repairing Caerlanwood's chapel?"

"For my tenants, of course," Graham answered, somewhat truthfully. "With the road washed out half the year and several without the means to travel regularly to Annan even when the bridge is passable, I deemed it a priority to repair the chapel and find the clergy to man it again."

"I see." William gave a curt nod.

"And if need be"—Graham admitted, not meeting William's eye—"if Sophie's safety were threatened we would have the means to marry quickly. If it came to that, I would still give her my name for protection. And then I would leave to protect her from me."

William's eyes narrowed, and he pursed his lips in a thoughtful manner. "Well, then. I shall have to amend my prayers in a way I never before considered. I shall pray for a visit from the viscount."

Thirty-Seven

"OH!" THE STARTLED GASP FROM Ayla had Sophie turned around faster than she would have believed possible, especially considering that she was kneeling on wet sand.

"What is it, Ayla? Did something hurt you?" Sophie's eyes quickly roamed over the girl, searching for injury.

Ayla shook her head—a positive addition to their still-limited communication. In the week since she'd received her doll and cried in Graham's arms, she had begun answering Sophie's queries with nods or shakes of her head. It was a vast improvement over her former blank stares.

She shook her head now and pointed to what had been one of three Egyptian pyramids. Sophie followed her gaze. Half of the third pyramid was gone, caught up in the tide that had swept in.

"Oh, dear," Sophie said sympathetically. "They were so lovely. You did a splendid job smoothing the sand to make such perfect angles."

"I'll fix it," Matthew offered, waving a spoon that Sophie had borrowed from the kitchen.

Ayla shook her head and held a hand out to block him from coming any closer.

"Let's finish yours instead." Sophie took Matthew's hand holding the spoon and guided him back toward a very leaning Tower of Pisa, which also looked to have been affected by the most recent wave.

Sophie glanced at the sky to confirm what she'd only just realized. The rising tide meant they had stayed out here *much* longer than she'd intended. Mornings were usually reserved for the beach or other outdoor play, but this afternoon during their geography lesson—she had decided to teach them the subject until such time as another tutor could be located for herself—she'd had what she believed to be a most brilliant idea. After a brief stop in the kitchen, she had ushered the children back down to the beach for a more interactive approach to their topic of study.

They'd all been having a glorious time of it too. *Until now. Drat the tide.* And the setting sun. At the least, they might be late for dinner. At worst, they'd already missed it. The long daylight hours of summer, combined with her enthusiasm for today's lesson, had made her completely forget everything else. It returned in a rush now, as she imagined the look of displeasure on Graham's face if they did not show up for the evening meal.

"Come, children. I'm sorry, but we'd best go in." Sophie stood, then bent to retrieve the various utensils and cups and bowls she had persuaded the kitchen staff to lend to her today.

"Mine's not done," Matthew complained, his bottom lip jutting forward in a pout.

"Nor is mine," Sophie said ruefully. If only they were not expected up at the house, she'd be more than happy to stay here as long as the children desired. Though the rising tide and the path from the sea gate to the beach could be dangerous at night. That was reason enough to conclude their lesson.

"Ayla, will you collect our book, please?" Sophie nodded to the copy of *Architectural Wonders of the World* that she had discovered in Caerlanwood's library. She'd found it a fascinating volume but had decided that the children would learn about the magnificent places and wonders more thoroughly if given the opportunity to replicate them. The wet, sandy beach had been the perfect medium, and it had been a delightful afternoon.

Let's hope the tide is the only thing to spoil it. Graham's mood the past week had been sourer than ever, something she would not have believed possible before, and she hoped their tardiness would not cause him to be irritable with the children.

Ayla picked up the book, and with a last look at their creations and a promise to the children that they could build them all again another day, Sophie led them up the path, Matthew's hand clutched tight in her free one. He bounced and bobbed and skipped along beside her, his complaint of a moment before already forgotten. He was like that more and more with each passing day—easygoing and carefree, just as a little boy ought to be, and it made Sophie's heart swell with joy.

She glanced back at Ayla, a step behind them. She, too, seemed to be healing, though much more slowly than her brother. *I can be patient.* Sophie smiled encouragingly at her. "Thank you for carrying our book, Ayla."

They reached the sea gate without incident and stepped through it to the stone stairway that led up to Caerlanwood. Sophie closed the gate behind them, then turned to look up at the house. Light blazed from the main tower, including the dining room, leaving little doubt that they were late for the evening meal—and in no state to be eating anything without first washing up and changing their clothes.

She trudged up the long flight of stairs, her damp skirt bunched in the same hand that held Matthew's. "I fear we are late to dinner and will miss taking it with your uncle this evening. We'll go directly to the nursery. Then I'll return to speak to him long enough to make our apologies." No need for the children to see Graham upset with her. *Maybe he won't be.* The past week it seemed he'd been going out of his way to avoid her more than ever. "I'm sure Finella will bring trays up to us."

"I'm hungry *now*," Matthew said.

Me too. "I'm certain we won't have to wait long," Sophie assured him. "And while we are waiting, we can wash."

They reached the back garden and walked through a second gate, then made their way to the house. It was quiet—not unusual, as the workers had gone home for the night, and the staff was probably down in the kitchen enjoying their own meal.

She avoided the hallway that led to the dining room, instead heading straight for the nursery. They ascended the stairs, meeting a surprised Lucy at the top.

"Miss Sophie, thank goodness," she exclaimed. "His Grace has all the servants searching the house for you and the children."

"I lost track of time," Sophie said. She tugged Matthew forward, placing his hand in Lucy's. "We are none of us fit to dine downstairs tonight. I'll go and make my apologies, if you'd be so kind as to take the children to the nursery."

"Of course," Lucy said. "You'll be wanting baths, I suppose?" Her nose scrunched as she looked over both the children and Sophie.

"Yes, please. I'll be along shortly," Sophie said to the children. "And I'll ask Finella to bring food," she added upon seeing Matthew's pout.

Leaving them in Lucy's care, she hurried back down the stairs, made a quick stop in the kitchen to request trays for the children and herself, then walked somewhat more slowly to the dining room. She paused in front of the double doors, then grasped the handles, pulled them open, and entered, stopping just inside.

The room's vast size, as tall as it was wide, had never intimidated her before, nor had the man sitting at the head of the long table. *Not much, anyway.* Tonight he sat stiff and unmoving, his fork midair as he stared at her, his brows drawn together sharply and his lips pinched. Such a cold look seemed in contrast to the room itself, warm now with tapestries restored to the walls, candles blazing in the sconces, and the glow of the fire in the hearth.

William and Elizabeth both looked up briefly. Elizabeth's eyes widened, and Sophie thought that William's twinkled with amusement, but she could not be certain from this distance. Both quickly returned their attention to their meals, as if nothing was amiss. As if Sophie were not three-quarters of an hour late, not at all dressed for dinner, and missing the two children who were supposed to be accompanying her.

As was usual, there were no servants in the hall—loitering about and eavesdropping when they could be useful elsewhere, as Graham would say—so she held her hands behind her to catch the heavy doors as they closed once more, sealing her inside to face her fate.

"Where are the children?" Graham's voice was deceptively quiet, but his scowl spoke volumes about his mood. He was more than displeased. Perhaps her tardiness and the children's absence had caused him embarrassment in front of his guests. Not that William or Elizabeth were the sort to care. And it wasn't as if she hadn't embarrassed herself and Graham in front of them already, on the very day they had arrived.

"I sent Ayla and Matthew to bathe and asked Finella to serve them dinner in the nursery." Sophie drew in a deep breath, pushed off the doors, and straightened to her full height, somewhat helpful in restoring her confidence, as the others were all seated. "I apologize for their absence. We became so engrossed in our lesson that time got away from us."

Elizabeth sent her an encouraging smile. "You must have been having a lovely time together."

"We were." Sophie returned her smile, grateful for the support.

"I thought their lessons took place in the mornings," Graham said, his fork finally lowering.

"In the absence of my own teacher"—*Your fault*, she might have said, still disappointed over having lost the most interesting Mr. McTavish—"I have added geography to their curriculum. Today we were learning about the great architectural feats of the world. Instead of simply viewing the pictures in a book, I thought that recreating such wonders would be more enjoyable for them." For herself too, if truth be told.

"How was that accomplished?" William asked, sounding genuinely interested.

"Indeed," Graham said. "Am I to find hammer and nails strewn about the house or more stones missing from the walls?"

"Of course not. Matthew has not dislodged any additional stone from the upstairs hall *or* the nursery." None that Sophie knew of, anyway. She'd had a hard time scolding him when Graham had pointed out his discovery—that Matthew had been prying loose stones from their places and hiding his treasures found at the beach behind them. It was exactly the sort of thing she would have done as a child—or as an adult. But she also understood the importance of maintaining a roof over their heads and the walls around them. So she had encouraged Matthew to search for loose floorboards instead.

"Well?" Graham asked, obviously still expecting more of an explanation.

Sophie moved a few steps closer to the table. The food smelled heavenly, and she *was* hungry. "We found the wet sand at the cove perfect for creating our masterpieces. You should have seen them. First we built a length of the Great Wall of China, and then Ayla made the pyramids. Matthew and I worked together on—"

"You were at the beach? Just now? *Alone?*" His brows pulled together again, giving his entire face a pinched expression.

"I take the children down to the beach every day." He knew this.

"At midmorning," he said. "When I can keep watch over you. *Not* in the evening when the sun is setting, the tide is high, and no one knows your whereabouts."

He watches over us? She wasn't certain how she felt about that. It seemed both chivalrous—and stifling.

Sophie folded her arms across her middle, then wished she hadn't when a handful of sand cascaded to the floor. She took another step forward, attempting to cover it. "I was not aware that I had to inform anyone of our every location each day. Though in this case, I did. I told the kitchen staff that we would be borrowing some utensils and cups to use at the beach."

"I would never have allowed that."

"I'll wash them thoroughly before I return them," she said, exasperated. Was he truly so stuffy about some old dishes? It wasn't as if she'd borrowed the silver. Though, maybe there was no silver at Caerlanwood. She'd never seen anything remotely fancy on the table, and if Graham's father had pilfered the paintings and furnishings from the castle, no doubt he'd taken everything else of value as well, especially that which was obvious, like the silver. Maybe that was why Graham was so sensitive about a few spoons and cups?

"It's only a few dishes," William said in a tone Sophie suspected was meant to placate. "As a child, did you never play at the same, building castles with the sand?"

"I don't care about anything you borrow from the kitchen or anywhere else," Graham said, still looking at Sophie. "Anything at Caerlanwood is at your disposal. It's you and the children being at the cove so late that I disapprove of. Have you any idea what might have happened?"

"We might have gotten wet." Sophie held up the hem of her skirt, darker than the rest of the garment for having been doused by the tide.

"You or the children might have been caught up in the tide and drowned, or slipped on the rocks and fallen on your way up to the gate. Someone might have rowed into the cove and taken you."

"*Or* I might fall and break my ankle on the crumbling stairs while heading to my room tonight," Sophie said, barely managing not to roll her eyes.

"I'll fix the stairs soon. There are other things"—Graham cast a warning look at William—"other places at Caerlanwood that demanded my attention first."

"I'm not truly worried about the stairs." Sophie gentled her voice. "And I *was* watching the children closely. I care about them, too, but I'm not going to keep them under lock and key. They are children and need to be outside exploring. We are all here now and all quite safe. But I shall make certain not to take them to the beach again in the evening, if that is your preference."

"It is." Graham brought a hand to his head as if it pained him. "Not that you'll need to go there at all, as it appears you brought half of it back with you. I can only imagine what the children look like."

"I suggest you don't imagine that," Sophie said with a grimace. She was rather the worst for keeping them clean. They were frequently messy after a few hours in her care. *Exactly how children should be.*

"I won't." Graham waved a hand in her direction. "You are more than my imagination can handle."

She cringed inwardly, guessing her appearance was worse

than she had feared, but why should he be so cross about a little sand? Heaven knew enough other things were a bit off or a little odd around here, and he seemed to tolerate those just fine. More importantly, *she* tolerated them. Not once had she complained about the odd state of Caerlanwood at their arrival. True, it was slowly improving, but it was still not up to a standard most of the ton would consider acceptable.

Perhaps that is why I like it so much.

But it was obvious tonight that Graham was not in a mood to tolerate her.

"Given that my appearance offends you, I'll bid you all goodnight and take my leave." Sophie gave a slight curtsy, then grimaced as more sand drifted to the floor. "My apologies, again, for the children missing dinner. I'm certain they will be more than eager to see you for stories later."

"We are almost finished reading *The Swiss Family Robinson*," Graham said, not arguing, as she had hoped he might, against her statement that her presence offended him.

"I know," Sophie replied. "Matthew recounts to me each morning all that you read to him the night before. I'll leave it up to you which book you select to read to them next."

"There will not be a next," Graham said. "You may read them a volume of your choice when we have finished this one."

"No. I can't." She shook her head, scattering sand in either direction. She'd hastily brushed the front of her skirt before entering the house but hadn't thought to check her hair. "The children look forward to that time with *you*. They are subjected to my company for much of the day. Nighttime is your special time with them, and it is important. You are their family and will be a part of their lives forever, whereas I am— a governess is—only temporary."

"Have you plans to go elsewhere?" Graham asked, his tone sharp and accusing.

Elizabeth shot him a disapproving look. "Of course she hasn't. Isn't that right, Sophie?"

"I had not thought to leave anytime soon." Sophie's gaze slid to Graham. "Unless that is what you wish." *Does he?* "But someday I shall have to. They won't be children forever, and . . ." *And what?* What place did she have here other than as their governess? *None.* That was abundantly clear, more so of late. The thought filled her with sorrow. She'd been at Caerlanwood less than two months, and already it felt more like home than any other place had. She loved the quiet of the woods and the roar of the ocean. She loved Matthew and Ayla.

Her gaze swung to Graham. *And you.* Tears stung her eyes at the idea of leaving this magical place and each of them behind. But that was her inevitable future—sooner rather than later if this tension between them continued. Ayla, at least, had become aware of it. On more than one occasion Sophie had noticed the girl watching her and Graham, no doubt paying close attention to their mannerisms and words. The feelings of discontent between them would not help Ayla's recovery. She needed stability and a warm, safe home, free of strife.

"I do not wish for you to leave," Graham said quietly. "Seeing as the children are not here at present, perhaps we ought to discuss what the future holds."

"I believe we shall retire early this evening." Elizabeth set her napkin aside and turned to her husband.

"Yes," William agreed, rising hastily. "It has been a long day." He pulled his wife's chair out.

Elizabeth squeezed Sophie's hand as they walked past, and William winked. Sophie waited until they had left the room before looking at Graham and speaking again. "I believe they misunderstood your intention."

He nodded. "I am sure of it. William is concerned for your safety and my vulnerability—with regards to the law—if we do not marry. He does not wish to see you returned to your father or see me imprisoned for abduction."

"I would tell anyone who accused you of such that I came here of my own free will. Indeed, it was I who first invaded *your* carriage."

"So you did," Graham said, an almost wistful smile briefly interrupting his serious expression.

"Do you wish I had not?" Sophie queried. "Have I caused no end of complications for you? Would you prefer that we had never met?"

"No." His swift answer and vehement shake of his head reassured her somewhat. "What you have done for the children . . . You have my undying gratitude. I shall be forever in your debt."

"There is no debt. If there were, it would be mine, for your saving me from marriage to Lord Newsome."

"It is what any honorable man would have done." Graham stood, leaned forward, and pulled out the chair closest to him. "Will you sit with me?"

Sophie came forward with as much grace as possible—not easy in a partially wet and somewhat muddy skirt—and allowed him to seat her. Across the room the doors had closed, leaving them alone together.

Sophie started to smooth her skirt, then thought the better of it, fearing she'd only dislodge more sand. Instead, she clasped her hands in front of her, attempting to silence her suddenly growling stomach. The aromas of roast meat and fresh bread wafted from the table, reminding her that it had been hours since she'd eaten. It was good that she'd requested a tray to be brought to her room as well.

"You should eat." A corner of Graham's mouth quirked. "It's obvious that you are hungry."

"I will wait," Sophie said. "I should return to the nursery

as soon as possible to help with Ayla and Matthew. It is my fault they are in need of baths again."

"No doubt." Another quirk. "Lucy can look after them. It's not as if she's spending a great deal of time tending to you, of late." His gaze drifted over her lazily, and the smile that had been threatening grew. "Are you certain you did not roll in the sand today? It seems to be covering you head"—he reached out and brushed some from her loose curls—"to toe." He looked pointedly at the floor by her chair and the small pile of sand there.

Sophie sighed. There was no point in being embarrassed. He had seen her at her worst before, the night they were caught in the storm, and he had teased her then, too. Tonight she supposed she was deserving of such censure.

"Matthew was rather clumsy with his digging and distribution of sand. I'm afraid much landed on me instead of its intended target. At one point, he tripped when he was carrying a full pail, and I was right in his path." She touched the top of her head and grimaced as she felt the grains there. A quick glance down at her shirtwaist confirmed that it was no longer white, but streaked with dirt—probably the result of leaning over their model of the Taj Mahal as she'd carved the Yamuna River beside it. "I really should go upstairs. I am not fit to be here." She made to push back her chair, but Graham's hand on the back held it fast.

"Stay—please." The sparkle of amusement was gone, replaced by the seriousness she'd viewed in him so often of late.

Sophie gave a nod of acquiescence and waited as he poured wine into her glass. She placed her napkin in her lap, then took a sip of the sweet, dark liquid. The hunger she'd felt dissipated beneath Graham's gaze, which she met head-on with her own. It was replaced with a need more fierce and persistent than any she had ever associated with food.

"Keeping the children out too late tonight may have been a mere mistake, a miscalculation on your part, yet it would seem consequences are in order." He swirled his own glass thoughtfully, much as he had that night in her father's townhouse. *Right before he did something rash.*

A beat of panic, along with a thrill of anticipation, thrummed through her.

"On the other hand," Graham continued, swirling his wine, "you *are* the best thing that has happened to them."

And you? She wanted to be the best for him as well. "I care for Ayla and Matthew a great deal. I know that you feel the same, and I am truly sorry to have frightened you tonight." Sophie straightened in her chair. "If there are to be consequences, I must insist they be mine. The children are not at fault for their tardiness. I am."

"I have no intention of punishing the children."

"Good." She nodded her approval, showering the table with additional grains of sand, then hastily brushed them to the floor.

Graham rose from his chair, picked it up, and placed it directly beside hers. He seated himself once more, then turned to face her. "May I assist in removing some of the—uh—larger deposits of sand from your face before you eat?"

"My face?" Sophie's hands flew to her cheeks as she felt them warm. "I ought to have looked in a mirror before coming in. I only meant to apologize and then return to my room."

"How dull the meal would have remained." Graham took her as-yet-unused napkin and dampened it with water from the vase of flowers on the table.

Silently Sophie applauded his practical solution—one that would have appalled any other member of the gentry.

"Close your eyes," he said quietly. "So you won't get any sand in them when I brush it away."

Sophie's pulse escalated, but she obeyed. Her eyes closed, and she sat perfectly still. The cool cloth touched her brow and began its gentle descent over the contours of her face. Though he wasn't touching her directly, her skin tingled everywhere his fingers passed. Her imagination took flight, and she envisioned him tossing the napkin aside, cradling her face in his hands, and kissing her deeply.

A sigh of pleasure—half imagined, half real—escaped her lips, but then she realized he was no longer touching her. Sophie forced the fantasy away and her eyes open. Graham sat as close to her as he'd been that day in Gretna Green, at the inn when they had pretended to be newly wed. It had been difficult being so close to him then, but this—this was much worse. That day they had only been play-acting, and she had at least looked the part. Now she was a mess—inside and out. If he intended to punish her, she could not think of much worse than this. Spending the night locked in a dungeon would have been preferable to having him so agonizingly close and not being able to act on her desires.

"What were you thinking just now?" Graham brushed the cloth gently down the side of her face once more. "When your eyes were closed?"

Unabashed, Sophie met his gaze. "I was wishing that you would kiss me again. And again. And again."

A strangled sound came from the back of his throat. "Your honesty will be the death of me yet." But he did not move away.

Sophie's breath quickened. *So close.* "What consequences did you have in mind?" she asked, her voice low and soft.

His hand covered hers on the table. As a precaution lest she decide to bolt? "I thought to make you understand how I feel, to know a fraction of the torment I suffer beneath. But with your confession, I wonder if you know such madness already."

She gave a slow nod. "I did not mean to add to yours." She boldly reached her free hand up to touch his cheek, feeling genuinely sorry that she had caused him worry about the children. "I wish only to bring you happiness. If you would but allow it."

"Day and night—especially the nights—you haunt my every thought." His voice was thick. "I cannot escape the sound of your laughter, the image of you skipping about with the children, the memory of the smile you gave to me at your father's house the night we met. I cannot forget the feel of your lips on mine, or the way you clung to me and responded so willingly."

"You don't have to forget," Sophie said, her own resolve to let him be slipping from her mind as easily as the grains of sand had fallen from her clothes. "I'm here. I will always be here, if that is what you wish."

"I do—my Sophie." He bent his head to hers, and she leaned up to meet him. Their lips touched briefly once, twice, before igniting the same blazing inferno that had begun weeks ago.

Sophie's eyes closed, and her heart soared as his mouth moved over hers in a series of loving caresses. *My Sophie. His.* At last he was claiming her, giving up on the ridiculous notion that they could not be together. Joy swept through her like wildfire, with passion quick on its heels. Graham's hands cradled her face as she had imagined, and her own hands twined around the back of his neck, pulling him closer.

The chair back poked into her side as she turned fully toward him, but she didn't care. He loved her—he had to, if he wished to kiss her in the state she was in. The tears she'd felt earlier pricked behind her eyes, but this time they were those of absolute happiness. Never had she wanted anything so much as this man, and now, finally, she was to have him.

"Oh, Graham," she murmured as their kiss stopped momentarily so they could catch their breath. "I do love you so."

He froze suddenly, his back stiffening, eyes opening wide. He pulled his hands from Sophie's face, glancing at them, as if he was unsure what they had just been doing.

"Graham?" Sophie laced her fingers behind his neck, determined to hang on to the moment they'd just been having. "I meant what I said, and that shouldn't surprise you or scare you." She moved her head about until he was forced to meet her gaze.

"I love you," she repeated, an almost giddy smile curving her lips. "You know that was not my intention when we met. I never wanted to marry and never thought I would care for any man. But you are not *any* man. You are Graham Murray, the most extraordinary human I have ever met, and I love *you*." Finally saying what had been burgeoning within her brought great relief, and she felt like shouting it to the world.

"You don't. You can't." He shook his head as he reached up to remove her arms from around him.

Sophie held fast. "Don't do this," she warned. "Don't—"

When she wouldn't let go, he ducked beneath her grasp, pushed his chair back, and stood.

Sophie followed, her chair crashing to the floor in her haste to jump up. "Graham—" Her voice held a desperate, pleading note that she hated, but she couldn't let him undo the beauty that had just happened. Once, at the cottage, had been hard enough. But with the weeks since then and their growing feelings—how could he deny this? Their kiss was only an outward manifestation of affection and commitment that ran much deeper. She was prepared to give herself, to give everything to him for the rest of her life. He couldn't dismiss that.

"I'm sorry." He held a hand out as if to ward her off, then backed away, as if fearing she might attack.

I might. She wanted to scream and shake him, but instead she stood frozen as a searing pain scorched her heart and spread outward. He hadn't said he loved her. Had he only intended the kiss as a consequence, to hurt her as she'd hurt him this evening?

"I never should have kissed you," Graham said, his voice, his expression, even his body sagging as if heavy with regret. "It was wrong of me. I'm so sorry. You cannot love me, Sophie. And we cannot be together. You know why."

"I know that you are stubborn and foolish, and I love you anyway."

He shook his head. "You have to stop saying that and thinking it. I am *not* a loveable man."

"You're right," she said hotly and brushed at the first tear trailing down her cheek. "A man who is loveable wouldn't play with my feelings as if they were a ball to be tossed to and fro." She turned from him, storming toward the doors.

"I'm sorry," Graham called after her.

She continued her march, then stopped abruptly and whirled around, practically running back to him, stopping only when they were nearly toe-to-toe, as close as they had been when they'd kissed.

"I do *not* accept your apology." She folded her arms in front of her, as if to hold in this latest hurt. "There are many other things for which you might, and should, apologize—like keeping me at a distance since our arrival when you had professed to being my friend, leaving me essentially on my own to help the children and to figure out my place here, in a house and among people foreign to me. You ought to apologize for telling me our first kiss was forgotten, or for watching me at the beach with the children when you could have joined us—"

"My sins are many," Graham admitted. "As I just told you, I am unlovable."

She ignored him and continued her tirade, eager now to list her grievances against him. "Those are things you ought to apologize for and for which I might consider forgiving you. But I will not accept your apology for finally acting on your feelings, for reciprocating mine and showing me I've not gone mad these many weeks imagining this attraction between us."

"You haven't imagined anything." Graham braced his hands on her arms, so that he held her in place. "But I would not dishonor you with anything less than marriage, and I care for you too much to put you in the harm's way that would bring."

"Am I not in harm's way now?" she demanded. "What is to change if we marry? There are no vows that I am aware of that ensure violence."

"No vows, but time—a sickness. I am my father's son."

"His *son*, but not him." Sophie leaned closer, forcing his gaze to hers. "Listen to me, Graham. Would your father have sailed to Saint Kitts to rescue two orphaned children? Would he have come all the way to London to save me? Did he treat his staff fairly and kindly and with the respect that you do? I think not," she said, without waiting for him to answer.

"I wish you could see the man you are—far removed from your sire. You are your own man, making your own decisions, and those he made have no weight in yours. But as you cannot seem to believe that, if you cannot have a little faith in yourself, then have some in me, and trust that I would not stay if you mistreated me." Sophie shrugged free from his grasp and took a step back, wanting to flee before more tears could surface.

"Your mother sounds like she was the loveliest person— gentle, softspoken, meek. I am none of those. Were you to ever, even once, raise a hand to me or the children, I would take them and go somewhere you would never find us—right *after* I shot you, and not in the hand!" As if to make her point, she whirled away and ran to the doors, bursting through them even as she heard him calling after her.

Thirty-Eight

"Looking for this?" William dangled the key to the glass-fronted liquor cabinet in front of him as he strode into Graham's study.

"Finella will have your head if she learns you've offered it to me," Graham warned him, surprised to find he wasn't all that tempted to indulge.

"She told me as much already." William raised one leg, showing the broom marks on his trousers. "And emphasized her point up front."

Graham smiled briefly. "Finella has been looking after me since I was a lad. She saw my father at his worst and will do everything she can to keep me from becoming like him."

"A woman of great influence, no doubt." William deposited the key in his pocket with a look of longing at the wares behind the glass. "I'll not drink in front of you. I'm a better friend than that."

"I'll send a trunkful of the best home with you at the end of your stay," Graham offered. "It will taste even better for your having anticipated it so long."

William dropped into a chair. "The same could be said of other pleasures. And there is another woman of influence in this house who I'm certain could ensure you toe the line."

Graham's eyes narrowed as he looked at William across the desk. "You've been eavesdropping again."

William shrugged. "It was my own influential wife who bade me do it—for your sake and Sophie's, of course."

"Of course." Graham gave a slight shake of his head and roll of his eyes. "I take it you heard every word of my well-deserved dressing down."

William nodded. "Hence, the offer to lend you the key."

"Thank you, but I need a clear head right now."

"As you contemplate your demise?" William crossed one leg over the other and settled into his chair as if warming to the topic. "Do you think Sophie would really shoot you, or was that just bluster?"

"Sophie doesn't bluster. She doesn't do things by half or speak falsehoods. What you see is exactly what she is. She *would* shoot me. I'm half surprised she hasn't already."

"You might not want to push your luck much longer," William suggested.

"Aye." Graham propped an elbow on his desk and rested his chin on his hand. "But what *to* do?"

"Haven't you just answered your own question?" William uncrossed his legs and leaned forward earnestly. "You know Sophie to be a woman of her word, therefore you know she would not put up with your harming her or the children. Your mother never had the wherewithal or the courage to leave, but Sophie would find it. *Not* that you would harm any of them," he added.

Graham gave a slow, thoughtful nod. "I have no argument for that nor for her declaration this evening. But . . ." He exhaled, attempting to release some of the heavy thoughts plaguing him.

"It is a lot to ask of any woman, even one as extraordinary as Sophie, to take on the likes of me. I want to believe that I'd never harm her or the children. I promise myself now that I won't. But the fact remains that I deal in melancholy and anger too often. I admit it has been much less, and I have felt far better in her presence, but there are still too many days and nights when I feel the guilt of my childhood and youth will bury me. When the injustices of the world anger me so much, I would act to end at least some if given the chance—as I did on Saint Kitts. At those times I am the poorest of company."

William gave him a look filled with sorrow.

"Even if Sophie does ensure I toe the line from here on out, there is always a possibility that my past actions, or even those of my father, may come back to haunt me—to haunt us, if Sophie is my wife. She has changed me for the better but not so much that I dare believe the demons of the past and those at my core are gone for good."

"She seems to consider you worth the risk," William said.

Graham shook his head. "I cannot fathom why."

"Love." William held up a hand. "I have come to believe the statement that love is the most powerful force of nature."

"Powerful enough to overcome all that is my past—and perhaps my future, if the Raymond curse proves true?"

"Yes." William nodded emphatically. "If you will allow it."

"I am not certain that I can." Graham rested his head in his hands again. He was tired. So tired of the fight within himself. *Against* himself.

William said nothing for several long moments. The room fell silent, the air chill as the fire had not been lit. A single candle burned in its holder on the corner of the desk, its flickering shadow a solitary dance on the wood-paneled wall.

At last William rose from his seat. "I am sorry for you, my friend. For if you cannot give love a chance then you have already lost—lost out on a life of happiness and untold joy, lost out on the bliss of holding the woman you love in your arms every night and waking beside her every morning, and the joy of raising children you have created together. You've lost laughter—and at times sorrow and the opportunity to comfort one another. You've lost out on the very essence and purpose of life—to love and lift another, to give of yourself until you're spent yet fulfilled and overflowing with happiness.

"Similar to a court of law, all of life is a risk. But without court, one is not even given a chance but merely doomed to his fate—a life of exile and drudgery, much as you have existed these past years. Either way a man has already lost, when he might at least have had a chance. You have a chance, Graham. I pray you will not throw it away."

William turned and exited the room, pulling the door shut behind him. Graham sat alone in the near dark for several hours more, wrestling with the fears and demons in his mind.

When dawn tinged the sky, he at last pulled his weary body from his chair and made his way to his bedchamber in the east wing. He was tired of staying by himself in this solitary part of the house, and he was tired of being alone. As he climbed the steps, William's words echoed in his mind as they had throughout the long night. *You have a chance.*

I have a chance. He repeated the words in his mind. *Take a chance. Take the risk. What if I ruin everything? What if I destroy her?*

You won't. Give yourself over to love, as I did. Trust her. Trust yourself, Graham.

He turned his head, certain a voice other than his own had spoken.

"Katherine?" he whispered. Was he hearing ghosts now?

Take a chance, Graham. Sophie loves you, and she is strong enough for the both of you and anything that is to come. Give her your love.

Graham stumbled on the stairs, though they were in better repair than those in the tower house. He fell to his knees in the upstairs hall, his head lifted, eyes straining through the dark, but no apparition appeared. He was alone, but the feeling that his sister, his guardian angel, had visited him remained. Countless nights as a boy he had trembled in her arms as she offered comfort while elsewhere in the house his father raged at their mother. Even in her own times of distress, when she had been forced to wed and move far away, her letters had brought him comfort, had guided him, had made him feel not quite so alone. Half a world away she had been fighting her own crusade. And for a while, it seemed she had won.

Was it worth it? Would she still be here, if she hadn't chosen to love? He thought of precious Matthew snuggled into his lap each night, his tiny hands patting Graham's cheeks to gain his attention, the chubby arms thrown around him in a fierce hug. Had Katherine not loved . . . *There would be no Matthew.*

The thought pierced him. Graham brought a hand to his chest, as if to rub the pain away. He didn't want to imagine a world without sweet, adoring Matthew.

How much have I missed already, withholding my love from him? From Ayla?

From Sophie?

William was right. Sophie was too. Already on his knees, Graham fell forward, a prayer for courage falling from his lips.

Thirty-Nine

SOPHIE HELD HER SKETCHPAD AT arm's length and studied her drawing of the pergola. She'd never been particularly accomplished at art, but she felt a need to get these sketches right. It was all she would have to hold Caerlanwood in her memory after she left.

William and Elizabeth were returning home next week, and she was going with them. They had said she might stay in their home as long as needed, until she was able to find another position as a governess—on the continent or even in America. No one in England would hire her, and she wouldn't be safe from her father there either.

She could hardly bear to think of leaving—this place or the children or Graham—but neither could she stay with the tension between her and Graham as it was now. Two full days had passed since their kiss and argument in the dining room, and she had not seen him once. He hadn't even come to read to the children at bedtime.

It wasn't fair that he obviously felt the need to hide out in his own home. Her absence would free him of that, and hopefully he would renew his efforts to be close to Ayla and Matthew.

Satisfied that her drawing of the pergola and the surrounding garden was good enough, Sophie closed her sketchbook and gathered her belongings from the blanket. She rose to her knees and would have pushed up to her feet, but a strong hand at her elbow lifted her first. Startled, she looked up into Graham's eyes.

Neither said anything, but she felt as if paragraphs or even pages of words passed between them as they stood staring at one another.

He is changed. The dark circles were gone from beneath his eyes, the worry lines surrounding them eased. Hope and apology shone from their depths, the dark gray lightened to a brighter hue, as if some burden deep within him had been flung off.

If she'd thought the emotion between them bare and charged before, now it was stripped of everything—raw and exposed and utterly captivating. Sophie couldn't have torn her gaze from his if she'd wanted to, and she wanted anything but that.

Graham's hand slid from her elbow to her hand, pulling her closer. She allowed herself to be reeled in, fully aware of what was coming. There was no other logical conclusion.

"Sophie, I—"

She leaned forward, raised on tiptoes, and silenced him with her mouth, accepting whatever apology or explanation he had with her actions rather than words. Graham's arms came around her waist, pulling her against him, and Sophie's hands curled into the cloth of his shirt, holding him tight as their lips melded.

There was nothing gentle about this kiss. It was filled with an urgency the others hadn't been, and a confidence and surety that they belonged to each other. Graham's lips parted as his mouth slanted against hers, and he kissed her like he possessed her already. He did. Body, soul, mind. He could have everything she had to give, and he was giving her everything he had as well, for the first time holding nothing back.

She felt like weeping again, and for some reason that made her smile amidst their kiss. Who did he think he was, turning her into a weak-kneed, weepy, swooning female?

Everything. He is my everything. Graham's lips turned up to match hers, and then they were both laughing as he lifted her off her feet in a fierce hug.

Sophie flung her arms around his neck and then, when he had set her down, pulled his face close to kiss her again. This time their urgency slowed to a lingering exploration and discovery. Long minutes passed as they stood swaying in each other's arms, healing, trusting, and learning what it felt like to be loved and cherished.

At last they broke apart once more, each breathless. Unwilling to lose their connection, Sophie swept her fingers up Graham's cheekbones and across his brow.

"I don't have a fever, though it may feel as if I do just now." Graham's smile was lazy and his gaze perusing as he brushed his own thumb across her cheek.

What had changed him? She held back the question. There would be time enough for him to tell her later. For now . . .

Graham cradled her face in his hands, then bent his head to hers once more, making up for lost time.

UNABLE TO STAND IN ONE place as he told Sophie the full extent of his wretched childhood, Graham paced back and forth in front of the pergola. "So many times I thought he'd killed her," he said, speaking of his mother. "I wonder now—I am almost certain of it, given what you said the other night—"

"I meant no offense." Sophie reached a hand out to him as he passed by. "I should not have criticized your mother. That was not my intent. I only meant that I am neither patient nor long-suffering as she appeared to have been."

"Long-suffering, certainly." Graham touched Sophie briefly as he strode toward the edge of the pavilion. "What you said made me think—about how my mother was when I was younger and how she changed over the years. I believe she must have sustained permanent damage from my father's abuse—how could she not?" He scoffed and shook his head. "A doctor was rarely called, and my father beat her terribly. It must have done her mind harm, long before that last push down the stairs." He paused, then turned and retraced his steps back toward Sophie.

She leaned her head against one of the pillars, her arm wrapped around it, as if for support. "I'm so very sorry for all that you've endured."

He could see the weight of his unburdening taking its toll, and he hated that he'd had to share such gruesome tales with her. *But if she is to be my wife . . .* She needed to fully understand who he was and why, what demons he still wrestled with, and the memories that haunted him.

As he drew closer, Sophie moved away from the pillar and reached both arms out to him. He stepped into her embrace, resting his head against hers, feeling her strength as she wrapped her arms around him and held tight. *She is strong enough for the both of you.* He hoped that was true. Until two months ago, he'd believed himself strong. Capable, fearless. But somehow loving Sophie and the children had exposed his every vulnerability, leaving him frightened and, at times, incapable of moving forward.

He'd been so driven for so long. The purpose, the work, the searching, the accumulating of wealth, severing ties with his father's colleagues, securing freedom for those in Saint Kitts, carrying on Katherine's work, ending his father's that had been nefarious. There had been no end to the list of tasks he'd set for himself. And while they might not have been fulfilling, they had at least filled the hours, days, weeks, and then months and years. Until two letters had changed his life. The first, from Saint Kitts, had led him to Ayla and Matthew, and the second to Sophie.

Ayla and Matthew had weakened his resolve to stay aloof and apart from everyone and everything he might find dear. He'd tried his best to hold them at bay, but they'd found a way into the cracks in his armor.

Then Sophie had come along and completely torn it asunder. Sophie, with her headstrong will and unique perspective. Sophie, with her honesty and determination.

"Sophie." Her name came out as half whisper, half sigh.

"Yes?" She tilted her face to look at him, and he felt an almost desperate need to kiss her again.

"Why did you kiss me earlier? I hadn't apologized or said anything to lead you to believe I had changed my mind about us."

"You didn't need to say anything." She smiled. "Your eyes, your manner, your stance, your very being said it all. The man I fell in love with on our journey here came back to me, but even better this time, as he'd left his self-doubt behind."

"I am trying to." Graham pulled her close again. "But now you know some of what I am up against."

She snuggled deeper into his embrace. "It is good that you told me. My father was not a beacon of love, but never has he struck me or my mother or sisters. If anything, he was and is indifferent to us as individuals, as humans with feelings and desires of our own. We were mere objects, either used for his purposes or eliminated because we were in the way. But your father knew you were real. He knew your heart and he purposely sought to destroy you, both physically and emotionally. What you endured is so much worse."

"And it is over." Graham repeated the mantra he'd been telling himself the last two days. It was over. His father was gone. Caerlanwood was his. So were his father's properties in England, but he needn't live there and had only to see that they continued to run smoothly. He and Sophie could stay here and make this into the happily-ever-after of a fairy tale. He need only marry her so that she was his and safe.

Gently he stepped back from her embrace. "I'm not the only one who has been changed since our meeting in May."

"No, indeed." She brought a hand to her chest, fingers splayed in a feminine gesture. "I've become a swooning, crying female who kisses men with wild abandon. Books, which were always my true love, have been largely left on the shelf."

He grinned at her pun. Then his smile turned to a scowl. "*Men*? Who else have you kissed? Did McTavish try something?"

She laughed as she shook her head. "No. I've kissed no one but you. You were my first."

"And last." Graham gave a possessive growl, then raised her hand to his lips and allowed them to linger several seconds until a delightful flush of color crept up her cheeks.

"Is it possible that your aversion to wearing a wedding ring has also changed?"

Sophie nodded. "I believe it has. I should quite enjoy wearing one, if it was from you."

Graham reached into his pocket and withdrew the velvet jeweler's bag. He recalled the day he'd purchased the ring inside. He'd been in a hurry and hadn't particularly cared what ring he bought, so long as it passed as an engagement ring. All the while he'd been wondering if he was a fool to even continue the ruse, when it was entirely possible Sophie—Miss Claybourne, then—had already fled his carriage. Nevertheless, he intended to visit her home under the guise of calling on her, as soon as he had purchased a ring.

He'd located one quickly and instructed the clerk to package it for him. Then, while wandering about the store as he waited, he'd glimpsed *this* ring, in the case near the back. Graham remembered pausing in front of it, staring at the diamond-and-ruby creation that somehow seemed perfect for Miss Claybourne. Her personality was as vibrant as the ruby, a cut above and so different from those of the ton. He'd known that even then, after fewer than twenty-four hours in her presence. And the diamonds . . . Those surrounded the ruby and rested just below the surface of the main jewel, much as he suspected there were a myriad of other talents and genius that Miss Claybourne hid in her desperation to avoid marriage.

He had instructed the clerk to put the other ring back and to package this one instead.

"Are you certain, Your Grace? That ring is the most expensive piece in our collection."

"Then it will be perfect for my wife," Graham had insisted.

The jeweler nodded. "Very well. You have impeccable taste. Miss Claybourne—if the papers this morning are correct—should find this most pleasing indeed."

Except she hadn't. Graham chuckled, remembering her gasp of horror and almost palpable fear of the ring when he'd asked her to wear it during their travels.

As he loosened the cord on the velvet bag now, he wondered why he had insisted upon this particular setting, why it had mattered, when he'd had no hope—no desire—to marry Sophie. Maybe Katherine really was his guardian angel and had nudged him to it.

He took the ring from the bag and held it up.

"I never told you," Sophie confessed, her hands clasped in front of her. "But I thought this the most beautiful ring I had ever seen when you gave it to me before."

"I thought it terrified you." Graham smiled, recalling her reticence to put it on.

"It did." Sophie nodded emphatically. "I wasn't certain whether or not I could trust you, and I wondered if somehow we would end up married during our time in Gretna Green."

"It was always your choice," he said, reaching for her hand.

"And yours," Sophie added. Her breath caught as he slipped the ring on her finger. "It's even more beautiful than I remember."

"Much like its new owner," Graham said. "You have grown more beautiful to me every day this summer." He brushed the loose strands of hair from her face. "It's not just your lightened hair or the freckles sprinkled across your nose." He touched it playfully. "It's seeing you with the children, seeing you carefree—set free, unbound from the restrictions that were holding you back. You have blossomed before my eyes."

"Now it's your turn to bloom." Sophie reached her arms around his neck once more.

Graham arched a brow. "Are you calling me a flower? I believe that comparison only works for a—"

"Woman," Sophie finished with a roll of her eyes. "I see that I still have much work to do as you progress from being an ogre to a prince."

"King," he corrected. "After all, we live in a castle. You said so yourself once."

"So I did." Sophie kissed him again, until he felt very much like a king.

Forty

"I CANNA BELIEVE IT. SEEMS too good to be true that Graham has found himself a woman to love and is allowing himself to find happiness." Finella blew her nose loudly into a handkerchief as Lucy and Elizabeth helped with the final touches to Sophie's wedding trousseau.

Lucy tucked a last, discreet pin into Sophie's veil. "I never thought I'd be dressing Sophie for a wedding—at least, not hers and of her own choosing."

"If the two of you are surprised, think how *I* feel." Sophie looked again at the ring on her finger. "I never intended to marry. It was to be the spinster life for me, and I was most content with that." Upon waking this morning, she'd half expected to feel nervous or uncertain about her decision, but joy had been her only companion, a bright, bubbling happiness and the feeling that today her life was truly beginning.

"I knew the first moment I met you that you were destined to marry Graham." Elizabeth finished fastening the last pearl button, then stepped back from Sophie. "I just didn't realize it would take the summer to accomplish it."

"Ach." Finella waved her hankie. "Summer is nothing. Took my man much longer to come round to the idea of weddin' me. Men are always slower to know their minds."

Sophie turned to her. "I would agree, except that I am trying to encourage less prejudice toward females from my soon-to-be husband, so I had best not disparage the male population."

"Isna disparagin' to speak the truth!" Finella declared.

Sophie laughed along with the others.

"Look at yourself now." Lucy turned Sophie toward the long mirror.

The elegant reflection staring back at her, with hair swept up in a mass of curls beneath the lace veil, eyes sparkling, and lips eagerly awaiting their next kiss, was familiar, but in an unexpected way. "I look like Torie." Sophie marveled at the transformation. She hadn't spent much time in front of a mirror during the past weeks, but still—how could she have changed so much?

"Torie?" Elizabeth questioned.

"My sister Victoria," Sophie clarified for both Elizabeth and Finella.

"Graham told me about her, about your loss, when you first came," Finella said. "He wanted me to know your heartaches so I'd take care with you."

"As you have." Sophie smiled at the older woman and turned from the mirror to grasp her gnarled hands briefly. "Just as you took care of Graham for so many years."

"Aye, the rascal," Finella teased. "He wasna a bad child, but Caerlanwood was the only place he was free to *be* a child, so he had to pack a year's worth of mischief into the weeks he was here each summer. None of us minded much, though. He was a good lad, too, always concerned for his mother and sister. He's the same with you and Katherine's wee 'uns. Always watching o'er you, ready to banish any threat."

"But he is marrying you for far more than that," Elizabeth chimed in. "At first, protecting you was his goal. But now he's marrying you because he cannot live without you."

"Let's hope he can live *with* me." Sophie laughed, feeling

the first pang of nerves she'd had all day. Though they had spent the last two months near or around each other, it wasn't the same as the intimacy they were about to experience as husband and wife.

"You'll both do fine." Lucy met Sophie's gaze in the mirror, reassuring her with the wisdom of one married four years.

"But I've never looked like Torie before." Sophie studied her reflection again. Her hair was lighter from her days beneath the sun, and her skin held a healthy glow. But it was more than that. Something in her eyes. *Love. I look like Torie did when she was with Jonathan.* A sense of warmth and comfort enveloped her. If Graham's sister was his guardian angel, then perhaps Torie was hers.

"Another truth about men is that they don't like to be kept waiting," Elizabeth said. "If you're ready now, we should go."

"I'm ready." Sophie turned toward the door. When next she stood in this room, it would be with her husband by her side.

"Now am I forgiven for not repairing the stairs right away?" Graham whispered as he walked beside Sophie toward Caerlanwood's newly restored chapel. The recently whitewashed stone sparkled beneath the rays of afternoon sun, and the new glass panes shone brightly. The flowers surrounding the small building were in full bloom, and the blue sky above made the entire scene appear as perfect as a painting.

"Forgiven," Sophie whispered, leaning into him a bit more than was proper for a bride. "Though you already were."

He turned to her. "Had you seen it?"

She shook her head. "Not since my first week here. I'd

dismissed it as a ruin and had not bothered to return. I had no idea you were working so hard to restore it." She angled her head to look up at him. "Why did you? If you had decided we could not marry?"

"My head had decided that. My heart..." Graham placed his free hand over his chest, then dropped it to cover Sophie's hand on his arm. "My heart knew better."

They made their way together past the tenants and staff lined up on either side of the road cheering them on, then reached the stone path where Ayla and Matthew, Elizabeth and William stood, along with Graham's friends from Annan, some of whom she had met on their journey here.

"I see that you're taking care with Graham's heart," Cameron whispered, patting Sophie's arm briefly.

"Always," Sophie vowed. She understood so much more now what Cameron had meant and what that entailed.

She took Matthew's hand, and Graham took Ayla's, and the four of them crossed the threshold into the quaint chapel.

Candles glowed from the altar in front and in each of the sconces on the wall. But they were hardly needed, with the afternoon sun slanting through the west windows and illuminating the small chamber.

Sophie and Graham walked to the front, helped Ayla and Matthew to settle on the nearest pew, then faced each other, neither able to contain their smiles as they waited for those behind them to file into the chapel and squeeze onto the benches. Unlike the large, ornate cathedrals in London, this church was cozy and intimate. *Peaceful.* A place one might come to feel God's presence. Graham had been right to give this building his attention before turning to the other needed repairs on the estate.

He took her hands in his, and the ceremony began with a blessing. Sophie felt only peace and a surety that she was exactly where she belonged. Yet how strange and fortunate that fate had led her here. *If Father hadn't arranged my betrothal to Lord Newsome—*

It seemed sinful to think of the viscount when she was about to pledge her life and love to another; nevertheless her mind returned to the fateful night she'd met Graham. If he hadn't had reason to save her, would they have ever spoken? Would they ever have met?

Not if Mother hadn't written that letter . . . A pang of longing for her mother struck deep. *If only she could be here to see my happiness. If only she could know that I forgive her for not helping Torie. I'm so grateful she helped me.*

Graham squeezed her hands, and Sophie lifted her eyes to his, her melancholy fading. She was here in a house of God with the man she loved. Today they left their families and the past behind, unbound from all that had tethered them in place, and formed a new family. *Ours, alone.* One the world would not be allowed to touch.

The priest finished his blessing of marriage, and it was time to speak their vows. Graham's eyes were a clear gray as he spoke, his voice low but firm.

"I, Graham Murray Raymond, do solemnly promise before God and man to be your husband, to care for you tenderly, and to love, honor, and cherish you, body and soul—so long as we both shall live. Thereunto I plight thee my troth."

Sophie's heart thundered at the thought of him fulfilling those vows. *To be cherished . . .* It was something neither had experienced, until now.

Her own voice was strong and clear when her turn came. "I, Sophia Marie Claybourne . . ." *Raymond now. The Duchess of Warwick.* It was unlikely she would ever have to perform the duties of a duchess. This little corner of Scotland suited them both far better than London or elsewhere in England. Here they could simply be Graham and Sophie, just as they wished to be, without worry over what was proper or how others might judge them.

The priest accepted their vows, then turned to Graham once more. Graham stepped closer, his thumbs circling the back of her hands.

"One more pledge, from me to you, as is tradition for the Murrays."

Sophie hadn't been aware of this, but she nodded and kept her gaze locked with his.

"*You* are the star of each night and the brightness of every morning. You are the breath of my *very* life, and now the report of this land." His thumbs ceased their caress, and his grasp tightened. "*No* evil shall befall you, neither on hill nor bank, in field, valley, nor on a mountain nor in a glen. I will lay down my life for you if necessary, and I dedicate that life to your well-being forevermore."

"Amen to the Murray chieftain," the congregation murmured. "Long live the Murray and his lady."

"Amen," Sophie whispered as a chill made its way down her spine. The seriousness of his words and the intensity of his gaze troubled her. She didn't want him laying down his life for her. She was used to looking out for herself, and she never wanted to be the cause of him being harmed. They were a team, and they would face any future challenges together.

GRAHAM'S ARM WRAPPED AROUND SOPHIE'S waist as they turned around in the reel. "Have I ever told you why we were caught in the storm on the way here?"

"Because it rained?" She laughed. "Or is the Murray chieftain able to control the weather?"

Before he could answer, she was passed off to another dancer. He waited not-so-patiently, smiling at each of the women who clasped his arm and made their way through the circle. At last he caught Sophie again and hurriedly spoke his answer.

"I cannot control the weather and was in great doubt of my ability, that night, to control my emotions if we danced together at a cèilidh. *That* is the reason I risked the storm. Because I was afraid to dance with you."

Her mouth opened with a reply as she was swept away again on the arm of another man. Graham frowned and wished for a dance where a man might keep his wife at his side the entire time. Before he could claim her again, the reel ended. Over the heads of several people, he watched as she accepted greetings and congratulations as she tried making her way toward him again.

Instead of fighting the crowd, Graham stepped back and circled around, coming up behind her and pulling her near to him.

"Obviously I don't scare you anymore," she murmured, turning into his arms as a waltz began.

"Oh, but you do." He bent down to whisper in her ear. "And you have since that same night I had to undress you to save your life."

"A just reward for depriving me of the joy of a cèilidh. Tonight has been most delightful."

"I agree." He took her hand in his and placed the other at her waist, claiming her as his and only his as they swirled around the floor.

Forty-One

Sophie tugged Graham's hand, leading him away from the front of the house.

"The guests are all gone. We can go inside now," he said, attempting to pull her back toward the door.

"Not yet." She gave him what she hoped was a mysterious smile.

"We're not cleaning up," he insisted. "Not tonight, anyway. If there is still work to be done in the morning, we can help."

"Cleaning isn't what I have in mind." She pulled him around the side of the house, then to the back garden, where two glowing lanterns waited at the top of the steps to the sea gate.

"Sophie?"

Instead of answering, she let go of his hand, laughing as she began to run across the lawn. She stopped at the lanterns, picked one up, and looked at him. "It's high time you stopped watching others play at the beach and had fun of your own."

"Now?" He shook his head and started toward her. "The tide's too high this time of night, and if the fog comes in it can be difficult to find the way to the gate. The switchbacks can be treacherous."

She sashayed just out of his reach. "We aren't going all the way to the shore. The dunes are perfectly safe." She started down the steps without him.

Graham snatched up the second lantern and followed, grumbling about this being their wedding night, not the time to build sand castles.

Sophie ignored his protests and hummed as she picked her way down the stairs. She'd only gone down a few when Graham caught her, holding his arm out.

"Hold onto me, at least. I don't want you falling."

"Too late." She circled her arm through his. "I've already fallen madly and passionately in love with you. I'm afraid it's quite incurable."

He shook his head at her again, but Sophie glimpsed his wide smile in the lantern light. She was acting like Torie had around Jonathan, like Elizabeth and William had too, but tonight she didn't care. It seemed that Graham didn't mind either.

They made it down the stone steps to the sea gate, and he unlatched it, then pushed it open ahead of them.

Sophie paused to take off her slippers, though they were already wet and dirty from dancing. "Shoes off," she ordered, looking up when she'd finished.

Graham stuck a bare foot out. "Already done."

Sophie straightened, then leaned up and kissed him on the cheek. "Thank you for indulging me."

"Of course." His tone was less reluctant. "I suppose you shall have to be indulged often. You're a duchess now."

"Not here, I'm not." She echoed words he had spoken to her before. "At Caerlanwood I am just Sophie, and you're Graham, and we can do whatever we wish the way we wish, without being bound by any silly rules or worrying what anyone thinks." Proving her point, she danced out in front of him, hands thrown wide as she twirled in a circle.

He caught her around the waist and pulled her close. "Have you *ever* worried about what others think of you?"

"Never."

"Which is possibly one of the very first things I loved about you." He dipped his head and kissed her until she was breathless.

"Graham." Sophie clung to him, her balance thrown off by the intensity of his kiss. "My plan wasn't to stand by the gate all night."

"There's a plan?" He sounded amused now. "*Most* women don't have a plan on their wedding nights, other than to survive it."

Sophie stooped to pick up her lantern, then leaned her head back to look up at him. Her other hand rested on her hip. "Most women are fools, then. I plan to *enjoy* it. Or, at least, I hope to." Her courage faltered slightly as images from her cousin's anatomy book filled her mind.

Graham leaned close and whispered, "I plan to see that you do." He glanced longingly up at the house, at the window that was henceforth to be *their* bedroom.

"Come along, then," Sophie urged. "It's getting chilly out." She moved ahead of him on the path, leaving him little choice but to follow if he wished to be with her.

About two-thirds of the way down, she veered off the trail, through the tall grasses to a space beyond where, nestled among the dunes, she'd prepared a bed of quilts and pillows atop the soft sand.

Graham came behind her, parting the tall grass, then stopped short when he saw her creation. Without saying anything, he set the lantern down, then brushed the sand from his feet one at a time and stepped onto the blanket. He held a hand out to her, and Sophie accepted it, then flew forward as he tugged her toward him. A second later she landed on top of him, the blankets and sand beneath cushioning their fall.

"Was this what you had in mind?" His eyes twinkled as he looked up at her.

Sophie pushed the hair back from her face and rolled off of him. "Yes. Mostly."

"*Mostly?* What else am I missing?" He rolled to his side and propped his head on his hand as he looked at her.

She shrugged. "I thought we could look at the moon and the stars, and we could close our eyes and listen to the waves cresting on the shore, and . . . I don't know exactly." She frowned. "You know how I detest not knowing something. I tried to find a book in your library that would prepare me but . . ."

"You couldn't?" His eyes were definitely twinkling now—with mirth.

Sophie folded her arms across her middle and looked up at the sky instead of him. "You find my lack of knowledge about what occurs on one's wedding night amusing?"

"I find it a relief," he blurted, reaching out to her.

Sophie rolled away, nearer to the edge of the blanket.

"Had you discovered a text, I fear I would have been subjected to very specific directives when, really, I just want it to happen as it will."

"*What* to happen?" Sophie demanded, her earlier calm and bravado slipping significantly. Torie had always been silent about the particulars of what went on in the marital bed. And Sophie had never had cause to ask her mother such advice. She'd considered questioning Elizabeth but didn't feel comfortable, given the newness of their friendship. And while Sophie believed she had a fairly good idea what was to take place, she was not certain she was correct or, if she was right, how such a feat was to be accomplished.

"What is going to happen is me showing you how much I love you," Graham said quietly, the teasing gone from his voice. He sat up. "Come here, Sophie—please."

She knelt, then crawled across the blankets to him.

Graham faced her away from him, then pulled her back against his chest and wrapped his arms around her. Sophie leaned into his warmth, relaxing again. "I dislike not knowing how things work," she mumbled, her voice fading as he began to massage her back.

"After tonight, you'll always know," he promised. "But just this once, allow me to be your teacher." He brushed her hair aside, then trailed a line of kisses along the side of her neck.

"Do you promise to be as entertaining as Mr. McTavish was?" Sophie asked, feigning indifference, though she was not at all surprised at the possessive growl Graham uttered at the mention of her former, and brief, teacher of geography.

"I promise to show you places you've never explored and territory you never dreamed existed."

"Oooh." A shiver of delight rippled across her back as Graham's kisses moved lower, to her shoulder.

"Uncharted territories that we'll discover together," he promised. "And it will be just the two of us on this expedition."

Sophie turned in his arms and met his gaze bravely, her momentary uncertainty forgotten as she looked up into his gray eyes. "I'm ready for our adventure."

He leaned forward to kiss her. "Me too."

HOURS LATER, GRAHAM LAY ON his back watching the moon's progress as Sophie lay curled up beside him, asleep after the very prolonged and intimate journey they had taken, coming to know one another as husband and wife.

Below, the roar of the surf had subsided with the shrinking tide, but the sound was still mesmerizing, as was the crescent moon overhead and the brilliant display of stars. But even their magnificence and light paled compared to Sophie. *My wife.* Tonight she had shone brighter than he could have ever imagined, a charming mix of shyness and curiosity as she'd allowed him to be her tutor. She'd plied him with questions all throughout their lovemaking, and the only way to get her to cease had been to kiss her until she was breathless. They had kissed a lot.

Of course, those kisses had rendered him breathless too—and almost senseless—and by the time he recovered after each, she had another question or five—about his anatomy, about why her body responded to his as it did, about why they had waited all summer to marry, and was it permissible to engage in these types of explorations frequently. He adored her last question—adored her. A hundred times more than this morning, if such a thing were possible, and he'd no doubt he'd love her a hundred times more than that by the time the sun rose.

She stirred in his arms, and Graham tightened his hold, relishing the feeling of her body pressed close to his, her head on his chest, her long hair spilling across his arm behind her. She was his now. He'd done it. *They* had done it—two people least likely to ever marry had found each other, and the result was perfection. How had he ever imagined that he could leave her? He would hold onto her, to their love, and keep his vows—both spoken and unspoken.

Graham lowered his head, kissing the top of hers. "I promise," he whispered, knowing this was a vow he would move heaven and earth to keep, "never to give you reason to shoot me."

Dear Reader,

I hope you will not wish to shoot *me* for ending *Love Unbound* at this point, with many things still unresolved. For months I tried (really, really tried) to wrestle this story into one (way too long) book. But both readers and my editor felt the ending was rushed and still missing some important elements. No amount of rewrites seemed to address this problem until I finally realized that I had so much more story to tell that Sophie and Graham needed a second book. *Love Undying* picks up where *Love Unbound* ended, and it will also include Olivia's (Sophie's younger sister, for those who may have forgotten) love story. I hope you will continue with me as Sophie and Graham face the demons of their past and try desperately to hold onto each other. Sophie's every wit and reserve will be tested as she is truly called on to be strong enough for both of them, and Olivia will discover that those things she deemed important with regards to love are not what matter the most. Continue the journey with these brave, strong sisters to see how each gets her heart's desire. *–Michele*

SNEAK PEEK!

Love Undying
A Hearthfire Romance

One

Caerlanwood Estate, Scotland
October 1831

SOPHIE BENT TO WIPE THE bright stain of berries from Matthew's mouth, cheeks, chin, and generally everything in that vicinity, right down to the collar of his shirt. "Did you enjoy your tart?" she asked, laughing as his tongue darted out, attempting to claim the last of the treat from the cloth in her hand.

He nodded and rubbed his stomach. "Can I have more?"

"May I?" she corrected, then shook her head. "Not yet. The men still need to eat. Then, if there are leftovers, you may have another." Turning from Matthew, Sophie held a hand up to her forehead, shielding her eyes from the rapidly descending afternoon sun. In the distance, she saw Graham, shirtsleeves rolled to his elbows as he worked one end of a crosscut saw. He had explained that part of the harvest festival, a long tradition at Caerlanwood that he had reinstated, was preparing for winter—in part accomplished by the various teams of men who competed throughout the day, cutting peat and as many logs as they could from the trees felled over the all-too-short summer months.

Summer was fleeting. Sophie pulled her shawl tighter around her as the chill of evening crept ever closer. Though the temperatures had cooled significantly already, she didn't mind, as the cooler weather had changed Caerlanwood's gardens and trees from lush greens to a brilliant display of yellow, red, and orange. She'd loved every one of the nearly five months she'd been here, but so far October was her favorite.

Though it was the season when the world braced for winter, and animals and people alike retreated to places of warmth and safety, she felt almost like it was spring, and the world was alive with possibility. For her it was, with her love for Graham and the children—and now the new life growing inside of her that would make his or her appearance late next spring. She'd only known for certain for the past two days, after she'd missed her second cycle of menses, and she'd yet to tell Graham. She wasn't certain exactly why she was waiting, other than that she wanted the moment to be just the two of them alone, and to be perfect. She worried he still had fears about being a good father, though he was a wonderful one to Ayla and Matthew.

In the months since their marriage, the four of them had become more of a family. They took all of their meals together, and Graham joined them on their adventures as often as he was able. Sophie and the children helped him with the projects to restore Caerlanwood whenever they could, working in the gardens, painting walls, hanging curtains and tapestries over windows and in halls that had long been bare.

Ayla still had not spoken, but her nightmares had all but ceased, and she responded to conversation by nodding or shaking her head and with hand gestures and facial expressions. A time or two Sophie had even caught her smiling.

Progress.

Evenings were Sophie's favorite. After the children were in bed, she and Graham spent long hours alone in their room, reading to one another, talking—sometimes on opposite sides of a subject—touching, loving in a way neither had ever realized was possible only a few short months ago. On clear evenings, they often wandered down to the beach and walked along the shore hand in hand, or sometimes they brought a blanket and headed for their favorite place among the dunes. Life was beautiful, nearly perfect. And she was oh, so happy.

SOPHIE'S EYES FLEW OPEN, AND she sat up in bed, ears straining to discern what had awoken her. *Ayla?* Beside her Graham slept, undisturbed. Odd, since Ayla's infrequent cries usually woke both of them.

There were no cries now, but, certain she'd heard something, Sophie eased herself out of bed, put on her wrap, and left their room. The hall was dark, but light from the full moon illuminated the nursery enough for her to see both children sleeping peacefully. Matthew's rocking horse stood beside his bed, and his hand hung off the edge, resting atop the horse's head. Ayla lay curled on her side, her doll tucked safely in her arms.

They were both the picture of innocence and childhood. *Exactly as children should be.* Content that all was well here, Sophie retraced her steps and was approaching her own bed when the cry, accompanied by what sounded like someone pounding on the front door, came again.

Graham was out of bed at once. He tugged on pants and boots in record time, then reached to the top of the wardrobe, where he kept two loaded guns. He tossed a set of keys to

Sophie, and she went to her bedside table, unlocked the drawer, and removed her own weapons. She hoped never to have to use either the gun or the knife, but she would if it meant protecting herself and her family.

"What do—" she started to ask as she turned around, but Graham was already gone.

Sophie rushed from the room to follow but stopped long enough to close the children's door. Whatever the disturbance, they need not have their sleep interrupted too.

In the dark, she crept down the stairs still in need of repair, the sounds of a woman's hysteria and sobbing reaching her before she'd come halfway.

"They shot him! And Ethan's alone at the cottage. They breached the gate, and they won't be far behind."

Lucy. Gooseflesh sprang up along Sophie's arms and the back of her neck, pinpricks of fear and foreboding. She ran down the rest of the stairs and into Graham coming up.

"Take Lucy, rouse everyone, and leave by the kitchen door. Then run into the woods as far as you can and hide. I'll bring the children."

"Hurry." Sophie touched his arm briefly as they passed on the stairs, not wanting to be separated from him. She reached the bottom and located Lucy by the sound of her crying. "Are you hurt?"

"Adam is," Lucy said tearfully, then doubled over, clutching her stomach as water gushed onto the floor beneath her. She gasped. "No! It's too early."

"Is it your baby?" Sophie wrapped her arm around Lucy.

She nodded. "This is what happened last time, but it's too soon. I'll lose them both, them all, on the same night." She grabbed Sophie's arm. "They shot Adam, and Ethan is at the cottage by himself," she cried again.

"We'll send someone to get him." The thought of the

toddler alone frightened Sophie too. "*Who* shot Adam? Can you tell me what happened?"

"I don't know which one shot him. From the window I saw maybe five or six men. Adam took his time answering their shouts and summons to open the gate. I don't know what was said when he went outside, only that Adam had turned back toward the cottage when one of the men shot him. Adam fell—and didn't get up again." Lucy's hand covered her mouth.

Sophie turned Lucy toward her and pulled her into a hug. "It may be that Adam is all right. If those men believe him dead or seriously wounded they're not likely to bother with him again. The smartest thing for Adam to do was to stay down."

Lucy bobbed her head. "He's a smart one, my man."

"He is." Sophie took Lucy's hand. "We need to be smart, too, and hurry."

They took three steps before Lucy gave an agonized moan and leaned forward. "This baby's coming."

We're not going anywhere. Not out in the woods, anyway. "You'll have the baby here, then," Sophie said with a calm she didn't feel as she turned Lucy back toward the stairs. "You can use my bed."

With her arm around Lucy, supporting her more with each step, they climbed the stairs, encountering Graham at the top, holding a sleepy Matthew in one arm and Ayla in the other.

"Lucy's about to have her baby," Sophie blurted before he could ask why she hadn't left yet. "She can't make it to the woods, and she can't give birth on the lawn."

"Take her upstairs," he said. "Lock yourselves in our room. Don't let *anyone* in. I'll send the children with the servants and be back."

"Be careful," she admonished, the words sounding hollow.

"Stay upstairs," was his only reply.

As he disappeared, Sophie turned her attention to Lucy, who was bent over and sobbing.

"You need to leave," she said, her breath short. "They're here for you."

"Who is?" The gooseflesh reappeared, raising the hairs on the back of Sophie's neck. "My father?"

Lucy nodded. "And Viscount Newsome."

"I am married. They can do nothing." Sophie attempted to push aside her fear. After so long, she hadn't believed they would come for her. Was her father really so vindictive? One daughter's death hadn't been enough for him?

Inside the room she locked the door, set the gun on the bedside table, and helped Lucy onto the bed. She was propping pillows behind her when more shouts and pounding came from below. A minute later banging sounded on the bedroom door.

"Open the door, Sophie. Let the children in."

She ran to the door.

"He told you not to open it," Lucy cried from the bed.

"I know my husband's voice. Graham is on the other side." Sophie threw back the bolt, then reached her hands out to take Matthew from him as Graham pushed the door open and strode into the room.

"They're here. There's no time to leave. *Stay* upstairs, keep your gun with you, and don't let anyone in this room." Graham deposited Ayla, looking much more awake now, on the edge of the bed, then ran into the hall.

Shifting Matthew to her hip, Sophie secured the door once more, then turned to face Ayla and Lucy.

"Lucy's going to have her baby tonight. Isn't that exciting?" Sophie forced a smile she did not feel. "Ayla, Matthew, you two may rest over here on the window seat." Sophie carried Matthew over to the seat, then tucked a blanket around both children as soon as Ayla had made her way over as well.

Lucy groaned and arched her back. "Birthing's a messy business. We'll need some hot water and towels for later."

Sophie headed toward the fireplace, grateful there were still embers and enough wood to build the fire up again. There was water in the pitcher too. "Tell me what to do," she said, then added a silent prayer. *Show us all what to do.*

MICHELE PAIGE HOLMES IS THE author of eighteen published romance novels and at least a dozen more, as yet unpublished books lingering on her hard drive. She has also written five novellas for the Timeless Romance Anthologies. She loves history and all things romantic, though the reality of her life is often less so, with piles of laundry to be folded, meals to be cooked, and dishes to be washed. She finds those blessings too, or evidence of the blessings in her life—her husband, five, mostly grown children, and five charming, high-energy grandchildren (four of whom reside in her home).

She is married to her high school sweetheart, a true Ironman who considers doing ultramarathons and triathlons fun. The only time Michele logs serious miles is at Disney theme parks, but she and her super-fit husband have been happily married for thirty-five years, in spite of her lack of coordination and lagging fitness levels. She is happy to continue her role as cheerleader and race support.

While her husband is out running, biking, or swimming, Michele's furry companion Sherlock Holmes—a Cavapoo strongly resembling a teddy bear—keeps her company and keeps her feet warm during the cold winter months in Utah.

In recent years Michele has enjoyed traveling to some of the locations she writes about. This summer she will be returning to Scotland to do research for upcoming Hearthfire Historical novels.

You can find Michele on the web: MichelePaigeHolmes.com
Facebook: Michele Holmes
Instagram: Michele Paige Holmes
Pinterest: Michele Paige Holmes